A PROMISE
to Azfal

PETER TEIXEIRA

NEWMAN SPRINGS PUBLISHING
320 Broad Street
Red Bank, NJ 07701

First originally published by Newman Springs Publishing 2018

ISBN 978-1-64096-191-3 (Paperback)
ISBN 978-1-64096-192-0 (Digital)

Printed in the United States of America

Acknowledgments

To my family and friends, thanks for all the support!
To Allison Fraser and Jessica Rubecindo, I am forever grateful for the help!
Thanks to the Authors who inspired me to write;
Mario Puzo, Walter Dean Myers, Donald J Sobol, and Roald Dahl

"Live it up!" – Kevin Fidalgo

Chapter 1

On the twenty-third of October, in 1992, Azfal Saad Ansary was filled with joy as he welcomed his first grandson to the world, Jassim Ibrahim Azfal Ansary. The grandfather couldn't stop looking at the adorable little boy; he experienced a faint psychic sense that the godsend was destined for greatness. The reverent patriarch was the best at calming the baby after one of his usual tantrums; Jassim seemed at peace in his caring arms. The connection between the two was undeniable, but it was Nadje who first noticed that the baby listened attentively whenever the *Qur'an* was recited. Her husband believed it was a sign of the child's natural faith. Azfal chanted *Surah* 2, *Ayah* 252, "These are the signs of *Allah*. We rehearse them to thee in truth: verily Thou art one of his Apostles."

The transitory peace that existed between his two sons after Jassim's birth ended on April 28 of the following year. It was a significant day in Iraq—Saddam's birthday. Ibrahim, the loyal supporter, insisted on a glorious celebration to commemorate the president's birth. His younger brother Saady, the agitator, was intent on doing all he could to ruin the day for his jubilant sibling. The turncoat slept for most of the morning while the rest of the family gathered by the peach tree in the spacious sun-drenched arid backyard for a cookout. A sweaty Azfal manned the stainless-steel gas-fire grill as was the custom. He wiped his face with a towel since the heat from the grill intensified the ninety-degree temperature; the rubber soles of his sandals stuck to the asphalt whenever he stood still.

"Why don't you give the grill a break and just cook the meat on the ground?" the chiseled Ibrahim joked.

It was late in the afternoon when Saady finally decided to grace the family with his presence; he didn't even bother to shower. With crust still in his eye, Saady stepped into his tan leather sandals and grasped the headboard for assistance lifting his heavyset body from the mattress. Still in his red pajamas, he stepped out of the house, and before he could put down his second foot, an enraged Ibrahim addressed him.

"Why has it taken you so long to come help us celebrate this great day? And why are you still in your pajamas?" he scolded.

Saady, annoyed, looked at his brother with disgust. "Great day? Great for who? Why don't you tell us—I curse the day your TET was born—terrible, evil tyrant." The free spirit had an annoying habit of using acronyms that he created on the spot, then explaining what they meant.

Ibrahim was incensed. "Why don't you get out of here if you're not going to honor the greatness of Saddam?"

"What greatness? He's an alliterated triple B—big, bad bum! Your dictator ruined this nation and caused nothing but suffering for all Iraqis." He spat on the ground before turning and walking toward the door. He stared menacingly at his brother. "I don't need to join your celebration—death to Saddam!"

Ibrahim was absolutely infuriated. "Look at the revolutionary. What a great man! It is he who will take the power from Saddam."

"What a shame. Look at little Jassi dressed in that disgraceful uniform. What a double H, F you are, horrible hate-filled father."

A fed-up Azfal stepped between the men and separated his sons. "That's enough. I will not sit here and have my day ruined by the two of you. I don't care what either of you thinks about Saddam. This is the last time that your pettiness will disgrace our family, remember the words of *Allah*. *Surah* 5, *Ayah* 9 states, 'O ye who believe, be steadfast in the cause of *Allah*, bearing witness in equity. Let not a people's enmity toward you incite you to act contrary to justice; be always just, that is the closest to righteousness. Be mindful of your duty to *Allah*; surely, *Allah* is aware of all that you do.'"

The two brothers remained angry but decided to stop their fighting, and the family attempted to salvage the rest of the day by forgetting the unnecessary argument. It was a few minutes before sunset when Ibrahim entered the house to use the bathroom. While he was inside, Saady removed the camouflage soldier's uniform from Jassim and confiscated the toy gun. The little comrade began to cry, causing the caring uncle to give him a mini green, red, and black soccer ball, which was more to his nephew's liking. It was a replica of the official Iraqi Soccer Association ball. Saady was playing with Jassim when Ibrahim returned. He kicked the ball then scurried to the grill, which was no longer in use. Enraged, he removed the rack before igniting the flames.

In spite, Saady defiantly threw the uniform into the fire along with the toy gun. The blaze rose three feet, increasing the temperature in the backyard to an unbearable degree. "Down with the dictator, no more CTC—corrupt, tyrannical conscription."

Ibrahim was livid. He screamed, "That's enough! I'm tired of your disloyalty to Iraq. From this day forth, I don't want to have anything to do with you, and I don't want to be around you anymore." Banging his fist against the bricked exterior of the house, he continued, "I no longer have a brother! You'll be lucky if I don't tell Saddam about your betrayal." He paused and carefully chose his words. "I don't agree with your 'lifestyle' anyways." He turned and stormed into the house, slamming the door.

Nadje, with a face full of tears, grasped for her heart and turned to her youngest child. "I don't know why the two of you need to fight constantly. Why must you provoke him Saady? I swear on the *Qur'an*, my sons will give me a heart attack."

The distraught son felt as though he was being unfairly blamed for the argument. Saady wanted to defend himself, but he stopped once he thought better of the situation. The tension in the air caused everyone to remain silent. Saady, feeling as though he were an outcast, hung his head in shame and walked out.

For the next nine months, the two warring brothers did not exist to one another. Ibrahim would leave his parents' house anytime Saady walked in, never acknowledging his sibling's presence. Wisely, he was reluctant to ban Saady from the second floor apartment. The bullheaded father was mindful not to disrupt the relationship between his obstinate brother and Jassim, but anytime Saady made his way over, Ibrahim locked himself in the bedroom, remaining there until his "son's uncle" departed.

⸺◈⸺

The family gathered for Jassim's first birthday party, and for the first time since the major blowup, the brothers were forced to be around each other. Neither of the men wanted to miss the momentous celebration, but the tension in the room created an unfestive atmosphere.

"Saady, try and fix things with your brother. It doesn't make sense for the two of you to fight over nothing." Nadje pleaded in private.

Saady sighed deeply. "Why do you always blame me? Talk to him. He's the one with the problem."

Later in the evening, Nebet attempted to convince her husband to mend the relationship, but he wouldn't hear of it either.

"What are you talking about? Everything's fine. I like how things are."

He was content to continue ignoring his younger brother, and the family sat in the unostentatious living room with the tension mounting. The only lavish piece of furniture was the lovely *settee*, a gift to Ibrahim from President Saddam Hussein. Everyone was taking turns playing with the birthday boy when the moment finally arrived for the cake to be brought out. Ibrahim gladly volunteered to retrieve the *kahqa* from the kitchen; he was extremely proud of the decoration. There was one large candle above a picture of Saddam in his military uniform, and the inscription read, "Happy Birthday, my future soldier, Jassi!"

Saady was boiling inside when he saw the picture. He knew Ibrahim purposely created the theme in order to wind him up, but the younger brother did his best to keep composed. To his credit, Saady did a good job of managing his discontent.

Nebet was aware that her husband used the decorative pastry to anger her brother-in-law, but there was nothing she could do. Nothing could've prevented him from carrying out his conniving scheme.

Azfal helped Jassim blow out the number-one-shaped candle, but the picture of Saddam remained intact. Ibrahim carefully cut around the dictator's image, and Nebet passed out the pieces.

"Here's a nice big slice for Jassi's favorite uncle."

"No thanks, sis, I won't be having any."

Nadje, alarmed by the volatile atmosphere, lovingly pulled Saady to the side.

"Just eat the cake. Remember that today is about Jassi. Don't let your pride ruin his first birthday party."

Saady decided to heed his mother's advice in an attempt to keep the peace, but he was fuming inside and struggled to keep his cool. He accepted the piece and ate a small bite, but every time he looked at the photo of Saddam, Saady grew more enraged, ultimately losing control of his emotions. With the cake cutter still in Ibrahim's grasp, Saady seized a knife from the drawer, and in an uncontrollable rage, he made a slash across the dictator's neck.

He scooped a piece with his fingers and winked at his shocked brother. "Now that's a piece I can enjoy. The tyrant is surprisingly DF—deliciously filling."

The ominous action set in motion another distasteful war of words, which spilled into the living room. Nadje grew tired of their bickering and forced Azfal to interfere. The patriarch falsely believed the conflict between the brothers was the result of Saady's secret desire to have the gorgeous Nebet for himself. He stood up from the *settee* with its lovely patterns and recited *Surah* 17, *Ayah* 84, "Everyone acts according to his manner; but your Lord best knows who is best guided in path."

Before either son could take in the verse, Azfal continued, "This is ridiculous. The two of you will not continue this childish behavior. Saady, you are to move from the house until you and your brother begin to act civilized."

Saady didn't say anything. He simply snatched his jacket from the closet hanger and headed for the door; it slammed violently upon his exit. He ran down to his room and gathered a few of his choice belongings before disappearing for several days.

A week later, Saady's best friend Mahmoud pulled up to the house in his beat-up jeep. He was a short, thin, jovial man whose mission was to gather the remainder of his friend's belongings; the defeated Saady refused to return to the home. Yet he called every Saturday in order to keep in touch, only speaking with his mother. If Azfal answered the phone, he would hang up and call back at a later time. The worst aspect about Saady being away was the fact that he missed Jassim, but the boy's stubborn uncle refused to be around his "jerk of a brother."

Even though Saady knew it was wrong to allow his bickering with Ibrahim to keep him away from his nephew, he was inflexible and kept his distance. There was no anger toward Azfal, but the prodigal son was disappointed because he felt his father was on the Ibrahim's side.

"When are you going to return home?" Nadje asked.

"I don't know, maybe never. Give my best to Dad." The weekly phone calls usually ended the same way.

It was in the middle of December when someone obnoxiously knocked on the Ansary's first-level door. Azfal and Nadje were both in deep sleep when the unexpected visitor woke them from their slumber.

"Who could that be? It's not Ibrahim or Nebet. They would have used the back entrance." She deduced.

She cautiously approached the door. "Who is it?"

"Me," replied a familiar voice.

The excited mother hurriedly opened the door and was elated as she saw her prodigal son standing in the entrance. She enthusiastically invited him in and called Azfal from the bedroom as she hugged her child.

Father and son embraced, and Saady whispered, "I am SUS— super ultra sorry!"

"None of that is important. All is in the past and forgiven. I recite to you, my son, *Surah* 17, *Ayah* 24, 'Thy Lord has commanded that ye worship none but Him and has enjoined benevolence toward parents. Should either or both of them attain old age in thy lifetime, never say: Ugh. To them nor chide them, but always speak gently to them.'"

Saady took in the inspirational words. He always marveled at his father's ability to recite the appropriate passages from the Holy Book, but he had a purpose for the unexpected visit. He was the bearer of bad news. Reluctantly, he announced his pending move to Amman, Jordan.

"Mahmoud's Uncle Assafa lives in Amman, and he has arranged jobs for the two of us. We will be working construction under the guidance of Assafa, and the job will begin on the first of January. I was afraid to tell you that I was moving and put it off as long as I could, but I knew I had to let you know what was happening in my SCL—super crazy life."

Nadje was disheartened by the sad news. She was expecting her son to announce his plans to return home, but he was moving further away. Azfal too was saddened, but he understood that the young man had to choose his own path in life.

After a short awkward visit, Saady went upstairs to visit his nephew; the first time he saw the lively toddler in two months. It was great for him to play with the boy, but he was mindful to leave before Ibrahim returned from work, not wanting to cause any conflict. Prior to his departure, he asked Nebet to notify his brother of his plans to move to Jordan.

"I'll tell him. Hopefully, the two of you can have a conversation before you leave."

There was no response. Her brother-in-law simply smiled before exiting.

She wanted desperately for the quarrelling brothers to stop their fighting and prayed that her husband would make an effort.

There was an uneasiness during dinner that was apparent to Ibrahim. His wife barely touched the lamb chops on her white unadorned china.

"What is wrong?"

She wasn't sure how he would react and spoke almost in a whisper, "Saady stopped by today. He's moving to Amman with Mahmoud. Apparently, his Uncle Assafa has a construction job for them." She didn't look at him after speaking.

Ibrahim didn't have a reaction. It appeared to his wife that the rift between the bothers would never be mended, but in reality, he was worried about the possibility of losing Saady forever. He didn't know how to respond at first but eventually opened up.

"I plan on saying goodbye to my brother in person before Saady leaves for Amman. I don't want our quarrelling to affect the family any longer." He hoped to fix their relationship so his brother wouldn't leave with them still on bad terms.

A couple days before Saady was to leave Iraq, he and Mahmoud began to pack.

"My mother said she was coming over to help us."

"Great! She can take over; I'm already sweating profusely. I hate packing!" the stocky and balding friend replied.

Nadje woke up early to prepare for the day and patiently waited for Ibrahim who gave her a ride to Mahmoud's house on his way to work. She wanted to help the men "properly" pack their belongings.

"How many things are you bringing? It looks like you're the one who is moving," Ibrahim joked while helping his mother load the trunk.

"I just brought some household items for him to take, mostly sheets and towels."

It was the beginning of the rainy season, and drops were pelting the car on the drive to *Az Kazimiyah*. Ibrahim slowly navigated through the crowded streets and arrived at Mahmoud's safely. He desperately wanted to go inside and speak with his brother but didn't know how to begin the process of mending their troubled relationship. After emptying the contents from the car onto the cracked walkway leading to the front door, he hugged his mother goodbye.

"I'll stop by tomorrow to wish Saady a safe journey."

Nadje spent the entire day at Mahmoud's.

"It's getting late. I have to go home and make dinner for Azi, assuming he hasn't eaten already."

She said goodbye to her troubled son and headed for the jeep after a long embrace. "You be sure to take care of yourself. And don't forget to pass by the house before you leave."

Mahmoud was in the driver's seat warming up the vehicle in preparation for the trip, but he was concerned about the decrepit wipers since the rain was progressively worse than in the morning.

"Please drive careful, Mahmoud. The roads will be slick and very dangerous. We don't have to rush. Azi can wait for his dinner."

Mahmoud was having a hard time seeing the road but didn't say anything to Nadje since he didn't want to alarm her.

"Are you sure you can see the road?" she worriedly asked.

"Yes, everything is fine. The wipers are better on my side than on yours," he fibbed.

He slowly drove east from *Az Kazimiyah* to the Ansary home, first heading south toward the center of Baghdad before crossing the Tigris River and heading north in route to *Al A'zamiyah*. The torrential downpour made visibility almost impossible. Mahmoud wasn't able to see five feet in front of him, but he did his best to navigate the slippery roads.

"Maybe you should pull over until the rain slows down," Nadje suggested.

"I think you're right. The rain is getting worse. There's a gas station coming up at the next intersection. I'll stop there, and we can wait out the storm."

"Thank you."

Mahmoud noticed Nadje's trembling hands and could see that she was anxious. "You're just like my mother, always worrying," he said while shaking his head.

"And you're just like my sons, never listening," she responded with a smile.

They laughed and he patted her left hand with his right one. "Don't worry. I'll get you home in one p—"

"Watch out!" she screamed, interrupting the driver.

It was too late! Mahmoud didn't notice the stop sign. He drove through the intersection and a massive big rig T-boned his raggedy jeep. The trucker wasn't able to stop his momentum. As he swerved, the mammoth vehicle rammed into the passenger-side door of the jeep causing it to spin across the road and smash into a parked sedan.

Mahmoud suffered a concussion, and several minutes elapsed, after the initial impact, before he gained consciousness. After gathering his bearings, he looked around and realized that they were involved in a terrible accident. The deafening sound of a siren filled his eardrum as an ambulance approached the scene. He turned to the passenger side and saw the trail of blood trickling down the right side of Nadje's pale face. Her hair was filled with shards of glass, but he couldn't tell if she was breathing.

"Nadje," he said in a faint whisper.

There was no response. He attempted to reach out to her but couldn't manage because of his dislocated right shoulder. After the paramedics arrived, he was carefully removed from the smashed vehicle. Mahmoud was whisked away before Nadje was attended to so he had no idea what kind of condition she was in.

"Is she going to be all right?" he asked. There was no response from the technician. He wanted to ask again but didn't have the strength. He drifted off into sleep.

Azfal was exhausted and ready for bed. He was aware that Nadje would have a difficult time letting go of her youngest child. He didn't expect for her to return early and ate dinner at Ibrahim's house. The fact that his wife was still out at such a late hour surprised him, so the worried husband decided to dial Mahmoud's number to find out how long before she planned on returning home.

"Hello," Saady answered.

"It's me. I just want to know what time your mother plans on coming home."

"Mahmoud left a few hours ago. He should be arriving AFM— any freaking minute."

Azfal grew worried and knocked frantically on Ibrahim's door. "We have to drive around in case Mahmoud is having car trouble."

Ibrahim agreed that the road conditions were horrible. He thought it was possible the old jeep could've had a flat tire. Father and son headed south toward the center of Baghdad on the most likely route in search of the vehicle.

A mile from the house, they arrived at the scene of a horrific accident. Ibrahim immediately recognized Mahmoud's rusted jeep.

"*Allah*, help us!" he exclaimed.

It was apparent that the fire department had to use the Jaws of Life to rescue its occupants. Azfal turned to his son and spoke in a barely audible voice, "Hospital."

The distraught man drove as fast as he could without the car hydroplaning, and they arrived at the emergency entrance of *Al Nuaman* General Hospital after the short trip, figuring Nadje was taken there since it was the closest in proximity to the crash site.

The two men worriedly ran inside after parking the car half-hazard into two spaces. They approached the reception desk and were completely out of breath. "Please can you tell me where my mother is?"

The cranky receptionist required more information. "What is her name?"

He collected himself. "Nadje Ansary."

She had the reaction of someone who knew a juicy secret, and he instantly realized his mother was seriously injured. The reception-ist pointed to the waiting area. "Have a seat and I'll find out where she is."

Panic set in, and Azfal almost fainted once he saw her expres-sion. He just about collapsed to the ground, only able to make it to an open seat with Ibrahim's help.

The apathetic emergency room receptionist picked up the phone. "Doctor *Sharif*, they're here."

After a few moments of waiting, Ibrahim combatively returned to the desk and demanded to see his mother, but his insistence didn't help. The cold receptionist simply ignored his demands and contin-ued to focus on the screen of her laptop. The unsympathetic woman clearly wasn't going to be of any help, so he begrudgingly sat down next to his grief-stricken father in the cold-deserted waiting area.

About ten minutes later, a triage doctor walked out and approached the receptionist. He asked her to identify the family members, and she pointed out the two men.

The compassionate surgeon approached them nearly in slow motion. "Hello, gentlemen. I'm Dr. *Sharif.*"

He noticed that Azfal was in no condition to talk, so his focus was on Ibrahim. "Is Mrs. Ansary your mother?"

"Yes, my name is Ibrahim, and this is my father Azfal."

"And is Mahmoud your brother?" he further inquired.

"No, he's my brother's best friend."

Doctor *Sharif* paused and took a deep breath. "There was a terrible accident due to the horrible road conditions. Mahmoud has a dislocated shoulder and several tiny fractures in his right leg. He is in surgery as we speak. Thankfully, he is expected to make a full recovery."

The doctor took a deeper breath, but he didn't have to say anything for Ibrahim and Azfal to know what was about to come out of his mouth. "Mrs. Ansary caught the brunt of the impact since she was seated on the passenger side of the vehicle. Her legs were wedged under the console and were crushed. The responding EMTs did everything that was in their power, but I am sorry to inform you that she did not survive the accident. She was pronounced dead on arrival."

The words stung Azfal. He felt the pain of the many parents who answer their doorbell and find two military men standing with an American flag, only to hear that their child would not be coming home from the war. The old man was aware that his cardiovascular disease, because of narrow blood vessels, put him at risk of a heart attack. He wasn't strong enough to take in the news. The dedicated husband immediately fainted.

Tears began to roll down Ibrahim's face. He resembled a cardboard cutout, sitting motionless in the hard-unpadded chair. Unable to move, he attempted desperately to comprehend what had taken place.

Azfal stared at the picture of two smiling children that hung, directly in front of him, on the white brick wall. He couldn't comprehend why they were so happy at such a morose moment. Slowly, he regained his composure. Neither of the men could muster up the energy to leave the hospital and remained seated in their devastated state. Azfal didn't feel like he had a reason to continue living because Nadje was everything to him and five hours elapsed before Ibrahim was courageous enough to identify the body. Her husband refused to see the lifeless corpse. His fragile heart wouldn't be able to handle entering the hospital morgue.

The silent drive home was the longest they ever experienced. Nadje was the glue that held the family together, and the men weren't sure how to cope with her untimely death. Nebet was driven to tears when her husband woke her up to deliver the horrific news; Nadje was her closest friend. It was she who immediately welcomed Ibrahim's beautiful wife into the family, careful never to treat her like an in-law.

Ibrahim cried uncontrollably on the drive to Mahmoud's house as he attempted to figure out what to say. He wanted to deliver the dreadful news to his brother in person.

"Ibrahim!" Saady said quizzically. "Why are you crying—what's wrong?" He thought that his sibling had reached a moment of enlightenment and was there to apologize for the many years that he was a jerk.

Ibrahim struggled to speak. "I have some bad news."

The happy expression on Saady's face was replaced with a look of terror. "What happened?"

"It's Mom. They were in an accident. She didn't survive."

Saady fell to his knees. "What about Mahmoud?"

"He's hurt badly, but he'll be okay."

Ibrahim lifted his brother, and they embraced one another tightly as they desperately attempted to cope with the pain. At that instance, the rift between them no longer mattered; neither man uttered a word.

Nadje's funeral was the worst day of his life. Azfal's new disheveled appearance bothered everyone but himself. He was always recognized for his well-groomed attire and stoical demeanor but no longer cared to keep up his looks. A week went by, and there was still no progress in his mood. He secretly blamed Saady and Ibrahim's fighting for the death of his loving wife, so he couldn't stand to be around either of them. The bereaved father would not speak to his sons directly. He felt disrespected because the turmoil between them still existed. The siblings attempted to be civil to one another, but their pretense didn't fool Azfal. It was obvious to him the boys still detested each other after overhearing Ibrahim yelling at his brother while on the phone. The way the men avoided each other at the ceremony was another clear sign.

A month later, Ibrahim parked the family car in the narrow driveway. The rear door swung open, and Nebet walked out. She opened the passenger door and offered to assist the phlegmatic Azfal.

"Hold my hand, Papa. Let me help you out."

The driver's side rear door opened, and Ibrahim grabbed little Jassim from his car seat. They planned to sit down for dinner as a family, but Azfal refused. He wanted to be alone; he was completely heartbroken. Never in his life had he felt so much pain. It was as if a group of cannibals carved open his chest and consumed his heart while he watched.

"What's the point? There is no need for me to be a burden on anyone."

The alarmed son turned to his wife as they watched the forlorn old man walk into his apartment. "I really hoped the trip to the zoo would have lifted his spirits. I don't think he will ever come out of this funk."

"Of course, he will. We just have to be there for him and help him get through it."

<hr />

Saady postponed his move to Amman in order to allow his best friend to fully recover. The two of them remained close buddies.

"I want you to know that you are not at fault. It was an accident."

"Thank you for saying that. It means a lot." Mahmoud looked down at the tiled floor. "I feel horrible. I think your dad hates me."

Saady placed his hand on his wounded friend's chin and lifted his head. "No, he doesn't. He's just having a hard time dealing with the pain. He knows it wasn't your fault."

The guilt-ridden son wasn't sure if he should go through with his move to Jordan since it was the reason for the tragedy. He wasn't one hundred percent sure if Azfal blamed his departure for Nadje's death, but the silent treatment he received seemed to be a clear indication of how his father truly felt. There was a desperate desire to repair their relationship before he left the country, but he was aware that time was running out. Nebet continued to try and lift her father-in-law's spirits, yet nothing seemed to work.

"Papa, can you watch Jassi for me. I have a lot of errands to run, and I won't get everything done unless I leave him behind. I won't be long, I promise," she fibbed.

The young matriarch secretly hoped the baby would somehow be able to bring him out of his depressive state. Azfal loved his grandson, but he was constantly in a sour mood, which caused him to lose the connection that the two were building. Feeling as though he didn't have a choice, he reluctantly agreed to care for the "little diaper filler."

Her plan worked marvelously. Azfal was forced to interact with the child, and the more he engaged his grandson, the better he felt. It was the first time he smiled since the accident. Nebet returned to the house a few hours later and found him bouncing the blissful child on his knee while they both laughed. She was extremely happy to see her "papa" in a better frame of mind and proud to be able to think up the successful plan.

Azfal finally gave his blessings for his son's move to Amman. The rejuvenated old man recited *Surah* 2, *Ayah* 149, "From whencesoever Thou startest forth, turn Thy face in the direction of the sacred Mosque; that is indeed the truth from the Lord, *Allah* is not unmindful of what ye do."

"I promise that I will always remember to adhere to the traditions of the prophet," he replied prior to exuberantly leaving with the recovered Mahmoud.

Nebet was glad to see the family beginning to get back to some form of normalcy. Even Ibrahim and his father's relationship improved slowly with time. Although Azfal still blamed his sons for Nadje's death, he did his best to forgive them. With a better grasp of the situation, he assured the family friend that he was not to blame for the accident. The kind gesture was a huge weight off Mahmoud's shoulders. The tension that he felt during Saady's weekly phone calls home dissipated. Each call brought the family closer, but the relationship between the brothers remained rocky.

Azfal knew his boys would never fix their differences, but he was happy that they at least didn't completely despise one another. He continued to hold out a semblance of hope for them to become loving siblings once again, but it would take a long time. The brothers spoke on the phone on a few occasions, to their father's delight, but they had a difficult time letting go of the past. Azfal spent every waking moment with his grandson and each day his condition improved; they were inseparable.

<hr />

Five-year-old Jassim continued to be Azfal's best friend, but trouble was on the horizon since the "golden child" was finally old enough to enroll in school. The learned grandfather taught his grandson how to read, write, and calculate simple math problems at an early age; the boy was thoroughly prepared.

"I'm worried that once Jassi heads off to school, Papa's condition might regress," Nebet said.

"I have the same fear, but you were able to help him get through the initial hurt, so I'm sure we will figure out a way to help him again."

The child excelled in school as expected, but the downside was Azfal's slow descent back to his depressive state. Jassim's parents were called to the school for a meeting after the first week of classes. To their surprise, his teacher and the principal informed them that he would be promoted to the first grade due to his advanced intelligence.

Azfal was proud of his grandson, but the loneliness he felt slowly resurfaced. Nebet noticed that he was returning to his sad state and once again asked Ibrahim to think of a solution.

"Something has to be done immediately."

"I got it! He always wanted to move to Italy but chose to stay in Iraq so he could raise a family with Mom. Maybe a move will help his condition."

She agreed it was a good idea, and they approached him in the evening.

"Dad, I think you should consider moving to Italy. I know it was a lifelong dream of yours, and I think now is the time for you to fulfill it. Living in Rome for a few years may be beneficial to you since it is what you always wanted to do. I know you gave up your dream for our family and it's time for you to do something wonderful for yourself."

Azfal initially felt his condition would worsen if he moved away from his grandson, but Ibrahim assured him that the two of them could talk on the phone regularly. They could chat for hours about their daily experiences.

"He can live vicariously through your experiences. Think of how exciting that would be for Jassi."

Azfal eventually warmed up to the idea of moving to Rome, the more he thought about it, but he was sure to discuss his possible departure with Jassim before ultimately agreeing and called the boy into the kitchen. The mature child's positive reaction was a pleasant surprise; the boy expressed excitement for his grandfather.

"Azi, I can't wait to hear your stories of how great Rome is when we talk on the phone." He was also excited about eventually visiting his grandfather in the ancient historic city.

Azfal promised that they would keep in constant contact and that he would visit Baghdad as often as he could. Jassim was a little saddened by the fact that his best friend was leaving, but his parents did their best to explain the situation to him.

"You have to understand that this has been Papa's lifelong dream, Jassi, and we need to be supportive."

"I know, Mom. Once I'm old enough, I will visit Azi in Rome!"

His grandfather gladly agreed to pay for the future flight.

Chapter 2

The city of Rome was everything Azfal thought it would be. The first two months were spent exploring the ancient historical sites and traveling through the boot-shaped nation. He was able to save up a large sum of money for his retirement along with the substantial check he received from the life insurance policy. He visited every glorious site that he studied during his time in Cairo and spent his days touring the country while his nights were designated for his journal writing. The detailed entries were scribed so he could relay his experiences to Jassim during their extensive weekly phone conversations.

When Azfal grew tired of traveling through the boot-shaped nation, he decided to settle in Rome. Although he loved most of the Italian cities, Rome was his absolute favorite. It was the only city that he wanted to live in. Soccer was his sport of choice as a youngster. He played it often, but wasn't very talented. The men in his family always gathered around the television and watched the World Cup matches with each person cheering on his respective team. Italy was the nation he supported, but his favorite player was *Pele*, who played for the Brazilian squad. He was aware that *Calcio* was a very important sport to the Italians and decided to attend his first league match at the *Stadio Olimpico* in Rome. An Englishman stood behind him in the crowded ticket line, and the two men struck up a conversation.

"The names Ralph. You a big fan of Roma?" the Londoner said as he extended his right arm.

"Nice to meet you. I'm Azfal. This is my first game," he replied, shaking the polite man's hand.

"First match? You're gonna love it! Gets about as rowdy as Wembley Stadium back home!" Ralph said, oozing enthusiasm.

"I know football is a big sport in Italy, so I wanted to experience the thrill—beautiful stadium!"

"Hey, Asfel, did you know they built Olympic Stadium for the 1960 Olympic Games in Rome?" The tourist with a fanny pack wondered.

Azfal didn't bother correcting the mispronunciation of his name. "That's interesting. I had no idea."

"Yeah, but now they use it as the home field for two clubs in Italy's *Serie-A*—*AS Roma* and *Lazio*. They're bitter rivals the game is called *Il Derby Capitolino*. You're lucky that the Rome Derby will be your first game."

Azfal was excited and approached the ticket booth, asking the young man sitting inside for a ticket to the game.

"*Quale squadra ti supporto?*" the attendant asked.

The question threw him off since he didn't have an allegiance to either side.

"Rome," he replied, deciding to support the team named after his favorite city. He was in for a treat. The match between the hated rivals was the soccer equivalent of a Civil War.

The attendant handed him the aforementioned ticket on the *Associazione Sportiva Roma* side of the stadium.

"Even though the team is named *Roma*, it's also called '*i Lupi*,' '*i Giallorossi*,' and '*La Magica*.' It's important to sit on the side of the team you support because there is usually some hooliganism that occurs in the stands," Ralph added.

"Thanks for the info. You've been extremely helpful," Azfal said while shaking the Englishman's hand before walking toward the stadium's entrance. *The wolves, the yellow reds, and the magic one*, weird names he thought.

Azfal purchased a program, and an usher helped him locate his seat in the nearly filled to capacity arena. His section was a great distance from the field, but he fell in love with the pandemonium that exploded in the festive atmosphere. Ralph was right. There were a few scrums fights that had to be broken up in the sections closest to the opposing side. The players put on a fantastic show, displaying their creativity with the ball, and there were several great scoring opportunities. One Roma player electrified the fan base by scoring on a strike from thirty yards away. Azfal shared high fives with several of the people sitting near him. He couldn't remember the last time he had so much fun. The match was a great experience, and he loved cheering on Roma, which quickly became his favorite team. The game finished with Roma winning *uno a nessuno*. The victory gave him a sense of belonging, and he truly believed he was a good luck charm.

On the taxi ride to his hotel, Azfal read the detailed program and learned about the historic rivalry between Rome's two clubs. His good luck must have truly been real since Roma eventually won the *Scudetto* in 2001, taking home the cherished golden trophy. Roma lost in the championship game to a club named *Juventus* in 2002, but the team was having another successful season and hoped to make a return to the championship game. The wonderful experience of his first game was unlike any other, and he planned on introducing Jassim to the splendid world of Italian club soccer after his arrival.

"The game was superb. I learned that the word *Scudetto* means a small shield and it looks like a golden champagne glass."

"Wow, Azi. The game must have been really exciting. When I visit Rome, I want us to go to a Roma match," Jassim said enthusiastically.

"Of course, we will. I can't wait until you are old enough to visit."

<hr />

The Inn at the Spanish Steps was Azfal's dream hotel ever since discovering it while studying in Cairo. He wasn't familiar with the history of the steps and sought out a guide who was very informative.

"The *Scalinata*, completed in AD 1725, is Europe's largest staircase with 138 steps and is unmatched in length and width. The Spanish Steps connects the Holy See to the Bourbon Spanish Embassy, and the Roman Catholic Church used these steps as a major source of income by selling indulgences to Catholics for a small fee. The laity paid to climb the *Scalinata*, saying a prayer on every step and the amount of money they dished out determined the length of time that would be reduced from their stay in purgatory."

Azfal thanked *Benjamino* for the information and decided to reserve a luxurious seven-night's stay in the hotel's most expensive room. He planned on eventually renting a permanent apartment but wanted to have the greatest experience of his life subsequently. The hotel stay was better than he could have ever imagined. Dining on the rooftop, marveling at the lovely décor, and enjoying the hospitality of the helpful staff would be everlasting memories. On the third day, he spoke with the helpful concierge, inquiring about any hidden treasures that he might recommend.

"There's an ancient Etruscan town east of Rome, which I consider the jewel of ancient Roman Civilization. The lovely town sits at the base of the *Monti Prenestini*, a range in the central *Apennines*," Marco informed.

The adventurous Azfal arranged for a private car with a gregarious Italian driver for the ride to Palestrina.

"Take me to the elegant Renaissance *Barberini* Palace so I can visit the National Archaeological Museum of Palestrina," he requested.

The Egyptologist's interest was picqued when the knowledgeable Marco described the beauty of the Nile Mosaic of Palestrina, located in the museum's third floor exhibit. The breathtaking scenery of the mountains bordering the town was visible from a third floor window, and he thought, *Marco was one hundred percent correct. This is possibly the best view in the world.*

Luciana Mancuso, a distinguished fifty-eight-year-old lady, the museum's director, noticed that Azfal knew more about the Egyptian mosaic than the guide. She inherited millions of dollars from her parent's estate and was an only child who devoted her free time to helping less fortunate people. The gentlemanly Azfal was immediately attracted to her. She didn't have the most beautiful face, but her commanding presence captivated him. His attention was split between her and the mosaic. She was very impressed with his erudite familiarity with Egyptian history.

"I believe the information attached to this artifact is incorrect. As far as I can ascertain, the soldiers are misidentified. They are not Alexander and his Macedonians but, in fact, Ptolemaic Greeks. I am certain of it."

Luciana arranged for the piece to be reexamined by experts, and Azfal's claim was confirmed six days after his first visit. He was invited to have lunch with the stunning director in order for her to reveal their findings. Ms. Mancuso offered him a position in the museum, and the scholar was interested, but he revealed his desire to find an apartment in Rome. After some persuasive banter, the temptress convinced him to move to Palestrina and accept the job as the museum's second-in-command.

"This is the great home available for rent I was telling you about. It's only a few streets from the museum," his new boss informed.

"It's perfect. Thanks again for helping me find a place to live."

The sleepy town grew dear to his heart within his first week of living there. Palestrina became his new home away from Iraq, and he slowly assimilated into the Italian culture. He was excited for Jassim to visit the magnificent former outpost.

As soon as Azfal settled into his new place, he called his cheerful grandson and revealed the good news during their hour-long conversation. He arrived in Italy at the beginning of September and was not accustomed to the colder weather but felt he would eventually adjust.

In October 1998, he returned to Iraq for the celebration of Jassim's sixth birthday, but he could only stay a week before heading back to brave the Italian wintry weather. During the visit, he recommended that his grandson visit during the cold so the boy could experience the splendid snowfall. Azfal looked forward to his second winter in Italy and was the only resident of *Via Veroli* who excitedly anticipated the backbreaking chore of shoveling snow.

During the fall of 2002, Jassim anticipated celebrating his tenth birthday with his best friend, but Azfal called a week prior to his flight to Baghdad.

"Jassi, I have some terrible news. Luciana can't find a replacement for me at the museum, so I won't be able to visit next week. I will make it up to you, though, I promise."

"That's okay, Azi. Maybe I can go visit you soon," Jassim understandingly replied.

He was clearly disappointed. Azfal's arrival had been circled on his calendar since his grandfather's last visit. The old man could hear the hurt in his grandson's voice and wondered if he was doing the right thing.

The morning of his birthday, Jassim ran to the front door to answer the bell. He was filled excitement, thinking that it was a package from Azfal. The naïve boy fell for the sly trickster's hoax.

"Azi, you made it!" an overjoyed Jassim shouted and jumped into his grandfather's awaiting arms.

"I wouldn't have missed it for the world, Jassi."

Number 10 turned out to be Jassim's favorite birthday.

Prior to leaving, Azfal promised his grandson he could visit Italy the following year, and the young man was thrilled. He couldn't wait to see his grandfather's new home and explore the museum exhibits that were described so eloquently during their phone conversations. Although he loved Rome, Azfal's main reason for leaving his native Iraq was the fact that his best friend went off to school, which cut down their quality time.

Ironically a month after his departure, Nebet and Ibrahim decided that it would be in their son's best interest if he left the school to be homeschooled by his mother. She was very intelligent and possessed a degree in physics from the *Ibn Al-Haitham* College of Science in *Al A'zamiyah*, teaching the subject at a local high school for a few years. At the time, raising her child became more important, so she decided to become a stay-at-home mom.

Nebet regained her desire to teach and walked with Jassim to the *Ibn Al-Haitham* campus daily for his instruction. She was an independent thinker who usually kept her off-putting comments to herself, but she ensured that her son was well aware of the atrocities committed by Saddam against the Iraqi people, refusing to allow him to grow up in admiration of the "evil totalitarian." It would have pained her greatly if he grew up agreeing with his father's ideology. These clandestine political lessons were obviously hidden from Ibrahim who would have been irate if he found out.

Jassim was taught by his mother during the morning but attended the newly constructed Saddam Hussein Language Institute in the Center of Baghdad. His lessons were daily from four to six. The institute was only operational for two years prior to his enrollment and constructed by President Hussein at the suggestion of Ibrahim, his most trusted translator.

The ultimate goal was to create a crop of the best linguists in the world, allowing for Saddam to have the ability of communicating with every single world leader. Instructors were flown in from all over the globe, and students were enrolled as early as age five. The school instructed each pupil to select two languages, which were learned simultaneously. Each class was an hour long and met daily. Jassim chose English and Italian as his first selections so he would be able to understand the citizens of Italy when he visited his grandfather. He also wanted to have the ability to read the array of books, which Ibrahim brought back from his many visits to America. Each language was taught for a five-year period, after which the students chose two different idioms for another five-year phase. Jassim planned on learning Spanish and French for his two subsequent dialects since he believed them to be fairly popular.

His fifth year at the institute ended in December of 2002. Ibrahim was proud of both the successful institution and his studious offspring who was fluent in both English and Italian. At the time, the majority of Iraqis worried that the United States might invade their motherland and the Ansarys were among them. His cautious parents agreed to send Jassim for a visit to Italy in January until the threat of war dissipated. Azfal was elated but suggested the child be sent to Amman to visit Saady for a week before flying to Rome. To everyone's astonishment, Ibrahim agreed with his father's idea, but it

was his wife who notified her brother-in-law of his nephew's sojourn.
The rift was still not completely mended.

"Hey, Saady, I have some good news. We are sending Jassi to
Italy to visit Dad, but first, he will ride to Amman so the two of you
can spend a week together."

"I can't wait! That is the BNE—best news ever!"

A black armored sedan was arranged by Ibrahim to transfer
his son on the five-hundred-mile journey. A capable soldier from
Saddam's *Fedahim* guard named *Amar* accompanied him. Jassim slept
for the majority of the time since Amar was not the best companion.
The military man had a repulsive personality and an apparent hatred
of children. The soldier was highly regarded by his commanders but
possessed little social skills, which Jassim quickly discovered.

"If you don't stop bothering me with your annoying questions,
you will not make it to Amman, I assure you," Amar threatened.

The driver, a burly man named *Fahid*, was a soldier as well. He
was even more of an introvert than Amar. These men were clearly
chosen for their ability to keep Jassim safe since they were intrepid
fighters and not for their companionship. Fahid was familiar with
Amman and easily navigated the confusing streets to Saady's apartment complex.

Jassim rushed out of the car, and the soldiers gathered his luggage from the trunk, placing them in front of the unassuming apartment building. Thrilled to see his uncle, the boy animatedly ran
to the front entrance and pressed the lit buzzer labeled "Saady and
Mahmoud."

"Who is it?" boomed Saady's voice out of the deafening
intercom.

"It's me, Jassi."

"It can't be Jassi. My nephew is a little baby, not a GYM—
grown young man."

Jassim laughed since he was the only person who enjoyed Saady's
irritating acronyms. "Uncle Saady, it's me. Open the door."

The buzzer sounded, and Jassim opened the single-pane door.
He entered the empty foyer and kept an eye out for his uncle who
took a couple minutes before running down the large center stairway

and hugging his nephew. The lobby was immaculate and lavishly decorated; the wide-eyed boy thought his uncle was living in a palace.

Amar and Fahid entered the building, each holding a suitcase. When Jassim was settled, they quickly said goodbye and headed back to Iraq.

Uncle and Nephew enjoyed a week of reestablishing their friendship. Even though they spoke twice a month, the separation made it difficult for them to connect. Mahmoud was on *hajj* to Mecca and was expected to be away for another three weeks. A "lucky" Jassim was allowed to sleep on the dingy living room couch.

"You can have Mahmoud's bed," Saady said.

The couch wasn't comfortable at all but better than the floor, or so he thought. The faint daylight entered through the only window in the unstylish apartment, which was barely furnished other than the couch; the small, unvarnished kitchen table had two mismatching chairs. There was no television set, and the bedroom only had an old queen size bed in it. However, the boy's attention couldn't avert from the tinge of urine that seemed to attack his nostrils.

The capital was filled with great new discoveries for Jassim. The buildings were a mixture of ancient and modern architecture, and he was in awe of the sites. The ancient citadel, the Roman amphitheater, and King *Abdullah's* mosque were among his favorites. It was at the mosque that he snapped the most pictures with the small digital camera that Ibrahim purchased so he would be able to record his first adventure. The photos from Amman were e-mailed to Azfal who lived vicariously through his grandson's escapade. Jassim loved the triangles atop the dome of the King *Abdullah* Mosque.

"You know what, Uncle Saady? When I am old enough to have my own house, I plan to build it using the same design as the mosque."

The week seemed to fly by; Jassim was sad to leave his uncle, but he was excited to finally be heading to Rome. He always viewed Saady as a great man, and the experience only strengthened his admiration, but he wondered the same thing as his mother.

"Uncle, why don't you have a wife?"

"I'm a bachelor. Me and Mahmoud have too much fun living the single life for us to get a LJS—lifelong jail sentence."

The perceptive boy found it hard to believe that Mahmoud slept on that uncomfortably awful couch since it was the worst night sleep that he ever had; he decided to drop the subject. After the first night of tossing and turning, he chose to move and take his chances on the hardwood floor.

It was a short drive to the relatively small Queen *Alia* International Airport. Its smoke-filled lobby was not a welcoming place for a child, but nothing could be done. The attendant at the *Alitalia* Airline counter, a middle-age widow dressed in a black *burqa*, assisted with the check-in.

"I'm sorry, sir, but you cannot accompany your nephew to the gate—only ticketed passengers are permitted," she said.

Saady was comforted when she managed to call one of the flight attendants to the main desk for assistance. Her name was Nira, and Saady noticed how stunning the Brazilian was, but he did not reciprocate when she flirted. She moved to Italy and decided to work for the airline to travel the world. The appreciative uncle hugged his nephew goodbye and watched as the lovely attendant led Jassim through the crowded security check.

"Don't forget to call your SGU—super great uncle—when you arrive!" he yelled vociferously.

Nira arranged for Jassim to be the first passenger to board the plane and named him an honorary attendant. First class was completely booked, so she placed the youth in a first row window seat in the coach section. He thoroughly enjoyed the flight to Paris and was given all the pretzels and cold drinks that he desired. She noticed his blue stuffed dragon and instantly fell in love with it.

"Hey, nice dragon, kid. I loved dragons when I was about your age. Are you going to leave that with me as my special gift?"

Jassim squeezed the dragon tightly. "No, my grandfather gave it to me. It's my favorite toy."

She put on a sad puppy-dog face, and he laughed. The honorary attendant was given the duty of picking the in-flight movies as part of his "duties." The lengthy flight was scheduled for five hours and ten minutes, allowing for two movies to be featured. He selected *Shrek* and Steven Spielberg's *AI: Artificial Intelligence*; Jim Carey's *The Majestic* was left for another flight. As the plane reached the "city of lights," he peered out the window and noticed the Eiffel Tower rising above the Parisian skyline. The competent pilot pulled into the terminal fifteen minutes early, extending Jassim's half-hour layover. Luckily, he didn't have to leave the plane. The time went by rather quickly, and he was off to Rome on a relatively short flight—only two hours and five minutes. It was impossible to keep his heavy eyelids open, and he nodded off about ten minutes after they reached cruising altitude.

Chapter 3

Azfal sat in his white leather La-Z-Boy and devotedly read his *Qur'an*. It was a nightly custom that began after his move to Italy. He placed the Holy Book on the nightstand and prayed to the Lord.

"*Allah*, please allow for Jassi to have a safe flight from Amman." He stood up and raised his hands, nearly touching the low ceiling and continued to plead, "And please help me to get a good night's sleep. Thank you for allowing me a respite from the depressing nightmares, and please continue to keep them from reoccurring."

Opening the top drawer of the wooden nightstand, he pulled out an electronic sphygmomanometer to check his blood pressure before nestling his seventy-three-year-old body into the warm acacia sleigh bed. Azfal tossed and turned fervently in the darkness of his single-window room; the excitement stalled his sleep. He was determined to figure out the best way to make his grandson's visit a lasting memory. Italy had much to offer, and he wanted Jassim to enjoy the full experience. The covers eventually fell to the floor, and he finally managed to drift into dreamland at two o'clock in the morning.

"No!" Azfal screamed in terror.

He sat up and removed the sweat-drenched pajama top. Part of his hopeful prayer wasn't answered since he experienced the same dreadful nightmare yet again. The usual remedy was a hot cup of green tea, which he fixed for himself before drifting back to sleep.

The gleaming morning sunlight filled the room, waking the aged man who was full of energy despite the many distractions during his slumber. He stretched out his five-foot-eleven-inch slender frame before performing his customary morning exercise routine.

His apartment consisted of one bedroom with a convertible brown leather couch in the living room, which he referred to as his guest room. The loss of sleep didn't curve his excitement since he was on his way to Rome's *Leonardo da Vinci* Airport to pick up his grandson Jassim who was visiting from Baghdad. January eleventh had finally arrived, and Azfal was eager to see his best friend. The two didn't get to see much of one another since his move to Italy in 1997, and he couldn't sit at home and wait until the flight's evening arrival. His impatience forced him to ease his enthusiasm by going to the terminal early to get in some light reading Homer's *The Odyssey*.

Azfal drove his 1994 forest-green *Fiat Punto* into the ES Park at *Termini* Station in the bustling center of Rome and slowly pulled into the first available space a few minutes before noon. The parking lot was his best option since central Rome's streets have very few public parking spaces; most credible travel guides warn vacationers against the pointless rental of a car. The forty-seven-minute trip from his apartment in the antiquated Etruscan town of Palestrina felt quicker than usual. The lush backdrop of the Italian countryside appeared more picturesque, and the rolling landscape mirrored the paintings of the great French impressionist Claude Monet. The ride made him wonder if Monet was attempting to capture the rolling landscape as it must have appeared to a horseman who was riding swiftly through the pristine scenery.

The handling on his old *Punto* seemed sharper. It was as though the finest formula one racing crew worked on it overnight. Even the gasoline gauge seemed to linger around the F longer than usual; everything was improved. He noticed the temperature in Rome was warmer than it was at his home after stepping out of his modest car. He grabbed his golden-yellow and maroon *AS Roma* scarf from the headrest and draped it around his slumping shoulders. A gift from his boss, the scarf was his pride and joy. She knew how fond he was of the team and wanted to welcome him to "the family," a moniker for the museum staff. The door of the car squeaked loudly as he slammed it shut, and Azfal immediately unbuttoned his black trench coat before heading toward the opening in the chain-linked fence.

The sweet aroma coming from a nearby *friggitoria* called to him, but he was able to resist the temptation of buying one of the fried treats. The previous week's six inches of snow had completely dissolved, and there were no traces of *neve* remaining; only small clumps of deicing snow salt scattered everywhere. The trip to *Fiumicino* was easier by shuttle from Termini Station, so he leisurely walked toward the depot and entered the *Via Giovanni Giolitti* main doorway. The white *kufi* on his head was the only distinguishable representation of his faith. His European features and clean-shaven face would have allowed him to blend in seamlessly otherwise.

Azfal warily strolled the short distance through the packed vestibule of Termini Station to the ticket desk and entered the quickly moving line. The large smile from the attendant seemed fitting for the special day. He purchased a shuttle ticket before moving on to the departure area. There was a white minibus parked near the exit, but the door was closed, and he could see through the tinted windows that it was empty. The driver was not standing around, so he walked over to the cold empty iron bench to sit down. Soon after the grumpy driver with *Luca* on his shirt appeared, the door to the shuttle opened suddenly, and Azfal handed over his ticket before situating himself behind "*Signore Scontroso.*" The minibus wasn't scheduled to leave for another fifteen minutes, so he peered out the window observing the scampering people.

A young American couple, most likely in their twenties, approached the shuttle. The athletic looking man's sweatshirt read, "University of Maryland 2002 Men's National Champions."

"*Buon pomeriggio,*" he said in a horrible Italian accent, walking past Azfal who returned the greeting.

The bosomy girlfriend followed, but she didn't attempt to speak Italian. She simply uttered, "Good afternoon," in her southern drawl.

"*Buon pomeriggio,*" replied the awestruck Iraqi, whose thick Middle Eastern accent overpowered his fluent Italian.

They chose the backbench and sat down but seemed to be unhappy as they waited for the shuttle to depart. The princess refused her paramour's attempt at handholding, coldly turning toward the window.

Must have had a terrible trip, Azfal thought.

The next person to approach was a middle-aged Italian woman dressed in an Easy Terra car rental uniform. She rudely handed the driver a ticket and walked past Azfal without acknowledging him. She sat in the middle row on the passenger side, and her attention was quickly focused on his *kufi*. In her thick Italian accent, she said, "You're not going to blow the shuttle up, are you?"

Not wanting to cause a scene, he politely smiled and responded in Arabic. The portly woman assumed he didn't understand Italian and rolled her eyes.

The motor roared, and a well-dressed businessman waved for the driver to hold up. The door opened, and the man thanked Luca while boarding. He settled in behind Azfal who turned to face him. "*Fortunato.*"

"*Sì!*"

"*La navetta prossimo non lascia per un'altra mezz'ora.*"

"*So.*" He knew he was lucky to avoid the half-hour wait.

The lady's jaw dropped, and her eyes averted Azfal's defiant look. Luca closed the door and drove off.

Thirty-eight minutes elapsed during the quiet ride to *Fiumicino*. The shuttle passed a large statue of *Leonardo da Vinci* at the entrance, and Luca bypassed the first two terminals, pulling into the first destination—terminal C. It was ten minutes after one when they arrived at the international terminal. The minibus pulled up in front, and the first to exit was the businessman. He appeared less debonair in his haste since the back of his fine Italian suit jacket had a few new wrinkles. Azfal remained seated, allowing the young couple to get off first. He turned to the hostile woman.

"*Allah, mi scusi! DIO, vi benedica.*"

The antipathetic woman ignored him and remained seated since she was headed to the rental car area.

He entered the crowded terminal, noticing the changes since his arrival in 1997. It was a familiar place for him due to his numerous flights to Baghdad. The airport, previously in disrepair, lacked sufficient public seating, and he was happy to see the renovation had finally been concluded. Terminal C seemed more open with an expanded area for travelers to relax. Azfal made his way toward the information desk and protected himself from the indiscriminate bumping of strangers mumbling, "This must be what it feels like to be in a rugby scrum!"

He wanted to find out if there were any designated areas where he could sit down to enjoy his novel and asked a wide-eyed attendant with a welcoming smile.

"Yes, there are several places. I can walk you around until you find somewhere suitable."

"No, that won't be necessary. I don't want you to get into any trouble. Francesca, right?"

"Yes, perfect pronunciation. Don't worry about me. As long as you are happy, everything will be okay. If I get fired, I can always get another job."

Azfal felt bad but the altruistic attendant wouldn't take no for an answer. She stepped out from behind her post and led him to the Grand Café Panorama, enthusiastically pointing out the magnificent view it provided.

"If this isn't to your liking, I can take you to some of our smaller cafes."

"Thank you so much, Francesca. You have been too kind. This will be fine."

The Grand Café Panorama, with its massive windows, offered the best views of the airstrip, but he thought it was too noisy and continued to walk through the enormous terminal. Azfal backtracked a little in order to look at the wooden sculpture of *da Vinci*, which they passed on the way to the café.

Jassim's flight was scheduled to land ten minutes before seven, so he had a lot of down time, but there was no need to seek out more artwork since he didn't really notice any pieces other than the two renderings of the austere airport's namesake.

An enervated Azfal finally spotted a quaint café across from gate 17C. It had round mahogany tables that were mostly empty. Each table was set up for two people, and the rear was completely deserted. It was the perfect location he thought, and he placed an Arabic-Italian dictionary and his newly purchased Italian translation of *The Odyssey* on the table, resting his bag on the floor against table leg.

The Iliad was an enjoyable read, and he couldn't wait to begin Homer's second great epic. It had been a lengthy, adventurous morning, and he was in need of a snack. The depleted man headed toward the spotless counter and looked over the menu with its few overpriced options. Luckily, he found what he wanted. The sugarcoated *tarallo* had become his favorite treat since arriving in Italy. Behind the counter stood a young, fresh-faced Italian lady with *Falavigna* on her name tag, and she could tell he was ready.

"May I please take your order, *Signore?*"

"I'll have a *tarallo* and a large cup of green tea please."

There was a painting of the map of Italy encompassing the entirety of the back wall, and he placed his snack on the table and sat facing the map. With his back to the café's entrance, he took a moment to study the atlas. After locating Palestrina to the east of Rome, he grabbed *The Odyssey* and his trusted dictionary, which he needed for the more difficult words. The snack was enjoyable and complemented the tea perfectly. He returned to the counter three more times for a refill of the green tea, buying another tarallo with the fourth cup. Each time, before getting another cup, he walked toward gate 20C for a restroom break; his seventy-three-year-old bladder was working tirelessly.

At five o'clock, he felt the need to use the restroom for the sixth time, turning to *Falavigna* as he passed the counter.

"I think I need to stop drinking."

"You're getting better. You almost lasted a full half hour this time," she said, smiling.

The airport security guard was dressed in a neatly pressed white shirt, navy blue khaki pants, and a navy blue hat with the words "*Sicurezza Fiumicino*" written across the front. The misanthropic guard was armed with a walkie-talkie and his trusty flashlight. The gold badge covering his left shirt pocket sparkled as the light reflected from it. On the right side, he had a nameplate that read, "*Raggio.*"

The guard immediately noticed the *kufi* when Azfal first walked in. *Raggio* was keeping a close eye on the stranger since he felt the diadem as a red flag. He also noticed that Azfal was heading toward the restroom for a sixth time and assumed "the Muslim" was definitely up to no good, possibly planning a suicide mission.

As he walked out of the restroom, the guard accosted the innocent man who appeared utterly confused.

"Why are you bothering me? What have I done? Why are you being so aggressive?"

"What is your business at *Fiumicino*? SIGNORI!"

"I am just reading a book in the café, waiting for—"

"Be quiet," Raggio yelled. "You are not going to bomb my airport. Understand! Not while Raggio is on duty."

The irrational guard was in no mood to hear any explanations. He grabbed Azfal's wrist, warning him not to move, and picked up his walkie-talkie, calling for police backup. Azfal was accustomed to the bigotry that existed against Muslims, but he never expected to be arrested due to his faith.

A few minutes went by before two police officers eventually appeared, identifying themselves as officer *Pirozzo* and officer *Maresca*.

Pirozzo was a short pudgy man who couldn't out run an old lady in a foot race, while Maresca was tall and athletic. They appeared to be no-nonsense type of people, so Azfal expected the situation to worsen.

"What is going on here?" Officer Maresca asked sternly.

"This Muslim has been behaving very suspiciously. I think he is possibly trying to set up a bomb in the bathroom near gate 20C. He has been going in and out for the last four hours."

Maresca turned to the accused and asked if the allegations were true.

"I was excited about picking up my grandson who is flying in from Amman today. I was overly anxious, so I decided to get here early and read while I wait for him to land. I can show you my things."

He led the officers into the café where Officer Pirozzo questioned Falavigna, who corroborated his statement. The apologetic officers were disappointed with Raggio and begged Azfal's forgiveness for the guard's racist behavior.

"You are very welcomed in this country. There are only a few Italians who are ignorant. Do not let the ignorance of some taint the courteousness of many," Officer Maresca said warmly.

Azfal thanked the officers for being understanding and sat back in his seat. They heatedly walked over to Raggio, and as far as Azfal could determine, the nescient was on the receiving end of a stern reprimand.

The officers stood outside the café as Raggio angrily approached Azfal's table and—in an insincere manner—said, "I am sorry for the misunderstanding, no hard feelings, right?"

There was no reply, and as Raggio walked away, he stopped and turned to face "the Muslim."

"I am keeping an eye on you, Osama. The officers may believe your lies, but I know what you are up to. You cannot fool Raggio."

Azfal knew that some people were not able to change their ignorant ways and was reminded of *Surah* 6, *Ayah* 49: "And (as for) those who reject Our communications, chastisement shall afflict them because they transgressed."

He returned to reading *The Odyssey*, not allowing the incident to ruin his day. At six-thirty, he gathered his belongings and headed toward the exit, addressing Falavigna before leaving.

"Thank you so much for the wonderful *torallo* and the delicious tea. Also thank you for your assistance with the two officers."

She smiled. "*Di niente.*"

With his grandson due to arrive shortly, he left on his way to the baggage claim.

Chapter 4

Jassim slept through the short flight to *Fiumicino* due to exhaustion. Nira awakened him from his peaceful siesta, and he gazed out the plane's window, just in time to see the famous Roman Colosseum. He was excited to start exploring the old city once he reunited with his grandfather. The exquisite flight attendant gladly escorted him through the frantic terminal, and as a perk, he was allowed to bypass the custom's line. The new friends were in route to the baggage claim area to meet Azfal, but there was still one question that remained.

"If the airport is called *Leonardo da Vinci*, why is the airport code FIU?" the astute boy asked.

"Yeah, that confuses a lot of people. The airport is commonly referred to as *Fiumicino* because of the town it is located in. Most of the locals still use the name," Nira informed.

Jassim quickly scanned through the multitude of faces, finally spotting his grandfather who was seated near the exit leading to the taxis and shuttles.

The tickled grandson dodged through the sea of passengers and ran toward his Azfal with the agility of a midfielder cutting through the defense on his way to scoring a game winning goal. The old man stood up with a smile as wide as the *Shatt al Arab* when he recognized the boy.

The loving grandson jumped into his waiting arms, and they shared a long-awaited embrace.

"Look at you. You're a grown man. You're even taller than you were when I last visited. Look at that, you still have the little powder blue dragon. I can't believe you traveled with it." He ran his fingers through his grandson's hair.

Jassim quickly moved away to avoid ruining his haircut. The ten-year-old was already five feet three inches tall and growing rapidly.

"Of course, I did, Azi. I take it with me everywhere. Ever since you gave it to me, it has protected me. Dragons are my favorite creatures, and my father brought me many books from America."

Azfal was more comfortable speaking in Arabic since he exclusively spoke Italian after leaving Baghdad, except when talking to his family on the phone.

"Azi, I can't wait to see your museum and everything else. I really missed you a lot."

He was the only person who called Azfal, "Azi." It was the pet name given to him by Nadje, and his grandson's use of the name helped to ease the pain that he felt when she died. In a way, Jassim's love replaced Nadje's.

Nira stood near them and admired the love that they shared. She patiently waited for Jassim to introduce her.

"Azi, this is Nira. Thanks to her I received the VIP treatment during my trip."

Azfal thanked her for helping his grandson on the long journey and invited her to join them for dinner, but regretfully, she was unable to. She gave Jassim a tender hug and headed back to the gate for a red-eye flight to London.

The bags took about fifteen minutes to appear, after which they made the walk to the shuttle pickup since Azfal already purchased two tickets for the trip to Termini Station while he was waiting for Jassim to arrive. Prior to exiting the terminal, he retrieved a winter coat from his shoulder bag that he purchased in a Palestrina shop for the unprepared boy who had never experienced the cold of an Italian winter.

The shuttle arrived, and they were the last two passengers to board. Jassim was excited to see Rome but disappointed to learn that all the snow from the previous storm had melted. He was looking forward to experiencing his first *nevicata*. Reenergized from his nap, he was ready to take in the sites; most of which Azfal identified as they appeared in the distance. The large statue of *Leonardo da Vinci* was the first that the inquisitive boy marveled at on the scenic drive to the center of Rome.

The highlight of the ride happened when the considerate driver made a detour by the massive Roman Colosseum. Jassim was amazed by its grandeur and couldn't take his eyes off of the ancient structure.

"Azi, the Colosseum is the first place I want to visit when we explore the city."

"You're going to love it, Jassi."

The shuttle arrived five minutes to eight, and the passengers cleared out the minibus. After grabbing the luggage from the rear of the vehicle, they walked in the opposite direction, away from the station. Their destination was the ES Park lot.

"Jassi, let's put the bags in the car before we go to the restaurant. Last night, I reserved a table for two at nine o'clock, at *Monte Caruso*. It's only a penalty kick's distance from Termini Station. It's a small family owned place, and I hear the food is great."

They made the short walk from the parking lot to the quiet *Via Farini*.

"Azi, look at the great logo of an angel riding a fork."

The entrance had two golden lamps on each side of the door, and the interior was decorated with old Roman art.

"Great décor. I feel as if I am in ancient Rome!" Azfal exclaimed.

The restaurant was not very large, only accommodating fifty patrons, and consisted of three rooms that were furnished with small wooden tables. Each set up had two matching wooden chairs.

Monte Caruso was a traditional Italian restaurant in every sense. There were small white vases on the tabletops that contained a single red rose. The staff was extremely friendly. Azfal and Jassim felt as though they were part of the family. Most importantly, the food was exceptional.

"I feel like an emperor! Did you enjoy the meal, Jassi?"

"It was delicious. That's the best spaghetti and meatballs I have ever tasted! Thanks for the wonderful dinner, Azi."

While they sat to allow their food to digest, Jassim asked his grandfather to tell him about Nadje since he didn't really know his grandmother's history and wanted to learn as much as he could. The request brought a smile to the seventy-three-year-old's face.

"It is very pleasing to hear that you want to learn more about your grandmother. Family has always been important to me, and I see that you feel the same way."

"I've always wanted to learn about her, but I wasn't sure if it was all right for me to ask."

"Of course, it's okay. You can always ask me anything, you know that."

Azfal leaned back in his chair and started at the beginning.

"My father always taught me that education was very important. He said that it would be my ticket to anywhere in the world. He never forced me to study but regularly reminded me that if I wanted to be successful, it was up to me to push myself. I finished my senior year in high school at the top of my class, and your great-grandfather Saad was very proud of me. When I told him of my decision to further my education in Egypt, he supported me one hundred percent. My mother was very sad the day I left Baghdad mainly because she didn't think I would ever return. She said that I had an adventurers' spirit and thought I would continue to travel the globe for the rest of my life."

A large smile appeared on his face as he reminisced about his mother.

"I have to say that she was probably right since I didn't have any plans on returning to Iraq. My focus was to finish my studies and move to Rome, which to me has always been the greatest city in the world. I learned to speak Italian in high school and also took classes in college. It was always a dream of mine to live in Rome and find a job working at a historic museum."

Jassim was enthralled. He could feel the enthusiasm as his grandfather spoke.

"I loved my family and intended on visiting them frequently, but I never wanted to move back home. Cairo University was a great school, and I earned a degree in Egyptian studies with a minor in Italian.

"I decided to stay in Cairo for my graduate studies. The day I walked across that beautiful stage with my master's degree was very special because my parents were able to attend the ceremony." His smile was already wide but somehow seemed to grow wider as he mentioned his parents.

"I was offered a teaching job at the university and had to decide whether to take it or move to Rome. I didn't have too much money while living in Cairo, but I didn't accumulate any debt either. My schooling was covered by scholarships. In order to earn a few dollars for spending money, I worked at the campus bookstore. I was also able to put away some pounds in my savings account. I probably could've moved to Rome, but I chose to stay in Cairo and work for a few years as a professor so I could save a good amount of money before leaving.

"Things changed during the second week of my first semester as a professor. I scheduled all five of my classes on Tuesdays and Thursdays, which was a load, but I had the other five days of the week to myself. It was on a Monday that I went to my office in order to prepare the lesson plan for the upcoming week. I spent most of the day setting up the schedule, and as I walked out of my office, I saw the most beautiful woman I had ever laid eyes on. She appeared to float down the hallway as though she were an angel. I struggled with the key since my palms were sweaty but did my best to keep as cool as possible. Later, she revealed to me that it was obvious that I was nervous."

Jassim laughed as he pictured his grandfather nervously fidgeting with the lock.

"Smooth, Azi!"

"It wasn't easy. You'll understand when you get older," he said in an attempt to salvage his masculinity.

"When she reached my office door, I could smell her lovely jasmine scented perfume." Azfal closed his eyes and sniffed the air; he recalled her scent.

"I can still smell her whenever I close my eyes. I stood frozen by her beauty, and she smiled speaking in a soft voice. '*Salam*, can you tell me where the mathematics department is located.' I was mesmerized by her and could barely speak. I told her that I knew where it was but that it was on the other side of campus. She was flustered because she was told it was in my building. I could tell she was having a difficult time navigating through the confusing campus, so I decided to be her knight in shining armor and offered to walk her to her destination."

"Now that's really smooth!" Jassim exclaimed while his grandfather adjusted his clothing and posed as if there were a photographer directing the Casanova's movements.

"I understood why she was having difficulty finding her classroom since all the buildings looked similar. We had a nice chat as we made our way through the different paths. I learned she was also from Iraq and was a *Shi'a* Muslim from *Basrah*. I told her that *Sunni* was the true branch of *Islam,* in the tradition of the prophet, but she vehemently disagreed.

"We arrived at the math building after a pleasant walk. I wanted to see her again and was ready to ask for her number, but she beat me to the punch. She asked to exchange numbers in case she found herself lost again, and from that day on, we became close friends, usually meeting during the week to have lunch in the cafeteria.

"It was during her junior year that the course of my life was changed. Moving to Rome was no longer in my future plans. We were still inseparable, but things changed when she returned to campus after the summer break. We made plans to have dinner on August 26, the night she arrived from Iraq. I always wanted to ask her to be my girlfriend, but I wasn't sure how she felt. Her father was a wealthy and influential man in *Basrah*, and he would've never allowed for his only daughter to date a *Sunni*. Most importantly, I also didn't want to risk ruining our friendship.

"The dinner was enjoyable, and the night was perfect. I decided to take a chance and ask her if she wanted to go on a date, and she immediately began to laugh, which was devastating. I couldn't believe her reaction. I mistakenly thought she was laughing at me but was overjoyed to hear the five most wonderful words come out of her mouth."

Once again, he closed his eyes in order to recapture the moment.

"I can hear her voice now. 'What took you so long?' She felt the same way but assumed that I didn't like her, and in those days, it was unheard of for a woman to ask a man on a date. She almost lost hope, but we became a couple that night, and I knew instantly that she was going to be my wife.

"I was very proud of her when she graduated with a degree in chemistry. Your grandmother was a very intelligent woman. I saved up a good amount of money during my tenure as a professor, and we decided to move back to Iraq in order to start a family. We agreed to live in Baghdad, rather than *Basrah*, since her father disapproved of me. Our first apartment was very small and modest, but we loved it. Our bedroom window faced the banks of the Tigris River. I taught at Baghdad University, and your grandmother taught in one of the local high schools.

"It was four years after we moved back to Iraq that we discovered she was pregnant with your father. We decided to move to a larger home and found the perfect place in *Al A'zamiyah*. Nadje didn't mind that it was a predominantly *Sunni* territory. She was just excited to have a place where we could raise a family. I was making a decent amount of money, so I continued teaching while she stayed home with little Ibrahim."

Jassim excitedly interrupted, "Are you talking about the house we live in now, Azi?"

Azfal nodded his head affirmatively and continued the story. "Saady was born a few years later, and I continued to work at Baghdad University in the history department. We had enough *dinars* saved up to allow your grandmother to stay home with the boys, and when your parents got married, we converted the house into a two-family."

"Is that when Uncle Saady moved out?"

"No, Saady continued to live with Nadje and me for a while." The old man's mood shifted; he became more serious. "Your uncle and your father always had problems. They constantly fought with each other, but after you were born, things improved between them for a short period. I was hopeful, but eventually, the fighting escalated again several months later. I grew tired of the arguing and asked Saady to leave. That's when he moved in with his friend Mahmoud.

He didn't speak to your father or me for many months. It was your first birthday party that brought the family together again. The night was going well, but the tension between them resurfaced, and they fought once more. Two months later, Saady came by the house and revealed that he was moving to Amman in order to work. We were devastated to have him be so far away, but we wanted him to be happy. The worst day of my life was the day Nadje went to help Saady pack his belongings at Mahmoud's house. It was a rainy night, and while driving her back, Mahmoud lost control of his jeep, and they were involved in a fatal accident." Azfal began to choke up, and a tear rolled down his cheek.

Jassim was also teary-eyed. "You don't have to continue if it's too difficult, Azi."

"No, Jassi, you should hear about your grandmother. When your father and I reached the hospital, we were devastated to discover she didn't survive the crash. That was a very difficult day for me. I was depressed for a while. Till this day, I still have reoccurring nightmares about the accident. In fact, I had a terrible one last night. I get them about once a month, but I think they're getting better, and hopefully with you around, they'll stop.

"I secretly hated the boys after her death. I know it was wrong of me, but at the time, I blamed their fighting. I was barely alive after she died, just merely existing. Your blessed mother tried everything to improve my condition. Initially, nothing worked. But one day, she decided to leave you with me, making up some weak excuse about having to run errands. I stared at you, and something happened inside. I could feel Nadje's spirit inside of you, and looking into your eyes was like looking into her eyes. A few months after your first birthday was when you first called me Azi. You were speaking a little, and I was trying to get you to say Papa, but you said 'Azi.' I immediately began to cry because you said it the exact same way that Nadje did."

Jassim listened intently, and they remained teary-eyed. The waitress was heading to the table but stopped suddenly when she noticed they were having an emotional conversation. Their table was in the back corner of the room, away from the kitchen, allowing for them to have privacy.

"How long are those two going to sit there? I don't want to be here all night," the owner's lazy nephew complained.

"Why are you in such a hurry, Luzio? You don't have anywhere important to go. Let the nice old man and his grandson enjoy the evening. It's the boy's first night in Italy. Can't you see they are having a meaningful conversation? Just straighten up around them. This family hasn't been in business for the past century by kicking out our customers."

Angelo was always patient and grew to be good friends with the two patrons who returned at least once a month to their favorite *ristorante*.

"From that day forward, my depression slowly improved. The two of us were inseparable during my recovery, and my relationship with your uncle and father slowly improved. I even stopped blaming the boys for Nadje's death, and we began to heal as a family. I thought my depression was completely gone, but when they enrolled you in school, it slowly returned. That's when I realized that I needed to find happiness within myself and not rely on someone else.

"Moving to Italy was never a choice. It was something that I had to do. If I didn't make the change, I would have never fully healed. I also wanted to take the opportunity to fulfill my dream of living in Rome since I gave up that part of my life in order to raise my family. I felt that *Allah* was rewarding me for a job well done. It is he who guides our lives. *Surah* 6, *Ayah* 104 reads, 'That is *Allah*, your Lord; there is no good but He, the creator of all things; so worship Him alone. He is Guardian over everything. Eyes cannot reach him, but He manifests Himself before the eyes. He is the Imperceptible, the All-Aware.'"

Jassim stood up and gave his grandfather a big hug, whispering in his ear, "Thank you, Azi."

The embrace was released after a minute or so, and they sat back down. Azfal decided it was time to go and asked for the check. The circumspect waitress walked over and placed the bill on the table. She had a concerned look on her face.

"Is everything okay?" *Silvana* asked compassionately.

He assured her everything was fine and thanked her for her exceptional service. Grandfather and grandson always shared a close bond but grew even closer after the dinner. It was almost one o'clock in the morning when they made their way from *Monte Caruso* to the parking lot. The cold temperature was below freezing, and Azfal was thankful he remembered to grab his *AS Roma* scarf from the car.

The drive to Palestrina was quiet and peaceful. There were no words spoken during the trip. Jassim thought about his family history while he stared at the starlit sky, and Azfal focused on the winding road, with his mind on how great it felt to share Nadje's story with his grandson.

During the drive, Jassim didn't get to see much of Palestrina since he fell asleep and didn't wake up until Azfal parked the car in the driveway. He woke up early the next morning from the guest room couch, quickly getting dressed and devouring his cereal. His eagerness to explore all that Italy had to offer caused the fired-up boy to forcefully knock on the unpainted wooden bedroom door; his grandfather was already awake.

"Come in, it's open," he shouted, sitting in his favorite chair, reading the *Qur'an*.

Luciana agreed to give him the week off. She often told him he was doing a great job and called him an excellent addition to the museum. It was almost certain she would agree because the crush she had on him wasn't very discreet. He never turned her down but let her know that Nadje's death was still difficult for him to get over. She understood and they continued to be good friends, but Luciana always held out hope for romance in the future. She was ecstatic to have the opportunity to finally meet his "precious grandson," who Azfal spoke fondly of almost daily.

"Jassi, I think we should focus our sightseeing in the great city during this first week, and you can explore Palestrina on your own while I work."

Rome instantly became the child's new favorite city. It was everything his grandfather had described and more. In the middle of the week, Azfal had a special surprise for his grandson. He noticed how thrilled Jassim was when they spoke about his visit to the Inn at the Spanish Steps, so he arranged for them to stay there for one night. The experience was thoroughly enjoyable.

"Azi, the artwork is just like you described it. This hotel feels like I'm in ancient Rome. Can we race up the Spanish Steps?"

"If you want to, go ahead. I won't be racing up anything. Maybe you can get my good friend Marco to race with you."

Azfal was cramped up from laughing while watching the slow middle-aged concierge attempt to chase down his athletic grandson. Jassim outpaced Marco by at least forty steps.

"Thank you, my old friend, for being such a good sport. But, Marco, I don't think you will be trying out for the Olympic stair-climbing event anytime soon. The least I can do is ask you to join us for lunch," he said, still laughing.

The out-of-breath silver medalist gladly accepted. "Thank you, my friend. That is very gracious of you. I would love to join the two of you. Just let me get some water first!" They all laughed.

The week of exploration in Rome was another bonding experience for them. Jassim filled up his memory card halfway through the week, taking a picture of everything. Luckily, Azfal bought him a new one, and he continued snapping away. It was during this time in Rome that the passionate *Roma* fan passed on his die-hard support to his grandson who was quickly hooked after attending a match. The thoughtful Luciana bought two tickets, for the AC Milan match, as a welcome gift for Jassim.

During the match, things got a little too exciting. A belligerent, wasted *Roma* fanatic had to be removed from the stadium because he struck a fan of "*il Diavolo.*"

Azfal, a proponent of nonviolence, quickly addressed his grandson, "That man deserves to be arrested. You never use violence. It is okay to have passion and support your club and celebrate their good fortunes, but one can never resort to violence. We must all learn to treat eachother with respect, understand, Jassi?" he said with an arm on Jassim's shoulder.

"Yes, Azi. I know what that guy did was wrong."

"Remember that you can always turn to *Allah* for answers. *Surah* 49, *Ayah* 12 states, 'Oye who believe, let no people deride another people, haply they may be better than themselves.'"

The unfortunate incident did not spoil the great experience. *Roma* scored in the eighty-seventh minute to tie the match at three goals. The Ansary men exited the *Stadio Olimpico* with a stronger bond, but Jassim was sad when the week ended. He knew his grandfather would be returning to work and wasn't looking forward to the lonely afternoons; however, he couldn't wait to explore Palestrina.

<hr />

It was Sunday the nineteenth when Azfal and Jassim sat at the small kitchen table for a discussion over lunch. He wanted to speak with his grandson about the plans for the boy's future since Jassim was not only a great student but also an exceptional soccer player. In Iraq, he was the best player in his youth league, and Azfal was amazed at his knowledge of the sport when they attended the match. The future forward was enthusiastic to play against the neighborhood children of Palestrina in order to gage his abilities against the stronger competition. Education was important, but Azfal wanted to encourage his grandson to strive for greatness in all his future endeavors.

"Tell me, Jassi, what do you want to do when you become an adult? How will you honor the talents given to you by *Allah* and achieve greatness in this world?"

Jassim thought about the question for a moment. "I want to be like the great *Pele*, who you told me about, Azi. I want to be the greatest football player of all time. I want to play better than he did."

Azfal often discussed *Pele's* greatness, and Jassim enjoyed watching the old soccer tapes of the Brazilian's games that his grandfather left for him. Jassim felt a connection to the soccer star since they shared the same birthday. Azfal purchased the highlight tapes so his grandson could see what greatness looked like.

"Yes, Jassi, becoming a great football star is an attainable goal if you work hard. What about school? Do you plan on dropping out in order to chase your fantastic dreams?"

It was clearly a test. There was no way he would support Jassim quitting school, no matter how great a player he became. There would always be a need for an education in his eyes.

"Azi, I will continue my education so I can have a backup plan. I will play football professionally after I earn my degree."

Azfal smiled and shook the boy's hand. "That's my boy. School is always first. What about the people? It is by the grace of *Allah* that you have such great talents. How will you repay him?" It was important for him to teach Jassim the concept of giving back, in order to improve the lives of those who are less fortunate; philanthropy would be imperative in his future. For a ten-year-old boy, he was very mature and understood the message. He knew soccer was a vehicle to be used for a free education and that he should always stay humble.

"I remember that *Zakah*, meaning alms giving, is one of the five pillars of faith in *Islam*, and I will always give back to the needy people."

"I see you are ready to take on the world."

Azfal loved being a Muslim but didn't become devout until he met Nadje. He never prayed five times daily and rarely fasted during *Ramadan*. Saad forced him to perform the religious rituals as a child, but he stopped once he moved out. He was happy that Nadje helped to make him a better Muslim, and when she died, his anger with God halted his prayer, but he eventually came to the realization that it was simply her time to go.

Ibrahim often avoided any religious rituals and raised his son to be more secular. It was Nebet who taught him about the Muslim culture and customs, but the family hardly prayed together. Although Jassim identified himself as a Muslim and enjoyed hearing his grandfather recite Quranic verses, religion wasn't a major part of his life.

As Azfal recovered from the loss of his wife, he turned toward God, and the *Qur'an* played a larger role in his life. It was *Surah* 17, *Ayah* 10–11: "Surely, this *Qur'an* guides to the way which is most firm and right, and gives to the believers who work righteousness the glad tidings that they shall have a great reward and warns that for those who do not believe in the Hereafter We have a grievous chastisement," which reaffirmed his faith and helped him comprehend Nadje's death.

Chapter 5

The following morning, the best friends ate breakfast, and Azfal gave the boy some *liras* for spending money before leaving.

"Don't forget to visit the museum at noon so we can meet for lunch," Azfal yelled before the door closed slowly.

Jassim sat on the couch and a sense of nostalgia gradually set in. He missed his parents but ignored the desire to go home since he was curious to explore Palestrina. The door swung open. Slamming against the wall, Azfal jumped up and down with excitement.

"Come outside, Jassi, quick," he yelled breathlessly.

Jassim ran to the door and witnessed a wondrous vision; a thick layer of snow covered everything. The wooden rack crashed to the ground as he hurriedly snatched his coat. He put on his boots, gloves, and woolen skullcap, banging the door shut as he bolted outside. It was his first snowfall.

"Azi, the street looks just like the postcard you sent me. It's the most wonderful thing I have ever seen."

Azfal packed a tight snowball and hurled it at the unsuspecting boy, hitting him on the left shoulder. Jassim attempted to retaliate, but he didn't know the proper technique and ended up sprinkling his grandfather's *kufi* with harmless flurries, causing him to laugh.

"Do you want me to teach you how to make a snowball, Jassi?"

"Yes, teach me great master snow ninja," he said, bowing to show his respect.

Azfal laughed and picked up a handful, demonstrating how to properly pack a snowball. The novice was a natural, and they stood across the street taking aim on the doorknob each trying his best, but their errant throws missed wildly.

"I forfeit and humbly declare you the winner of the first annual 'Snow Ball Doorknob Target Competition.'" Azfal conceited. He couldn't stay much longer since he had to be at work shortly.

Palestrina was a very safe town, and Jassim could freely explore the ancient sites without Azfal having any concerns; the ancient Etruscan settlement would be his playground. The young adventurer grabbed his trusty camera before closing the door. He was off on his first expedition. He stepped onto *Via Veroli*, which was a one-way street, and walked toward the corner.

Before he reached the end of the block, the terrified child was frozen in his tracks. There was a menacing-looking dog standing in the middle of the road barking at him. The thought of running past crept into his mind, but he thought better of the idea. He had to decide between running back to the house and hoping he had enough time to unlock the door or attempting to jump into a neighbor's yard.

"Don't worry, he's harmless. He's just a mutt. He barks at everyone, but his bark is a lot bigger than his bite."

Jassim turned toward the angelic voice coming from the house across the street. A girl's head was hanging out the first floor window, but he wasn't certain he could trust her.

"Are you sure? He looks pretty mean. I never saw a harmless German shepherd before."

She could see that he was scared and vanished from her window. A few seconds later, the large red door to her house swung open, and she came running out onto the street.

As soon as the dog saw her, it stopped barking. The expert snow thrower picked up a handful and packed it into a tight ball. She heaved it at the dog's head, striking it directly on the nose.

The German shepherd let out a whimper and ran into an open gate at the end of the street.

"I told you the big bad wolf is really just a sheep?" she said.

Sabatina laughed at how frightened Jassim looked and walked over to him. The overly dramatic boy graciously thanked her for "saving my life" and introduced himself as "Jassim."

Her eyes lit up. "My name is Sabatina. Jassim? You're Jassi, Azfal's grandson, right?" Jassim nodded affirmatively. "How long are you staying with him?"

"I'm not sure how long I'm staying. My parents wanted me to leave Iraq because they fear there will be a war there. I won't be going home until they think it's safe for me to return."

She processed the information. "If you're from Iraq, how can you speak Italian?"

"I took classes. I can speak English too."

Sabatina was impressed with the polyglot's multilingualism. "Where's your grandfather?"

"He's at work and left me to explore the city on my own."

She also spoke fluent English as well as French since her father advised her that anyone who wanted to be successful in the world must learn the "important" languages.

"I want to learn Spanish next," she said.

"Me too!"

"I was born in *Reggio di Calabria* on Italy's toe, across from Sicily. My father's a brain doctor at Rome American Hospital in Lazio. Because of his job, we move to a different city whenever he gets a better offer. This is the fourth city I've lived in."

"Wow, all that moving must be rough?"

"Yeah, we've only been here for about a year. It's hard to make friends."

Sabatina didn't really know too much about Azfal, but he was friends with her parents and ate dinner at the Moretti home on a several occasions. The adults usually conversed in the living room while she retired to her room to watch television. Salvatore usually listened in as his wife discussed artifacts with their guest. She often visited the museum.

The ponytailed, auburn-haired girl offered to give Jassim a tour of the town, and before they left, she invited him into the house to meet Anastasia who was a housewife.

"Mother! Where are you? Azfal's grandson is here."

Anastasia, who had the same auburn hair, appeared at the top of the stairs. "I'll be right down, Tina."

Jassim turned to Sabatina. "Does everyone call you Tina?"

"Yeah, I guess."

A few moments later, Anastasia sauntered down the stairs. She was a classic Italian beauty with mesmerizing bright blue-sapphire eyes and dressed in the latest designer fashion. Her long hair reached the small of her back. Her doting husband provided everything her heart desired. She looked at Jassim with a welcoming smile.

"Jassi, it's nice to finally meet you. You're grandfather has told me a lot about you. Welcome to Italy. I'm Ana."

Jassim thanked her for the kind welcome, and after a brief conversation, the two youths headed for the door.

"Jassi, be sure to tell your grandfather that I invited the two of you for dinner tonight. We'll be expecting you guys."

"Okay, Ana, I'll remember."

The children ran off without closing the door, causing her to shake her head. Jassim was a few months younger than Sabatina, who turned eleven on June 10. They spent several hours exploring the ancient town. It was a simple place where people knew one another. Sabatina introduced Jassim to most of the locals, and he was welcomed by all. The nostalgia that he felt during the morning began to dissipate.

"It's getting close to noon. I have to meet Azi for lunch. I'm sure he won't mind if you join us."

She gladly accepted, and they walked to the museum, where Jassim approached the information desk and identified himself. The lady behind the counter was expecting him.

"Mr. Ansary is located on level three. The guard will open up the elevator for you," she called out to the security guard. "Fabio, you can let them use the employee elevator."

The doors opened to the third floor, and they searched for his grandfather. He was standing in front of one of the exhibits and explaining its significance to three Japanese tourists.

The children explored the other artifacts while they waited, and when Azfal was ready to leave, he walked over to the Nile Mosaic where they were standing. Jassim recalled most of the information given to him and was serving as Sabatina's personal guide. They were speaking English when the old man approached.

"*Solo Italiano, non Inglese.*"

The children laughed; he was happy to see that Jassim was getting along with his friendly little neighbor since he worried the boy might end up spending most of his days in Palestrina alone. They were promised a full tour after eating, and the threesome headed toward a little café a block from the museum.

During the meal, the conniving youths spoke in English whenever they wanted to have some privacy, which annoyed Azfal who felt as if they were talking negatively about him. The duo discovered the use of English would be an invaluable asset in the future. Lunch was delightful, and the new friends returned with full bellies, excited to see the exhibits.

The tour began on the first floor where the main attraction was the ancient sculpture of the Capitoline Triad.

"This is a statue of the Etruscan divine triad. It has Jupiter, king of all gods; Juno, his wife; and Minerva, the goddess of wisdom." Jassim and Sabatina thought it was the best piece in the museum.

"It was recently discovered in *Guidonia* and is the only example of the Triad in which the gods are preserved virtually in their entirety." They also learned a bit of background information about Palestrina. "In the past, the town had a history of problems with some of the popes. Palestrina was a fiefdom in the late thirteenth century, and the disgruntled owner revolted from the pope's control. In retaliation, Pope Boniface VIII viciously ordered the town to be destroyed. But the people rebuilt it in the early fifteenth century until Pope Eugenius IV ordered it to be destroyed again. Palestrina was rebuilt and sacked once more. Eventually, the town was sold to the Barberini family. This is the location of the former palace of the Baron, and the museum was built inside the massive structure. Parts of the city were destroyed during WWII, which allowed for the ancient ruins to be uncovered in the damage."

Azfal continued the informative tour, which concluded back at the triad sculpture.

"Sabatina, you should take Jassi to see the summit hill about a mile away from town. The city was built on the ruins of the gigantic Temple of Fortune, and the hill provides the best views in Italy. From the top, one can see Rome, the Alban Hills, and *Monte Sorrate*."

Filled with excitement, they headed for the exit, but he called for them to come back. Luciana, who had the day off, entered from the employee's side entrance. He got her attention and waved her over. She was pleased to see Jassim.

"It is nice to finally meet you, Jassi. I have heard so much about you. I feel like I've known you all my life," she said and gave him a big hug.

"Nice to meet you too. Thanks for the great seats at the Roma game. We were so close, it felt like we were playing."

Luciana was a very kind lady and genuinely seemed to care about the boy, and they instantly connected. She turned her attention to Sabatina.

"Hi, Tina. You're looking lovely as always."

Sabatina knew Luciana well since the director accompanied Azfal to her house for dinner on several occasions. "Thank you."

Luciana concurred that the children should visit the summit. They excused themselves and exited through the revolving doors.

Jassim was alone when Azfal arrived from work; he was too tired to prepare a meal.

"Jassi, get ready so we can go out for dinner."

"Don't you remember, Azi? I told you that Ana invited us for dinner."

"Great! I completely forgot. I wasn't really in the mood to travel to a restaurant."

Azfal was a devout Muslim but struggled with his desire to experience the Italian culture. He never attended a mosque believing that his personal relationship with God and own interpretation of the Holy Scripture was sufficient for entrance into heaven. He somewhat observed *Islam's* anti-alcohol policy by not consuming beer or hard liquor but did enjoy the occasional wine with his dinner. His defense was the Quranic *Surah* 5:14: "Truly the Righteous will be in bliss: on thrones will they command a sight: Thou wilt recognize in their faces the beaming brightness of Bliss. Their thirst will be slaked with wine sealed."

Enjoying a glass of wine was a habit that he developed after moving to Italy. He decided to walk to a nearby store and purchase a bottle of *vino* since he didn't want to show up to his neighbors' home empty-handed. Azfal selected a bottle of *Castello di Monastero Chianti Superiore 2001*, which was a safe choice since the wine could be served with a variety of foods.

Sabatina answered the door and welcomed the guests inside. They joined Salvatore and his daughter in the living room. Shortly after, Anastasia popped in from the kitchen for a quick hello. Salvatore was seated on the dark leather couch while watching the news, and Azfal sat down beside him. The children played cards on the ground while the men discussed the news reports about the impending war in Iraq. Sabatina taught Jassim how to play the Italian game "*Scopa*," which he picked up fairly quickly.

Salvatore stood up and walked toward his bar cabinet to grab a bottle of Johnnie Walker Black Label scotch. He sat down, placing two glasses on the coffee table.

"Will you J-Walk with me?"

"Sal, you know I can only drink wine."

The doctor had been told on numerous occasions that his neighbor didn't drink hard liquor but always offered a glass of his favorite whiskey to Azfal who was starting to think that Salvatore was purposefully trying to get him to break the laws of the *Qur'an*.

"Sorry, Azfal, the Muslim thing right. I always forget. That's too bad. This is the world's best whiskey. I think if your prophet had some black label, he might have allowed alcohol."

The revolting comment didn't sit well with the believer. Salvatore noticed that he was clearly being insensitive and instantly apologized profusely.

"I know you didn't mean to be offensive, but my faith is very important to me."

The message was clear, and the jovial mood shifted. After a brief moment of awkwardness, Azfal broke the tension.

"I don't know about good whiskey, but I do enjoy a good sneeze every now and again."

Salvatore laughed and went to the kitchen. He brought back a glass of the *Chianti*.

"I couldn't find anything to make you sneeze. I hope the wine will be okay."

The guest nodded affirmatively and grabbed the glass. The taut episode, resulting from the host's crass comment, was broken, and the men continued their discussion while they waited for dinner.

"Okay, everyone to the dining room. The feast is finally done."

The extended family shared amusing anecdotes as they enjoyed Jassim's first home-cooked meal in Palestrina.

"Ana and Sal, I would like to thank you for inviting us to your home for this lovely dinner. Everything was delicious as always. And I'm happy to see the children getting along. I was worried that Jassi would have trouble finding a playmate."

Jassim also thanked his hosts for the warm welcome and deliciously filling meal. He was thoroughly enjoying his first couple weeks in Italy and understood why his grandfather loved the country so much. His thoughts of permanently living in Palestrina were revealed during the walk home for the first time.

"Maybe I can live here with you, Azi."

Azfal didn't want to encourage the notion and simply laughed it off.

Jassim and Sabatina grew to be very close friends. All their free time was spent together. They either explored the hilly streets; some of which were basically cobblestone stairways or kicked around a soccer ball. Traveling through the small town was a tiresome undertaking, which the children considered their daily workout. Salvatore enjoyed showing off his dribbling skills whenever he happened upon the athletes as he arrived from work. He was a die-hard supporter of Lazio, which had a following of Rome's upper class, opposed to *La*

Magica whose fans were from the rowdier lower class. He often joked that *AS Roma* was the "dark side."

Jassim was considered a member of the family and spent more time at the Moretti home than at his grandfather's. It was the middle of January when he arrived from Iraq. After a month and a half, Ibrahim still didn't feel it was safe for his son to return to Baghdad. In fact, things were getting worse in the country, and the threat of war was a real possibility. The boy was torn because he missed his parents and his home, but he loved living in Italy and wasn't sure how he was going to feel when it was time to leave.

The next morning, when Jassim woke up, Azfal had already left for work, so he poured himself a bowl of *Nicoli* Bran Flakes and read the note on the table.

"Jassi, I purchased some plants for Ana. She has welcomed the two of us into her family, and I wanted to thank her. Take them over to the Moretti's house and thank her for me."

He noticed a bag from *Pierluigi's* flower shop against the wall, and when he finished his breakfast, he grabbed it and headed down toward the end of *Via Veroli*.

Sabatina answered the door, and he found Mrs. Moretti sitting in the living room.

"What is this?"

"My grandfather wanted to thank you for being so nice to us, so he sent it over."

She opened the bag and pulled out two plants. They were ponytail palms, causing her to be overcome with bliss.

"He remembered!"

"Who remembered?" Sabatina asked.

"I once told Azfal how much I loved these plants because your grandmother had a friend who brought back the seeds from a trip to Mexico as a gift. It was the first plant that we grew together. They're so beautiful and unique. I like the fact they're easy to maintain."

Azfal recalled her story and asked Mr. *Pierluigi* if it was possible for him to obtain a couple of the plants. It took three weeks, but he was finally able to acquire the foreign flora. She took the gift into the kitchen while the children played in the backyard. They were building a snowman. A neighbor peered over the fence after overhearing them.

"Hey, Tina, whose your little friend?"

"His name is Jassi. He's Azfal's grandson."

The bigot didn't realize Jassim was a non-Italian due to the boy's European features. A look of disgust appeared on his face.

"Why is a beautiful Italian girl playing with a little terrorist?"

An appalled Anastasia heard the despicable comment as she opened the back door to check on the children.

"You should be ashamed of yourself, Giacomo."

Her cold stare rendered him speechless. Giacomo was deeply embarrassed since he always had a strong attraction to the gorgeous housewife. He often attempted to impress her whenever he found an opportunity. He secretly coveted her, hoping that one day she would betray her marriage vows. The jerk was sadly mistaken. Anastasia Moretti was a loyal wife who was desperately in love with her husband. The unspeakable incident truly shook her up, and she was never cordial to the hate-filled neighbor again.

Inside, Anastasia attempted to explain to Jassim that only some Italians were ignorant and he understood her message.

"Don't worry, Ana. Everything is fine. Azi already prepared me to deal with hateful comments." He knew there were intolerant people in the world but was too young to understand why. Azfal made sure to sit him down and explain the bigotry he might encounter.

Later on in the day, Anastasia walked over to the house so she could personally apologize for her Giacomo's repulsive comment. She didn't want either of them to think she shared the neighbor's ill-bred views, and Azfal let her know that there was no need for her to apologize. He went on to reveal the many occasions in which people were unpleasant toward him, and she was happy to see that he didn't allow a few ill-mannered citizens to ruin his experience in the beautiful country.

When Anastasia left, he spoke to Jassim, "Jassi, the *Qur'an* prepares us for these religious attacks. I want you to remember *Surah* 15, *Ayahs* 95 and 96: 'Surely we will suffice you against the scoffers, those who set up another god with *Allah*; so they shall soon know.'"

The next day, the boy called his grandfather into the kitchen, and the two had an important conversation. The thought of staying in Italy permanently was the major topic. Jassim loved Iraq but felt that he found a new home in Palestrina, and he believed Azfal would be able to give him the same education that Nebet provided. He wanted his grandfather to help him convince Ibrahim that living in Italy would give him the best chance to succeed in life. He would continue to be homeschooled and could improve his chances of succeeding as a soccer star; the skill level of the players in Italy was unquestionably greater.

Jassim never had any really close friends in *Al A'zamiyah* since he didn't attend school and only saw the children while playing soccer in the streets. Sabatina was his first true best friend, and the two were imparted. She became the closest person to him other than his grandfather, and he didn't want to be separated from her. Azfal understood where he was coming from and was sympathetic, but he believed the responsibility of raising a growing boy fell on his parents. He knew Jassim was not experienced enough to make such an important decision and explained the reasoning behind his assessment.

"Not only should you be with your loving parents, but most importantly, you must remember that Ibrahim would never allow his son to skip out on the duty of serving in Saddam's military."

The service requirement had completely slipped Jassim's mind. He knew there was no way his father would permit him to stay in Italy.

"The world is a different place. It's not like when I was growing up. You and Tina live in a new age where you can contact people from anywhere on the planet, even from space. You can talk to her every day on the computer, and the two of you can speak on the phone occasionally. I am certain your friendship will not be affected once you go back home. When you get older, you'll realize why staying in Italy won't work out."

Jassim never really thought he would be able to stay. It was basically a shot in the dark since he was dreading the distance that would exist between him and his best friends. Azfal didn't agree with the dictator's conscription policy and didn't want his grandson to put his life at risk for the sake of Saddam, but the decision wasn't his to make. He could see that Jassim was worried about the forced military service.

"I know that you're sacred, but I assure you there is nothing to be concerned about. Ibrahim will guarantee that you'll be safe."

They shared a hug, and the talk helped to put his mind at ease. His focus was shifted to enjoying the time he had left in Italy.

"Thanks for the talk, Azi. You always know what to say."

"Anytime, Jassi, anytime."

Jassim grabbed his soccer ball and headed out the door. The Moretti's doorbell rang, and he ran into the street with his ball. Sabatina ran out to join him.

"Mittens!" her observant friend yelled.

"Thanks, I always forget them." She ran into the house.

The children kicked the ball back and forth for a while, but there was a strange silence between them. He grabbed the ball and walked closer to her so they could discuss the talk he shared with Azfal. She was accustomed to moving from city to city and never had a close friend either. He was the only person that she considered her true friend since she was always the new girl, finding it hard to fit in. The friends had been avoiding the talk about his imminent departure. Although she was dreading it, they had to have the uncomfortable dialogue.

"I also have some bad news," a teary-eyed Sabatina said. "This morning, Mom told me that Dad was offered a better position at another hospital, and we may have to move again. She didn't tell me where, but I'm sure it won't be Baghdad."

Salvatore still hadn't decided on whether or not he was going to accept the offer. He was very aware of how the constant moving affected his family. The family grew to love Palestrina, and for the first time, he saw that his little girl was feeling at home. The doctor also loved the fact that she had a close friend, so the family planned on discussing the matter over dinner in the evening.

"I was sad when my mom told me about the possibility of moving again because I didn't want us to be separated, but in the back of my mind, I always knew you were leaving, so it really doesn't matter," she said with a shrug.

"Yeah, I guess," a slumping Jassim replied.

The children sat in silence for a while. They weren't in the mood to play anymore and decided to call it a day.

"Tina, let me know what the family decides," Jassim said sadly.

"Okay, I'll tell you tomorrow."

She walked home, but Jassim remained on the curb, waving goodbye. She waved back and slowly closed the door. The saddened boy sat on the cold pavement and thought about the day's events. It was a lot to take in for a ten-year-old, and he couldn't understand why life was so difficult. Eventually, the cold finally became unbearable, forcing him to walk home.

The resounding doorbell woke Jassim the subsequent morning. He stepped into his golden-yellow and maroon *Roma* slippers and listlessly walked to see who it was, still saddened by the previous day's bad news. It was Sabatina, and he invited her in. They sat in the kitchen, and he anticipated more "great news."

"When my father came home yesterday, we sat down to dinner, and he let us know what the offer was. You know he's a brain doctor at a hospital in Lazio, but he wants to be in charge and was offered a job to be the boss at a hospital in America. He said it's in a city called Boston." She had a quizzical look on her face as if the city was on the smallest moon, of the furthest planet, in a faraway galaxy. "I don't know where that is, but he said it is nice, so we all agreed to move there once the school year is over. I really didn't want to move again, but since your leaving, I guess it doesn't matter if we stay or not. I always wanted to live in America anyway, so I think it will be a good move. I'm tired of being the new girl at school, but he promised that this was the last time."

Jassim wasn't glad to hear the news, but he knew they were going to be separated regardless. "I think America sounds exciting, and I guess Azi was right. It will be better if I move back to Iraq since either way, we'll be able to remain friends."

Sabatina agreed and revealed that she had to go shopping with her mother. She asked if he wanted to accompany them, but he wasn't in the mood to leave the house.

"I will come back once we return from the shopping plaza."

"All right, I'll see you later."

"Okay, bye."

The two friends decided to forget about their future separation since there was nothing either of them could do to change the situation. They agreed to enjoy as much of the time together in Palestrina and made promises to visit one another in the future.

Chapter 6

On March 17, American President George W. Bush suspended all diplomatic efforts and issued an ultimatum to Saddam Hussein. The Iraqi dictator was given the choice of leaving his country or remaining and suffering the consequences. Bush set a deadline of two days for the regime to make a decision, but Saddam refused and continued to urge Iraqis to prepare for a fight against the invading military. Azfal called home and asked Ibrahim to leave the country, but the hard-line loyalist, with a voracious loquacity when discussing Saddam, would do no such thing.

"I'm not afraid of the Americans. I will stay and fight for Saddam and the dignity of Iraq. We will be victorious."

Azfal was horrified. He couldn't believe his stubborn son would risk his life for the "evil tyrant." He feared Ibrahim's allegiance to the Iraqi president would be his downfall and gave up any hope of convincing the bullheaded offspring to leave. He was also dreading the fact that the beautiful and devoted Nebet would never leave without her husband.

Jassim was called into the room. His worrisome grandfather handed over the phone and left the kitchen for the solitude of his dimly lit bedroom, where he sat in his La-Z-Boy, picking up his *Qur'an* from the acacia nightstand for comfort.

"Hello, hello! Father, are you there?" Jassim asked anxiously while whimpering.

A confident Ibrahim did his best to assure his son that everything would be fine. "Yes, my son, I am here. Why are you crying?

You don't have to waste your tears. Don't worry about the nonsense you hear on the news. We are safe here. Saddam will guide us to a triumphant victory over the foreign infidels. I will call you in a few days to check in on you. Be sure to listen to your grandfather." He handed the phone to his wife.

Nebet did her best to sound confident in order to assure her child that they were not in any harm's way, but deep down, she felt Saddam would lead Iraq on a path to destruction. The loving mother spoke with her son for half an hour. She informed him that they were moving to a safer location and not to worry if she was unable to call for a few days. Saddam provided the couple with access to one of his many bunkers where they would be shielded from the expected bombings, which comforted Jassim.

"Tell your grandfather that we love him."

"Okay, I will."

"Remember that we love you," she uttered affectionately.

Jassim heard the trembling in her voice and nervously replied, "I love you too."

He hung up the phone and went into Azfal's bedroom, where they sat together in the faint light of a candle, praying for God to keep the family safe.

Two days later, Jassim and Sabatina were in the middle of the cobblestone street kicking around his soccer ball when Azfal arrived from work and signaled for them to enter the house. There was a troubled look on his face as he watched them run toward the opened white door. The three of them sat down on the couch, and he turned on the television set.

"Saddam refused to listen to the ultimatum, and the maverick American president ordered his generals to commence the bombing of Baghdad," Azfal informed with tears rolling down his cheeks.

The ambitious military campaign began with a few strategic air strikes designated for previously determined Iraqi military strong-holds and the city power generators. The goal was to kill the non-compliant dictator and knock out power throughout the city.

Azfal and the ten-year-old looked on in horror as a barrage of missiles rained down on the city. He attempted to call Ibrahim, but the phone lines in Baghdad were down. Jassim was visibly troubled, and his grandfather did his best to reassure the child that his parents were safe. The mature boy put on a front as if he believed what he was being told, but it was obvious to him that his parents were in danger.

The bombing continued the following evening with the obedient Iraqi Minister of Defense insisting that the soldiers not surrender. Full of misinformation, the unregenerate demagogue used his lies to assure his supporters that the Americans were being defeated and would soon retreat.

A compassionate Luciana thoughtfully decided to give Azfal time away from the museum because she knew he would not be able to focus on anything other than the war in Iraq. She usually arrived at his home after work to cook dinner. Sabatina watched the coverage by Jassim's side daily. She didn't want her best friend to be without a shoulder to cry on. Anastasia also joined the "Ansary Boys" during the afternoons, in a show of support, but the housewife usually went home in the early evening to prepare dinner for Salvatore. The helpful ladies performed the household chores so their friends could focus their attention on the news reports.

The good doctor didn't make it over as often as he would have liked because he was always tired from his busy work schedule, but he always popped over for a quick hello so he could offer his best wishes to his extended family.

On the third night of "Operation Iraqi Freedom," the American president announced the implementation of the "shock and awe" campaign. Salvatore called to inform his wife he would not be able to make it home in time for dinner; he was performing surgery and had to stay in Rome.

"Please give my best to Azfal and the Jazz-man. I don't know what this shock and awe will be, but I hope their family members are safe."

Anastasia spent the evening at Azfal's along with Luciana and Sabatina. The five of them sat in front of the television observing the news coverage.

"Azi, what is shock and awe?"

"I never heard of the term before, Jassi," a puzzled Azfal replied, shrugging his shoulders.

The unfortunate citizens of Baghdad had no idea what they were about to experience; a procession of bombs covered the city.

"This must be what it was like when God destroyed Sodom and Gomorrah," the impressed anchorman stated.

The United States and Great Britain unleashed history's largest single air strike on the ill-fated city. Baghdad was blanketed by utter destruction as a devastated Azfal looked on with a face full of tears. He slowly placed his head in his hands. He wasn't strong enough to bare watching anymore. Luciana placed his head on her lap and soothingly rubbed his back. After a few minutes, he was unwilling to remain in front of the television and excused himself.

A tearful Anastasia stood up after noticing the horrifying look on Jassim's face and turned the set off. He remained in a state of shock, and Sabatina wanted to help out her best friend, but there was nothing that she could do. The shock and awe campaign lived up to its name. It was a night that the five of them would remember for the rest of their lives.

Jassim left with the Moretti's and slept in the guest room of their house, leaving Luciana to care for his grandfather who was in a deep depression. Azfal instantly fell asleep after plopping into his comfortable bed. The concerned "friend" found it impossible to leave and kicked her feet up in the La-Z-Boy, slowly drifting to sleep.

On April 9, American soldiers gained control of Baghdad, and they were shown toppling a mammoth statue of Saddam in *Firdos* Square. It was also the day the bold despot emerged from his bunker to make his final public appearance. Azfal was heartbroken. His beautiful city was destroyed, and he developed an even deeper hatred for the ousted president, blaming him for the "invasion."

He was elated to see the colossal statue of the oppressor torn down but troubled by the fact that he didn't know if his family was safe. In a state of panic, the patriarch attempted to call everyone he knew who lived in the country, but no one answered. His concern was increased when he couldn't reach Saady in Amman. To his surprise, the operator informed him that the number had been disconnected. There was no way for him to contact any of his family members. He continued to reassure Jassim that his parents were safe, but the boy remained skeptical. In reality, Azfal was trying to convince himself that they survived the foreign military onslaught, but each day that he failed to contact them, their survival seemed less likely.

Luciana visited *Via Veroli* every day after work. "I want you both to know that I will always be here to help with anything that is needed."

"Thanks, we won't be able to make it through this horrible ordeal without you, Lucy."

Luciana loved the nickname since Azfal was the first person to use it. It had been a month without him stepping foot in the museum, but she let her best employee know that he did not have to worry about work. "Contacting your family is the most important thing now."

Her companionship comforted Azfal who was beginning to fall for his boss, but he was afraid to express his feelings partly since he didn't know how Jassim would react. He didn't think it was the appropriate time.

———※———

The twenty-third of June was a very emotional day for the Ansary men, along with Luciana. The Moretti family had been a major source of support for them. The time arrived for Salvatore to move his family to Boston, and their flight departed in the evening. Everyone anticipated the day arriving, but they weren't prepared for how difficult the separation would be.

Azfal decided it was best for him and Jassim to accompany the family to *Fiumicino*, which was also beneficial since he barely left the house after the beginning of the war. He was at risk of falling back into a deep depression because he was consumed by the war coverage and still hadn't received any news of the family's whereabouts.

Luciana prepared breakfast for her "favorite guys" and was basically living at the house, only going home to change clothes. She slept on the extremely comfortable La-Z-Boy every night. Although she wanted to sleep in the bed, she was mindful not to add any more drama to the emotional turmoil that Azfal was dealing with. He wanted to ask her to sleep on the bed as well but didn't think he was psychologically prepared to handle the situation. He was deeply grateful for her undying compassion.

"I like taking care of my favorite guys. It's definitely something that I can get used to," Luciana said, as she stared longingly into Azfal's brown eyes.

He understood her insinuation and flirtatiously responded, "We love having you around, Lucy. You really know how to spoil us. I don't know how we'll survive when you leave."

She knew he was struggling with his feelings but felt he was slowly falling for her. Neither of them discussed the matter.

The director had to be at work in the afternoon but accompanied them to the Moretti home where everyone was in a solemn mood. The six strangers grew to be a family during their time together in Palestrina, and Luciana was the first to shed some tears. Anastasia was next to cry, followed by Sabatina, but Azfal and Jassim were all cried out. The manly Salvatore, wanting to be strong, fought to control his emotions. Luciana was only able to visit for fifteen minutes before heading home to prepare for work.

"When the family is settled, be sure to give me a call," she said after an emotional goodbye.

The flight to Boston was scheduled to depart at 9:00 p.m.; therefore, the Moretti's didn't need to leave for the airport until five-thirty, allowing them the time to enjoy their last day with the Ansary's. Azfal promised that the next time Jassim visited Italy, the two of them would fly to Boston for a week's visit. He always desired to visit America, "the land of the free." Ibrahim was the only family member to make the journey to the United States. Azfal always peppered his son with questions about the experiences.

Each person shared his or her favorite memories, and the day was both joyful and gloomy. The highlight of the afternoon came when Jassim imitated his grandfather's failed attempt to explain an exhibit to American tourists at the museum.

"*Theesa eesa statua ova Roma mana, ona heesa horses.*" He mimicked.

Salvatore almost wet his pants. "You sound just like him, Jazz-man."

When it was finally time to leave, everyone pitched in to help pack the rental van, which Azfal would return. The drive to *Leonardo da Vinci* Airport, in the air-conditioned van, was a very quiet one, causing Anastasia to turn on the radio so they could listen to a station that played classic Italian folk songs.

The Moretti family used the drive to take in a final view of the picturesque Italian countryside. They wanted to create a lasting memory of Italy's beautiful landscape. Salvatore made a detour through central Rome to take in the ancient architectural masterpieces for one last time. The statue of *Leonardo da Vinci* at the airport's entrance grew larger as they approached.

"Almost there."

There was no response; no one else was in the mood to speak. He drove to terminal C and parked near the curb just ahead of the entrance. Everyone slowly exited the van. The reality of their division was setting in, and the children seemed to be the most affected.

Azfal already lost his true love Nadje, but he had Jassim and Luciana to help fill the void. Anastasia and her husband were still very much in love and looked forward to the next chapter in their lives together. The companions barely spoke a word to each other the entire day. It was difficult for them to look at one another since they were losing the only real friend that either of them ever had. Their silence continued as the skycap helped unload the luggage. Salvatore opted for the curbside check-in to save them the hassle of the long lines.

The group agreed to keep the goodbyes short so the pain would be lessened, and the two best friends hugged for a long while, each secretly hoping there would be a way for them to stay together. Although Jassim and Sabatina swore to keep in touch, they knew there was a strong possibility they might never see one another again. Her face was drenched in tears, and he was completely dejected, managing to release a tear, which rolled down his left cheek as the two dear friends released their embrace.

"I'll call you as soon as I get a chance," a barely audible Sabatina uttered.

Jassim just smiled as she walked to join her parents. The Ansary's stood by the van and waved to their family, who vanished in the midst of the frantic terminal.

The heartrending ride back was a long one, in which neither of them spoke at first. They were trying to take everything in.

"Azi," Jassim mumbled, his face covered in tears.

"Yes, Jassi."

"Do you think we will ever see them again?"

In a confident voice, he responded, "Of course, we will, Jassi. Before you know it, we'll all be dining together in Boston, listening to Sal explain the different labels of Johnnie Walker."

Jassim cracked a faint smile. His grandfather's comment actually lifted his spirits a little.

"What about my mom and dad?"

Azfal tried his best to remain positive and cautiously pulled the car over to the side of the road, turning to his anxious grandson.

"They are fine, Jassi. *Allah* will protect them. There are problems with the phones because of the bombings, but as soon as Ibrahim is able to call, he will send for you, I'm sure of it. As long as we have *Allah* on our side, everything will be okay. *Surah* 41, *Ayahs* 30 through 32 reads, '(As for) those who say: Our Lord is *Allah*, then continue in the right way, angels descend upon them, saying: Fear not, nor be grieved, and receive good news of the garden which you were promised. We are your guardians in this world's life and in the hereafter, and you shall have therein what your souls desire and you shall have therein what you ask for: A provision from the Forgiving, the Merciful.'"

Jassim smiled as if he believed that his parents were safe, but he knew his grandfather was simply trying to stay positive, and he was grateful. The Quranic verses helped to put him in a better mind state, which his grandfather's recitation of the Holy Book usually did.

He hugged Azfal affectionately with the thought of never seeing his parents lingering in the back of his mind. They continued the remainder of trip in complete silence. Jassim couldn't prevent from tearing up as he thought about Sabatina. She was the one person who kept him sane while his parents were missing, and her departure left an empty hole in his heart. It was during the drive that he realized how much she truly meant to him.

The twenty-second of July was a disheartening day. Saddam Hussein continued to evade captivity, and Azfal still held out hope that Ibrahim and Nebet were in hiding with the dictator. It was the only way that he could convince himself of their safety.

The breaking news revealed that Saddam's two sons, Uday and Qusay, were killed in a firefight in the Iraqi city of *Mosul*. They were in line to be Hussein's successors, and Azfal figured the chance of Ibrahim and Nebet surviving was slim since the country's leader was unable to protect his own sons. He tried to keep a positive outlook, but it was difficult. He focused his attention on continuing the boy's homeschooling while they awaited news from Iraq.

Sabatina kept her promise, remembering to call as soon as the family's home phone was installed. Her voice helped to raise her best friend's spirits since he was becoming more depressed as the war raged on. Jassim hadn't heard from his parents since the beginning of the March, and he felt lonely in Palestrina. Although he spoke on the kitchen phone, he was able to have privacy because the conversation was entirely in English.

The two friends would speak every weekend since Salvatore vowed to bring home a twenty-dollar calling card on Fridays. The phone call was the most exciting part of the week for Jassim who often mimicked his grandfather's English.

"*Iya nowa. Iya lika theesa showa too.*"

Azfal's hilarious American accent was a combination of Arabic, Italian, and English. His attempts at copying the boy's words brought instant comic relief. Sabatina could overhear him speaking over the phone and couldn't stop laughing at his pitiful effort.

"That's the funniest thing I've ever heard. Gramps is hilarious," she said.

"How's Boston?"

"It's okay, I guess. I really like the teachers at my new school."

The friends continued to talk until the minutes ran out. Even though they were living on different continents, their friendship remained strong. They also contacted each other through e-mail and instant messaging.

———◉———

During dinner one evening, Jassim decided to learn more about his family history.

"Azi, why did my father always fight with Uncle Saady?"

"Ibrahim is a hard-line Saddam loyalist who admired him faithfully since the day he took power, and Saady is a free spirit who always butted heads with his older brother, usually regarding Saddam's tyrannical rule of Iraq. I'm pretty sure that your uncle secretly had a crush on Nebet, which I believe exacerbated the situation."

"I know I wasn't around, but after visiting Saady, I'm pretty sure he didn't like my mother."

Azfal shrugged off the comment and continued, "My sons had conflict from an early age, and I think their rivalry began when Ibrahim noticed that your grandmother had less money for him since the arrival of his brother. Things escalated when Saady entered high school and felt he was his brother's equal. The confrontations eventually turned into fistfights. I had to step in the middle of the slugfests on several occasions, but my efforts were futile since they towered over me, since Saady's six-three and your dad's an inch taller. At the time, Ibrahim was a lot stronger due to his military training, and he usually won. They stopped the physical confrontations eventually but couldn't be in the same room without one of them seeking out an argument. Their disagreements usually ended with Saady getting angry and storming out of the house and your father calling him an 'unpatriotic coward.'"

"Why did he call him that?" a slightly angered Jassim asked.

"Ibrahim fervently agreed with President Hussein's policy to force all males into military service. He felt it was the duty of all patriotic citizens to support their 'great leader,'" Azfal said, as he made air quotes.

"Ibrahim viewed Saddam as a hero, a sentiment not shared by the rest of us. We usually avoided talking about politics on most occasions, but Saady was the exception. He would purposely bring up the dictator in order to get your father riled up. He had a deep hatred for Saddam and strongly disagreed with his policy of conscription."

"What is conscription?"

"It's when someone is forced into service," he explained, as Jassim nodded understandingly.

"Saady arranged for Dr. *Ajman Tariq*, who was a family friend, to provide him with fabricated medical records which exempted him from serving in the military. Ibrahim never forgave his brother for what he called 'an unpatriotic deception,' which is why he often called your uncle a coward."

"Although I agree with Saady and never really understood why your hardheaded father liked Saddam so much, I did my best to remain neutral. I just wanted them to put the family first and forget about politics. I was also full of optimism when Saddam first came to power, but the dictator's repulsive actions changed my views. I have a deep hatred for the former American President George H.W. Bush as well since I lost many friends during 'Operation Desert Storm.' I love America, but I hate its foreign policy, and I feel strongly that George W. Bush's motive is his desire to continue the invasion of Iraq that his father started in 1991. I don't understand why he would want to invade our country since the only terrorist is Saddam. There is no Iraqi connection to the 9/11 attacks on America. Bush's claim that Saddam was working with *Al Queda* is unfounded and simply not true. Saddam was no saint, but he hated extremism and did not allow *Al Queda* to operate inside Iraq. It is my hope that Bush will shift his focus to Afghanistan and leave our country alone."

"This is all too confusing. What about the fighting?"

Azfal shook his head understandingly and returned to the story about the boys. "Saady was basically unemployed, which caused further turmoil between him and Ibrahim. He mostly performed menial tasks, here and there, for neighbors when the opportunity presented itself. He had the ability to work hard, but his undying hatred for Saddam was his downfall. Whenever he managed to arrange a steady job for himself, he would find a way to lose it since he was quick to leave work at a moment's notice, never notifying anyone, in order to attend 'important' clandestine anti-Saddam meetings. Your uncle had it in his mind that his destiny was to remove Saddam from power and save the Iraqi people from the dictator's tyrannical rule, but the 'important' meetings turned out to be nothing more than a group of men getting together to create outlandish plans that none of them would ever be willing to carry out. Saady and Ibrahim always got into their biggest disputes whenever he was fired from a job."

"I didn't know their problems began so early. I thought it was over something recent. I guess they will always fight," Jassim said, shaking his head.

"I came to that realization a long time ago," Azfal replied with a look of despair.

A week later, Azfal had just finished giving his grandson his daily lesson when the doorbell rang. They were both surprised since Luciana had her own set of keys.

"Get the door, Jassi. I wonder who it could be."

Jassim answered the door, and standing outside was a forty-four-year-old, short, stocky, and slightly balding Catholic priest.

"Hi, my name is Giuseppe De Luca. I am a friend of Luciana's. She asked me to visit with you and your grandfather."

He was led to the kitchen, and the boy introduced him to Azfal who completely forgot that Father De Luca might be paying him a visit. Luciana felt it would be beneficial for him to speak with the compassionate priest. Jassim dismissed himself and went to watch television. Azfal was tolerant of other religions and didn't mind the meeting, expecting that Giuseppe could possibly offer him and Jassim a different perspective on how to deal with their missing family members.

"How long have you been a priest?"

"I was ordained in my hometown of Milan and moved to Rome five years after joining the priesthood. I've lived here for the last three years. The bishop of Milan was vastly impressed with my commitment to Christ and flawless understanding of church theology, so he gave me a recommendation to live in Vatican City, where I could further my theological studies."

Azfal learned a lot from talking with the priest, whom he invited to his home often so they could sit and converse on Saturday afternoons. The clergyman enjoyed talking with his gracious host, who was always sure to provide the *Taralli*, which the portly priest was also fond of, along with some complementary tea. They grew to be good friends, although Azfal was careful not to fully trust the Catholic since he wasn't sure of Father De Luca's true motives. His father *Saad* taught him that all Catholics secretly desired to convert the world's Muslim population to Catholicism. Azfal developed his own views as he grew older, but the lesson was ingrained into his subconscious.

⸻ ◈ ⸻

United States President George W. Bush unwisely committed an egregious folly of epic proportions during a mid-September speech to Congress. He brazenly called the war in Iraq a "modern-day crusade." The ignorant president continued, "This is a war against a new kind of enemy. We will rid the world of evil doers."

The message spread throughout the Islamic world faster than an email worm, and the White House attempted to cover up the mistake, but the damage had been done. Muslims began to see the American invasion of Iraq in a new manner. The prevailing thought was that it was a religious war, which diminished any opportunity for peace, and Azfal was genuinely hurt by the comment. Although he didn't agree with extremism over diplomacy, he felt Bush's comments, "Will force all believers to act." He wanted the international community to stop "the American" from waging a religious war. He preferred the use of brain instead of brawn, but when he heard Bush call the invasion a "crusade," he was livid and convinced of the Catholic Church's involvement. He turned to Jassim.

"It is the pope who guides Bush's bombs! We must always beware of Father De Luca. He appears to be a good friend, but we can never be sure of his motives."

The comment confused his grandson who didn't understand why his grandfather was questioning the friendship of the charming priest. Ultimately, he didn't doubt Azfal's judgment and heeded the warning, growing wary whenever he was around the priest.

———◈———

October 23 was Jassim's eleventh birthday, but he wasn't looking forward to any celebration because there was still no news of his parents' whereabouts. His excitement did slowly increase as the day progressed since Azfal invited Father De Luca and Luciana to the house so they could cut a small birthday cake. Luciana purchased it from a friend, an accomplished virtuoso, who owned a specialty bakery. The decoration was a picture of Jassim wearing an *AS Roma* jersey, which blew him away.

"Wow! That's the best cake I've ever seen. Thanks, Luciana."

"You're welcome, Jassi," she replied after releasing the big hug that they shared.

Each adult presented the grateful boy with a gift. From Luciana, he received a remote control race car. He thanked her with another big hug. Jassim couldn't wait for the following morning so he could play with toy on the sidewalk since it was too fast to be operated inside of the house.

A new soccer ball was the gift presented by Father De Luca. He had noticed that Jassim's ball was raggedy and barely inflated. The future star was elated and hugged his grandfather's new friend with excitement.

Azfal vicariously enjoyed his grandson's lifted spirit. It had been a while since he saw Jassim's bright smile. He handed the birthday boy a large duffle bag. It was a practical gift. He needed the bag to carry his soccer equipment and was blown away when he unzipped it open.

"Wow, an official *Roma* jersey!"

It was the one gift he truly desired. He immediately put it on and began dribbling his new ball in the kitchen's small space. Considering the circumstances in Iraq, his birthday was a great success. He enthusiastically answered the phone before it rang a second time.

"Happy birthday!" yelled Sabatina.

Mr. and Mrs. Moretti also took turns briefly wishing him a *"Buon Compleanno."* The best friends talked on the phone for the remainder of the night, and he bragged about his gifts, and Sabatina was elated to hear him almost sounding normal again. It was the first instance that he didn't seem depressed. The absence of his parents dampened the celebration, but number 11 turned out to be a special birthday nonetheless.

In comparison to the American forces stationed in Iraq, Italy had a minor presence in the war-torn nation, but the conflict became personal on November 12. The first Italian soldier was killed in a suicide bombing against an Italian police base in the southern city of *Nasiriyah*, near Nadje's hometown of *Basrah*. Azfal feared the repercussions that Muslims living in Italy would experience. The inability to hear from neither Ibrahim nor Nebet, and the threat of harm to him and Jassim began to take a toll on his health.

The sickly man grew weaker each day as his cardiovascular disease worsened. Jassim closely monitored his grandfather's health, along with Luciana. Later that week, an unexpected call interrupted their dinner. The boy optimistically answered the phone and was surprised to hear a familiar voice coming through the receiver.

"Azi, it's Nuri!" he exclaimed and handed over the phone.

The dentist was the first person from Iraq who was able to make contact. Nuri was a neighbor who lived three doors from the Ansary's home. He grew up with Ibrahim, and they remained close friends.

The two men exchanged pleasantries and some small talk. Azfal was stalling to avoid hearing the real reason for Nuri's call, anticipating bad news since he could tell from Nuri's tone the conversation would probably not be pleasant. He prepared himself for the worst and inquisitively asked.

"Have you heard any news from Ibrahim or Nebet? I can't get in contact with either of them. I also attempted to call Saady, in Amman, but his phone was no longer in service."

Nuri made a loud sigh, which Azfal knew wasn't a good sign.

"I thought you knew Saady came to Iraq for an extended visit."

"No, he didn't tell me."

"Yes, when he arrived, he said the visit from little Jassi made him realize how important family was. He wanted to reconcile with Ibrahim in person and arrived with his 'good friend' Mahmoud on March 18. He wanted to talk with his brother before the war began. I guess I was the only person he notified of his plans. I scooped him up from the airport and drove him to your house where we all sat in the living room. Saady began with an uncharacteristically heart-felt apology to his older brother. The two of them talked for several hours, and everything that was said seemed genuine and honest. I looked at Nebet, and we knew the conversation marked the end of their rivalry. The plan was for Saady, Ibrahim, and Nebet to fly to Rome and surprise you and Jassi. Saady saved up a good amount of money from his construction job and planned on footing the bill for what he called the SST—super secret trip."

For the first time in his life, Azfal was glad to hear one of Saady's annoying acronyms, but he was shocked to learn that the boys were able to put their differences aside.

"When the war started, Ibrahim arranged for all of us to stay in Saddam's nearest bunker, located right here in *Al A'zamiyah*. The construction of the new tower on the *Ibn Al-Haitham* campus was a front. They were actually building an underground bunker for Saddam. When we arrived, Ibrahim showed his identification card, and they let us in. There was a large weapon stockpile and what appeared to be a year's supply of food and water. The bunker was filled with the family and friends of Saddam loyalists, and we spent the first week of the foreign invasion safely inside."

The news made Azfal feel better, but he was still anticipating the worst.

"The entire structure shook every time a bomb landed in its vicinity. We were all terrified, but the soldier-in-command assured us that the structure was capable of sustaining a direct hit. When the bombings finally stopped, we left and went to inspect our homes, finding an impressive amount of destruction. Thankfully, our street avoided the heavy attacks, and most of the houses were still standing, but we weren't allowed to stay out for more than five hours, and after grabbing some essentials, we returned to the bunker.

"On April sixth, to everyone's surprise, Saddam arrived and remained with us for three days. He was so paranoid and didn't trust anyone. In order to ensure his safety, he only stayed in the same location for a few days. He also wanted Uday and Qusay to be in a different location than his to insure all three of them would not be killed in a single attack. On the ninth, he gave his final public speech then left. A group was assembled to leave in order to send a message from the president to the commander of a nearby bunker. There were four of us who were each given an AK-47, and we used a hummer for transportation. We safely made it to the other bunker without facing any obstacles and delivered the message. We spent the night and headed back the following morning, unaware how desperate the invading army was to kill Saddam. They received intelligence that his hiding place was a bunker in *Al A'zamiyah*, and it was correct but slow since Saddam had already left. On the drive back to our bunker, we saw a relatively large air strike. It was off in the distance so we were unable to determine the location, but we knew that whatever the target, it was completely decimated."

Azfal listened; an awful truth seemed to be dawning.

"We were horrified when we reached the bunker. The crater that was created spanned seven square blocks. The new bunker-buster bombs penetrated the structure leaving nothing in its wake. There were obviously no survivors, and we were devastated." Nuri's voice trailed as he spoke. It was obvious that he was crying.

Azfal couldn't handle what he heard. He felt the same sense of loss that the Greek hero *Achilles* felt when he saw the dead body of his friend *Petroclus*. The phone released from his grip and crashed to the ground. He grabbed for his chest and began convulsing. He was having a heart attack.

Luciana rushed to his side and yelled for Jassim to call for help. The boy quickly jumped from his seat and grabbed the phone, hanging it up and calling for an ambulance. He was crying as he attempted to keep his grandfather alive. Luciana was also in tears. She felt helpless since she didn't know what to do.

The ambulance arrived in a relatively short time, and the EMS technicians were able to stabilize his condition. He was in no further danger and taken to Rome American Hospital in Lazio. Luciana followed, arriving shortly after the ambulance, and Jassim was comforted that his grandfather would be at Salvatore's former place of employment. A battery of tests were performed, and the diagnosis was alarming. He needed an immediate heart transplant and was placed on a donor list, but the chances of him finding one before his heart gave out were slim.

The news was demoralizing to his loved ones. They sat motionless at the side of his hospital bed with no one uttering a word. It was the longest night of the child's life. Jassim knew the news from Iraq was terrible, but he still wanted to hear the details. In the morning, he anxiously asked his grandfather about his parents.

"Azi, what did Nuri say?"

With tears in his eyes, he looked at his grandson. "Saady was in Baghdad with your parents, and none of them survived." He was too weak to reveal all the particulars and slowly closed his eyes as he attempted to cope with the physical and mental pain from the horrific news.

The overwhelmed boy placed his head in his palms and continued to weep. Luciana also cried. It took a couple of days before everyone could regain their composure. It was then that Azfal had enough strength to share the complete story with his grandson. Jassim required a few days before he was strong enough to deliver the news to the Moretti's.

"Hold on a second. I'll ask my mom if I can go visit," Sabatina said.

After a few minutes, she returned to the phone. "She said I can't miss school, but if Luciana doesn't mind, she'll let me visit during the Thanksgiving break."

"What's Thanksgiving?"

"It's an American holiday."

"Oh, hold on a second." He turned to Luciana and asked if it would be okay for Sabatina to visit during the school break.

"Of course, she can. We'll pick her up from the airport," Luciana said.

Jassim was pleased and returned to the phone. "She said it's all right."

"Great. I'll see you soon."

"Okay. I'll talk to you later. We're about to leave for the hospital."

"Okay. Tell Gramps I said hi."

———

Sabatina's arrival couldn't have come soon enough. Jassim barely slept in anticipation. On the date of her flight, Luciana drove to Fiumicino from the hospital. Sabatina's presence helped Jassim focus on his bright future rather than his great loss. His best friend's words helped, and he was happy she was able to visit, but he was basically inconsolable. The trip solidified their bond, which would never be broken. He didn't cry as much as he did when his parents first disappeared since he had already assumed they were dead, but he was in a deeply depressive state.

Azfal was very surprised to see Sabatina enter his room since he had no idea she was coming.

"*Eetsa mya besta frrend. Alla tha waya froma Ameriga.*"

The children laughed at his pronunciation, and he believed it was God who joined the two of them in friendship. He felt a sense of relief knowing that Jassim would not be left alone when he died.

"*Allah* has blessed us with wonderful friends," Azfal said with a faint smile.

———

Sabatina was distraught when she departed for America at the end of the week but vowed to visit again. She didn't get a chance to do any sightseeing while in Rome, but that wasn't the reason she made the journey across the Atlantic Ocean. Her visit assured Jassim that he still had family and the best friend possible.

Jassim never left his grandfather's side, and Luciana was unable to work, taking a leave of absence from the museum. She chauffeured the boy back and forth at least once a day so he could grab a change of clothing. After weeks in the hospital, Azfal was moved to his permanent room in the cardiology wing, but he didn't want his grandson to spend the entire day in the room, so he forced the child to stay with Luciana in her guest room.

The museum director was finally able to go back to work after a couple weeks, but she returned with a heavy heart. Father De Luca looked after Jassim during the day. The priest replaced his ailing friend as the boy's primary educator since Azfal did not have the energy to continue. Jassim was trying to make the best of the new circumstances, but it was a difficult period in his young life. He always knew Father De Luca to be a kind and gentle man during his weekly visits to the house, but the priest's strict teaching style came as a complete shock. The inveterate instructor was a martinet with a laconic approach to education. Jassim was growing more annoyed with his method, which was entirely contrary to how his mother and grandfather taught him. The short-tempered priest's disparaging comments were unhelpful.

"I can't think straight if you keep yelling at me."

"Don't be a baby. You're not working hard enough," Father De Luca yelled.

———— ◈ ————

Jassim complained to Azfal, "Azi, I can't learn anything from him. All he does is yell."

"You have to understand that De Luca's austerity is aimed at getting the best out of you. I know it seems like he is torturing you, but he realizes your potential and wants you to achieve the greatness that you desire."

Azfal wanted him to learn how to thrive in any adverse situation. He believed the boy would benefit from the priest's firmness.

———⊷◉⊷———

On December 13, U.S. troops captured displaced Iraqi president Saddam Hussein in a spider hole, in the city of *Ad Dawr* near his hometown of *Tikrit*. The news of Saddam's capture put a smile on Azfal's face. He hoped for Iraq to recover and prosper under a new regime. He expected the foreign military forces to leave Iraq since the dictator was no longer on the run, but when it was reported that they planned on staying, he was angered. The untrusting Iraqi was sure the Americans had a hidden agenda. He believed the "greedy foreigners" wanted to strip Iraq of its many resources and felt that the country, its people, and its culture were in danger of being extinguished by the Catholic Church's "modern crusaders."

Jassim visited his grandfather every day after his lesson, usually traveling on his own whenever Luciana had to work. She provided him with enough cab fare, and he was careful to make the forty-seven-minute trip to Rome safely. The old man's heart condition worsened daily, but he was still intent on ensuring that his grandson would have a "great future." Azfal wanted the boy to be prepared for his imminent death, instead of giving him any false hope of a recovery. It was during one of these daily talks that he introduced Jassim to the *Shi'a* concept of *taqiyya*, which would shape the rest of the obedient child's life.

The death of his entire family turned Azfal into a bitter and vengeful old man with a heart filled with hate. He desired nothing more than to take down the "crusaders," spending every waking moment devising his grand scheme until he determined it was foolproof before presenting it to Jassim. Nadje was the one who explained *Taqiyya* to her husband while they were still in Cairo, and Azfal was careful to speak in Arabic to avoid anyone overhearing him.

"The first thing I want to do is thank you. I never updated you about the nightmares, which completely stopped after you arrived. I guess you're my lucky charm. I think you helped to replace the emptiness that was in my heart.

"I'm glad to hear that they stopped." Jassim was also happy to learn that his grandfather was giving him credit.

"I also want to say that I love Luciana. She has been a true blessing to both of us, and it is by the grace of *Allah* that she entered our lives. She has also helped to remove part of the emptiness that has existed inside of me."

Jassim was amazed to hear his grandfather speak so frankly about his feelings for Luciana. He never understood why it was such a secret.

"Father De Luca has been a very great friend as well. I want you to look to him for guidance, but always remember that he may not be completely trusted since we don't know his true motives."

Jassim nodded understandingly.

"You must understand the fact that *Shi'a* Muslims and *Sunni* Muslims are the same people. Both groups follow the teachings of the Prophet *Mohammad* and have the same aim of righteousness. The split happened in the year AD 632 after the prophet's death. He did not assign a *caliph* to lead our people, causing some followers to believe that *Ali*, who converted to *Islam* at the age of eleven and eventually married the prophet's daughter *Fatima*, was the his true successor. Yet others believed *Abu Bakr* to be the rightful successor. *Abu Bakr* was followed by *Umar* and *Uthman* in the *Sunni* tradition. When *Uthman* was assassinated, *Ali* was finally selected to be the fourth *caliph*. The *Sunni* Muslims believed that *Ali* should have punished *Uthman's* assassinators, which he failed to do, so they were angered and a split was created. The followers of *Ali* became known as *Shi'a* Muslims and are convinced that he is the prophet's only true successor."

Jassim knew a lot of Muslim history but wasn't familiar with all the details. He was very interested to listen to his grandfather's enlightening lesson.

"It is important to understand that Judaism, Christianity, and *Islam* are the same religion essentially. They all come from the same tradition, which serves *Allah*. The Jewish people were the first people of the book. It is through the prophet Moses and many others that *Allah* delivered his laws to them. Unfortunately, they added many inaccuracies when constructing the stories of the *Torah*, which is their Holy Book. Later, *Allah* sent the prophet Jesus to the people of the book. His undertaking was to correct the misinformation that is contained in the Jewish scriptures. Jesus taught the people the true word of *Allah*, but those who were assigned to record his teachings added their own falsities. Finally, *Allah* sent the prophet *Muhammad* to the people of the book. He provided us with the Lord's true word, and us Muslims believe the *Qu'ran* is *Allah's* unaltered message, revealed to the prophet. Do not allow ignorant people to confuse you. God and *Allah* are one and the same. *Allah* is simply the Arabic word for God. Jews and Christians serve the same God as Muslims, and those of them who speak Arabic use the word *Allah* when referring to the Lord."

Azfal's explanation helped to clear up a lot of misconceptions that Jassim was confused about, but his temperament grew more serious as he continued.

"The world is no longer a safe place for Muslims. You have a great goal to achieve. I want you to convert to the Roman Catholic Church."

Jassim was shocked by what he heard. "Azi, there is no one that I know who is a more devout Muslim than you. Why would you ask me to become a Catholic?"

"You must learn all that you can about their customs. Father De Luca is the key, and he is the vehicle that you will use to become a Catholic. The religion will keep you from harm, and you must remove all your own beliefs. You must accept what they teach. Follow their laws and become the best Catholic that you can."

Azfal paused. He grabbed his bewildered grandson's shoulders and stared into his eyes.

"I want you to become a priest so you can help to change the views of the Catholic Church from within. You must help to improve the relations between the Catholics and Muslims. With Father De Luca's help, you may possibly elevate to a powerful position in the church, maybe even become a bishop. Our friend, the helpful priest, will guide you with your assimilation into their culture, but remember that you can never trust him. In the future, he may try to keep you from helping Muslims. I have known since I held you as a child that you were destined for greatness, but it wasn't until recently that I realized it won't be on the football pitch, as we had hoped. It is through you that *Allah* will protect the believers. This will be your *Jihad!*"

Jassim listened intently as his grandfather spoke so he wouldn't miss any important details.

"The Catholic Church has many flaws. You will learn what they are and correct them. I also want you to study the *Rastafarian* movement. I don't agree with all their customs and beliefs, but the reasoning for their rejection of the Catholic Church is very revealing and pertinent to your undertaking. I believe that it is important for all Muslims to read the Bible since the prophet *Muhammad* was familiar with the Jewish and Christian traditions. We should follow in his example. There are many references to their Holy Scriptures in the *Qu'ran*. *Surah* 4:157 reads, 'That thy say, we killed Christ Jesus the son of Mary, the Messenger of *Allah*.'

"Knowing the Bible stories will allow you to better understand the *Qu'ran*, but before you set forth on your task, you must learn what *Taqiyya* means. It is essential that you listen carefully to everything I say."

Jassim knew that his grandfather was preparing to reveal something that was very important, so he gave his undivided attention. For about two hours, Azfal went into painstaking details in order to fully explain *Taqiyya*. The mature boy asked questions whenever the lesson became too confusing, and his grandfather took the time to further elaborate.

Taqiyya was revealed, and the boy understood exactly what his knowledgeable guardian was asking him to do. His heart was set on fulfilling the task. He grabbed Azfal's hand, looked into his eyes, and spoke with all the passion that was in him.

"I promise to do as you have instructed Azi. I will complete the *Taqiyya*, but I am confused. I thought you told me *Jihad* was an inner struggle to improve one's self?"

"Yes, that is the 'greater *Jihad*,' Jassi. There are two *Jihads*. The 'lesser *Jihad*' is the struggle against enemies of *Islam*. Both are important. You must always strive to be a good Muslim and follow the teachings of the prophet. The 'greater *Jihad*' is a lifelong struggle. In this instance, I am referring to the 'lesser *Jihad*,' which will be your personal struggle against the 'crusaders.' You must remember that *Allah* promised to punish the slanderers. Let me recite *Surah* 104:

> Woe to every slanderer, defamer, who amasses wealth and considers it a provision (against mishap); He thinks that his wealth will make him immortal. Nay! He shall most certainly be hurled into the crushing disaster, and what will make you realize what the crushing disaster is? It is the fire kindled by *Allah*, which rises above hearts. Surely it shall be closed over upon them, in extended columns."

Jassim comprehended his grandfather's lofty expectations, and Azfal knew the blessed child would be successful in completing "the promise."

There was only one more event that Azfal wanted to witness since he was resigned to the fact that he would miss the upcoming *Il Derby Capitolino*, which he could do without watching. He wished that it were possible for his heart to hold on long enough so he could witness the execution of Saddam Hussein. It was obviously wishful thinking because the Iraqi judicial process was very slow. He asked Jassim to be sure to witness it for him. In his eyes, it was the evil Saddam Hussein who was responsible for the death of his sons and daughter-in-law. The devoted boy swore to his grandfather that nothing would keep him from watching Saddam's death.

Jassim was exhausted from taking in all the information. He knew it was a monumental task that he was about to undertake, so as he always did, he hugged Azfal.

"I love you, Azi."

He left the hospital and headed to the cabstand for his ride back to Luciana's house. He entered a white taxi and gave the serviceable driver directions to his destination.

Azfal was very weak, but he managed to survive through the cold Italian winter. Bad news was relayed on the day of the Spring Equinox. He was given less than a month to live. Jassim and Luciana visited every morning and didn't leave until late in the evening.

On the first of April, noticing that she had nodded off, a fading Azfal whispered to his grandson, "Remember the promise! I will be with you always. I will send a sign."

Jassim nodded, assuring his grandfather that he would complete the mission, but he did not reply as a tear rolled down his cheek.

"You are like *Diomedes*, the true hero of the *Iliad*. While *Achilles* was sulking on the beach, he was taking on and wounding the Olympian gods. I see his determination in your eyes, and I know that you will succeed, even though I place before you an unimaginable task. Let the Holy *Qur'an* be your sword. Remember *Surah* 23, *Ayahs* 1–3: 'Successful indeed are the believers, who are humble in their prayers, and who keep aloof from what is vain.'"

The following morning, Jassim and Luciana returned to the hospital, but Azfal's room was empty. They began to walk out on their way to find out where he was and *Rosalia*, his assigned nurse, walked into the room. The motherly Italian was teary-eyed. She grew to be good friends with the Egyptologist. Immediately, they knew he didn't survive the night and cried as they held each other.

"I always enjoyed listening to his stories about the grandiose lives of the ancient pharaohs. I told him that once he got out of this hospital, I wanted a personal tour of the museum. The way he described the Nile Mosaic made it seem lovely," Rosalia said.

"It was Azfal's favorite piece in the museum. You should stop by and see it for yourself. Let me know whenever you decide to come by, and I'll arrange a guest pass for you."

Rosalia accepted Luciana's offer and sat with them for a moment leaving. Outside, Jassim turned toward the hospital. He could have sworn that he saw Azfal looking at him from the window of room 617, but when he looked again, the apparition was gone.

At the time, Jassim was reading the "Epic of Gilgamesh" assigned to him by Father De Luca. The student wished he could honor his grandfather the way the hero Gilgamesh honored his good friend Enkidu. He wanted to erect a monumental statue in his grandfather's memory.

Chapter 7

Azfal's slow death helped to prepare Jassim for the looming grief, but it was still painful. He previously notified Sabatina of his grandfather's impending passing. The Moretti's were prepared to receive the phone call informing them that he died, but the family was still heartbroken when the actual call arrived.

"Hey, Jazz-man, I know you want Sabatina to visit Italy, but I think it would be best if you move to Boston and live in our home. We are your family."

It was a difficult decision for the eleven-year-old to make. He had to choose between staying in Rome to be an apprentice of Father De Luca's and moving to America to be with his best friend again.

Luciana and the Moretti's were his only remaining family, but he still felt as if he were alone in the world. It was definitely something to consider since the move to the United States would provide him with a stable home environment for the first time since he left Baghdad.

The major hurdle was the fact that he wasn't sure he could rise through the ranks of the church from Boston, so he consulted with Father De Luca. The priest assured him that the archdiocese was more than capable of preparing him.

"Your ascension will be based on your understanding of church theology and not on location."

Everyone involved was in agreement, so he accepted the offer, knowing that the promise he made to his grandfather would still be an attainable goal. The promise was the one thing that kept him connected to Azfal, so Jassim was committed to carrying it out.

Father De Luca was well aware of the young man's plan to convert to Catholicism and also told of his desire to become a priest in the church.

"I am pleased that you aspire to join the priesthood, but serving the Lord is for those who are called and a lifelong commitment. You should experience life before you make such a big decision. If you feel the same way when you are older, I will help to prepare you."

Father De Luca knew that Jassim wanted to become a great soccer player and encouraged him to continue to pursue that goal as well.

"I understand. I will experience life, and if God calls me, I will be ready to serve. I'll follow whichever path he sets me on."

Azfal didn't want to be alive to witness his grandson's conversion, so it was agreed that Jassim would wait until after he passed away before making the change of faith.

He was buried atop a large hill, overlooking his new hometown, with a great view of *Monti Prenestini*. After his body was properly buried, Jassim met with his mentor, on May 1, to finalize arrangements for his baptism, which happened in the Church of *Santa Rosalia* in Palestrina. He officially joined the Roman Catholic Church on the ninth. Jassim felt that Mother's Day was appropriate in honor of Nebet.

Although Father De Luca and Luciana were named his godparents, he didn't feel comfortable using the terms because the death of his parents was still difficult for him to deal with; godmother or godfather reminded him of them. Luciana sat him down for a talk about the sensitive matter.

"I understand why you don't like the terms, and I will notify Father De Luca that we should avoid using them when you are in our presence. The plan will be for you to stay in Rome so you can learn about the teachings of Christ from your mentor, and then you can fly to join the Moretti's in Boston at the end of the summer."

Jassim was having a difficult time adjusting to life without his grandfather and often asked Luciana to take him to *Via Farini* for dinner at *Monte Caruso*. The restaurant held a special place in his heart since it was the first place he and Azfal sat down for a meal in Italy. *Monte Caruso* became his favorite destination in the Rome.

Father De Luca was impressed with the dedication and eagerness to learn that Jassim displayed, but he wanted to understand what the boy's motives were.

"Why did you decide to convert?"

Jassim sat in deep thought for a couple minutes. "I was impressed by how tolerant you were toward me and my grandfather. We are Muslims, but you took the time to not only help us but to also get to know us. Our religion never seemed to matter to you. I feel Jesus Christ reached out to me through you. I think he was calling for me to serve in his church. They say God works in mysterious ways, so maybe my parents were taken so I wouldn't have anyone to stop me from converting."

Father De Luca was impressed with his thoughtful response. He was skeptical at first but realized it was possible that God had indeed called the child to serve.

The summer went by swiftly, and Jassim became more familiar with the teachings of the Catholic Church, serving as an altar boy during the month of August. It was finally time for him to make his voyage to America. On his final night, Luciana reserved a table for three at *Monte Caruso* so the three friends could have a memorable dinner.

They enjoyed a lovely meal. It was unforgettable but also somber. Jassim was excited by the fact that he was preparing to enter the next phase of his life. The thought of moving to Boston was scary, but he couldn't wait to see Sabatina. His godparents were also excited that he would finally regain some stability in his life. They knew Salvatore and Anastasia would be great guardians.

In honor of Azfal, they all ordered his favorite dish, *penne all'arrabiata*. The spicy meal was a challenge for Jassim who asked for two refills of his apple juice in order to finish it. The adults shared a bottle of the finest *Vino Valpolicella*, and they all toasted to their fallen loved one and a safe trip to America. The witty boy held up his glass and couldn't stop laughing as he mimicked his grandfather's English.

"*Gooda lucka ina Ameriga*, Jassi."

Luciana and Father De Luca held up their glasses and laughed over the sound of clinking glasses. It was the first time since taking the responsibility of educating the child that Jassim saw the priest carrying on jovially. He was pleasantly surprised since he had grown accustomed to the priest's sternness. The night was one that neither of them would ever forget.

———⬦———

Azfal willed all his estate to Jassim and named Luciana as the executer; the boy wouldn't have control of the money until his eighteenth birthday. The estate was worth a little over $290,000 since he took out a quarter-of-a-million-dollar life insurance policy after the growing tensions against European Muslims.

The Moretti's lived on the outskirts of Boston in the town of Newton, and Sabatina attended Beaver Country Day School located one town over in Chestnut Hill, Massachusetts. Luciana sent a check to Salvatore for her godson's tuition at the prestigious private institution. He would join his best friend at the school in the fall.

Jassim promised to take care of himself and to keep in contact with his godparents. Both of whom accompanied him to *Fiumicino*. The three of them shared an emotionally heartfelt goodbye. Father De Luca gave him an inspirational verse from the Bible.

"Always remember first Chronicles chapter 22 verse 13: 'Only then shall you succeed, if you are careful to observe the precepts and decrees which the Lord gave Moses for Israel. Be brave and steadfast: do not fear or lose heart.'"

The new Catholic convert was moved by the priest's inspirational words. The gesture reminded him of Azfal since he loved to hear his grandfather recite *Quranic* verses. Luciana and Father De Luca watched as the teary-eyed boy made his way through the labyrinth leading to the metal detectors. As he walked through the security checkpoint, his mentor yelled, "Practice your dribbling!"

Recognizing the voice, Jassim turned and gave a thumbs-up to the man who always encouraged the future soccer star to practice his craft. He then walked toward his gate and was surprised to see a familiar face exiting gate 31C. Nira immediately recognized him, and they embraced.

"What are you doing here?"

"I am on my way to America to visit a friend." He didn't want to bring up the death of his family members, not wanting to discuss his loss.

"Hey, where's your dragon?"

Jassim removed his backpack and unzipped it to reveal his stuffed dragon. "Right here! I don't travel without it."

They both laughed and chitchatted for a little bit, but Nira was in a hurry; a friend was picking her up from the terminal, and he was due to arrive shortly.

"Have a safe flight. Remember to tell Ingrid that you know me and she'll give you the VIP treatment."

"Okay, I will. Thanks."

———— ◈ ————

The entire Moretti family traveled to greet him at the airport. It was agreed they would meet at the baggage-claim area. Sabatina was the first to spot her best friend as he descended on the escalator. She ran toward him, and they embraced like a wife hugging her soldier husband who just returned from the war front.

"How was the flight?"

"It was great. Remember the lady I told you about that I met on my flight from Amman?"

"Nira?"

"Yeah. I ran into her while I was walking to the gate, and her friend Ingrid let me help with the announcements. It was great."

His new guardians welcomed the bright-eyed boy to America, and after retrieving his bags, they all walked through the sliding doors toward the parking garage.

The United States was an immediate culture shock, and Jassim did his best to take everything in. He was excited to explore his new home. The trip from Logan Airport to the town of Newton was only fifteen minutes on the Massachusetts Turnpike. Salvatore drove into a driveway at the end of a cul-de-sac, leading to a house with an exterior of white siding and black trim. The newcomer was amazed by its grandeur.

"Is this the white house?"

They all laughed. "No!" Sabatina replied.

Salvatore gave him a quick tour of the grounds and pointed out some of the unique features.

"This beautiful domicile was constructed in the original American style and modeled after the Old Ship Meeting House located in Hingham Massachusetts," he said, impersonating a tour guide.

"Thanks for the info, sir," Jassim replied and they laughed.

"You can look it up online and see the resemblance, Jazz-man. This house was built in the seventies, but the designers of the original building were ex-shipbuilders. Look at the roof. You can see how they flipped the hull of a ship upside down to create it. You see how it is hipped with a widow's walk?"

"I agree it's a beautiful house, but that explanation is way too technical for me. I have no idea what a hip has to do with a widow on the roof, and I don't think I want to know, Sal."

The boy's comments humored Salvatore. They returned to the garage to unload the luggage. Sabatina gave Jassim an abbreviated tour of the house, finishing by directing him to his room, where he couldn't believe his eyes.

"It's huge! I have my own bed, and a computer, and an-I-don't-know-how-big flat-screen TV."

"It's forty-two inches," she informed him before bursting out laughing.

Jassim joined the Moretti's in the dining room for their first dinner as a family, and the massive painting that hung in the living room over the mantle captivated him.

"Wow, that's a big painting!"

"It's not an original. Sal commissioned a local artist to create this replication of John Singleton Copley's *Watson and the Shark*, originally painted in 1778. The piece became our favorite painting ever since we saw it at the National Gallery of Art in Washington, DC."

"I learned a little about art from my grandfather. I'm impressed with the artist's use of *char-curo*."

"I think you mean *chiaroscuro*, and I'd say I agree with you. We wanted a copy of the significant painting because it was inspired by a real event. A shark attacked a fourteen-year-old orphan who miraculously survived, and we also like the fact that it's the first positive portrayal of an African American in a painting."

Jassim was immediately reminded of the biblical story of Jonah and the whale. He also thought the erroneous portrayal of the shark's lips was comical.

It took two weeks for him to adjust to life in America. He was able to talk to both Luciana and Father De Luca. Their godson informed them how much he enjoyed the first day of school, even though he didn't feel challenged by the easy workload. His homeschooling was well ahead of the regular curriculum, causing him to stand out a bit, but he became fairly popular due to his prolific soccer skills. The new life was great, but every so often, he would be saddened when reminded of losing his family. Luckily, the reliable Sabatina was always there to cheer him up. Beaver Country Day was a fun school, but Jassim wanted to transfer to Trinity Catholic High School after he completed the eighth grade. The parochial school seemed like a better fit for him.

The Moretti's attended Sunday mass at the chapel on the Trinity Catholic Campus, and he struck up a friendship with the mercurial Father Mike, who was a caring man that inspired him; the priest also assisted with his Bible interpretation. The church's new altar boy became familiar with the faculty, making for a seamless transition once he switched schools. He was a devoted young man who quickly became a fixture at the parish, and Father Mike replaced Father De Luca as his daily mentor.

———◦◦◦———

April 2, 2005, was the one-year anniversary of Azfal's death and a significantly sad day for all Catholics around the world. News reports announced the death of the beloved Pope John Paul II. April

19, the conclave elected a new pontiff, who chose the regnal name Pope Benedict XVI. He was a German and a former member of Hitler's Youth. The new pontiff was chosen because he shared many of the same views as Pope John Paul II and the cardinal's wanted to continue the policies of the previous pope.

Jassim didn't think it was a coincidence that the pope died on the one-year anniversary of his grandfather's death. He wasn't sure how to make the connection but felt that in some way it was a sign from Azfal to continue with his *jihad*.

He was consumed by grief for most of the day but able to find a sense of peace in the chapel where he sat in the first row of pews and stared at the gold plated cross above the altar.

"Azi, I know you are watching over me. I can feel your presence, and I am motivated even more to fulfill the promise that I made to you," he whispered, as he looked up toward the large wooden rafters.

Sabatina found him alone in the church and was amazed to see that he was no longer in a sad mood.

"I feel like I have a guardian angel watching over me, and I don't see the point of grieving. Azi will always be there for me."

They exited through the main entrance of the Trinity Catholic and walked the several blocks to the house. He enjoyed walking over the Mass Pike because he felt a sense of danger with all the cars speeding by under the grate of the pedestrian bridge.

The school year ended successfully, and he helped out at the church as much as he could during his summer vacation. Father Mike grew to be a very close friend and confidant. The obliging priest helped him to prepare for his ultimate goal of becoming a member of the clergy.

Jassim was also readying himself for his first year in high school. The placement test that he took when he first arrived would have placed him in the ninth grade, but his guardians agreed that it would benefit him to have a year in junior high so he could adjust to life in America with Sabatina to assist him.

She remained at Beaver Country Day for high school since she didn't want to have to adjust to a new environment. She loved the teachers and looked forward to her final four years at the institution, but Jassim went through with the transfer to Trinity Catholic High School. The soccer coach was also excited to have him join the squad since the star striker's abilities were revealed during practices with the team during the summer. He was the only freshman that was skilled enough to be placed on varsity, and his teammates immediately welcomed the "new guy."

The first day of school was a bit nerve racking for him. Jassim sat in homeroom awaiting the teacher's arrival. After the pledge of allegiance and the morning prayer, all the students were ordered to stand against the wall. Mr. Fallon placed them in alphabetical order with the first seat being assigned to Jassim Ansary, who sat next to Mario Aponte.

"Hey, I'm Jassim," he said, extending his arm.

"Mario."

"Like the video game? Super!"

"Yeah, I guess. No pun intended, right?" The boys laughed.

Mario had an athletic build and always had a new haircut every week. His parents were from Venezuela, but he was born in Boston and lived in the city's South End section. The two boys became fast friends, spending most of their days together. Jassim wanted to learn two foreign languages but was only allowed to register for one course, so he decided on the more popular Spanish. He would wait until college to study French. He invited his new friend to the Moretti's house after school and introduced him to Sabatina, who instantly got along with Mario. Within a month, the three of them became inseparable.

Jassim scored two goals in his soccer team's first game, leading Trinity Catholic to a 5-to-1 victory, and as word of his success spread throughout the school, he quickly became very popular. Mario was a member of the freshman football team, finishing practice at the same time as his new "best bud." They usually went over to the Moretti's after they were done, where the "triumvirate" helped each other with homework.

On the tour of the house during Mario's first visit, he jumped into the empty oceanic tub, inside the master suite, and—in a Montana-like accent vociferously—stated, "Who put this thing together? Me, that's who! Who do I trust? Me!"

"Hey, Tony, you want the Columbian or Peruvian *llello?*" Jassim replied in jest.

"Get out of there. Your sneakers are going to track dirt inside my parents' tub, and I'll be the one who gets blamed," Sabatina yelled.

"*You know whah your prolen iz pussy-cat? Ju got nothin' to do, your life. Why don't you get a job or sonthin'? You know. Do sonthin'. Be a nurssss. Work with bline kidz. Lepers, thah kinda thing.*"

The friends laughed at his great imitation of *Scarface*. The new friendship inspired the future priest to quote from the Bible. "My two best friends will remain with me forever. It's important for us to remember Ecclesiastes 4:9–10: 'Two are better than one, because they have a good reward for their labor. For if they fall, one will lift up his companion. But woe to him who is alone when he falls for he has no one to help him up.'"

Jassim decided to continue in the tradition of Azfal and quoted scripture whenever he felt it was relevant. His grandfather would live on through him. Anastasia didn't mind having Mario over. She drove him home in the evening because she wanted her "little star" to have an easy transition to life in America and felt the running back was a great friend.

Mario's football team had a modest year finishing with six wins and five losses, but his buddy faired much better. The star forward led his squad to the division one state semifinals, where the Falcons lost to the eventual champions, the Wolf Pack of Boston Latin School, by a score of 3 to 2. Jassim finished the season as the state's leading scorer, and the *Boston Herald* called him a "phenom." The *Boston Globe* labeled him, "The future of American soccer." He remained humble despite all the adulation and kept to his core group of friends, which mostly consisted of his teammates.

He continued to speak with Luciana on a weekly basis, and she was proud of her godson's accomplishments.

"The next time I call, I'll have Father De Luca present. It's been a while since the two of you spoke."

The apprentice looked forward to speaking with his godfather, even though the priest was a strict disciplinarian. He truly missed "God's enforcer."

Luciana was true to her word, and the mentor was finally able to speak to his pupil. He was elated to hear the wonderful news about the boy's soccer accomplishments.

"In America, they don't say football. They use the word *soccer* instead," Jassim informed.

"I like that word—*sucker!*" the priest repeated over and over again.

Each time he said it, Jassim nearly wet his pants. The foreigner's thick Italian accent made it difficult for him to pronounce the word properly. The conversation lasted for a while longer and ended with a promise from Jassim to keep in better contact with his guardian from Milan.

The triumvirate pushed one another to perform well in school, and all three finished on the honor roll. "Mr. Soccer" had the worst grades among them, receiving a B+ in his English class, which ended up being the only "B" the group would receive while they were in high school.

The attention that the star player received from the girls was growing with every goal he scored, and there was a reciprocal attraction, but he fought his inner desires, deciding to focus on his future in the church. He didn't want to taint his pious reputation, in preparation for achieving his ultimate goal. The future clergyman didn't think the foolish advances from the girls were worth the risk. Both Azfal and Father De Luca warned about the potential to lose focus when faced with the temptations from the opposite sex.

His grandfather cautioned for him not to allow a woman to come between him and his destiny, but he didn't understand the counseling until the females began to admire him. He also never forgot Father De Luca's words.

"If you can reject the temptation from women, then you will truly know the Lord has called you to serve. Remember 1 John 2:16–17: 'For all that is in the world, sensual lust, enticement for the eyes, and a pretentious life, is not from the Father but is from the world. Yet the world and its enticement are passing away. But whoever does the will of God remains forever.'"

Jassim turned down most of his suitors with the same excuse. "Sorry, but I'm already dating Sabatina."

She was a fixture at all his games and often walked to the school to meet the boys after they practiced. Most of the students were familiar with her. Jassim swore Mario to secrecy, and he was terrified she would be angry if she uncovered his lie. Luckily for him, the freshman year ended without her finding out.

The triumvirate finished the school year and enjoyed their summer vacation even though they were mostly separated. Mario worked at his Uncle Victor's barbershop for six days out of the week. His main duties consisted of sweeping up the hair from the floor and taking out the trash, and most importantly, he was in charge of the lunch order. The apprentice didn't mind having to work his way up because he loved cutting hair and wanted to be a professional barber. Victor was unwilling to allow him to practice on any customers but promised to give him a chance in the future. Mario was the exclusive barber for most of the boys on Trinity Catholic's soccer and football teams. He made a few extra dollars while practicing his craft by charging five bucks a cut. He wanted so badly to impress his uncle with his skill but understood that he would have to bide his time.

Sabatina was away for most of the summer at a sleep-away camp in Maine. She enjoyed the arts and crafts but hated all the outdoor activities and the insects. The many cans of bugs spray became her most prized possessions. She loved getting to know the other campers but missed hanging out with her two "best buds."

Jassim continued to help out at the church assisting Father Mike, mostly pestering his mentor with all types of inquiries pertaining to joining the priesthood.

"I am convinced you have a true calling simply by the sheer volume of questions you ask on a daily basis."

The future priest served as an altar boy for every mass held at the parish, including all the Saturday weddings. He closely studied everything that the priests were doing, and by the end of the summer, he was able to recite the entire mass, verbatim.

Sophomore year began with the boys joining their respective teams for the upcoming seasons. Jassim was again a member of the varsity team, with Mario moving up a level to the junior varsity squad. Sabatina missed a few of their games since she joined her school's choir. She didn't have a dazzling voice but was a quality singer and a welcome addition to the group. The triumvirate saw less of one another during the school week but hung out the entire weekend. Mario usually slept over from Friday night to Sunday afternoon. He wasn't religious, but his mother forced him to make it home in time to attend the four o'clock mass. Anastasia often joked that she had three kids and talked about converting one of the guest rooms to "a sanctuary for my third child."

On one Saturday night, "number 3" wanted Jassim's advice on impressing one of the girls from school. Her name was Kathy, and she was extremely religious.

"Give me a verse from the Bible that I can say to her so she will be impressed."

"Are you kidding me? You can't use the Bible to pick up chicks. Besides, it won't work. She knows you're not spiritual."

"C'mon, I know there's something you can give me."

"I guess it can't hurt. Hopefully, she'll be able to straighten you out." He grabbed his Bible and reluctantly flipped through the pages. "Here, read this to her. It's Sirach chapter 26 verses 13 and 14: 'A gracious wife delights her husband, her thoughtfulness puts flesh on his bones; a gift from the Lord is her governed speech, and her firm virtue is of surpassing worth.'"

Mario was very impressed, and he looked up at his friend. "Damn, that's pimp, but I'm not looking for a wife, playa! On second thought, that's not a bad angle to play up. I had no idea what I was missing. I gotta check out more of this Bible stuff. Do you know how many religious freaks I can bag with these verses!"

Jassim shook his head. "What have I done? I know Kathy will blame me for helping you. Give me that Bible so I can find a good line about forgiveness."

The soccer team enjoyed another successful season. The captain led the Falcons to the championship game, but the Cardinals of Madison Park High School defeated them on penalty kicks, three goals to one. It was a masterful performance, but the team didn't have enough skilled players to support the star. Jassim was basically a one-man team. For the second consecutive year, he led Massachusetts in goals scored. The mailbox at the Moretti home was constantly filled with scholarship offers from universities throughout the country, not to mention the seven professional club teams from different countries, which also contacted "Golden Cleats." He was humbled by the publicity and careful never to let it change his character.

Whenever asked about his favorite team during post-game interviews, the star player often mentioned the love for *AS Roma* that he shared with Azfal, and he was blown away when he received a phone call from *La Magica's* owner, offering an immediate contract. It was flattering, but he wasn't willing to drop out of school. The offer was open-ended, and the owner looked forward to talking with "*il franchesing*" after his graduation.

On December 30, 2006, former President Saddam Hussein was executed by hanging for crimes against the citizens of Iraq. The new Iraqi government handled the trial, and he was sentenced to death, which was carried out at "Camp Justice." Camp *Al-Adala*, located in Iraq, was a joint Iraqi-American military base. The U.S. leaders made the wise decision to allow the Iraqis to carry out the proper justice for the ousted dictator, and the gesture helped to improve relations between the American military and the Iraqi people. The execution was broadcast live over the Internet, and Jassim gathered with the Moretti's and Mario to watch it.

"I know Azi is watching, and he is pleased."

Witnessing Saddam's death was very emotional for him because he believed that the tyrant and Bush's arrogance were the two main reasons for his parents' death. Deep down inside, he wished that the execution was more torturous since he had an unforgivable hatred for the former oppressor. A concerned Luciana called the following day to check on how her godson was feeling. They talked for a short time, and he let her know that he was content to finally see the "devil's dictator" pay for his crimes.

Father De Luca also called to check in. He also wanted to know how the soccer team was doing.

"I'm happy to hear about another successful season. I was very pleased that you turned down the offer from *AS Roma* because I know that Azfal wouldn't have supported quitting school."

They were still unable to contact one another on a regular basis due to the expensive calls, so Luciana decided to teach the antiquated priest how to use e-mail. She set up an account for him, allowing them to communicate more frequently.

In one e-mail to his mentor, he expressed a desire to turn down all the soccer scholarships and professional contract offers in order to join a seminary after high school; he didn't see the need to waste his time at a university. Father De Luca explained to the ill-informed teenager that it was in his best interest to attend a Catholic University before joining a seminary subsequently. The pupil was also vacillating over the idea of quitting his high school team in order to devote more time to helping Father Mike at the church. The boy was assured that the church would always be waiting for him and not to rush the process; it was more important for him to keep all his options open.

"I understand what you are saying. The seminary will always be there for me once I finish with school."

In another e-mail, after giving the matter more thought, Jassim wrote: "I am having second thoughts about going to college. I'm already having trouble dealing with the temptations placed before me in high school and would rather avoid living on an enticing campus. I feel that it would serve me better to enter a seminary following my high school graduation. That way, I can avoid the temptation from the women and all the money that will be thrown at me from the professional teams."

"My son, if you are truly called by the Lord, you shouldn't worry about temptation. If your calling is true, you will be able to resist any temptation, no matter how enticing it may seem." The priest wrote in a response e-mail.

He was appreciative to have the counsel of the wise priest and knew, with his mentor around, sound advice was always within reach. Father De Luca was impressed that he was still devoted to becoming a priest since he didn't think the eleven-year-old boy he spoke to in Italy was experienced enough to make that decision. He knew the temptation would be difficult for his godson but held out that the light of God would continue to burn inside him.

Junior year was the most challenging for the school's celebrity athlete. At the beginning of the summer vacation, Victor promised Mario he would allow him to cut a customer's hair before the start of the school year. He did an exceptional job, so his impressed uncle offered to allow his favorite nephew to cut hair at the shop on a part-time basis. The job offer was for after school and weekends, and Mario accepted the weekend spot since he couldn't work during the week due to football practice.

It only took him a week to change his mind and quit the team because he was the fourth running back on the varsity team's depth chart and felt his time would be better spent improving his haircutting skills.

Sabatina wanted to add to her extracurricular activities in order to present a more impressive application to her perspective universities and decided to fill up her after-school and weekend schedule. She continued to sing in the choir, joined the track team, and was a member of the debate team. Her free time on weekends was also used to add to her community service hours. The triumvirate barely saw one another during the school year.

Jassim's year started off horribly. Someone initiated a vicious rumor about him that quickly spread throughout the Trinity Catholic hallways. Students were aware that he aspired to join the priesthood, but it was never a problem for him until some envious players on the football team decided to pick on the "attention stealing" soccer star.

They referred to him using homophobic slurs during each encountering in the locker room, and he did his best to ignore the abusive behavior but grew concerned when the taunting escalated to threats of violence. Boston was at the center of the pedophilia scandal that tainted the Catholic Church's image, and claims were being made that Jassim was a rape victim.

The disparaging comments turned the school into a living hell for the aspirant. His friendship with Father Mike was twisted into a torrid love affair in which he was a willing participant. Each day became more unbearable with the increasing harassment. The football players often ran out of the locker room claiming that he was steering at them while they changed. His performance on the soccer field began to suffer, and he was unable to focus in class; his grades began to slip. He was in danger of receiving another "B" or maybe worse.

For the most part, Jassim suffered in silence and didn't even tell Mario that some of the students were harassing him. On the Monday following his team's fourth game, he could no longer take the abuse and decided to quit the soccer squad. He didn't want to be anywhere near the football players. Coach Donaghy was speechless and tried everything in his power to change the star player's mind, but nothing worked.

"Sorry, coach. I know that you are disappointed, but I want to focus on helping the parish, and soccer is taking up too much of my time."

Anastasia answered the door later that evening and was surprised to see the entire freshman, junior varsity, and varsity soccer teams standing outside. The cocaptain Dave Bishop asked to speak with his teammate, and she called him to come to the door.

The boys were interested to know why the number 1 ranked high school junior in America was quitting the soccer team. Jassim attempted to lie to his teammates but broke down crying. He finally admitted that the discriminating harassment, mostly from the football players, was unbearable.

"I didn't want to quit, but I felt like I was forced to. When I started to lose focus in class, I had to do something."

Jassim was astonished at the support that he received from his teammates, who vowed to stand by his side and stop the harassment. The following day, the entire team surrounded him while in the locker room. The football players were careful not to say anything in front of so many witnesses because they didn't want to risk getting into any trouble, but as they walked by, they stared at him and smirked without saying a word.

Following practice, Dave walked over to the football team and made an announcement to Coach Richards in front of his players.

"It has been brought to my attention that some of your players have been harassing one of my teammates. I don't know if any of this is true, but if it is, it stops today. Got it!"

Dave turned and walked away. He could tell Coach Richards was extremely upset because of all the screaming. The entire football team had to run laps for half of the next day's practice as their punishment for violating team policy concerning hazing.

The harassment didn't stop completely, but Jassim was able to deal with the few students who continued to make insensitive comments. Knowing that his teammates had his back comforted him since he previously believed that everyone was against him. He was too afraid to ask for help and was thankful to Dave. He quoted from Sirach 6:16: "A faithful friend is a life-saving remedy, such as he who fears God finds."

Mario didn't hear about the harassment until a week later and was furious when he approached his friend.

"Why didn't you tell me that they were harassing you? You know I'll always have your back no matter what."

"I'm sorry. I was lost and didn't know what to do. It won't happen again. I know you have my back."

Mario wasn't a great athlete, but he was a tough kid and asked Jassim to point out the worst offender. The boy's name was Barry Thomas. He was the football team's star quarterback and a complete jerk. He walked around school as though the other students were beneath him. Barry was not necessarily homophobic. His main reason for attacking the school's top athlete was jealousy. He was supposed to be the big man on campus, but Jassim's success on the soccer field overshadowed the covetous quarterback's celebrity.

Mario approached the signal caller in the locker room while he was preparing for the day's practice. He made a point to yell during the confrontation because he wanted to make sure that all the players were paying attention.

The quarterback's nonchalant attitude angered him further. Mario reached back and swung with all his might. Barry attempted to parry the blow, but his heavy-handed fist landed square on his eye, and the football captain fell to the ground. Mario picked him up and slammed him on the cold concrete locker room floor, and as Barry lay squirming on the ground, he kicked him in the stomach.

"Don't ever let me hear that you are harassing anyone, or the next time, it'll be worse."

The ghastly comments ceased from that point on, but Jassim still received an occasional dirty look. The pacifist didn't condone violence but was comforted in the fact that he had a true friend in Mario. A few days later, the "amigos" were talking as they slowly walked to the Moretti home.

"Hey, do you ever read the Bible?"

"Na, man, that's not for me. The last time I touched that book was when you gave me that line for Kathy, which didn't turn out to well."

Jassim chuckled as he remembered the incident. "Didn't work out too well? She called you out in front of the whole cafeteria. That was the most embarrassing thing I have ever seen. 'How dare you use the Bible to get pickup lines. I hope you burn in hell!' I was waiting for her head to start spinning, she was so pissed."

"Shut up. It was all your fault. You didn't give me a good enough line."

"Yeah, I'm sure that was the problem."

"After that experience, I don't plan on going anywhere near that book. My mom always tries to get me into church and stuff, but I'm not feeling it. I don't really care what a bunch of people had to say a million years ago. I guess when it comes to the church, each year, I become more 'decited.'"

Jassim stared at his friend with a look of consternation. "'Decited?'"

"Yeah. It's a word, means to lose excitement gradually."

Jassim laughed. "Yeah, you should give Webster's a call in case they forget to add it into the next edition." Shaking his head, he continued, "The Bible's not as bad as you think. There are some interesting verses in there. Take for example Deuteronomy chapter 23 verse 2 about membership into the community. 'No one whose testicles have been crushed or whose penis has been cut off may be admitted into the community of the Lord.' Tell me that's not crazy."

Mario was stunned to hear what was actually in the Bible and nodded in agreement, and Jassim continued.

"Do you know what that means? There were a lot of people getting their penises cut off. They were thugged out back in the day."

"I got some biblical quotes for you since you're always quoting the Holy Scriptures. See if you remember this famous one. 'You know what they say. Salvation is a drink best served cold.' I believe that's Mike chapter 10 verse 16, if I'm not mistaking," Mario said facetiously.

"Of course, from the book of Mike. Who doesn't know that one?" Jassim responded and they both laughed. "Your comedy has a certain, *Je ne sais quoi*. I must say, you have completely reached the height of hilarity."

As the situation at school improved, Jassim was beginning to enjoy his junior year. The soccer team advanced to the state finals again. Sabatina sat in the stands, along with her parents and Mario, and they watched him lead Trinity Catholic to the school's first championship; a win over the Brockton Boxers. The star player scored four goals to improve his total for the year to an inconceivable ninety-eight goals, making him the new record holder for high school players in the nation. He surpassed the old mark of ninety-four, which was set in Pennsylvania during the 2002 season. The celebration was spoiled when a schoolmate of his ran into Sabatina after the game.

"You are so lucky. Jassim is so cool. He must be a great boyfriend."

Sabatina didn't know the girl's name but saw her from time to time. "He is cool, but we're just friends."

"That's not what he told me."

Later on that evening, she knocked on his room door. He let her in, and she began to question him about what the girl said. He never stopped telling students that she was his girlfriend, thinking that she would never find out. Sabatina was angry at first but calmed down after he explained his actions.

"I only said that we were dating because the girls were always asking me to go on dates and I didn't want to date any of them. You know I want to become a priest, so I figured if I said you were my girlfriend, they would leave me alone. Anyway, it's none of her business, why can't some people just mind their P's and Q's?"

She understood why he lied and decided it was okay for him to continue telling people that they were an item.

"By the way, what does 'mind your P's and Q's' mean?" Sabatina questioned.

"I'm not a hundred percent sure, but I remember someone saying that it has to do with Britain. I guess back in the seventeenth century, the drinks in the pubs came in pints and quarts, and whenever two people got into a dispute, the bartenders would say 'mind your P's and Q's' to the other patrons, basically telling people to focus on their drinks and mind their own business."

The triumvirate did not hang out as much as they were accustomed to. Jassim and Sabatina spent most of the weekends without Mario, who was always working. Anastasia would sometimes drive them to the barbershop so they could spend an afternoon with their employed friend on Centre Street in Jamaica Plain. Victor lived in an apartment above his shop and not in the South End with the rest of the family. The shop was very large and had three big screen televisions, and Victor didn't mind Mario having company as long as it didn't affect his work.

The triumvirate was paying close attention to the presidential election of 2008, in which Illinois Senator Barack Obama was nominated as the Democratic candidate. Neither of the students cared too much about politics, but they knew the year's election had the potential to be historic since there was a legitimate chance for an African American to become president for the first time in the history of the United States of America. They were swept up in Barack mania, along with a majority of the country, and signed up to join the local election committee as volunteers.

On the night of the vote, the triumvirate gathered in the Trinity Catholic School cafeteria, along with over a thousand Obama supporters to watch the election results. November 5, 2008, was a historic day. Barack Hussein Obama was elected the forty-forth president of the United States of America, and most of the people in attendance were in tears as CNN called the election. Jassim felt an extra sense of pride, although he knew that President-elect Obama was not a Muslim, he loved the fact that his middle name was Hussein.

"Now here's a Hussein I can be proud of!" he exclaimed to Mario and Sabatina.

For him, the name had always been associated with hatred and evil, but now it stood for "change." The election of Barack Obama gave him the confidence that he would be able to fulfill the promise to Azfal, and from that moment on, he believed that anything was possible.

Senior year was an exciting time for the trio. Obama was elected president, and Sabatina felt a connection to him since she was elected president of her senior class. Mario worked hard and was able to save up enough money during the summer to purchase a car, allowing him to drive to school in his newly painted black 1992 Honda Accord with eighteen-inch black Katana GR4 rims. Jassim was looking forward to leading the soccer team to back-to-back state titles and a third straight selection as "Mr. Massachusetts." The friends were almost certainly headed off to different universities, and senior year was possibly their final opportunity to be around one another on a regular basis. Mario and Sabatina applied for early admissions, considering they both had excellent grades, but Jassim was relieved to avoid the stressful process of applying to colleges; the universities were pursuing him.

The soccer season went relatively well. Jassim stood six feet two inches tall and was in top shape. He was considered the fastest soccer player in the state and the perfect striker. He unfortunately missed three games due to a severe ankle sprain and was unable to eclipse his goal total of the past season. The seasoned veteran was the archetypical team captain. He led by example and practiced indefatigably. Prior to the championship game, he stood up before his teammates, and they encircled him, taking a knee.

"We have worked hard to put ourselves in the position to repeat as champions. Remember the 2007 Pats. They had an opportunity to become the greatest football team ever, but they blew it. Instead of going down in history as the best of all time, they went down in infamy as the greatest choke artists in Super Bowl history. Be mindful that one loss can change everything. It doesn't matter how many games you win if you can't finish the job. We will not follow their example. We will be like the 1999 Broncos! Like the great John Elway, we will finish our careers, at Trinity Catholic, as back-to-back state champions. We will finish this season with an undefeated record. Take Deuteronomy 31:6 with you onto the field: 'Be brave and steadfast; have no fear or dread of them, for it is the Lord, your God, who marches with you; he will never fail you or forsake you.' Let's go out there and bring back another championship."

The Falcons stood up and cheered wildly. They ran out onto the field with the determination of champions. An inspired Trinity Catholic team dominated the game against the outmatched Boston College High School Eagles. Jassim, playing in his final high school game, gave the best performance of his career; he scored eleven goals. The previous single game state scoring record was completely obliterated. He dazzled the crowd with his unbelievable dribbling skills and displayed the agility of a Madagascan fossa, slicing through the slow opposing defense, which looked as if they were running against crashing waves. His most incredible score came in the opening moments of the game when he dispossessed an opposing midfielder and darted toward the goal. He dribbled between his legs and kicked the ball into the air with his heel. After which, he jumped as high as he could and bicycle kicked the ball passed the hapless goalie. The game was never in question, and the Falcons successfully defended their championship by a score of 15 to 2. The star player ended his soccer career at Trinity Catholic. He was the greatest player in high school soccer history.

———————⊙———————

Anastasia and Salvatore wanted to ensure that the election of President Obama remained in the triumvirates' collective memories everlastingly. They gathered the young adults into the family's SUV and drove down to Washington, DC for the Inauguration Day festivities. It was an exciting time for the nation, but the weather was cold, and the family had to brave the freezing temperature. They stood patiently on the National Mall, along with a record-breaking crowd of 1.8 million people.

January 19, 2009, was the beginning of "change," as the nation was in a deep recession and a majority of the people was hopeful that President Obama would revive the economy. On a personal note, Jassim hoped the new president would end the war in Iraq, which was a main concern of his. Salvatore managed to get enough tickets, and the fivesome arrived early enough to pick out a decent spot with a clear view of the swearing-in ceremony. They were able to capture many photos, and the trip was one that none of them would ever forget.

———————⊙———————

Jassim believed the best way for him to rise in the Catholic Church would be to move back to Iraq, in hopes of increasing the pope's influence in the region, but he was also aware of the fact that it would be a dangerous undertaking. In the winter, after his senior season, he decided to pray to Azfal for guidance. He truly missed his grandfather and wanted a way to feel his presence. The aspiring priest wasn't sure the prayer would work but thought that if he spoke from the heart, somehow, the message would reach heaven.

The biggest decision of his life was fast-approaching, and he needed divine guidance.

"Azi, maybe if you were here, you would want me to play for *Roma*, and you wouldn't ask me to continue trying to fulfill the promise that I made. I want to know whether or not I should continue to pursue fulfilling the promise."

The long prayer session lasted all night, and he spoke to both God and his grandfather. When he divulged all that was on his mind, there was an immediate sense of relief.

"Azi, please send me a sign that will help to guide my decision."

He didn't know if his prayers would be answered but was relieved to clear his head of the many confusing thoughts. Jassim slept wonderfully during the night and woke up in feeling refreshed.

The family ate breakfast together, and everyone noticed that he seemed in higher spirits.

"I spent the entire night talking to my grandfather in heaven. I had a lot on my mind, and it felt good getting everything out."

"I think it worked. Getting all your feelings off your chest can be therapeutic," Anastasia thoughtfully added.

After a hearty breakfast, Jassim turned on the television in his room in order to check on the situation in Iraq. He routinely followed the coverage to keep up with the latest developments. The CNN report almost knocked him off of his seat.

For the first time in recorded history, snow fell to the ground, covering Baghdad. The Iraqi people were stunned, and an eighty-year-old lady was asked if it was the first occurrence in her lifetime. She replied, "Yes." Jassim interpreted the snowfall as a sign from Azfal, telling him to continue the mission of carrying out the promise. The astonished boy instantly knew that his grandfather would watch over him.

"Thank you for the sign, Azi." He was even more determined to succeed.

Many people were optimistic that Iraq would be able to recover from the war, and the return of soccer games throughout the country served as an indication that a sense of normalcy was setting in, but things changed on the fifteenth of March. Sabatina called Jassim to the living room where she was watching the news. In Iraq, the events of the day became a major setback for the American soldiers who were waiting for the country to stabilize so they could leave.

During a soccer match in the southern city of *Hilla*, a spectator shot the opposing team's forward, in the head, as he was about to score an equalizing goal. The killing affected Jassim personally since he was also a striker, and optimistic that the conditions in the country were improving, there still existed a large enough faction that didn't want the Americans to get any recognition for removing Saddam and improving the lives of the Iraqi people. They were willing to kill in order to keep the country in a state of chaos, and their malicious attack caused the U.S. military forces to tighten its grip on the nation. The tension in Iraq was escalated.

"It's weird that this happened on the fifteenth of March," he mentioned.

"What's so weird about it?"

"Because it's the Ides of March. The date was made famous by the Shakespearian play *Julius Caesar*, in which his Senate assassinated the Roman leader on the fifteenth."

"Oh yeah, that's right, weird coincidence."

Mario was the first to receive an acceptance letter and decided to attend his first choice, Boston University. He celebrated with his family before driving out to Newton to share the news with his close friends. He had been unnecessarily worried that he wouldn't get in, and the letter was a big weight off his shoulders.

It took a week for Sabatina to hear from one of her schools. The first acceptance letter arrived from Providence College. She was excited, but the school wasn't her first choice, and she continued to anxiously await the decision from Boston College.

The letter from BC didn't arrive for two days. Anastasia knocked on the bedroom door and handed her restless daughter a large maroon envelope with gold lettering.

"Here what you've been waiting for. Open it up."

Sabatina was scared to open it at first but slowly gathered the courage to read the letter and jumped for joy when she saw that she was accepted.

"I can't believe it. I'm an Eagle!" she screamed.

She wouldn't be attending the same university as Mario, but they would only be a couple miles apart.

Jassim avoided announcing his decision because he was having difficulty making up his mind and didn't want to rush the process. He knew he wasn't accepting the offers from any of the professional teams since his education was very important. His final decision was between college and the seminary.

He was still unsure if attending a university was the right move, even though Father De Luca assured him it was. He seriously considered going against the advice of his informed mentor. In an e-mail to a Boston Herald reporter, he wrote: "I have a difficult decision to make, and I will carefully take all my options into consideration, weighing the pros and cons. I want to be vigilant, and I don't plan on making an announcement until after graduation. I will take a trip with a friend of mine and will hold a press conference upon my return. After giving my options serious thought, I will reveal my future plans."

The e-mail was circulated to all media outlets, and Jassim felt a sense of relief because he no longer had to worry about the difficult decision until after graduation.

Chapter 8

Graduation day was very emotional for Jassim. Luciana and Father De Luca flew in from Italy to attend. Family members scurried into the chapel to avoid getting drenched from the evening's rainfall. An eruption of cheers filled the room as the most distinguished graduate walked across the stage, with Azfal's *AS Roma* scarf draped over his gown. The stuffed powder blue dragon in his left hand was comical to most in attendance, but those who knew him best understood its importance.

He expressed a few inspirational words to a group of his closest friends after joining his classmates in the traditional tossing of the caps.

"I want to leave all of you with Jeremiah 29:11: 'For I know well the plans I have in mind for you, says the Lord, plans for your welfare, not for woe! Plans to give you a future full of hope.'"

Anastasia invited everyone back to the house for a joint celebration, and it was an enjoyable time for all. A few of the soccer players attended along with Coach Donaghy, who was glad to have been given the opportunity to coach "The greatest player I have ever seen play." When the celebration was over and all the guests went home, Jassim and Sabatina sat down for an overdue conversation.

The two of them talked for about an hour, reliving some of the great memories they had shared over the years. She enjoyed rehashing the old memories but had something important to reveal.

"I know you haven't made your decision about your future, and I wanted to get some things off my chest. You have been my best friend, and we've been inseparable since the day we met, but I haven't been completely honest with you."

Jassim wasn't sure what she was preparing to say, but he hoped it wouldn't ruin their close bond.

"You know how I always yell at my mom whenever she tries to say that we are brother and sister?" He nodded in agreement. "Well, I can't see you as my brother since I have strong feelings for you and they grow stronger every day. When I told you it was okay to continue telling people that we were dating, it was because I secretly wished that we were, and I suggested that we go to the prom together because that was my dream. I'm scared that you are going to leave me, and I'll be devastated if you go off to play soccer in Europe or go to a school that is far from here. I know you are under a lot of pressure, and I don't want to add to it, but I want us to stay together. Boston College has a decent soccer team, and I think you should accept their offer so we can go to the same school."

Jassim was speechless. He never suspected that she had feelings for him. He always thought she was the hottest girl in the world and desired to be with her but avoided the subject because he knew it would deter him from his ultimate goal. He thought she was even more attractive than Anastasia and was aware that every boy at her high school had a crush on the auburn-haired Italian; her perfectly proportioned body matched the beauty of her face. She had always been the object of his fantasies, and the feelings he had for her prevented him from calling the Moretti's "Mom" and "Dad."

He didn't know how to respond and became more confused than ever before. He couldn't even look her in the eye and fiddled with a stuffed bear while he spoke.

"I was called by God to serve his church, so I can't pursue a relationship with you. I think you're beautiful, but I don't want to confuse things by getting involved in a relationship, knowing that I will eventually join the priesthood."

She refused to accept his response and leaned in closer to him. They shared a passionate kiss. Jassim felt that he was in danger of giving into temptation and pulled away.

"You have to understand that joining the church isn't a choice but a true calling. We can't do this."

Sabatina got the message but secretly hoped to change his mind in the future. He seriously considered the option of attending a different school in order to avoid succumbing to his desire for her. He had a lot to think about, and his mind spun all night; the bewildered senior barely slept. The next day, Sabatina accompanied Anastasia to pick up Mario so he and Jassim could take the bus to New York from Boston's South Station.

"I really wished you could have joined us, Tina. I hope you have fun with your friends in Maine. I'll see you when I get back," Jassim said.

The trip to New York provided Jassim with enough time to plan his future before the scheduled press conference on the day after his return. New York City had the reputation of being a very tough place, and visitors were often warned to be careful when venturing to the "Big Apple." Women were reminded to be wary of purse snatchers, and men were told to be cautious of pickpockets. It was often said, "If you can make it in New York City, you can make it anywhere." The boys could attest to the validity of the quote after their experiences in "the city."

During their weekend visit, the friends found themselves riding the Greyhound bus into Manhattan—final destination Pennsylvania Station, on Thirty-Fourth Street. It was an enjoyable expedition, and they took in all the major tourist attractions, vowing to return. They both knew that Sabatina would have enjoyed the lively city and wanted to bring her along on their next excursion, but the big decision loomed on Jassim's mind during the entire trip. It wasn't until the bus ride back to Boston that he asked for Mario's opinion on the matter. He was able to narrow down the options to accepting a scholarship offer but wasn't sure where to go and wanted to know if joining Sabatina at BC was a good idea.

"I think you should go to Boston College. You loved the campus when we took the tour, and the coach is a great guy. You can't run away from the challenges that life throws at you. You're going to have to deal with Sabatina, no matter where you end up next year, so you might as well choose a school you love. Plus, that tour guide was hot! If you see her around campus, let her know that I'm just down the street."

Jassim knew that his girl-crazy friend was right, even though he did have a unique way of getting his point across. He used the remainder of the long ride, in the congested traffic, to further think about his future and was eager to get the decision over with. The stench emanating from the coach bus's restroom was unbearable, so getting off was the top priority.

Uncle Victor gave the boys a ride from South Station to Mario's house, where Mrs. Aponte cooked a feast fit for her "young princes." Jassim loved spending time with the family since he had the opportunity to improve his Spanish and eat the "best cooking in the world." Mr. Aponte especially was impressed with his ability to construct proper sentences and his correct pronunciation of the words. Mario gave him a ride to the Moretti's after the tasty meal.

"Hey, it's the Jazz-man and Super Mario! I can't believe you guys made it back in one piece."

"We almost didn't, Big Sal. I don't think the natives appreciated my Red Sox gear," Mario said.

"Yeah, he was getting the evil eye the entire time," Jassim added.

Anastasia and Sabatina were also happy to see the boys arrive home safely, but his best friend was eagerly awaiting his decision.

"So! What are you planning on doing next year?"

"I still have plenty to think about, and I'll make my announcement at the press conference. We can talk about everything afterward." In the meantime, he couldn't wait to tell her about their trip.

"Our hotel was a few blocks away from Penn Station, so we were pretty much in the heart of Manhattan, right down the street from Times Square. After walking around the very confusing Penn Station, we wanted to see New York's famous Grand Central Station, but in order to reach the historical landmark, we had to ride on the city's public train to Forty-Second Street, where the shuttle is located. We made our way through the busy terminal, following the blue circular ACE signs toward the train so we could go across town from the west to the east side.

"The city was filled with workers and students who were rushing to get to points unknown. We found that walking in New York City was an adventure within itself. People were often bumping into one another on the crowded sidewalks. I felt like I was a football player running through drills in practice with all the collisions. We could have walked the eight blocks uptown then across Forty-Second Street, but we decided to take the shuttle instead. We learned that on a daily basis, the shuttle makes its way back and forth hundreds of times, so we didn't expect a long wait.

"The A-train was first to arrive, so we jumped on for the short ride to the next stop, and when we exited, we made our way to the shuttle. The area was filled almost to capacity with impatient passengers crowding the underground platform due to it being rush hour. The shuttles were running as fast as possible trying to accommodate the large crowd, with a new train leaving about every three minutes. We weren't in a hurry and decided to wait until there were fewer people. Our wait was made bearable since we watched five teenagers using buckets as drums to create eclectic beats. The varying sounds filled the station, making for a soothing atmosphere, and people gathered around, throwing money into an old dirty baseball cap. As expected, Mario received many dirty looks from the New Yorkers because he insisted on wearing his new Boston Red Sox cap and a different Sox shirt every day."

Sabatina smiled approvingly since she was a die-hard Sox fan as well. The rivalry with the Yankees always seemed to be a big deal to the citizens of Boston, but Jassim didn't think it was as bad as the fans made it out to be. While in Italy, he witnessed a few savage beatings handed out to unlucky fans of *Lazio* by crazed *Roma* supporters. To him, the Red Sox and Yankees rivalry was good sportsmanship, compared to *Il Derby Capitolino*.

"Finally, after twenty minutes or so, we decided not to wait anymore because the natives were growing restless. The dirty looks were coming from more and more of the Yankee faithful, and the people who were still waiting to board a shuttle were growing more intolerant. There was no telling where the mass was headed, but it must have been an important place because of the increase in pushing and shoving. That station was definitely not the place for the faint of heart. As the next transport arrived, I managed to carve out a little space for us to stand, opposite the opened door of the glutted shuttle. The people just continued to file in. Observing the movement of the crowd brought up visions of Macy's employees opening the door during Black Friday and watching the bargain hunters push, shove, and claw their way through the racks, in hopes of finding the best deal."

Sabatina laughed. "Was it worst than last Thanksgiving at the mall?"

Jassim shook his head affirmatively and continued, "It was beginning to be very crowded as passengers crammed into any available space. I would certainly not recommend for someone with claustrophobia to attempt to ride the shuttle during rush hour."

Sabatina understood the picture that Jassim was painting, and she crowded over him, invading his personal space.

"Yeah, kind of like that but worse," he said while pushing her away.

"We were a lot closer to the citizens of NYC than either of us wanted to be, and the combination of sweaty people coming home from a hard day's work, all jammed into a confined space, created a unique aroma. If I tried to describe the pungency to you, I wouldn't do it justice."

"Yuck!" she let out, grossed out just thinking about what it could have smelled like.

"Wait! Remember that nasty smelling fruit that we found at that market in Palestrina?"

"Yeah, the durian. How can I forget? It was putrid!" She was repulsed as she recalled the nasally challenging experience.

"Well, I would gladly sleep in a room full of rotting Southeast Asian *durians* than relive the experience. Not to mention, I think I was sexually assaulted, but I can't be sure. Everything happened so fast," he joked. "The shuttle was almost filled when two distinguished gentlemen, probably in their early sixties, walked in. They were both dressed in fine-cut suits, covered in long trench coats, and each carrying a black-leather briefcase. New York City was a unique place because everyone rides the train. We saw a homeless man sitting next to a Wall Street multimillionaire."

"Are you serious? Rich people use the crowded subway."

"Yeah. These two men seemed to be the last to board, and the doors began to close. Suddenly, out of nowhere, a man ran as fast as he could and used his arm to stop the door from closing. This man was most likely in his early thirties and dressed in the latest hip-hop fashion, with baggy jeans, an oversized T-shirt, and a blue New York Yankees baseball cap that was at least two sizes too big.

"He barely made it, but there was no more room. Yet he was determined to push his way into the already overcrowded shuttle. His valiant effort was made more difficult because one of the businessmen was blocking the entrance, clearly trying to keep him out. The older gentleman was in a hurry and couldn't understand why the man wouldn't just wait for the next shuttle. 'Mr. Hip-Hop' continued to try and squeeze into the shuttle, but there just wasn't any more space, and it didn't help that 'Captain Wall Street' was slowly pushing him back onto the platform. This struggle between the two men continued for about ten seconds. It was an epic battle: Wall Street vs. Hip-Hop. The unnecessary effort was annoying the businessman's friend since another shuttle would be leaving in less than five minutes. We were completely enthralled and looked on in awe, eagerly anticipating what was going to happen next.

"Wall Streets's friend, whose facial expression was growing more intense, cocked back and made a fist. He swung with all his might in the direction of the young hip-hopper, hitting him squarely in the face. Mr. Hip-Hop stumbled backward and fell, hitting the white-and-black checkered platform flat on his back."

Sabatina was stunned; she couldn't believe what had occurred. She never expected a businessman to get into a street brawl in the middle of a train station. "I think I'm having second thoughts about visiting New York. I'm not sure I'll be able to survive."

Deep down inside, the story increased her desire to have her own "New York moment."

"To me, the most shocking part of this incident was the fact that not one person on the shuttle made any kind of reaction. Everyone behaved as if it was a normal occurrence. It didn't really bother Mario to see a Yankees's fan get punched in the face, but he was shocked as well. This was our first true New York City moment. The two seemingly civilized men turned out to be bona fide thugs. The term 'time is money' must capture the mentality of the average New Yorker, but the incident didn't scare us or make us feel unsafe. In fact, in a strange way, we were kind of excited that we were able to witness what transpired. I couldn't wait to come back and tell you about our crazy New York City experience.

"The fact that someone was attacked on a train wasn't what was so shocking to either of us. Growing up in Iraq allowed for me to witness all types of crazy events, while Mario, once riding 'the T' witnessed a heated argument between the bus driver and a passenger. The passenger finally left before the incident became violent, but he didn't exit without yelling, 'Next time I see you, I'll kill you!' The reason this encounter was so shocking is the fact that the man who initiated the violence was wearing a suit and looked as if he was on his way back from a multimillion-dollar transaction. The saying, 'Don't judge a book by its cover,' holds a lot of truth. We definitely made an assumption, judging the men by their clothing. Because of this incident, we'll make the effort not to make judgments before having all the facts."

"Hopefully, when I go to New York, I will come back with my own story, just as long as I'm not the one getting punched in the face."

"Good luck with that! How was the trip to Maine?"

"It was okay. We just hung out in the cabin for most of the time, nothing exciting."

The basketball gym inside the Trinity Catholic school building was the center of the sporting world. Soccer was not America's favorite sport, but the phenom's declaration captivated the nation. Jassim's high school highlights were a regular occurrence on Sports Center's Top Ten countdown. The media outlets crowded into the gymnasium, along with representatives from each of the professional soccer clubs that offered him a contract. The owner of *AS Roma* made the trip to hear the announcement in person, anticipating good news. The stands were filled with adoring fans. ESPN televised the press conference live with the star athlete sitting at the dais in front of several microphones and scattered tape recorders. A copy of his prepared statement was centered on the podium.

"First of all, I would like to thank God for blessing me with the ability to perform at a high level. And I would also like to thank ESPN for broadcasting this press conference. I have had a lot to think about, and I took the time to weigh all my options. After deep consideration, I have reached a decision. I am grateful to all the professional teams from all over the world who took interest in me, for offering a contract. I also want to thank all the universities who have offered me a scholarship. School has always been the most important thing to my grandfather Azi, and he advised me to use my soccer abilities to gain a free education. I cannot go against his wishes, so I will have to turn down the contract offers from the professional teams."

The representatives were extremely disappointed, but they understood that he was making the best decision for himself.

"I look forward to playing college soccer for the next four years, and if the professional teams still want me following my graduation, I will then consider the offers. I especially want to thank Mr. *Giordano*, who owns the *Roma* team, for making the long flight and attending today's announcement in person. I hope you understand the reasoning behind my decision. Although I have always loved *i Lupi*, I can't join your club at this point in my life, but I will always support your team. And maybe in the future, I will be able to suit up for *i Giallorossi*."

Mr. *Giordano* acted as if he understood, but he was fuming inside. He couldn't comprehend how anyone could turn down a multimillion-dollar offer. He was a businessman, and the bottom line was all that concerned him. The only thought that comforted him was the fact that Jassim would eventually join his club after his college career.

"I had many great universities to choose from, and I'm thankful to all the coaching staffs that pursued me. I feel that only one school is the perfect fit for me because of its great athletics' tradition and strong academic record. I also love the fact that the university is a religious institution."

Jassim reached down under the table and grabbed a cap. "Next year, I look forward to playing for Coach Johnson at the Heights."

He placed the Boston College hat on his head, proudly exclaiming, "I will be an Eagle!"

The crowd exploded with applause, and Coach Johnson, who was in attendance along with some of his players, thanked Jassim for choosing Boston College. The future star had to stick around and answer questions from the throngs of media to his chagrin. After the press conference, he joined Sabatina and her parents for a celebratory dinner and was filled with a sense of relief.

"I can't believe how many interviews I had to sit through today, the same questions over and over. I hope I never have to go through that again!" a tired Jassim proclaimed.

"Well, it looks like you'll have to, Jazz-man. The four years at BC will be over before you know it, and you'll have to pick a professional club," Salvatore reminded, as he took a swig from his glass of Johnnie Walker Black Label.

Later on in the evening, Jassim and Sabatina sat in her room to discuss their future. She was extremely excited by the fact they would be attending the same school.

"I know you are happy that we will be at the same school next year, but you have to remember that we can only be friends. My determination to become a priest is real, and I don't want to lead you on by giving you any false hope."

Sabatina was too excited to care. She planned on seducing him once they were alone on campus. She knew he had feelings for her and was determined to bring them to the surface, undoubtedly believing they were destined to fall in love.

The future Eagle consulted with his longtime mentor about his outlook. "I'm sure you heard that I am going to Boston College, but I am more concerned with selecting the best seminary."

The experienced priest was familiar with Saint John's Seminary located in Brighton, Massachusetts. "One of the retired cardinals who is living in the Vatican was the former leader of the Archdiocese of Boston and lived at Saint John's."

Father De Luca assured his godson that when the time arrived, he would ask the cardinal to assist with the transition to the seminary.

Jassim also met with some of the Jesuit priests on the Boston College campus in order to determine his class schedule. The priests were excited to see a talented young man who could possibly choose to serve God over fame and fortune. He also took the opportunity to register for French classes. He would finally be able to learn the romantic language.

<hr />

At the end of September, *AS Roma* announced plans for the construction of a new stadium, because the club was renting the use of the Olympic Stadium and the owner wanted a "true" home field. The new stadium would be constructed on the western outskirts of Rome. Jassim was excited for the future of his favorite club.

He remained determined to complete the promise that he made to Azfal, but a part of him desired to play for *AS Roma* in the new stadium. It was a decision that he didn't have to worry about for at least four years, and he hoped to discover another sign pointing him in a new direction. The new *Roma* Stadium was to be completed in 2014, a year after his graduation from college, which further caused him to seriously reconsider his future plans.

Freshman year in college was an easy adjustment for the triumvirate who helped each other as much as possible. Mario was on the Boston College campus on most weekends after working at the barbershop.

Jassim had a successful first season at the Heights. The men's soccer team was ranked seventh in the nation, entering the post season. The dominant Eagles only suffered two defeats during the season with their new star leading the way. He was the third leading scorer in the country. He also finished first among all freshmen;

however, Boston College was eliminated in their national semifinal game against the Tar Heels from the University of North Carolina. It was a disappointing defeat, but overall, the season was a successful one in which Jassim finished fourth in the voting for player of the year. His hard work was rewarded, and he was named newcomer of the year.

Sabatina attended all the team's home games, and the two friends often met for dinner afterward at Uncle Lu's Fill-Up on Bread Restaurant near the campus. The quirky uniqueness of the place was what hooked them. Uncle Lu's was more of a take-out joint than a sit-in restaurant; customers were fed a varied selection of bread while they sat and waited for their food to be prepared. The metal tables were small and designed to sit four. The matching silver stools swiveled over the hardwood floor, and the scintillating aroma of fresh baking bread invaded the nearby Boston College campus each morning. The students filed into Uncle Lu's, almost in a zombie-like trance, on a mission to fill their empty stomachs. The staff was professionally trained to create a variety of fresh breads from all over the world, and most patrons were full before leaving because the bread was so delicious. There was an overwhelming desire to try as many of the different types as they could stuff into their cavernous bellies. The take-out orders were named "later meals" since they weren't usually consumed until the following meal.

During the first semester, Sabatina's flirtation increased, and Jassim grew alarmed because she was becoming sexually aggressive. He seriously questioned his ability to resist her and did his best to avoid being alone with her, which was impossible because they were always around each other.

The nation was in an uproar over the new H1N1 virus. Anastasia called the children and ordered them to get their vaccinations, which were available at no cost on the campus. Later on in the day, after arriving at home, Salvatore called Sabatina to say that the flu shot wasn't necessary.

"The swine flu is pretty much harmless. I really don't understand why there is so much concern about an epidemic. Don't listen to the false news reports. Be sure to tell the Jazz-man."

Mario finished his first semester at Boston University with a perfect 4.0 GPA. Schoolwork had always come natural to him. He never received a grade lower than "A" from kindergarten on. Although he earned perfect grades, Mario didn't have a desire to stay in school because his true passion was cutting hair. He didn't see the point in continuing his education until after he perfected his craft. He met with his parents and his Uncle Victor over dinner at the Aponte home.

"School will always be waiting for me in the future. I know that my decision to leave BU is a little disappointing, but I have to follow my heart. I promise to return to school once I complete my goal of establishing my own shop."

"As long as ju return to the school, we don't have a problem. ¿Entiendes?" Mr. Aponte said in his thick Venezuelan accent.

With the blessing of his family members, Mario was excited to pursue his career. His two best friends were less stunned by the news that he was dropping out since he always expressed his dispassion for school.

During the winter break, Mario purchased a bottle of Johnnie Walker Black Label because he wanted the triumvirate to celebrate the completion of their first college semester. He drove to pick up Jassim and Sabatina from their home, and the three friends traveled to Victor's barbershop in Jamaica plain. The shop was closed for the night, so they decided it was the perfect place to hold the celebration since he had his own set of keys. To avoid Mario driving under the influence, they all brought sleeping bags and planned on staying the night.

"I'm not twenty-one, so I'm not drinking any. As much as I want to try Sal's good whiskey, I can wait until I'm of legal age. If I drink it tonight, I know it will be impossible to justify not drinking in the future," Jassim said.

His friends were disappointed, but they didn't try to convince him otherwise since they knew that his mind was made up. He wasn't the type to fall victim to peer pressure. Unfortunately for Jassim, the two rebels were inexperienced and couldn't hold their liquor. After three shots each, they became stammering winos.

Jassim was further annoyed after every shot because the intoxicated duo grew increasingly aggravating. Being the sober person in the presence of two drunks was an experience that he never wanted to suffer through again. The night became gradually more unpleasant because he was left to clean up the vomit-splattered bathroom since his inebriated friends were passed out on the cold linoleum floor. Victor didn't arrive until late in the afternoon, but another barber questioned Mario about the foul odor that emanated from the back of the shop.

"Hey, bro, what the hell is that smell?" asked Paco who was attempting not to breathe in the foul odor.

"Oh yeah, I crashed here last night and got food poisoning." The excuse was naively believed.

Mario enrolled at the Massachusetts School of Barbering and Men's Hairstyling in the neighboring town of Quincy. He continued to work at Victor's part time while he was studying for his barber's license. He searched online for a good place in anticipation of dropping out and discovered the school during his first semester. He requested a brochure and signed up for a campus tour, and Jassim accompanied "*El Barbero*" on the visit. Mario loved the school and couldn't wait to begin.

Uncle Victor loaned him the ten thousand dollars for his tuition, expecting that he would pay it back once he completed the courses. His barbering ability was already above average, but the school increased his skill level immensely. The novice learned the proper techniques, causing him to no longer question the justification for the large tuition payment.

Jassim never forgot Azfal's speech in room 617 at Rome American Hospital. He always wondered about the significance of the *Rastafarian* movement mentioned by his grandfather. He knew that Azfal would not have brought it up if it weren't important and decided to look into the subject since he had a lot of free time during the winter break.

He learned a great deal about *Rastafari* and decided to register for an anthropology course—Afro-Caribbean Religions—at UMass Boston during the abbreviated winter semester. Professor Waters was very knowledgeable, and Sabatina was interested to hear what Jassim discovered.

"The most important thing I learned is why the *Rastafarians* rejected Roman Catholicism, which is what Azi wanted me to focus on. I discovered that Jamaicans were looking for a way to improve their lives because they didn't find Catholicism helpful. They created their own spirituality. In their eyes, the Catholic Church is designed to keep the people poor.

"The poverty-stricken Jamaicans wanted to improve their economical and social environments and viewed the church as a deterrent to the necessary change because the missionaries focused more on receiving rewards in the afterlife. There was no mention of the religion providing any way for them to improve their lives on earth."

Sabatina shook her head understandingly.

"The *Rastafarians* decided to read the Bible and interpret it for themselves. The movement didn't see the need for priests to serve as middlemen for God. They believed that people should have a personal relationship with the Lord, which they call 'I and I.' To them, priests are considered representatives of Babylon, which are the evil forces trying to oppress people. Not to be confused with the ancient Near Eastern capital city, which was overtaken by Macedonian leader Alexander the Great in 331 BC. I know you just saw the movie about the great conqueror, and I don't want you to be confused."

"Thanks, 'Genius!' I was confused but not because of the movie," she remarked.

"*Rastafari*, all have a continuous connection with God. They believe that people should read the Bible for themselves and develop their own understandings. Reasoning is very important in the process, and *Rastafarians* reason with one another as they discuss the scriptures. They join together and discuss what they believe to be true and have gatherings called *Nyabinghi I-ssembly* in which the object is for all in attendance to reason with one another, with the goal of arriving at a universal truth. Their main goal is to reach *Zion* by interpreting the Bible and living their lives according to reason."

"What is Zion?"

"To *Rastafarians*, Zion is the Utopia. I am still a little confused as to whether Zion is a state of mind or actually the continent of Ethiopia. The *Rastafari* call Africa, *Ethiopia* because the slave owners created the word *Africa* and *Ethiopia* was the actual name for the continent used for centuries."

"Wow! That's interesting."

"That's why Azi wanted me to learn about the *Rastafarians*. He believed the movement was designed to help improve the lives of people, unlike the Catholic Church, which he felt promoted poverty.

"The only aspect of the movement that I have trouble agreeing with is the claim by the *Rastafarians* that God is actually the former Ethiopian Emperor *Haile Selassie*, who was crowned in 1930. The notion that *Selassie* is God came from the fact that Marcus Garvey said that a great king would rise up in Africa and lead the people to greatness, but he was falsely quoted as saying, 'The Messiah would return to earth in the person of an African King.' Once *Selassie* was crowned, the *Rastas* believed that he was God. The word *Rastafari* comes from *Selassie's* name. His family name is *Tafari*, and *Ras* is the *Ethiopian* name for 'prince.'"

"What about their use of marijuana? How is that sanctioned?" she questioned.

"I knew that would come up. Well, they believe that *Ganja* is for spiritual use. They smoke in order to free their minds so they can understand the wicked ways of Babylon. Marijuana is not used as a recreational drug. They feel that Babylon is trying to oppress the movement, and smoking ganja allows them to think clearly and uncover the treachery. They believe it's illegal because Babylon doesn't want them to have the capability to uncover the truth."

The two friends continued to discuss the movement during the night, and she asked a litany of questions, which he was able to answer for the most part.

"There was something else that I've always wanted to ask you. Everyone in your family called you Jassi, but in my *World Religions* course, I learned that the *Qur'an* is against the use of nicknames."

"There are some Muslims who believe that the *Qur'an* teaches them to avoid the use of nicknames, but my grandfather always taught us differently. He believed that the Quranic verses, which speak about nicknames, are referring to negative names that people use against one another. Azi's interpretation of the *Qur'an* allows for affectionate names to be given to family members."

"Thanks for clearing that up."

The new information about *Rastafarianism* inspired Jassim, and he was more driven to fulfill the promise that he made to his grandfather. He really began to enjoy the culture, learning to appreciate the music of *Bob Marley* who helped to spread the movement's message to millions of people.

———◆———

Tragedy struck on January 12, 2010. On the late Tuesday afternoon, a devastating earthquake of biblical proportions struck the impoverished nation of Haiti. Jassim sat in the living room along with Anastasia and Sabatina as they watched the news coverage of the catastrophe. The category seven natural disaster was the worst to hit the western hemisphere, and he was horrifically reminded of the time he spent sitting in Azfal's home watching his homeland be decimated by bombs. The young humanitarian was genuinely concerned and turned to Sabatina.

"We have to find a way to get involved."

When Salvatore arrived home from the hospital, he announced that he generously donated one hundred thousand dollars to the relief effort, which warmed the hearts of his distraught family. The hundreds of thousands of dead and displaced people inspired the friends to join students from Boston College's *L'Association Haitienne*, in the effort to organize donations for the survivors. The organization also arranged for volunteers to fly to the Dominican Republic, in order to help the neighboring country's Red Cross assist refugees who were encamped across the border. Jassim and Sabatina missed the first two weeks of their spring semester and joined the convoy. The disheveled appearance of the people and the large scale suffering that they witnessed filled the duo with empathy, but the gregariousness that existed throughout the makeshift camp near the city of Jimani, Dominican Republic, created a sense of hope.

One of his teammates, on the Eagle's soccer team, was a native of Port-au-Prince who lost family members that lived near the epicenter of the catastrophe. Jean-Baptiste was comforted by the fact that he had the support of his fellow students during the trying time.

"Hey, JB, don't hesitate to call me if you need anything. You're not alone in this." Jassim assured his courageous heavyhearted friend after they returned from the humanitarian expedition.

"Thanks, Jass, it's good to have supportive people to help me through this tragedy."

The powerful earthquake also closely affected the Roman Catholic Church. The archbishop of Port-au-Prince was discovered dead in the rubble at the archdiocese's office. Jassim asked the Boston College campus ministry to organize a candlelight vigil in honor of those who lost their lives and was blown away by the awesome show of support displayed by the BC community. Over thirteen thousand people joined in Alumni Stadium for the inspirational tribute. There was a lot of work to be done by the relief workers, but everyone held out hope that Haiti would recover from the enormous quake.

Chapter 9

T he summer, following freshman year, was a tumultuous time in the Moretti house. Salvatore was working longer hours and taking on more patients, adversely affecting his marriage. Anastasia noticed that he was barely at the house, often sleeping on the couch in his office. The new rigorous schedule began during Sabatina's junior year of high school, but his absence wasn't noticeable until the children were away at school.

In the past, Salvatore always maintained a small number of patients in order to spend more time with the family, and his increased workload worried his wife. On an evening in May, a week before Sabatina and Jassim were scheduled to return home, a suspicious Anastasia was home sitting on the couch awaiting her husband's late arrival. It was the fourth consecutive night that she had to dine alone.

She found herself snooping around in his home office and discovered a note hidden in one of his medical journals. On the envelope was written: "To my snuggy bear! Love, Amber." It was from one of the busty nurses who worked at Massachusetts General Hospital. Anastasia began to read:

> "Dear Salvatore,
>   The trip to Las Vegas was wonderful. I loved relaxing in the cabana at the Caesar's Palace pool. And I can still feel your strong hands."

The betrayed wife was angry and heartbroken. She couldn't read any further. Anastasia fell to her knees, sobbing uncontrollably with numerous questions running through her head. She locked the door of a guest room and cried herself to sleep.

Salvatore arrived at the house just after four in the morning and slept on the couch. He planned to tell Anastasia that he was extremely tired and fell asleep as he lay down to watch television. He expected she would have questioned him if he entered their bedroom at such a late hour. By the time he woke up the next morning, his enraged wife had already left the house not wanting to see him.

She was further infuriated because she always dreamed of going to Las Vegas and had hoped that Salvatore would bring her along on the trip. When he left without her, she was crushed, especially since the trip was during Valentine's weekend. Salvatore returned late on the Sunday night and found her fast asleep. He gave his best effort to make up for missing Valentine's Day, but it just wasn't the same for his disappointed wife. The excuse he used was the fact that he would be too busy with all the lectures and they would hardly be together.

Anastasia returned home once it was certain that the philandering doctor had left for at work, and she searched online for information about the "medical conference." To her surprise, there was no information about a February conference scheduled for Las Vegas. The only way for her to uncover the truth was to call the Venetian Hotel information desk, and she discovered that no conference was held there during the time of Salvatore's trip. She was furious and couldn't believe her "loving husband" traveled with another woman to Sin City during Valentine's weekend.

In a fit of rage, she grabbed the expensive bottle of Johnnie Walker Blue Label King George V from her spouse's home-office shelf and threw it out the window. The bottle smashed onto the asphalt walkway leading to the back entrance. The broken glass scattered everywhere, and she had no intentions of cleaning it up. Throwing the five-hundred-dollar bottle out of the window was a big relief; it was purchased for him and Jassim to enjoy after the young man's graduation from Boston College. The thought of destroying all his valued possessions crossed her mind, but she decided that revenge would be a more fitting punishment. It still took all her strength to keep from breaking everything else.

When she gained her composure, her thought process shifted to figuring out the best way of exacting her revenge. For the rest of the week, she kept up the façade that nothing was bothering her. She pretended to have headaches to avoid the cheater as much as she could. He was clueless to the fact that she had discovered he was a philanderer since his attention was too focused on his scorching love affair. He didn't even notice the missing bottle of whiskey.

Jassim and Sabatina returned from school on the following Monday morning, and they could immediately tell that something was wrong.

"Hey, Mom, what's going on? Something seems to be bothering you."

"Nothing's wrong, honey. I just missed you guys so much."

Sabatina dropped the subject for another day since she was only staying home for a short time before traveling to Maine on Friday for a weekend visit to her old camp. The campers were not scheduled to arrive until the beginning of July, but she wanted to meet with the coordinator in hopes of becoming a counselor.

On Saturday morning, after Salvatore left for the hospital, his scorned wife set her plot for revenge in motion. She put on a Santa baby garter skirt, sans panties, with a matching red bra; all recently purchased at Victoria's Secret. She stepped into a pair of red five-inch stiletto heels and checked herself out in the floor-length mirror. The outfit was her own creation, and she looked devilishly stunning.

Anastasia entered Jassim's room without waking him. "Jassi," she called out in a sensual whisper. On the third call, he woke from a deep slumber but was unsure what he was witnessing.

Anastasia turned around and bent over grabbing her ankles. "Santa sent me to give you your Christmas gift a little early. Have you been naughty? Do you like what you see?" she teased.

Her naked bottom was completely exposed to the unsuspecting and confused young man who couldn't comprehend why she was acting so whorish.

"What are you doing?" he asked, mystified.

Anastasia walked over to the side of his bed and sat beside him. She leaned in and began to softly kiss his neck while caressing his hair. Jassim tried to pull away, but she seductively pulled him in closer, softly kissing him on the lips.

As amazingly sexy and beautiful as she was, he knew he couldn't allow himself to give in to the temptation. Jassim managed to overpower her and jumped to the floor on the opposite side of the bed.

"Why are you doing this?" he asked in a stunned bewilderment.

She tried to convince him that it was what they both desired, but he didn't want to further complicate his life by sleeping with her. He was already having enough trouble resisting the advances of her equally arousing daughter. "The hottest mom on the block," was the object of most men's fantasies, but he knew that some lines were never meant to be crossed. Resisting his strong manly urges wasn't easy, but he did his best to diffuse the situation and jumped to the other side of the room.

The seductress walked slowly over to him, and he continued to back away.

"Why are you acting like this? This isn't like you. What's going on?" He was still trying his best to ward her off.

"Stop!" he yelled.

Reality finally set in. After realizing how foolish she was acting, Anastasia collapsed to the ground and broke down into tears. Jassim embraced and comforted her as best as he could. He ran to her bedroom and grabbed her bathrobe.

"Here, put this on. Why don't we go down to the living room and talk about whatever it is that is bothering you?"

"I'm so sorry. Thanks for not totally freaking out," she said, still with her head in her hands.

They sat on the couch, and he listened attentively to his humiliated guardian's explanation. "It all started back in February. Sal went to his conference in Vegas and didn't invite me to go with him. I was upset because I wanted to spend a romantic Valentine's weekend with him because our marriage was slowly falling apart and I thought the trip could help to rekindle the fire that we once had. Actually, the problem started once you kids left for school. I didn't really notice anything before because you and Tina were always around to help fill the void. But once I was alone, I felt that me and Sal were different people. He was almost never home."

Jassim was stunned. "I had no idea you and Sal were having problems."

"I barely saw him during the week, so the trip would have been perfect. When he returned from Vegas, I was mad as hell. He must have sensed it because he began to spend even less time at home. About a week ago, after staying late at the hospital for the fourth consecutive night, I began to snoop around in his office. To be honest, I didn't even know what I was looking for, but I was completely lost and felt I had to do something. I found this envelope hidden inside one of his journals. It contained a letter from a nurse that works with him." She grabbed the envelope from under the couch cushion and handed it to Jassim. He held it without opening it.

She continued and wiped away tears from her cheeks. "I couldn't read it. I only made it through the first few words. Do you believe he took some slutty nurse to Vegas with him on Valentine's Day?"

The aspiring priest was shocked to learn of Salvatore's infidelity, and he shook his head disapprovingly.

"I searched the Internet and discovered there was no convention. He made the whole thing up. I didn't know what to do. I know people cheat, but I didn't think it would happen to me, not after all these years. But looking back on things, I should have known he wasn't trustworthy. I always catch his eyes wandering whenever we go anywhere. I am such a fool. I don't know why I thought he loved me, and I guess in my fractured state of mind I thought the best way to get back at him was to start an affair with you. I guess I hoped that one day he would walk in on us and experience the heartache that I am dealing with. I was wrong for involving you, and I deeply apologize. I hope you can forgive me."

The two of them sat in silence for a moment, but he finally gathered his thoughts.

"I don't think you should assume that he doesn't love you. People always make mistakes, especially ones who have a good deal of wealth. I think that you should sit down and have a talk with Sal. You don't have to stay married but at least listen to what he has to say. Maybe you can still salvage the marriage. It is important to remember that forgiveness is a vital part of relationships. You took vows once you married him, and you said for better or worse, and right now, you are experiencing the worst of the worse. Maybe it would be best if you speak with Father Mike. I think he can probably give the two of you some helpful counseling. I know for a fact that he has helped other couples work through difficult situations. Don't throw away your marriage because of a mistake. If there is still a deep love existing between the two of you, the marriage can be salvaged. You have to remember that he is and will always be a man. When he looks at other women, it's just a natural reaction that we men have—we can't help it. It takes total concentration for any man to avoid looking at a beautiful woman.

"My grandfather explained it to me like this. Let's say that you go to the best bakery in town and the owner is there. He offers you a deal. You can eat dessert for free at his bakery, but the catch is that you can only eat the desserts from his menu. You are forbidden from eating any other dessert. You can't eat homemade desserts either. You are allowed to take home all the desserts you want from his establishment, and your supply is unlimited. You decide that it is a good offer, and you agree to his conditions. The first thing you do is stock up on desserts. You buy a freezer, put it in the basement, and keep it full. Every time you go on a trip, you bring your desserts with you to the hotel. You know that you have a great deal and you'll never break the agreement. To you, there is no dessert in the world worth breaking it. That doesn't mean that you won't look at other desserts or that you won't desire other desserts. Men are the same way. We have an agreement with a woman that we can have sex with her and only her. We still have the natural desire to look at other woman, even though

146

we know we won't have sex with them. Sometimes, even the best of us makes a mistake and eats the foreign dessert."

Anastasia understood his unflattering point. "I get what you're saying, and I have a lot to think about. Again, I'm sorry for acting inappropriate. I haven't been myself since discovering the love letter."

Jassim left her with a verse from the Bible. "It says in Matthew 6 verses 14 and 15, 'If you forgive others their transgression, your Heavenly Father will forgive you. But if you do not forgive others, neither will your Father forgive your transgressions.' Try to find it in your heart to forgive Sal. He's a great guy."

They agreed to never tell anyone about her moment of weakness.

"Thanks, Jassi, this conversation has helped me a great deal."

<hr />

Salvatore returned home in the evening and was startled while taking out the trash. He noticed his prized bottle of Johnnie Walker was smashed to pieces, and the sight of the broken glass angered him.

"Hey, Jazz-man, do you know anything about the broken bottle out there?"

"Yeah, Ana broke it."

Salvatore knew instantly that his wife must have discovered his extramarital affair.

"I take it you know everything," he said sheepishly, and the young man nodded. "I guess I deserve what is coming. I owe you an apology as well. I was really looking forward to sharing that bottle with you. Hopefully, I can make things better, and we can get another one," he dejectedly said.

The two of them spoke about the incident, and surprisingly, Salvatore was completely open. He listened to Jassim's suggestions. He was inspired by the future priest's insight and loved the inspirational verse that was given to him before he left.

"Sal, remember that God is forgiving. Psalm 32:1: 'Happy the sinner whose fault is removed, whose sin is forgiven. Happy those to whom the Lord imputes no guilt, in whose spirit is no deceit.'"

The couple had a long discussion, and the contrite husband admitted his transgressions. He agreed to go to marriage counseling in hopes of saving their marriage. Anastasia wasn't sure if she wanted to stay with him, but she didn't want to make a rash decision without giving counseling a chance. Jassim was called down from his room, and he was thanked for the words of wisdom. Salvatore felt that he not only cheated on his wife but also on the entire family. He seemed truly remorseful and swore to immediately end the affair. He called Amber and delivered the news to her. He also apologized for leading her on since she was under the impression that he was going to leave his wife for her. When Sabatina returned home on Sunday evening, the entire family sat down to discuss the issue, and she was absolutely heartbroken to hear that her father was disloyal.

"I have to say, I am completely disappointed by your actions, Dad. It's going to take a good amount of time for our relationship to be repaired. I hope we can learn to trust you again."

"I totally understand, Tina. I will do everything in my power to keep our family together."

Salvatore's self-improvement occurred moderately, and he eventually returned to being the uxorious husband that Anastasia had always known. Their marriage was not completely mended, but signs were pointing to things getting back to how they were "supposed to be." Sabatina ultimately found it in her heart to forgive her father, and he was happy to have his little girl back. The remorseful Salvatore became a better father than he was previously and, more importantly, a better man. He constantly canceled hospital commitments in order to attend her concerts and Jassim's games, making the family his top priority.

Sabatina continued her love of singing and joined "Against the Current," a Boston College Christian *a cappella* group. Anastasia developed a deep admiration toward Jassim. She was grateful for the maturity that he displayed in handling the awkward incident.

The Eagle's star forward was excited to begin his second season at the Heights. He was named cocaptain along with the team's goalie, Amari. He had always played in a 4-4-2 formation as one of the strikers, but Coach Johnson wanted to give him more scoring opportunities, so he made the switch to a 3-6-1 formation.

In the new, more aggressive attacking formation, Jassim would be the only forward with six midfielders to get him the ball. The experiment worked perfectly, and teams were unable to defend Boston College's unstoppable offense. He led the team to a victorious College Cup, completing the university's first undefeated season in men's soccer. It was also the soccer team's first ever national championship. "The great goal scorer" was named most valuable player for the tournament. He was also voted player of the year, topping off the perfect season. The team's cocaptain was also recognized for his great play and was named to the all-American team along with Jassim. The Moretti's invited the players over to the house for dinner, and the striker gave a speech.

"I would like to thank all of you guys, because without your support, I wouldn't have received so many accolades from the writers. I want to give a special thanks to Amari. You were the best goalie in the nation, and we wouldn't have won the national title without your many saves."

The guys cheered for their all-American goalie.

"I would like to thank the three backs and the defensive midfielders for their lackluster play. If not for their incompetence, I wouldn't have had the opportunity to make so many great saves," Amari said jokingly, causing the room to erupt in laughter.

———

The spring of 2011 was a momentous time in the Middle East. American President Barack Obama helped Iraq transition into a sovereign nation, and plans were initiated to remove all foreign troops from the country by the beginning of the summer. The United States would shift the concentration of its military operations to Afghanistan. The new Iraqi government created its own Constitution, which granted citizens freedom of religion. The removal of U.S. troops surprisingly happened smoothly without incident. The religious freedoms afforded to the people were not really implemented, and the Catholic Church was hoping to establish a strong foundation in the country, but the government leaders were wary of Catholics gaining power in Iraq.

Christians continued to be persecuted throughout the country, and most of the churches were vandalized. Many of Iraq's Catholics hid their faith. During the same period, tensions between Israelis and Palestinians were at an all-time high, and suicide bombings were occurring more frequently in Jerusalem. Rockets continued to fly into the West Bank and the Gaza Strip in retaliation for the attacks. Peace in the region didn't seem probable, and Jassim kept a close eye on all the events that were transpiring. He was excited that Iraq was once again a free nation and hoped that the new regime would be able to improve the lives its people.

Mario established a reputation for being the best barber in Victor's shop. He was saving up his money in hopes of one day opening up his own place, and his uncle was proud of his nephew. Victor encouraged him to grow the family business, as long as Mario's shop wasn't too close. Victor didn't want to lose any of his loyal paying customers, but there was nothing to worry about since the new shop would be in the South End.

Jassim went to Centre Street to visit the barbershop because he was in desperate need of a haircut and wanted to talk to his friend about a problem. Sabatina was able to get a single dorm room, so whenever he found himself alone with her, he always noticed that she was wearing fewer clothes than the previous time, especially if he notified her in advance that he would be going over. He was devoted to becoming a priest, but as a man, he had natural urges that he was finding increasingly difficult to suppress.

"I've been doing an excellent job of resisting Sabatina's tempting sexual advances, but she is becoming more and more aggressive. You have to help me figure out a way to avoid having another conversation with her about us remaining only friends. I'm literally afraid of going to her room."

"I think you should just do your best to avoid the subject and leave things as they are. I don't think she can handle another rejection. Talking about her unrelenting flirtatiousness will only make her upset. She will feel unwanted."

"I don't think you understand how bad it's gotten. She always manages to bend over in front of me, exposing her voluptuous breasts because she never wears a bra under her loose shirts. Usually whenever I find myself being tempted, I will automatically come up with an excuse and leave. I really want to ask her to stop, but I'm not sure if that is the best way to handle this situation. I'm more frustrated than a motorist, stuck in traffic, behind an accident, in the HOV lane, on I-93, during rush hour."

"Damn! That's some serious frustration," Uncle Victor, who was listening to the conversation, chimed in. "Why don't you stop being gay and just bang the broad?" he continued.

Sabatina often visited the shop with Jassim, and he thought she was "The hottest chick that ever walked in here."

"I can't understand how you can turn down a fine thang like that," added Paco.

A regular customer was also in agreement with the terse assessments, but Jassim agreed with Mario's advice and decided to just continue to do his best to ignore her advances.

With only two years remaining at BC, Jassim realized that he was going to have the difficult task of explaining to the world why he wanted to choose the seminary over the fame and fortune of playing professional soccer. The media pestering him with a barrage of annoying questions was not something he looked forward to. The last thing he wanted was to sit through another exhausting press conference. The striker knew that he could compete with the world's best players and didn't have a desire to prove it to himself. His main focus was to carry out the promise that he made to Azfal. Anything else was meaningless to him, and he wanted to avoid any major distractions. During the summer before the junior season, the team captain had to figure out a way to get his mind off the over-whelming decision.

Jassim had control over his inheritance since the day he turned eighteen, during the fall semester of his sophomore year. Other than the purchase of gifts for everyone that he loved, he didn't really spend any of the money. With Mario working full time and Sabatina in Maine working as a camp counselor, the soccer star planned a return visit to Italy. He wanted to see his godparents and also meet with Cardinal Rose who was the former head of the Boston Archdiocese. Most importantly, he needed to get away in order to clear his mind of the looming decision.

The time in Italy with his godparents was enjoyable, and they were elated to see him.

"Thank you for introducing me to Cardinal Rose, De Luca. He gave me some sound advice and has agreed to write me a letter of recommendation."

Jassim's future as a priest was pretty mush solidified due to the strong support he received from his mentor and his new friend. Prior to his return, he called Coach Johnson to deliver some horrifying news.

"Hey, Coach, I'm afraid I have some terrible news. I was playing soccer with some of the local kids here in Italy, and I hurt my knee. I had an MRI, and it revealed that I completely tore my ACL and MCL. They performed surgery on me, and I'll most likely be able to walk again, but it looks like my soccer career is pretty much up in the air. I was deeply depressed at first, but I guess the Lord works in mysterious ways. Maybe this injury is a sign that my true calling is to serve the church," he said in a distressed voice.

The coach was speechless but hopeful that his perfect athletic specimen would make a speedy recovery. He didn't say anything initially but eventually gathered himself.

"I hope you make a speedy recovery since your health is what's most important. I also want you to know that you will always be a member of the team, whether or not you return to the playing field." The star player could tell that his coach was devastated even though he attempted to remain poised.

"Coach, I will do all that I can to make a full recovery."

"Okay, Jass, we'll see you when you get back. Have a safe flight."

The Boston College men's soccer team was aware of their leader's ill-fated injury since Coach Johnson spoke with them prior to the season's start. The Eagles were disappointed to see Jassim walk onto the practice field with a knee brace and the help of crutches.

"I want to hang around and be a part of the team, but sitting here watching all the guys running around is too difficult for me. I can't deal with the fact that I won't be able to play. It'd be better if I stayed away, but I will continue to pray for your success," he said before slowly limping away from the artificial turf of Alumni Stadium. He would never play again, to the dismay of the Eagle family and the displeased *AS Roma* owner.

Most predictions of the "end of the world" have pointed to December 21, 2012, as the day of reckoning, with the ancient *Mayans, Nostradamus,* and other prognosticators agreeing on the same date. Levels of fear were escalating as the day grew nearer, and Sabatina was finding it hard to concentrate on her schoolwork. She didn't see the need to work hard for a future that would never come to fruition. After the Thanksgiving break, she returned to school and continued struggling to focus on her studies. While she was trying to prepare for her upcoming finals, the only thing on her mind was the impending "doomsday."

Jassim gained the ability to walk without the help of crutches but still wore the supportive knee brace. One night in mid-December, he was fast asleep when his phone rang. The frustratingly resounding ringer eventually awakened him.

"Hello," he answered in a raspy voice.

It was his distraught friend, crying on the other end, frantic and incoherent.

"Calm down. I'll go over to your room. Just relax."

After quickly getting dressed, he rushed across the campus. He struggled to figure out what was bothering her because he couldn't understand her unrecognizable utterances. A panic-filled half hour elapsed before she was able to finally calm down.

Sabatina revealed that she was worried about the end of the world. "I have been saving myself for 'Mr. Right,' and I don't want to die a virgin."

"Don't worry about that. The prophecies aren't real. The worst that will happen is a Wicked Nor'Eastah."

His horrible imitation of a Boston accent brought a smile to her face. "You're an idiot, but the world is ending. I know it."

He continued to try and convince her otherwise, but nothing worked. She remained adamant that the prophecies were right. "I don't think you understand what I'm saying. I've been saving myself for you, and I want us to have sex tonight."

She stood up and dropped her robe, revealing her perfect body. He wanted to tell her that they couldn't, but he wasn't strong enough. At that instance, Jassim understood how his grandfather felt when he was standing outside of his office, watching Nadje approach. The beautiful auburn-haired Italian caused his palms to sweat, and he did his best to keep his cool, but he was as nervous as Azfal. In a moment of weakness, he gave in to her advances, and they shared an unforgettable night of passion.

Sabatina was the first to wake up the next morning, and she just lay in bed holding her lover in her caressing arms. When he finally woke up, Jassim wasn't sure what to say and remained silent while she expressed her undying love for him.

"I am happy that we had the opportunity to share at least one great night together, and I look forward to the next couple weeks. Even though the world is ending soon, I'm glad we get to spend the rest of our time on earth as a couple."

Jassim wanted time to think everything over, and his paramour didn't argue when he left because she was still glowing from the previous night. Sabatina didn't want to force their relationship. She wasn't bothered that he avoided her for the next few days.

On December 21, 2012, Anastasia asked the children to spend the night at the house. The family wanted to be together in case the world indeed ended, but the night passed without incident; there was no "Apocalypse." It was time for the lovers to have the talk he was cowardly avoiding. Jassim honestly hoped the world had in fact ended in order to avoid the difficult conversation.

Sabatina was excited, in anticipation of finally hearing Jassim express his undying love for her. They agreed to meet on campus and sat above the 126 steps of the Higgins Stairs.

"Why do they call these the million-dollar stairs?" she asked.

"Because students created a myth that the stairs are internally heated to melt the snow, which they believed cost a million bucks."

"I always wondered why. I thought it was the prize money given to all champion stair racers! I was going to give you a rematch of our race on the *Scalinata*."

"You're not faster than me," he said while laughing. "You only won because you cheated."

"You might be faster than me on the ground, but on the steps, I become a different person. I was built for this sport."

"We can race right now if you want."

"No, I'm officially retired."

The conversation became more serious, and Jassim spoke from the heart, "You have to understand that it's difficult to turn down fortune and fame in order to follow my true destiny, but I really have a strong calling from the Lord to serve. It is not a 'choice.' It's complicated for others to comprehend how powerful God's call is, unless they have a firsthand experience. I'm not perfect, and as much as I'm trying to ignore all the distractions in my life, I can fall victim to temptation like anyone else. It wasn't easy for me to turn down multimillion dollar contracts and except the scholarship, especially since I have always been a huge fan of *Roma*, but that decision pales in comparison. The biggest temptation and the one with the only chance of preventing me from fulfilling my duty to God is and has always been you."

The comment warmed her heart and brought a big smile to her face.

"I am so attracted to you. In my eyes, you are the most beautiful woman in the world, and I have to fight with myself every second that I am around you to prevent from tearing your clothes off. You need to understand that I'm not rejecting you. I'm not choosing the church over you. I'm simply following the path that the Lord has chosen for me. We, as humans, have moments of weakness, and I am no different. Trust me, everyone has them, and mine came the other night when I gave in to your temptation, but we can't continue to pursue a relationship. I'm going to become a priest, and you have to allow me to do that. We can never tell anyone about what happened between us, not even Mario. You have to swear to me that you will never reveal what we did. I will always remember the night we shared, but it has to remain a memory. In the book of Isaiah chapter 1:18, he writes: 'Come now, let us set things right, says the Lord: Though your sins be like scarlet, they may become white as snow; though they be crimson red, they may become white as wool.'"

Sabatina understood where he was coming from. She never knew how strong his devotion to the church was until that day. She previously assumed that he was just using the priesthood as an excuse because she felt he was afraid to ruin their friendship. For the first time, she truly agreed to stop pursuing him. Although she was hurt, she promised to never tell anyone about their shared intimacy.

———◈———

The two friends enjoyed the winter break without any of her usual advances. Sabatina kept her word. She felt like she had a new lease on life, and at the start of the spring semester, she was open to meeting someone new for the first time. As she walked around campus, the beautiful Italian found herself noticing the guys; her interest in other men was at an all-time high. A week into the semester, she was studying in the O'Neill Library when her attention was focused on a work-study student who was reshelving books. Her eyes followed his every move, and her interest in him increased throughout the day.

Her interest was obvious, and he walked over. "Do you need any assistance?"

"No, just looking."

He introduced himself as Eric and asked if she would go on a date with him. She feigned interest at first but finally agreed.

"Great! Do you want to meet up tonight so we can get to know each other better? Have you ever tried Uncle Lu's?"

"That's my favorite place to eat. I have my own table there." She embarrassedly revealed to his amusement.

Eric was a senior journalism major, and they began dating exclusively soon after. Sabatina wasn't sure how Jassim would react to the news of her new boyfriend, so she avoided him for a week before introducing them.

To her delight, Jassim was happy for her, knowing that even though he had feelings for her, they could never be together. Her two favorite guys became great friends, and the threesome hung out frequently. Eric helped to form "the second triumvirate" in Mario's absence.

Eric was originally from Connecticut and usually traveled to his hometown for haircuts until before being introduced to Victor's shop. The new friends made the trip to Jamaica Plain so he could get a "quality" haircut, and Mario was happy to see Sabatina moving on.

"Well, Eric, it was nice to meet you. You seem like a great guy, although I don't like the fact that I am being replaced. Obviously, I'm not a big fan of the second triumvirate. I will take back what is mine, Antony!" the barber said facetiously.

They all laughed, and Eric became a welcome addition to the group. The semester seemed to fly by, and the friends prepared for the upcoming graduation.

Chapter 10

Graduation was the longest day of their collective lives. The metal benches of Alumni Stadium were scorching to the touch, from the hot afternoon sun. Boston College had a main ceremony for the entire graduating class on the football field, followed by smaller more intimate ceremonies throughout the campus in which all graduates had their names individually announced by their respective schools. Sabatina and Eric, along with Mario and the Moretti's, sat in a tent located in front of the new School of Theology and Ministries.

"This building looks fairly new," Anastasia remarked.

"Yeah, Mom, it was founded in 2008."

The group waited for Jassim's name to be called, and he was the fourth student since his surname was Ansary. He proudly wore Azfal's *AS Roma* scarf over his black gown as he did during his high school graduation. The maroon-and-gold scarf matched perfectly with the Boston College colors. Many people mistakenly assumed it was representative of the Eagle's soccer team.

He felt no shame as he walked across the stage with his stuffed dragon. There were a few comments questioning his manhood, but he was proud to honor his grandfather. Once his name was called and he respectfully received his degree, the group rushed over to the Conte Forum where the liberal arts degrees were being distributed. Sabatina and Eric found their assigned seats and joined the rest of their fellow graduates.

A three-year-old boy was seated in the row in front of Jassim's, and the child was fixated on the powder blue dragon. The accomplished young man decided that Azfal's gift had run its course and would better serve the child. He selflessly handed it over to the lively boy who was delighted to receive the mythical creature. The graduate realized that the memory of his grandfather wasn't dependent on a stuffed animal.

It took an hour and a half for Sabatina's name to be called since the school was the university's largest. Eric, whose last name was Kent, was called a several minutes before his girlfriend. Neither Luciana nor Father De Luca was able to attend the ceremony, but they each sent cards congratulating their godson on his academic achievement, and Jassim made them promise to try their best to attend the celebratory mass once he completed his studies at Saint John's Seminary.

Eric located his parents, and everyone met up for a celebration dinner at an upscale Italian restaurant in Boston's North End.

"Hey, Eric, why does Mario call you Ant?" his father asked.

"It's a nickname that he came up with because me, Jassi, and Tina call ourselves the second triumvirate. Mario was part of the first triumvirate, and I replaced him. He thinks I'm Marcus Antony."

Eric never mentioned anything, but he had always been wary of the bond between Sabatina and Jassim. He mainly felt there was some sexual tension that they weren't dealing with. His entire graduation day was ruined because of the aggravation caused by their overt display of affection toward each other. It was almost as if he were invisible to his girlfriend who focused all her attention on her "best friend." At dinner, it seemed as if they were a couple and Eric was the friend. The longtime chums sat side by side while Sabatina's peeved boyfriend was at the other end of the table seated between his parents.

The future journalist was further irritated when she refused to spend the night at his dorm room. Boston College allowed for all graduates to keep their rooms until two days after the graduation ceremony. Eric planned on permanently moving to Boston but was heading back to Connecticut for a month first. He had plans to enjoy his last two days at the Heights with his lovely girlfriend, but she failed to comply.

"I'm really worn out since it's been a long day. I really think it's better if I go home and you pick me up tomorrow morning. Then we can spend the entire day together."

Sabatina didn't need to return to the campus since Salvatore rented a moving van and gathered her belongings along with Jassim's; they were already back at home. A dejected Eric reluctantly agreed but felt that she was more interested in spending time with her "good friend."

At the Moretti house, the two men of the house sat in the air-conditioned and dimly lit living room, conversing, while they shared the exceptional replacement bottle of Johnnie Walker Blue Label King George V that Salvatore purchased for the special occasion. Jassim wouldn't turn twenty-one until October, but they agreed the occasion called for an exception to the law of the land.

"Wow, this is pretty smooth. This is the best thing I have ever tasted. I thought hard liquor was supposed to be disgusting and harsh. This was definitely well worth the wait. Is the regular Blue Label the same as this one, Sal?"

"Pretty close, Jazz-man, but this is a tad smoother. But honestly, you can't go wrong either way. And don't think that all hard liquor is this smooth. Most of it is really harsh. You're starting at the top of the mountain."

"Tina has to try this." Jassim stood up from the dark brown leather couch.

"Tina!" he yelled from the bottom step.

Sabatina came jostling down the stairs. "What?" she asked, annoyed that she had to get out of bed.

"You have to try this King George V Blue Label," he said after taking another swig.

Salvatore poured a glass for her, and she savored the taste, slowly sipping it. "Oh my God. This is really good. I thought the Black was smooth, but this Blue Label is my new drink!"

Salvatore was well aware that it wasn't his little girl's first drink. "I don't think so, honey. The bottle is about five hundred dollars more than the Black Label. This might be your last time Tina, so enjoy it!"

"I don't know. It might be worth getting a part-time job." They all laughed. "I'm going to get some ice, does anyone else want any?"

Salvatore jumped out of his seat animatedly. "Honey, what are you thinking! You can't put ice in the J-Walk, except for the Red Label, especially not the J-Walk Blue. Johnnie Walker is to be enjoyed neat! The ice waters down the distinct flavor. Ice in Blue Label? You might as well put it in a blender with ice cream and a protein shake."

Sabatina sat back down in the comfy love seat and playfully acted as though her feelings were hurt.

"Careful, Sal. You don't want to upset her. Chapter 25 verse 14 in the book of Sirach says, "No poison worse than that of a serpent, no venom greater than that of a woman," Jassim teased.

"You wouldn't poison your dad. Would you, Tina?"

"What about the green and gold labels?" asked Jassim.

"When you're J-Walking, as I call it, you may select whatever label you desire. I personally don't buy the Green Label anymore. I've had too many bad experiences with it due to its inconsistency. If you get a good batch of the Green, it's definitely worth the extra money, but you might as well purchase a Red if you end up with a bad batch. I've been burned too many times, so for me, it's just not worth the risk. The Black Label is always consistently smooth, though, and good enough for most occasions. On special days, I am fortunate enough to be able to afford the Blue Label," Salvatore said proudly.

"Geeze, I didn't know you took it so serious. I would like to apologize for my inexperience, Grand Scotch Master. I will never attempt to add ice again. I promise."

"You are forgiven. It is with great pride that I offer you the reward of this spirit, and you must exhibit great responsibility, my loyal apprentice."

They enjoyed the remainder of the world's best scotch and continued to exchange good-natured ribbings.

The next day, Eric's mind was a chaotic mixture of negative thoughts. He decided that it was time for him to question Sabatina about the nature of her relationship with Jassim. He called her to see if she was ready, and she wasn't, which was the first of the day's unfortunate incidents. His call woke her from her sleep.

"I was up all night hanging out with Jassi and my dad. I'll just jog over to your dorm and shower there."

He agreed but wasn't pleased that she spent the night with Jassim. The Moretti's home was about a thirty-minute run from the Boston College campus, so it wasn't long before she arrived.

She was out of breath when she made it to the front of his building and called him from her cell phone. Eric met her at the entrance, but he didn't say a word. She could tell that something was wrong but wanted to freshen up before dealing with whatever was troubling him. After forty-five minutes in the bathroom, she finally emerged.

"What's wrong?"

Eric slowly paced back and forth in the small space, trying to gather his thoughts.

"Is anything sexual going on between you and the Jazz-Man?" He was annoyed at the nickname that Salvatore used frequently during the celebratory dinner.

"Are you jealous of his relationship with me or my father?"

"Just answer the question and stop stalling!"

She was startled to hear him ask such a bold question and assumed he never picked up on her true feelings for her close friend. At first, she outright denied any such thing, but he was persistent and continued to pester her with questions until finally she broke down.

"Okay, I'll admit it. I'm still in love with him."

Eric wasn't sure what she meant. "What do you mean *still*?"

"I have been in love with Jassi for years, but he always refuses my advances. He really wants to become a priest."

"Did anything ever happen between the two of you?"

She paused for a second and was about to reveal the truth but remembered that she was sworn to secrecy. "No, he always turned me down."

Eric couldn't bear to listen to anymore since he honestly believed that Sabatina was going to eventually be his bride.

"I can't allow myself to stay with a woman who is in love with another man even if he becomes a priest."

He broke off the relationship, and she was heartbroken. Sabatina knew that she did the right thing by telling him the truth. She really wished that she could stop loving Jassim but knew it was impossible. She was lying to herself the entire semester. The relationship with Eric was a sham. She never stopped longing for her "best friend." The fact that she would be by herself saddened her. Eric was gone, and she knew that Jassim would always choose the priesthood over her.

"I'll never forgive you for this!" Eric yelled before storming out of the room and slamming the door emphatically. He didn't return until he knew she was gone, thus ended the second triumvirate.

Jassim spent the day in the barbershop with Mario, trying to relax since the stress of his final semester had worn him down. It was the first time in a while that he had the free time to visit the shop. Maria Soledad was proud of Mario's best friend and told her son to invite "*El Graduado*" for a family dinner. He gladly accepted since *Marisol* was a tremendous cook. He never left the Aponte home without filling up a Tupperware container with leftovers and enjoyed speaking Spanish in order to improve his fluency. He became a better speaker with every visit.

"*¡Muchas gracias por la amante invitación!*" The guest exclaimed as the family gathered at the lavishly adorned dinner table. He was confused as to why everyone began to laugh.

"Its *amable* not *amante*. You said thank you for the loving invitation, insinuating that my mother is your lover, dumbass," Mario said while chuckling.

Jassim was embarrassed, and his cheeks grew pomegranate red.

"Ju will have to fight me for the honor of my bride, *Yassi*," Mr. Aponte joked.

He was a very successful businessman, and the Aponte house was decorated with expensive furnishings throughout.

"Sorry, Enrique, but I was trying to say gracious invitation."

They all enjoyed a hearty meal, and Jassim thanked his hosts for a lovely evening. Mario gave him a ride back to Newton, and he wondered whether Sabatina was home or out with Eric. As he walked by her slightly ajar bedroom door, he could hear her sobbing; he entered. She was at the foot of her bed, with her angelic face drenched in tears, but she had no desire to discuss whatever was bothering her. He did his best to comfort her, and she ultimately revealed that Eric ended their relationship.

He asked if she wanted to talk about it, but the answer was an emphatic "No!" Realizing that she needed some space, he decided to just walk away.

"You know where to find me if you ever need to talk."

The next day, Sabatina was still in a funk and remained hidden away in her room, refusing to come out. Jassim didn't want to overstep his boundaries, so he respected her wishes, but later on in the evening, he decided that it was time for her to discuss the breakup. After fixing a large bowl of ice cream for them to share, he sat at the foot of her bed.

"I hate to see you like this. You're going to talk to me whether you like it or not. I won't leave until you do," he threatened.

She hesitated at first but decided it was best to deal with her problems rather than keep them bottled up. The ice cream was a pleasant treat while she revealed the facts to him.

"I jogged over to Eric's dorm room expecting that we were going to hang out. He seemed upset, so I asked him what was wrong, and out of nowhere, he asked me if I had any feelings for you." Jassim was immediately aware that he might have been the cause of their breakup. "I denied it at first, but I finally admitted the truth because I knew it would have been wrong to lie. When I told him that I was still in love with you, he was crushed, and I don't think he will ever forgive me for hurting him."

The aspiring priest was truly relieved when he thought that she had moved on. He was upset to hear that they were back to square one and tried to come up with the best way to handle the precarious situation.

"Eric will eventually forgive you. Maybe the two of you can reconcile once he gets over the initial hurt. I really think he cares about you a lot, Tina," he said halfheartedly, but she wasn't buying a word that came out of his mouth.

Sabatina wanted for him to make her feel better. "I never stopped loving you." She leaned in for a kiss.

He couldn't resist, and they made out for a while until he realized he was making a huge mistake and quickly pulled away.

"I can't do this. Nothing has changed. It isn't fair for you to keep complicating my life with your sexual advances," he said coldly.

She wasn't surprised at his reaction since she expected him to reject her. The good friends spent the entire night talking about life, with Jassim once again choosing to continue pursuing his fulfillment of the promise and living the modest life of a priest rather than entering into a relationship with Sabatina.

"Sorry, but you know I can't ignore my calling."

"I won't lie to you. It will be very difficult for me to move on, but I promise that I will give it my best effort. The last thing I want to do is cause a strain in our friendship, which is ultimately the most important thing to me."

"Thank you!"

Chapter 11

Sabatina was away for most of the summer, working at her old camp in Maine. She was aggressive in her job search and already secured a position at the corporate office for Bank of America prior to graduation day; the job was to start in September. Becoming an investment banker was her ultimate goal, and she was determined to work her way up the corporate ladder. Jassim divided his time, during the summer, between assisting Father Mike at Trinity Catholic and preparing for his entrance into Saint John's Seminary.

The first step was called the "internal discernment." He was well prepared to enter since he already had numerous years of church service as an altar boy. The idea was for him to look inside of himself in order to be certain that the hand of God touched him. It was his decision to answer the Lord's call; only men who were called could be accepted into the seminary.

Becoming a priest involved memorizing the sacred scriptures, learning how to minister to a parish, and understanding how to serve as a counselor to the laity. Saint John's specifically required their seminarians to have a strong devotion to the Eucharist and for them to express humility. Once Jassim completed his studies, he would earn his MDiv. The course work was not the only requirement for getting his degree. He was also required to perform community service, which was referred to as his pastoral assignments.

"After I graduate from the seminary, I will receive my conferral of the master of divinity degree in orthodox theology. The entrance requirements are pretty simple. I have to provide a recently taken photo of myself, along with a certified copy of my Baptism, a completed health examination, my SAT results, a detailed biographical essay along with a fifteen-dollar fee, and finally my official high school and college transcripts."

"Who knows, maybe I'll decide to sign up with you. I can be one of those priests who breaks all the rules and sleeps with all the women in the parish," Mario joked.

"Yeah, that's a great idea. I can't wait to hear you talk to the parishioners about the Gospel of Mike."

Jassim quickly became a favorite of the seminary priests. Only a small portion of his inheritance was used on essential purchases throughout his stay in America. In a show of his true commitment to becoming a priest, the seminarian arranged for $250,000 to be donated to Saint John's. He believed that he didn't need the money. So he didn't want it to become a distraction that could possibly deter him from carrying out the promise that he made to his grandfather.

The Morettis were wealthy and didn't need any of the money, and Luciana was also in no need of assistance. Mario was working hard to purchase his own shop, and he looked forward to the satisfaction of completing his ultimate goal without any monetary assistance. The inheritance money didn't really serve any purpose to him personally, so the decision was simple.

All members of the bishopric were blown away by his magnanimous donation. The bishop of the Archdiocese of Boston held a special mass in celebration of the thoughtful young man's gift to the church. His devotion to serving God and the community was undeniable, and his speech at a banquet in his honor ended with a quote from the book of Proverbs 19:17: "He who has compassion on the poor lends to the Lord, and He will repay him for his good deed."

The young determined seminarian devoted all his time to his studies and community service obligations. He was at the top of the class along with another standout from New Jersey who studied religion as an undergraduate at Seton Hall University in South

Orange—Gianni Malandra. He was baby-faced and stood five feet nine inches tall with an average build, and his devotion was also pure. Jassim thought his new neighbor resembled a Roman emperor with his curly black hair.

"You're not going to try and overthrow the pope and take control of the church, are you, *Caracalla*?" Jassim teased.

"I don't know. You better keep an eye on me!" Gianni joked.

The seminarians were placed in single rooms in order to allow them to spend time in seclusion for prayer and reflection. Gianni wanted to become a priest as far back as he could remember. His family migrated to America when he was three years old from their hometown of Florence, Italy. He grew up in Livingston, New Jersey. In the old country, they were extremely poor, but his father Tomaso always had a true devotion to the Catholic Church, and it was a priest from their local parish who arranged for the patriarch to find a job in America.

Tomaso was forever grateful to Father *Portella*, and it was a goal for his only child to become a priest in order for the family to pay back the church. He groomed his son for the priesthood and was proud when the boy displayed a deep loyalty to the church. It was no secret that his father wanted him to become a priest, but it wasn't until Gianni felt God calling him that the boy decided to make the lifelong commitment.

The two notable seminarians enjoyed discussing theology, and the consensus among the observant faculty was that both students were destined for greatness within the church. They helped one another memorize the scriptures and used their free time to get involved in the community. Their favorite place in the city was Chandler Pond, which was located a few blocks away from the seminary. The calm water and quacking mallards made for the perfect setting. They often sat on the grass and meditated, usually deep in religious thought. Most of the other seminarians preferred walking to Gallagher Memorial Park, which was in the opposite direction, but the two standouts loved the pond.

It was also a routine for them to discuss their lessons while jogging around the Chestnut Hill Reservoir during the customary morning run. Jassim visited the Boston College campus frequently since it was fairly close to Saint John's, and he remained active in assisting the campus ministry. His bread-loving friend introduced Gianni to Uncle Lu's and the Florentine loved their classic Italian bread but could never bring himself to admit that it was tastier than his mother's home baked bread. On most Sundays, the Morettis drove to the seminary grounds and joined the future priests at the weekly mass in the chapel. They often treated the two devout friends to a breakfast after the service.

Mario didn't get to see much of his good friend, but Jassim and Gianni traveled to Victor's for a cut about once a month in order to keep in touch. Gianni was pleased with the barber's work.

"Thank God you're friends with Jassi. I usually have difficulty finding someone who has the ability to cut my curls properly. Great job, Mario!"

"Just make sure you put in a couple good words for me with the man upstairs."

"Yeah, and don't forget to put a couple extra dollars in his pocket. The cuts aren't complimentary," Jassim added and the young men laughed.

The New Jerseyan was very grateful to meet Jassim. He missed his parents and was beginning to feel as if he was an extended member of the Moretti family. Salvatore was especially fond of Gianni since the Italian priest in waiting was a fellow "striding man."

"It was nice to meet you, G-man. Any friend of Johnnie's is a friend of mine!"

Jassim was careful not to reveal the feelings that existed between him and Sabatina. Although he trusted his new friend a great deal, he wanted his experience at the seminary to be pure and scandal free and couldn't risk the information slipping out in a moment of weakness.

In the year 2013, the United States of America observed a new federal holiday during the month of September. The eleventh marked the first celebration of Heroes Day and was also the grand opening of the Freedom Tower in New York City, which took seven years to be completed.

"The skyscraper stands 1,776 feet in honor of the American Declaration of Independence from King George III of Great Britain. The building is topped with an antenna encased in a spire that measures over four hundred feet and stands in a compound that also includes the Reflecting Absence Memorial in honor of the 2,986 citizens who died in the tragedy," the news anchor informed.

Jassim marveled at the site of America's new beacon of freedom while he watched coverage along with Gianni and their fellow seminarians. It was a very emotional unveiling for the native Iraqi because the attack on New York City's Twin Towers led to the invasion of his homeland—ultimately the death of his family members. To him, Iraq suffered a great deal because of the terrorist attack, and the building marked a new beginning for both Americans and Iraqis.

The room had a somber mood since Dave Stanley, one of the seminarians, lost a family member at Ground Zero.

"Uncle Tim was one of the 343 firefighters who bravely gave their lives during the rescue effort, and it was his death that inspired me to devote my life to serving the Lord."

Witnessing the unveiling created an everlasting bond between the future priests that lasted throughout their time at Saint John's. The first year was very successful for "J&G," and the friends were well on their way to becoming priests.

In June 2014, a majority of the seminarians gathered in front of the television to watch the World Cup held in Rio de Janeiro, Brazil. Jassim rooted vociferously for the host nation because of his connection to the great Brazilian star, *Pele*. Gianni gave his undying support to his home country, but to his dismay, the Italian squad was eliminated before the round of sixteen began. The Brazilian team was attempting to make up for its poor showing at the 2010 Cup held in South Africa.

The championship match was held in Rio de Janeiro's massive *Maracana* Stadium, which seated over a hundred thousand spectators. The Brazilians defeated Germany by a score of three goals to one, giving the country a record sixth World Cup Championship. A grand celebration ensued, and the victory parade was a larger festival than the country's famed: *Carnival*.

Jassim was happy to see his favorite team win the cup, but he wasn't the most gracious winner; unfortunately for Gianni, who caught the brunt of his overjoyed friend's celebratory exclamations.

"I was hoping the Italians would have fared better, but I enjoyed watching the matches nonetheless," Gianni said.

"I agree! And I think it was wonderful that your team scored that one immaculate goal. That's what World Cup Soccer is all about. You show up, score a goal, then watch the Brazilian's *Samba* their way to another cup victory," Jassim taunted.

The passionate former soccer star didn't let a day go by without mentioning how wonderful the Brazilians performed, but his friend didn't mind the good-natured ribbing. A few days after the World Cup was over, Gianni elatedly returned to New Jersey for the summer break since he missed his parents and looked forward to the quality time they would spend together.

<hr />

The seminary was able to put Jassim's gracious donation to good use. Usually, the annual retreat was a fairly modest trip, but for the first time in a while, the rector, Reverend Cessario, was able to schedule a top of the line escape before the end of the first year. The destination was the Poconos in Pennsylvania, where the rector was able to arrange for two lodges, which slept sixteen people each at Hemlock Point Lodge. It was the perfect location for the getaway since there were no homes nearby allowing for the seminarians to be alone with nature.

Gianni fell in love with the beauty of the lakeside lodge and lived close enough to the area for a return trip during the summer with his family. He knew Tomaso would enjoy the calm that was provided, so he explained how great the retreat was.

"You'll love it, Dad. The cabins are right by the lake, and all the necessary equipment is available for rent. We can fish right in the backyard. And the cabin had an old brick oven like the one in the picture of Grandma's old house in Italy."

"It sounds good to me. It will give the three of us an opportunity to catch up and spend some quality time together. I'll reserve a month's stay."

At the lodge, the nature-loving seminarian enjoyed the night's air, usually preferring to sleep in a tent near the water. He loved being away from the frenzy of everyday life and having the full experience of living in the wild.

One evening, just before he was about to turn in, Gianni was surprised to hear a strange noise in the distance. He ignored it at first, but eventually, curiosity got a hold of him, and he decided to investigate. Following the shoreline in the direction of the sound, he got closer and could tell that the cacophony was coming from a party. There was a group of college-aged kids hanging around a campfire in the middle of nowhere. He estimated there wasn't a lodge within fifty acres of their gathering.

It appeared to him that the rambunctious group was a jovial bunch, so he approached without any fear and discovered that most of them were college freshmen. To his amazement, he learned that a few of the teenagers claimed to be Amish, although they were dressed similar to the others; he undoubtedly believed their claim to be a lie.

The young adults were high school buddies who attended different universities and were celebrating their return home. They were consuming a large amount of both alcohol and drugs during the secluded jamboree. Most of the students were coupling up and disappearing into the thick woods. Sex was clearly taking place in the surrounding brush. Enamored couples were leaving on or returning from passionate excursions throughout his time there.

The human sin detector was flabbergasted to learn that the wildest of the group, a young man named Tobias, claimed to be a member of an Amish community. He was taking shots of gin while smoking a joint, and two baby-faced girls anchored him on each side. The threesome took turns French kissing. Every so often, all three would kiss at the same time.

"Why are you claiming to be Amish?" Gianni asked.

The stoned young man blurrily slurred, "Because I am Amish, man!"

Gianni assumed that Tobias was too smashed to create a rational thought, but Sarah, one of the girls who also claimed to be Amish, explained.

"We have a tradition in the Amish community called *Rumspringa*. It is a German word that means 'running around.' When an Amish boy or girl turns sixteen, we are allowed to take a respite from our faith. We are encouraged to leave the community and experience all that the world has to offer. We travel to large cities, experiment with drugs and alcohol, enjoy sex, etcetera. We can basically do whatever we want. We discover all the new technologies that are foreign to the Amish way of life and after experiencing much of what the outside world has to offer. After a short period of total debauchery, we must make a decision. We can either choose to reenter the Amish community and live according to Amish law, or we can remain in the secular world. Most of the youth decide to return to the Amish faith, but those who reject the community are banished forever. The hardest aspect for those who leave the community is the fact that they lose all their family members."

"Are you serious?" Gianni was blown away and didn't know how to react. He understood the concept but felt it was way too outrageous. Exhaustion began to overtake him, and he was ready to get back to his campsite. He thanked Sarah for the information and walked back into the woods on the moonlit night. He would never forget the eye-opening experience.

August 2, 2014, was an exciting day for Jassim. He plopped down in front of the television to watch *AS Roma* play against *AC Milan*. The game was the first to be held in the squad's new Franco Sensi Stadium, named in honor of the team's late president. The move was a welcome one for *Roma's* fans, who were hopeful that the team would return to glory, given that *i Lupi* hadn't won the *Scudetto* since the 2000/2001 season. The yellow-reds had the largest following in *Serie-A*, and the new 55,000-seat stadium was better suited for the team since it was designed after arenas in the English Premier League.

The track, encircling the field, at Olympic Stadium prevented the fans from being close to the action, but in Sensi Stadium, the fans were closer than in any other Italian venue. The followers were also happy to end the use of a shared home field with rival *Lazio*.

La Magica won the inaugural match three goals to one. The joyous revelers celebrated for an entire week. Jassim was happy to see his favorite team moving in the right direction, but he tried not to think about how it would have felt for him to play in that game.

———

The seminarians were excited to begin their second year, and Gianni shared his summer experience with his best friend who also had no idea that the Amish had such an "outrageous" ritual. He honestly didn't fully believe the story until researching *Rumspringa* and discovering it was a real occurrence. His perception of Amish people totally changed from that moment on.

As expected, J&G continued to outperform their fellow seminarians, and the second year went swimmingly. Toward the end of the year, Jassim was chosen to give a speech to an at-risk youth group in Jamaica Plain, just a few blocks away from Victor's shop. He was the top student in his class, and the speech was the first test of his mentoring and counseling abilities. As a priest, these speeches are commonplace, and it was an honor for him to be chosen. The seminarians were typically prepared for the speeches in their third year, and only one lucky second-year pupil was selected. The experience would be invaluable, and he prepared for a week. He was eager to meet the youngsters and looking forward to getting a fresh haircut.

Jassim met the group at Our Lady of Lourdes Church, shaking a few hands and chatting with some of the early arrivals before beginning the speech. He walked back and forth, staring into the eyes of every teen as he spoke.

"First of all, let me introduce myself. My name is Jassim, and I am a seminarian. That means I'm a student at a seminary where I am studying to become a priest. You can probably tell that we are required to dress modestly. We don't really have a dress code, but we must wear clothing that is clean and neat, with our shirts always tucked in. I'm not here to try and tell you to go to church every Sunday or to try and convince you to become priests and nuns. I want to talk about responsibility and choices."

The blank faces staring back at him didn't seem to care what the topic was. They clearly wanted to be somewhere else.

"Every decision you make in life requires a choice, and you are solely responsible for your actions. I often hear people say, 'I did what I had to do,' after committing a crime. I don't really understand what they mean by that statement. I'll see an interview with a ex-con, and he will say, 'I sold drugs 'cause I had to do what I had to do to feed my kids.' That way of thinking seems very illogical to me. What he is saying is that he is helping his family by risking his freedom. How can someone possibly help his family and provide for his children if he is locked up behind bars. Once a man is in jail, his children are left to be raised by a single mother, who is usually overwhelmed, or the children have to raise themselves, which is unfair.

"Personally, I'm afraid of jail, and I hope I never end up there, so I live my life accordingly. Anyone who commits a crime knows there is a possibility that he or she may end up in jail, and to me, it's just not worth it—crime is purely nonsensical. You have to live a lifestyle according to what you want. I know that you may think it is easy for me to sit here and preach to you because I am a seminarian, but I had to make difficult decisions throughout my life. I was a star soccer player. I was the best high school player in America, and after my senior year, I was offered millions of dollars to play professionally in Europe. But I turned down the lucrative offers because I wanted to become a priest. It may seem like that was a hard decision, but it really wasn't. I wanted to become a priest, so it was clear to me what I had to do. There is nothing difficult about it."

The teens were stunned to hear that a person could choose to become a priest over making millions of dollars playing a professional sport.

"Temptation is the reason why people make bad choices. You have to think about what you want and then make the choices that will get you to your goal, doing your best to avoid veering off course. If you aspire to become rich, you have to make decisions that will help you achieve your goal. Selling drugs or committing other crimes doesn't lead to wealth. It only leads to death or jail.

"I haven't heard of too many wealthy, retired ex-drug dealers who are basking in their glory. The aim should be education. You have to study hard and focus in school, and you'll be able to achieve any goal that you set for yourself. The key is to travel on the right path. I read all your bios and saw that most of you have family problems, but you can't allow an absent father or a neglectful mother to take you off your path. You must be the one to end the cycle of poverty and underachievement. Strive for excellence, and you will achieve it."

A twelve-year-old boy stood up and challenged the seminarian. "Na, man. *Smooth Killah* says you gotta get your grind on in these streets to get that 'gwock!'" he boastfully argued.

Jassim was very disappointed in the young man's challenge. "What is your name?"

"Mike Woodruff," he said, proud to represent his quote.

"You see, Mike. That's your problem right there. You are turning to rap music for guidance, which is a big mistake. Don't get me wrong. I don't have any problem with rap music. In fact, I enjoy it. I grew up in Iraq then moved to Italy and lived there for a little over a year before coming to the United States in 2004. My good friend Mario introduced me to rap music, and I enjoyed it quite a bit. My favorite group is the *Cash Money Millionaires*."

The kids were stunned to hear that he actually listened to rap.

"So what you, *lil' wodies*, need to understand is the fact that rap music is a form of entertainment. It isn't a guide to life. The music is simply to be enjoyed, not emulated. Rap is similar to movies. You enjoy the art form, and then you return to reality. You can't use the songs as inspiration. The characters are not real, and crime is not the answer. Hard work is the only way to succeed in life. Education has to be your goal, and there can be no excuses. The only person who can keep you from achieving your goals is yourself. And you can't follow in the example of those who are not successful. If you have someone in your life that hasn't achieved anything, it is probably a good idea not to follow in his or her footsteps. The key is to understand who is giving you advice."

A bold young girl with three ponytails in her hair rebelliously stood up and challenged his creditability. "I don't think you can understand what we're going through."

Jassim turned to her direction. "You may continue, but introduce yourself first."

"Hi, everybody. My name is Jackee, with two *E*'s, and I don't think you can put yourself in our shoes. You didn't grow up in the inner city, and you don't know how hard life is for us."

"One thing that you must truly realize is that you can't judge someone by how they look. As I look around this room, I see teenagers of all races, but everyone is in the same boat because poverty is color blind. You have to understand that there are many people out there who don't want you to succeed, but that doesn't mean you should stop trying. You have to persevere, and you can't rely on someone else to work hard for you. One misconception is that rich people are scared of gangsters. But that is totally false. Rich people aren't afraid of inner city thugs at all. In fact, it is the complete opposite."

He paused to look around the room and could see that most of the teens didn't agree with him.

"It doesn't bother them to see a group of inner city kids misbehaving in public because nothing could make them happier. The very sight brings a sense of warmth to their hearts. They love gang members because as they see it. Every gang member is one less person who can challenge their children for a spot in the best universities. They want you to become the best gangbanger that you can be."

"You mentioned that I haven't been in your shoes. What you don't know is that I grew up in Baghdad, and while I was visiting my grandfather in Rome, my entire family was killed during the bombings of 'Operation Iraqi Freedom.' And if that's not bad enough, when a family friend called after several months of not knowing where my parents were, my grandfather suffered a heart attack which eventually killed him. I think I have suffered through enough hardship in my life to stand here in front of you and speak from experience."

The mention of his struggles seemed to resonate as the kids sat up and began to focus on his message.

"As far as money goes, I don't need it because my goal in life is to become a priest. My grandfather left me almost three hundred thousand dollars when he passed away."

There was a loud murmur in the room.

"Since I am studying to be a priest, I didn't see the need for the money, so I donated it to the church."

"What! That's crazy," screamed out a teen sitting in the back.

"I know it may seem crazy to you guys, but that's the kind of decision I am talking about. You have to stick to your goals and forget about trying to live up to the desires of other people."

Jassim was getting more passionate and decided to switch topics before he lost control of his emotions. "Has anyone heard of the Amish?"

One of the older males raised his hands.

"Yes, introduce yourself."

"My name is Malik. Aren't the Amish the people who live like they did back in the day? You know, with no electricity?"

"Yes, you're right. Recently, I learned something very interesting about the Amish," the seminarian explained the traditions of the Amish to the group, and they were stunned.

"I don't agree with the way the Amish do things, but I like the fact that each individual makes his or her own decision. That's what I want you guys to think about. Make your own decisions and live with the consequences. Don't blame someone else if you decide to make a poor choice. If you want to be successful, choose to do the right things."

The students gave him a rousing round of applause, and Jassim opened the floor to questions, spending the remainder of the time giving the best answers possible. He left the group with a sense of accomplishment and truly believed that he reached through to a few of the students.

The group's mentor, a rehabilitated convict named Zachary Hart, was impressed with the message and thanked the seminarian for his heartfelt words of inspiration. Mr. Hart knew that Jassim was genuinely concerned for the well-being of the teens and believed that the speech seemed to penetrate the defensive walls the children usually put up. Jassim wasn't positive that his words were able to sink in, but he was hopeful, and the monsignor who oversaw the group wrote a review of the seminarian's speech in which he mentioned that the seminarian gave an exceptional performance.

He was elated and returned to Saint John's to immediately watch the replay of the *Serie-A* championship game, which he missed because of the speech. *AS Roma* captured the *Scudetto* to Jassim's delight. His favorite team opened the first season in their new stadium in style. The determined seminarian continued to excel in his studies and once again finished the year at the top of his class.

During his third year, Jassim was in the room studying when Gianni knocked on the door asking for his assistance. The anal seminarian noticed the chaos in one of the storage rooms in the basement and volunteered to straighten it up. The area was filled with random junk that had been discarded there throughout the year. Gianni was deathly afraid of mice, but the thought of coming across one while in the basement never crossed his mind since he hadn't seen one during his time at the seminary. When he began moving some of the larger items, he was startled at the sight of a mouse running from under a broken desk. The "manly man" nearly had a heart attack and ran out of the room as fast as he could. He refused to return by himself.

"I don't want anything to do with the clean-up effort because I am deathly afraid of the dirty rodents, but I'll help since you're such a good friend," Jassim said.

Their first course of action was to buy glue traps from a convenience store, which the two of them strategically placed throughout the room. It was a terrifying ordeal because of the small dark crevices that they were forced to target.

The following day, they returned to see if any of the traps were successful in capturing mice and found that only one of the ten yielded a triumphant result. Neither of them wanted to pick up the victorious trap. They argued back in forth trying to convince the other that it was his responsibility. Suddenly, Jassim heard a racket

coming from the opposite corner of the room. The terrified seminarians didn't want to investigate but knew they didn't have any
other choice. They were shaking as they made their way across the
shadowy room. In the corner, there was an old cast iron slipper tub,
to which Gianni pointed, confirming it was the source of the noise.
As they cautiously peered into the discarded tub, they saw a small
mouse running back and forth. It was stuck and couldn't jump out.
Jassim bravely grabbed the successful trap and quickly threw it into
the tub.

"What did you do that for?" asked a puzzled Gianni as he threw
his arms up in the air.

"I am hoping that the mouse will get hungry and attempt to eat
the food that is on the trap. He'll get caught, and we'll only have to
discard one trap."

Gianni didn't really see the logic. "Why didn't you just throw in
an empty trap and each of us could have thrown one away? You don't
make any sense."

They returned the next day and checked all the remaining traps,
but no other mice were caught.

"Time to see if the mad scientist was right," Gianni said.

"If they're both in the trap, you're throwing it away because you
doubted my brilliance."

Cautiously walking across the room, they peered into the tub
and were amazed to see that the free mouse must have been starving
because he ate the head of the dead one.

"Wow, cannibalism at its finest. I knew it!" Jassim said.

"What are you talking about, you said no such thing."

"I guess his survival tactics kicked in and the mouse did
what it had to do to live. It reminds me of the movie *Alive*, about
the Uruguayan soccer team that found themselves trapped in the
Andes Mountains without any food. The survivors carved out flesh
from the bodies of the dead and ate it. I guess nature is all about
survival."

A few days later, they found the mouse dead on the trap. It got
caught in the glue as it attempted to eat the remaining food after
managing to eat a good portion of the dead mouse's body. Luckily,

the rest of the cleanup went on without any more incidents, but it was a chilling occurrence that neither of them would ever forget.

—————◦◉◦—————

To celebrate the end of their third year as the seminary's top two students, Jassim invited Gianni to join him at the Moretti home for a celebratory dinner. Before eating, the friends hung out in his old room, and it was the first time that Gianni saw the enormous trophy collection.

"Why didn't you ever tell me that you were a soccer star?"

"I don't know. I guess it's a part of my past, and I'm focused on the future."

Jassim didn't want to spend time dreaming about how his life could have turned out if he had decided to play professionally. To his dismay, the young man's soccer career ended up being the topic of discussion for the remainder of the night.

Gianni felt sorry for his unlucky friend. He knew that the knee injury ruined what could have been an amazing professional career.

"I know it's hard to believe, but I don't feel that I missed out on anything. To me, the knee injury wasn't significant since I would never have pursued a professional soccer career. I was called to serve the Lord, and that is my intent."

Gianni was even more blown away by his friend's devotion to God. He was amazed that someone could choose to turn down fame and fortune in order to serve the church. On the ride home, he continued to pester the former star with questions.

"See. This is why I don't tell people about my past," an annoyed Jassim said.

The following morning, the friends decided to walk to Chandler Pond where they could read in the warm sun of the beautiful summer day. They wanted to take advantage of the lovely weather, and as they were sitting in the grass, Gianni noticed two men walking in their direction. They were holding hands, which he considered disgusting since he was a one hundred percent congenital homophobe. He truly believed that all homosexuals were going to hell.

Jassim wasn't accustomed to seeing two men holding hands, but he wasn't bothered by the sight because he believed that people should live and let live. Homosexuality was never a problem for him since he always suspected that his Uncle Saady might have been gay. Although he questioned his uncle's sexuality, it never changed the unconditional love that existed between them.

He couldn't understand why Gianni was being so intolerant. He never understood why people discriminated against those who were different.

"People are free to live their lives as they please. Only God can judge," Jassim said.

"Are you insane? Gays are going to hell, and that is that." He grabbed his Bible and opened it to the book of Leviticus, turning to chapter 20 verse 13: "If a man lies with a male as with a woman, both of them shall be put to death for their abominable deed; they have forfeited their lives."

Jassim knew the passage well and knew he would choose it. "I know the Bible, you don't have to read it to me. You're so predictable."

He wanted to further discuss the issue but knew that the Catholic Church was antigay and didn't want to risk his future by trying to convince others to be more tolerant. Later on that evening, he called Anastasia.

"I think people make the mistake of taking the Bible too literally. Azi always taught me to be open-minded, and as far as homosexuals are concerned, I learned too much about the great ancient civilizations to be homophobic. The Greeks and Romans basically lived in bisexual societies. I also learned from Azi that the Hebrews added the passages that banned homosexuality in order to protect themselves from being raped by the invading armies. The Romans had the custom of raping all the men after sacking a town because they saw the rapes as an act of humiliation. The Jews weren't accustomed to the behavior and wanted it to stop. I truly feel that all those who have a desire to serve God should be allowed to join the church, regardless if they are different in any way, but it isn't a platform that I am willing to support at the risk of affecting my future in the church."

"You have to understand that Gianni was raised differently. Don't let his narrow-minded views affect your friendship."

"Thanks for the talk, Ana. I'll see you on Sunday."

"Okay, bye, Jassi."

<hr />

August 7, 2016, was a tragic day for the Catholic Church. The summer was winding down, and the seminarians were looking forward to their final year at Saint John's. The community was saddened to learn that at the age of eighty-nine, Pope Benedict XVI, who was gravely ill, died of natural causes. It took fifteen days after his death for the conclave to decide on a new bishop of Rome.

Cardinal Anthony Thomas Rose of South Africa was the first African to be elected as the pope. It was assumed that he would chose the regnal name Peter in order to fulfill the prophecy of St. Malachy, who predicted that Pope Benedict XVI would be the second last pope, preceding "Peter the Roman," who was to be the last pontiff before the world came to an end. Those who believed in the prophecies were disappointed when Cardinal Rose chose the name Pope Nelson in honor of his country's hero, Nelson Mandela, who was instrumental in ending *Apartheid*.

The election of the African pope helped to ease tensions between Catholics and Muslims in the Middle East. The monumental selection was brilliant on the part of the cardinals, and the president of Iraq personally sent gifts to the new pontiff. The progressive-minded Iraqi also vowed to end the anti-Catholic sentiment that existed in his country. He even extended an invitation for the pope to visit Baghdad. Pope Nelson was pleased by the good-natured gesture and said he hoped to make a visit in the future.

Jassim was elated to see his country take a positive step toward religious freedom and saw an opportunity to help expand Catholicism in Iraq, inevitably throughout the Middle East.

"Times are changing, my friend," he proudly proclaimed to Gianni while they watched the news.

After centuries of warfare, it seemed that the world was heading toward peace, or at least that was his optimistic view.

"The election of the new pope isn't just a publicity stunt. He might be in charge of the church longer than Pope John Paul II," Gianni pointed out.

The cardinals were making a point to show the world that they intended for his eminence to serve the church for many years to come since he was fairly young, only sixty-seven years old. The Florentine seemed a bit dejected.

"Are you all right?" Jassim asked.

"Yeah, I'm fine. I'm just a little disappointed that he didn't choose the name Peter. It would have been great to see the prophecy come true," Gianni said.

"Are you insane? The prophecy predicted that Peter the Roman would be the last pope before the world ends. I don't want the world to end anytime soon. Why do you believe in St. Malachy's prophecies anyhow?"

"Well, so far, a lot of them have been correct. He first predicted that the pope would come from a castle on the Tiber and Pope Celestine II was born in a castle on the Tiber. He said the 267 pope would represent the 'Glory of the Olives' and Pope Benedict is from the Benedictine order called the Olivetans. I haven't given up yet because St. Malachy never said that there wouldn't be popes who will serve between the 267 pope and the last pontiff. We'll just have to wait and see."

"Yeah, I guess."

Jassim was really focused on becoming the best priest that he could entering his last year at Saint John's, causing him to see less and less of Mario. Sabatina visited the seminary on most Sundays with her parents so they kept in contact, but he was only able to visit the shop whenever he was in desperate need of a haircut. Sometimes, he lasted three months without getting a cut, and unbeknownst to him, Sabatina and Mario usually met once a week to have dinner.

They saw a lot of one another, and a romantic connection was slowly developing. It was on a rainy night that Mario went to her apartment in Boston's Back Bay section for their usual dinner date.

He decided to hang around to wait out the rainstorm, and the sexual tension between them was obvious. At fifteen minutes past two o'clock in the morning, after polishing off a couple bottles of wine, they finally succumbed to temptation. Their flirtatious behavior led to the bedroom, where they found themselves cuddled up under the sheets. Neither of them planned on having sex that evening, but they couldn't resist the urge.

The night of sexual experimentation was followed by a few more intimate encounters, which eventually turned into a serious relationship. They decided to keep their liaison from Jassim since they were positive that he would react negatively.

Mario saved up enough money for a down payment on his own shop, and his parents agreed to cosign the bank loan, which was promptly approved. Sabatina was proud of him and helped with the search for a perfect location, but the new couple continued to avoid telling Jassim about their relationship. When he heard from "El Rey de las Tijeras" that the search for a new shop had begun, he was excited for his old friend.

"Hey, I'll help you with the search. It will be great," Jassim exclaimed.

"Na, that's not necessary. I'd rather look on my own. I don't want to bother anyone."

The rejection was surprising, but he decided to let the matter go. The secret relationship grew more serious, and Sabatina stopped joining her parents on their Sunday visits to the seminary, which was a red flag to the young astute seminarian. He was beginning to think that something was amiss but couldn't put his finger on it. The search for a shop was more difficult than the entrepreneurial barber had anticipated. He had enough money, but the available spaces didn't suit his needs. Jassim became more suspicious of his trusted friends, and they found it more difficult to avoid him. It was obvious that he was close to discovering their torrid love affair.

Chapter 12

The two seminarians were excited to volunteer at the annual track meet between some of Greater Boston's best Catholic grammar schools. Thirty-two teams in all participated in the one-day challenge, consisting of forty different timed events. The meet was traditionally held during the third week of October, on the grounds of Saint John's Seminary in Brighton, Massachusetts. The boys and girls competed separately except for the one mixed-gender relay race, and at the end of the day, the school with the most victories was named champion.

St. Patrick's School in Roxbury earned the reputation as the team to beat because they have the most victories in the competition's history. Entering the year's meet, they were once again considered the favorites.

Jassim was in charge of time keeping for the sixty-yard dash, and Gianni was in control of the shot put. The meet was a great success, and as expected, St. Patrick's fought off all challengers on the way to capturing another first place finish. The students jumped and celebrated in a wild frenzy. The sportsmanship displayed by all the schools was what really made it an enjoyable event.

J&G enjoyed volunteering at the meet during their four years of study at the seminary. The best feeling was watching the children's faces light up after they received the ribbons.

"If I don't move back to Florence and end up staying in the Boston area, I'd like to keep volunteering at this event," Gianni stated.

"Yeah, me too. Maybe I can incorporate stairway racing since I'm a grand champion."

"You're an idiot. Anyway, I thought Tina said she beat you."

"She cheated. That race was never sanctioned. I retained my title."

A few weeks after the successful track meet, the seminarians traveled to South Boston for a conference of Roman Catholic clergy, which was held at the Boston Convention and Exhibition Center. They enjoyed meeting Catholics from all over the world and learned a great deal about what was expected of them once they became priests. Jassim especially loved the back and forth banter involving church policy. He did his best to display his vast knowledge of the Bible, which was clearly greater than the other seminarians in attendance.

Late in the afternoon, after the conference ended, the future priests decided to walk toward Downtown Crossing since it was a lovely autumn day in The Hub. They ended up walking to the Boston Common and stopping at the entrance to take in the scenery. The Common was filled with tourists taking pictures, loitering students, and business people hurrying to their "important" destinations. Jassim picked out a green paint-chipped wooden bench for them to sit down.

The seminarians enjoyed observing the vibrant city folk and discussing the key points from the conference, but Jassim was taken aback when he saw his buddy Mario walking hand in hand with Sabatina. They appeared to be a couple in love.

Sabatina laughed as Mario adoringly whispered into her ear, and the couple picked out a spot in the grass to unwind. Jassim was incensed. He tried hard to control his emotions, but Gianni could tell that something was bothering him.

"What's wrong? All of a sudden, your mood changed for no reason."

His friend just shrugged his shoulders. "Nothing's wrong."

Gianni looked around and finally spotted the couple lying in the grass, enjoying life as if they didn't have a care in the world. He had no idea that Jassim had feelings for Sabatina, so he didn't understand why he looked so flustered.

"It's just that I don't think Mario and Sabatina should be a couple, because if they break up, it will end up ruining the unity of the triumvirate," Jassim fibbed.

Gianni understood and looked on while the angered seminarian approached the unsuspecting lovebirds. Sabatina was the first to spot him, and she quickly alerted Mario. Panic consumed them.

Jassim didn't try to hide his anger as he greeted them. They could clearly see that he was not happy.

"*Et tu, Mario?*" he furiously stated.

His discomforted friend couldn't look at his face. Mario didn't know what to say.

"How long has this been going on?"

"A few weeks. It just happened. We didn't know how to tell you," Mario sheepishly replied.

"Is this the reason you didn't want me to help you find a new shop?"

Mario was confused. He didn't know if he should be angry with his buddy or if he should be ashamed. On the one hand, he was dating his best friend's one true love, but on the other hand, Jassim turned down Sabatina and was studying to become a priest.

"You know what. I think you're the one who is out of line because I didn't do anything wrong. You're the one who isn't being a good friend. You turned her down for the priesthood, and if you're a good friend, you'll be happy for us."

Sabatina didn't have anything to say. She remained silent and could barely look away from the freshly trimmed blades of grass. She knew that Mario was ignorant of the fact that she previously slept with Jassim. There was a sense that she betrayed both of them. It was wrong of her to sleep with the close friends, and she didn't want to be the reason they hated each other. Jassim could hardly look at her, but his anger was more focused on Mario's betrayal.

The barber became increasingly angered and stood up. "If you're not going to admit that you are wrong, we don't need to be friends!"

The two best friends continued to argue loudly, but Jassim didn't want Gianni to discover the truth behind their dispute. "I don't want to see either of you ever again. I should have known the triumvirate was a weak alliance. 'The evil man lies in wait for blood, and plots against your choicest possessions. Avoid a wicked man, for he breeds only evil, lest you incur a lasting stain.' That's from Sirach chapter 11 verses 32 and 33. You should read it, Mario. I know you like when I quote from the Bible, right, buddy!" He then turned and walked away.

Sabatina and Mario knew he didn't mean what he said. Jassim was just speaking out of anger, but they didn't chase after him, deciding it was better to let him calm down on his own.

Mario felt bad. "I said some horrible things as well, and I'll make things better when the time is right. We can't let the friendship end like this, not after all these years."

Jassim collected himself as he walked toward Gianni, not wanting to appear angry.

"What was all that about?"

"I tried to tell them that they were putting our friendship in jeopardy, but they didn't care. I got a little upset because I don't want to lose either one of them, but I guess in the end, it's none of my business."

Later on that evening, after giving the situation much thought, he called Sabatina to apologize for his poor reaction. Jassim realized that the conflict with his friends was irrelevant since it had nothing to do with his ultimate goal. He remembered that his grandfather spoke to him about being careful not to let the temptations of a woman take him off his course. Sabatina and Mario were together, and he gave them his blessing.

"I want to apologize for my harsh words, and I have a better Bible verse than the one I quoted this afternoon. It's from 1 John chapter 1 verse 9: 'If we confess our sins, He is faithful and just to forgive us our sins and to cleanse us from all unrighteousness.'"

Even though he feigned to accept their relationship, Jassim was incensed. Suppressing his feelings took a great deal of mental toughness, but the seminarian was prepared to deal with any situation.

Nothing would get in the way of his desire to carry out the promise that he made to his grandfather. From that day forth, the triumvirate would never be the same.

⸻ ◈ ⸻

Jassim was excited to complete his studies at Saint John's Seminary, but at the same time, he was saddened by the fact that he would be separated from the wonderful people who helped to create so many great memories, especially Gianni, his true friend. He was worried that they would most likely set off on different paths. The Florentine wanted to return to Italy and serve as a priest, hopefully in his hometown, while the Iraqi had aspirations on expanding Catholicism in Baghdad.

The future priests took the opportunity to strengthen their friendship during their final months at the seminary, and they truly enjoyed the short time that remained, but before either of them could be recommended for the priesthood, there were some requirements to be fulfilled. For the official review of his time at the seminary, Jassim had to sit through an informal interview with the institution's head.

The rector and president, Reverend Arthur Cessario, and the vice rector, Christopher Medas, conducted the interrogation. The apprehensive seminarian walked into the austere office and took a seat in front of the desk alongside Rev. Medas. The process commenced with Rev. Cessario commending the top student on an impressive record.

"I can't help but notice that maybe your record is too impressive. You are the only student during my tenure as the head of this seminary who has never been reprimanded for a single infraction. How is it possible for you to avoid breaking at least one rule? No one is perfect. It's impossible for any seminarian not give in to temptation at some point in the four years."

Jassim never had any disciplinary problems in high school or college either and respectfully defended his character. "I understand that it is hard to believe, but it is true, I haven't broken any of the rules. You have to understand that I have a true calling. I have known since the age of eleven that I was destined to serve the Lord. I was placed on this earth to serve his will, and I know that temptation is merely a choice. A person is responsible for making the decision to misbehave, and I have made the decision to serve God. I have been tempted more than any other seminarian. I was offered millions of dollars to play professional soccer, and everyone thought it would be a difficult decision, but I always knew where my heart was. Becoming a priest is worth more to me than any amount of money. I have lost every member of my biological family, and God is the only one that I have left, so I want to be as close to him as possible."

Rev. Cessario was touched by the speech, and so was Rev. Medas.

"It appears to me that the young man is indeed on the righteous path," the vice rector said.

The priests were well aware of Jassim's many achievements during his stay at the seminary and were further impressed with his devotion to God. Rev. Cessario thanked the accomplished seminarian for being a great example to the other students and wished him well. "The light of God resides within your spirit."

Jassim earned their unwavering respect and recommendation to join the priesthood. He thanked both of his superiors and exited the small room. Gianni was being interviewed while his best friend called the Moretti family and Luciana to deliver the great news. His godmother promised to arrange for herself and Father De Luca to attend the ordination ceremony. Jassim also delivered the news to Sabatina and Mario, but he kept the conversation brief.

The triumvirate became more of a twosome since "the great betrayal." Although he didn't keep in close contact with his old buddies, their presence at the mass was important to him. In order to avoid making the situation worse, by finding a new barber, he would wait as long as he could before getting a haircut from Mario. The two "friends" didn't have much of a conversation while he was in the barber's chair, which added to the awkwardness of their strained relationship. The heartbroken seminarian always made up an excuse to leave after the cut.

The class's other top student also had a successful interview, and the friends celebrated the completion of their studies by traveling to New Jersey and having dinner in the Malandra's beautifully adorned dining room. After tasting the homemade bread, he understood why Gianni was hard-pressed to admit that Uncle Lu's bread was better than *Simona's*. Mrs. Malandra prepared a tasty traditional Italian feast, which almost rivaled the culinary mastery of Marisol.

———◦◉◦———

The final step in the completion process was the confession of sins. Each nominee was required to confess all his sins to a priest of his choosing. Jassim entered the confessional and knelt before Father Davis. The young priest arrived at the seminary the previous year, and he thought it would be best to confess to a priest that he had the least connection with, lessoning the awkwardness of the event.

He decided to reveal only one of his major past deceits while in the confessional. Even though he knew that the priest wasn't supposed to divulge any of the details, the cautious seminarian was reluctant to give away all his sins, especially not the *Taqiyya*.

The glib confession began. "Forgive me, Father, for I have sinned. It has been an entire day since my last confession. I am not sure, even though I had good intensions, that the heavenly Father would approve of my actions. I was deceitful to everyone that is important to me. Not only did I lie to my friends and family, but I also lied to the Boston College family, specifically Coach Johnson and the members of the soccer team. I had an important decision to make upon the conclusion of my college career, and I didn't know how to avoid hurting anyone, so I decided to lie. I already knew that I wanted to become a priest and never wavered in my decision. The problem I was having was figuring out how to deal with the disappointment of letting so many people down. I was the most sought-after player in the world while in college, and I didn't want to disappoint my fans along with all the people who wanted to see me play professionally. After my sophomore year, I returned to Italy in order to clear my mind and figure out a way to deal with the impending decision. It was during my time there that I misled everyone. I bought a knee brace and crutches on the Internet and faked a career ending knee injury. I told everyone that I wouldn't be able to play soccer again and continued to keep up the ruse when I returned to America. I pretended to be injured by using the crutches for a few weeks and keeping the brace on for months. I know that no one was hurt by my actions, but I was not truthful. My decision was guided by the book of Sirach chapter 5 verse 10: 'Rely not upon deceitful wealth, for it will be no help on the day of wrath.'"

Father Davis advised him to repent. "You must repeat the Hail Mary thirty-three times, along with thirty-three Our Fathers. The significance of the number is for each year that Savior walked on the earth."

The young priest wanted the misguided seminarian to think of Jesus while he prayed. Jassim remained in the church for an hour, completing his penance. With the confession process finished, he began to prepare for the ordination mass.

———◦◉◦———

J&G had to serve as transitional deacons for at least six months before the bishop could officially ordain them into the Order of the Deacons. They were dressed in albs and diagonally worn stoles of the deacon. A parishioner was very interested to understand the process; Jassim gladly explained.

"It is up to each deacon to decide whether or not he wants to become a priest. Some of the deacons prefer to remain permanent, and they are allowed to marry while assisting the church but are not considered members of the ministry."

"The ministry consists of three levels. The lowest is the transitional deacon, which is followed by the second level, the priest. And finally, the top level, which is the bishop. The pope is the bishop of Rome. All the cardinals are bishops as well, they simply have more influence over church matters."

Luckily, the two new transitional deacons were assigned to the same parish, allowing them to serve their time in the diaconate jointly. Jassim's speech to the at-risk youth group was very impressive, so they were assigned to assist the priests at Our Lady of Lourdes Church in Jamaica Plain. The future priests learned a lot during their time as deacons, developing lifelong relationships with most of the parishioners.

The ex-all-American even helped organize a youth soccer league at the parish, which was a hit with the children. He continued to fake the injury to his knee and refused to play, but his knowledge of the game was impressive, and the eight-team league became a community success. It was a known fact that neither of the two transitional deacons would continue at the church, so volunteers were put in place to continue the league. Mr. Hart served as the commissioner. The six months were filled with great memories for the anxious priests in waiting and quickly flew by.

Chapter 13

In November, the ambitious seminarians joined eleven of their peers for the ordination ceremony. The parishioners of Jamaica Plain had a strong connection to their two deacons and were saddened by the announcement that they would be leaving the parish. Most vowed to attend the celebratory mass in a display of support. Invitations were sent to the family and friends of the ordinands. On the day of the ordination, J&G joined their respective loved ones, prior to the mass, at the altar of the Blessed Virgin Mary, located in the vestibule of the church. They were excited and proud of the two men for their commitment to the Lord.

Everyone was in awe of the large wooden cross, which hung over the main altar, in the grand chapel of Saint John's Seminary. On Sunday, November 26, 2017, the cardinal archbishop of the Archdiocese of Boston, Mike O'Malley, presided over the ordination mass, and the immaculate church was packed with parishioners. Some of the people knew the nominees while the others were well-wishers who regularly attended mass at the parish. The first row of wooden pews was reserved for the transitional deacons. The mass was like any other ordinary Catholic mass, except for a few ceremonial additions.

The "calling of the candidates" was the first aspect unique to the ordination process, and the cardinal called each of the transitional deacons by name. The respective ordinand stood up and responded "present" before stepping in front of the cardinal. Luciana was brought to tears when Bishop O'Malley said, "Jassim Ibrahim Azfal

Ansary." She knew Azfal would have been proud of his grandson and looked to the ceiling, knowing that he was watching over them from heaven. With the candidates aligned at the front of the chapel, the next phase began.

It was the "presentation and inquiry."

"Who will give testimony to the fact that these deacons received proper training and are worthy of ordination?" the bishop asked.

Reverend Cessario confirmed that the transitional deacons were worthy to join the ministry.

The next step was the "Acceptance," in which the archbishop said, "We rely on the help of the Lord God and our Savior Jesus Christ, and we choose these men, our brothers, for priesthood in the Roman Catholic Order."

The "approbation" followed. Everyone in attendance responded, "Thanks be to God," and a round of applause was given for the future priests.

The archbishop then performed the "examination of the candidate." He stepped in front of Jassim and asked if he was willing to serve Christ and the church.

The ordinand responded with "the promise of obedience" and grabbed the archbishop's hand, answering, "I promise to be obedient to the authority of the church and to my superiors."

The archbishop knelt and invited everyone present to kneel and join him in "prayer for the candidates," which included the Litany of the Saints.

"The chanting of the litany" was the most moving moment. The singing by the laity brought a tear to Gianni's eye. Tomaso also found himself wiping away tears, standing proudly, watching his son in front of the cardinal archbishop.

Jassim and the other ordinands lined up before Cardinal O'Malley and lay on the ground. They were all on their stomachs with their foreheads on their hands, forming a line from left to right across the altar. The thirteen transitional deacons listened carefully to the cardinal's words. Prayers were said in order to ask God and the saints to send the Holy Spirit to these men who were about to become priests.

The archbishop went on to perform "the laying of the hands," which was the most solemn moment and essential act. The bishop placed his hands on Jassim's head and prayed silently, invoking the Holy Spirit upon the new priest.

The membership into "the one priesthood of Christ" was then initiated. A proud father De Luca, with tears rolling down his right cheek, joined Father Mike and the multitude of priests who were in attendance. They placed their hands on the heads of each ordinand.

The clergymen performed the "vesting of the new priest." The deacon's stoles were removed, and the new spiritual fathers received their priestly stoles and chasubles.

The cardinal performed the "anointing of the hands." An assisting priest held up a bowl over, which Jassim placed his hands. The archbishop poured the oil of chrism over the ordinand's hands and said, "The Father anointed our Lord Jesus Christ through the power of the Holy Spirit. May Jesus preserve you to sanctify the Christian people and to offer sacrifice to God." He used the linen cloth to wrap Jassim's hands.

The "presentation of the gifts" followed, and each new priest was handed a paten and a chalice. The archbishop said, "Accept from the holy people of God the gifts to be offered to him. Know what you are doing, and imitate the mystery you celebrate. Model your life on the mystery of the Lord's cross." The mass continued as usual, and the new priests assisted with the distribution of communion. Before the proceedings ended, the thirteen new members joined at the altar.

The cardinal knelt before him, and Father Jassim performed his "first priestly blessing." The new priests stood at the altar and gave a blessing to their family and friends. At the end of the ordination ritual, there was a reception.

"I want to extend an invitation to all my supporters to join me next week for the celebration of my first mass as a priest, which is called the 'mass of thanksgiving,'" Jassim said.

Luciana and Father De Luca were scheduled to leave on Saturday, December 2, but extended their stay to attend the mass. She originally purchased the plane tickets, with Anastasia's thoughtful invitation in mind. The ordination mass was held on the Sunday before Thanksgiving Day, and the hostess invited Jassim's godparents to join the Moretti family for dinner. The distinguished Italian was aware of the American custom and was excited to experience the tradition for the first time.

Father Jassim perceptibly chose to celebrate his first mass at Our Lady of Lourdes Church with the parishioners of Jamaica Plain, and it was held on December 3, 2017. Father Gianni celebrated his first mass in the same location the following week, and his proud parents made the long drive up from New Jersey.

Tomaso looked up to the ceiling and prayed. "Thank you, heavenly Father, for guiding my boy to a lifelong commitment as your servant. Please give him the strength to avoid any evil forces, which can take him off the righteous path."

Father Jassim scheduled a meeting with Archbishop Cardinal O'Malley in order to plan his future in the church. The cardinal was in charge of deciding where each new priest would serve the institution due to his high position; only the pope had the power to overrule his authority. The new priest asked Father De Luca to sit in on the meeting since he knew that his mentor would be able to convince Cardinal O'Malley to allow him to go to Iraq.

Father Jassim wasn't sure how receptive the archbishop would be to the idea of expansion in the Middle East and wanted the extra support. The election of Pope Nelson and the decreasing tension between Catholics and Muslims in the country was exactly the break that the young priest needed. He spent a few days in counsel with his godfather, and they prepared a solid case to present to Cardinal O'Malley so he would allow Father Jassim to undertake the monumental task.

The cardinal, along with Reverend Cessario, met with the ambitious priest and his mentor in the modest rector's office at Saint John's Seminary. Father De Luca was the first to speak.

"Your Excellency, I have known this young man since he was ten years old. He has the light of God within his spirit, and it is his desire to serve the Lord as best as he can. It is my recommendation to you to allow him to help expand the reach of the church in the Middle East. He is the perfect candidate to serve in Iraq because it's his homeland and I can assure you that no one is better prepared than he is."

The cardinal took in the respected priest's commendation and allowed for the subordinate priest to speak.

"I believe that I am destined to help spread God's Word to my Iraqi brothers and sisters. I know that it will not be an easy undertaking, but I am ready. I have prepared for this since I converted to the church at the youthful age of eleven. God will help to guide me in my endeavor," Father Jassim said.

Reverend Cessario was in agreement that Father Jassim be allowed to go to Iraq as well. He knew that there would never be a better candidate than the young motivated priest.

Cardinal O'Malley realized that assigning Father Jassim to Iraq was the best option. He understood the expansion of Catholicism in Iraq could help the church become more influential in the region. He was aware of the priests desire to undertake the massive responsibility and spoke to Pope Nelson in regard to the matter prior to the meeting. The pontiff agreed with his assessment. The new president of Iraq was a supporter of the African pope, so the timing couldn't have been more perfect. Father Jassim was excited to learn that he would be returning to his homeland.

"Archbishop O'Malley, I want to thank you for allowing me to pursue my mission of spreading the teachings of Christ in Iraq. I won't let you down. I'd also like to thank my other superiors for believing in me."

Cardinal O'Malley received a request from the cardinal of Florence for Father Gianni to join the Florentine Archdiocese, and the new priest was notified of the cardinal's personal demand. He was ecstatic. His parents were proud of him and very thankful that he would be heading back to his hometown, although they would miss him.

The two friends made arrangements for their departures to be on the eve of the New Year, figuring it would be the best way to have a proper new beginning. The year's Christmas was an emotional one since the young priests were leaving their loved ones behind. Prior to his return to Italy, Father De Luca wished his young apprentice good luck in Iraq, and his godson promised to visit Rome as soon as he was able. Before leaving, the godfather said, "Take care, my child. Your future will be bright. If you do well, the cardinals will be grateful." They embraced and the novice priest took in the inspirational words.

Sabatina, a successful investment banker, received news of Father Jassim's assignment from Anastasia. She called to congratulate him, knowing that it was a major goal of his. Mario grabbed the phone and announced that he was lucky enough to find a location for his shop, but it wouldn't be functional until after his devout friend's departure.

"When you come back, I'll have a free cut waiting for you. Why don't you stop by the old shop before leaving and let me send you off in style? The guys will be excited to see you before you depart."

"That sounds like a good idea. I'll definitely swing by."

Tomaso and his wife accepted the offer to spend Christmas in Newton so the extended family could celebrate Christ's birthday together. Father Mike was also invited for their traditional Christmas day lunch, which followed the morning mass. Everyone had a great time, but the fact that the priests were leaving dampened the mood.

The newly ordained priests joined Mario and Sabatina on the drive to the South End for Christmas Day dinner at the Aponte home. Father Jassim was looking forward to enjoying Marisol's cooking for one final time. He was still angered by his friends' betrayal but didn't let it show. Father Gianni was asked to bless the food.

"Thank you, Lord, for the wonderful family and friends that we have. And thanks for the lovely dinner that our host has prepared."

Father Jassim took the liberty to give a toast and raised his glass. "To Sabatina and Mario's relationship. May they have a loving and long-lasting future together." Although the young priest appeared to be supportive, he was fuming inside. Watching Mario with his hands around Sabatina made him understand how Anastasia must have felt when she discovered Salvatore's infidelity.

The dinner was delicious as usual, and Father Gianni finally understood why his buddy always praised Mrs. Aponte's cooking. Marisol cried tears of joy while she watched her *padrito* leave on his way back to the Moretti house.

"I'm proud of you, *mi amor. Buena suerte en Iraq.*"

"Make us proud, Yassi," Mr. Aponte added.

The day before leaving America, Father Jassim and Father Gianni traveled to Victor's shop for one last haircut from the masterful Mario. He no longer worked at the shop since he was preparing to open his own place, but he had to send them off looking great, assuring they would make a good first impression on their new parishioners. Sabatina was at her parent's home when the priests returned from the shop, and Mario made the drive out to Newton as well. It was the last day that the triumvirate would be together.

Mario couldn't stay for too long. He had to get back to his shop and continue the preparation for his grand opening.

"Good luck in Iraq. Remember that I'll always have your back. I'm just a plane ride away. I know that you gave us your blessing, but I want to apologize for how things unfolded."

"Don't worry about it. I wish you guys the best. I'll definitely give you a call if things get too crazy in Baghdad." Jassim wasn't over the betrayal, but he was going to miss his friend.

Father Gianni's parents arrived from their hotel shortly after. They were ready to drive their son back to New Jersey so he could spend his final day at the Malandra house. He hugged everyone goodbye, and they all wished him a safe trip.

"Take care, old friend. After we rebuild the church's greatness from our hometowns, we'll meet again."

"I can't wait! Who knows, if you can't make it back to Italy, maybe I'll go down to Baghdad for a visit. Have a safe trip."

Father Jassim wished his loyal friend a safe trip as well, and they shared a strong embrace. The two novice priests were off on separate journeys.

The flight to Florence was departing from Newark Liberty International Airport, but *Simona* was too sad to make the trip see her son off, so Tomaso drove his son to Newark alone.

"Don't forget to thank Father *Portella* once you arrive in Florence," Mr. Malandra said.

"I won't. I'll call as soon as I land. Hopefully, you and mother can visit the old country soon."

On the morning of New Year's Eve, the Moretti family traveled to Logan Airport's International terminal. Salvatore was the only one who wasn't crying during the short emotional ride.

"I want to thank you for being a great addition to the family. It was a joy getting to know you. Take care of yourself, Jazz-man. We'll J-Walk when you make it back to the States!"

Anastasia hugged him tightly and whispered into his ear, "Thanks for being so mature and helping me through my weakest moment. I will never forget what you did." Father Jassim smiled as they released each other, and it was Sabatina's turn.

"Thanks for being the best friend a person could ever have. I'll always love you," she said.

He wanted to tell her exactly how he felt about her relationship with Mario, but he simply opened up his arms, and they hugged. "Me too."

After a weak embrace, Father Jassim headed toward the security checkpoint. Sabatina could sense that something was wrong. The hug was nothing like the one they shared at *Fiumicino* before she left for America. She knew that the liaison with Mario was a big mistake.

Father Jassim suddenly stopped in his tracks, and with tears in his eyes, he turned to his loving family.

"I promise to visit soon!" he yelled.

He waved and entered the roped-off line of the checkpoint.

Chapter 14

It was Nuri who met Father Jassim at the airport in Baghdad. They barely recognized each other among the scuttling travelers. "You look good, my friend. Looks like you put on a few pounds since the last time I saw you," the priest said, tapping his friend on the belly.

His long graying beard reached halfway down his chest. The old friends embraced, and Nuri took a step back.

"You were only ten years old when I last saw you. I see you have Ibrahim's height." He was looking up at the young virile priest.

Father Jassim continued working out vigorously even though he stopped playing soccer; staying in shape remained a top priority.

The mention of his father brought him to tears. It was difficult for him to return to Baghdad. The pain from his parents' death began to resurface, and he was extremely bothered by the fact that their bodies weren't recovered; there was no gravestone to visit.

The Catholic Church was not centralized in Iraq, and once the tension between the two largest religions escalated in 2011, the laity left the country to avoid being persecuted. There were only a few remaining parishes. Most were located outside of Baghdad, with St John's Church being the only one that still stood within the city limits.

The church was abandoned at the start of the U.S. invasion in 2003 and reopened in 2007, but the anti-Catholic sentiment forced it to be deserted once again. The election of Pope Nelson in 2016 led to another reopening. The followers of Christ were encouraged to return, and a few took up the offer. There was only a small devout assemblage of Catholics that regularly attended mass at the time of Father Jassim's arrival.

The young motivated priest hoped to reestablish a large congregation in order to impress the pope. His goal was to earn a visit from the pontiff. Father Jassim was aware of the new Iraqi leader's desire to have his holiness visit the country and arranged for a meeting with President Sa'dun Ahmed Allawi.

Allawi gained the support of the voting public by promising to spread acceptance in Iraq in an effort to elevate the country's world image. The religiously tolerant president struck up an immediate friendship with the young ambitious priest.

"I will do everything within my power to assist my young Christovert."

"What is a Christovert? I never heard that word before?"

"You were born a Muslim, but you converted to Catholicism. I think that anyone who converts to Catholicism should be called a Christovert. I coined the term based on the fact that they convert to follow Christ."

Father Jassim was elated to have the full backing of the country's chief, and to his astonishment, the church received a one-hundred-thousand-dollar grant from the generous Iraqi leader. Renovations began immediately on the decaying edifice. President Marzouk was impressed with the Catholic's character. He knew that Father Jassim would be successful in getting people to follow him.

The determined priest was given access to a weekly radio show, in which he reached out to all Catholics living in Baghdad. The attendance at the Sunday mass increased exponentially. The small pockets of Muslims who hated Catholics still existed, but the president's support helped to keep Father Jassim hopeful. Numerous arrests were made for crimes against Baghdad's Catholics because Allawi wanted to send a clear message that he intended to wipe out any anti-Catholic faction that remained in Iraq.

A year later, the peaceful celebration marking the reopening of St. John's Church was a clear sign of the priest's progress in the country. The soaring golden steeple atop the chapel became the crown jewel of the neighborhood. Proud Iraqi Catholics finally felt a sense of belonging, and Father Jassim quickly became a national hero. He dug deep within himself to find the courage to stay the course and was finally reaping all that he sowed. The hate crimes continued for two and a half years, with the population of Catholics tripling in the capital city since his heaven-sent arrival.

Father Jassim was the second most popular man in Baghdad. For the most part, Iraqi Muslims lived in harmony with their Catholic brethren, although a small extremist sect remained. The following year, the distinguished priest planned to celebrate the third anniversary of his return to Iraq. President Allawi donated fifty thousand dollars for the festivities, and the friendship between the two men continued to strengthen. The violence slowly dissipated, and the number of crimes against Catholics reduced by eighty percent.

On a chilly November evening, the celebrated priest went to visit the family of *Elisha*. She was a pure Muslim and the victim of a vicious rape by three assailants. Unfortunately, it was a case of mistaken identity. The extremists confused her plain dress to be that of a Catholic. President Allawi was furious. He gave a televised speech concerning the incident.

"I have given my word to the family of Elisha. I have ordered my best officers to seek out the perpetrators and arrest them as swiftly as possible. Iraq will not accept this deplorable behavior."

It only took two days for the criminals to be apprehended, and two of the men were sentenced to life in prison for their role in the attack. The third man, who devised the plan, was sentenced to death by hanging. Father Jassim drove to the family's home to deliver the good news in person.

"President Allawi does not tolerate such atrocities. I am happy to report that his men have arrested the three rapists. This country has come too far for us to allow the extremists to impede our progress. I wish you a speedy recovery."

The compassionate priest's visit helped to lift the spirits of the dishonored young lady. After a heartfelt visit, the priest headed back to the parish. Father Jassim wished the van had an automatic starter since the night air grew colder as he left the house. It took a few chilly minutes for the engine to warm up, and he was finally off. Three miles away from St. John's Church, his vehicle struck a land mine. The blue-and-white church van flipped over three times, landing on its roof, and the passenger side was completely smashed. By the grace of God, the airbag saved Father Jassim's life, but the blow knocked him unconscious. He was rushed to the hospital and suffered broken bones in his right arm and left leg, along with other minor injuries. The fortunate priest believed Azfal was watching over him.

"You are extremely blessed to be alive right now. The responding emergency medical technician said the car was completely destroyed. Luckily, you didn't sever any main arteries," Dr. *al-Maliki* said.

Father Jassim recovered in the hospital for six months. It was a slow painful process. The president was angered by the brash incident, and he knew the attack was the work of the anti-Catholic faction that remained in Baghdad. After three months of investigation, the responsible party was identified, and the Baghdad Special Forces rounded up thirteen radicals.

In order to keep with his message that Iraq no longer supported religious intolerance, President Allawi ordered for the men to be executed by firing squad at the mouth of the Euphrates River. Upon his release from the hospital, Father Jassim gave a speech to the Catholic congregation, assuring them that the failed attempt on his life would not deter him from continuing to promote peace in the country. He quoted Psalm chapter 27 verse 3, "Though an army encamp against me, my heart does not fear: Though war be waged against me, even then do I trust."

Father Gianni was thriving in Florence, and he was well aware of the progress that his friend was making in Iraq. They kept in contact through the Internet and used videophones on a weekly basis. The Florentine was worried for Father Jassim's safety.

"Archbishop Borgia, I request your permission to travel to Iraq in order to assist with peace effort. Father Jassim needs my help."

"If you are willing to brave the harsh atmosphere that exists in Baghdad, I will allow for you to travel there."

Pope Nelson was pleased with the brave young priest's ability to stabilize the church inside Iraq and cognizant of the fact that he was being mentored by his godfather. The pope recommended Father De Luca's elevation to the position of bishop to the Apostolic Nuncio. The sitting bishop of Milan was not able to perform his duties because of his weakening health, and Father De Luca was promoted to replace him. A disappointed Father Jassim wasn't able to attend the celebration of Bishop De Luca's new appointment but was proud of his mentor. He hadn't fully recovered from the wounds and wasn't cleared to fly.

Father Jassim called the pope to ask for His Excellency to visit Iraq, and Pope Nelson said he would take the request under consideration. He wished the injured priest a speedy recovery and continued success. The pope realized Father Jassim needed help if he planned to expand the Catholic Church throughout Iraq and agreed to support Father Gianni's move to Baghdad.

The Italian didn't speak any Arabic, so he was assigned a personal an interpreter from the newly renamed Iraqi Language Institute; Saddam Hussein's name was removed after it reopened in 2013. Father Gianni's translator was a short frail man named *Yusuf*, who didn't understand any of the Catholic traditions but was an excellent linguist. The two grew to be incredibly good friends.

While Father Gianni was left to head the Archdiocese of Baghdad, his fully recovered friend traveled the country establishing new churches in every major city. It was an arduous task that lasted four years, and the courageous priest also campaigned for the reelection of President Allawi during his travels, knowing that his success depended on the supportive leader remaining in power. In 2024, the president was reelected to a second six-year term and remained a key supporter of Father Jassim's.

The subsequent year, the native Iraqi finally returned to Baghdad to lead the expanded Catholic Archdiocese of Iraq. The anti-Catholic sentiment in the country was basically nonexistent, and the president, along with his favorite priest, spread a message of religious tolerance. The Iraqi Muslims and Catholics lived in relative harmony. Father Jassim's central point was that members of both faiths were people of the book.

Pope Nelson, along with Bishop De Luca, traveled to Iraq during the summer of 2025. Cardinal O'Malley and Reverend Cessario flew in from Boston to attend the historic mass. The proud president made arrangements, preparing for the pontiff's monumental visit. Iraq's famed Saber Stadium was the location for the pope's extraordinary mass.

Catholics from every corner of the country made the pilgrimage to Baghdad, and Saber Stadium, which was set up to seat over 110,000 people, was filled to capacity. The Baghdad economy received a big jolt, with the increased tourism from the influx of the faithful laity.

The mass was a complete success, and many of the followers cried when they laid eyes on his eminence. It was the largest religious celebration in the country's history. Father Jassim sat with President Allawi on the altar in the center of the empty stadium after the pope's mass concluded. They stared at the two massive Sabers at the stadium's entrance and reveled in the success of the event.

"You pulled it off, my young Christovert," Allawi said.

"We pulled it off. I couldn't have done it without your support."

At the beginning of their massive undertaking, neither man actually believed the pope would visit the country, but their diligence paid off. The following day, before the church leaders departed from Iraq, they met for breakfast at the presidential palace. Pope Nelson was especially impressed with Father Jassim's ability to end the hatred toward Catholics that existed in the country. The accomplished priest exceeded everyone's expectations. Father Gianni, who learned to speak fluent Arabic, was also commended for his role in the great achievement. *Yusuf* was no longer needed to translate for his priestly friend, but they remained close.

Cardinal O'Malley was proud of his young apprentice. He always thought Father Jassim would rise to greatness but wasn't sure he could succeed in the harsh environment of Iraq. He mostly worried that the young priest would die at the hands of extremists.

"I always knew that the two of you were destined for greatness," added Rev. Cessario as he put his hands on the shoulders of the proficient clergymen.

At the airport, as the planes took off, Father Jassim looked to the sky and knew Azfal was proud of him. The mission was unfolding according to his grandfather's script. A month after returning to Italy, an impressed Pope Nelson conferred the "red hat" on the newly appointed Cardinal De Luca at a consistory in front of the College of Cardinals. The young priests made the trip to St. Peter's for the ceremony, and Father Gianni brought along *Yusuf*, who was ecstatic to visit the Vatican. It was an experience that the young Iraqi would never forget. Cardinal De Luca was thrilled to become a "prince of the church" and enjoyed the meal at *Monte Caruso*, a gift from his godson.

Father Jassim also saw Jews as people of the book and encouraged them to move to Iraq. There were only a handful living in the country. The acceptance and success of the Catholic Church caused many Jewish people to seriously consider the invite. A small Semite community was established in Baghdad, and slowly, more Jews began to immigrate to the birthplace of civilization. The growth of the community was slow but steady, with the realization of the religious freedoms. In 2027, the population of the Jewish community exceeded three thousand in Baghdad, and a temple was built with money from a fund created by President Allawi, whose aim was to increase the capital city's diversity.

Chapter 15

Father Jassim was preparing to celebrate his tenth year in Baghdad, and the supportive Iraqi president planned a New Year's Day celebration to mark the occasion. Pope Nelson, along with Cardinal De Luca, flew from Rome to be in attendance. They wanted to support the flourishing priest but had an ulterior motive for making the journey. Father Jassim was to be appointed the new Archbishop of Baghdad and was considered the official leader of the Roman Catholic Church in Iraq. A special mass was held at St. John's Church in the new bishop's honor.

Luciana surprised her "favorite guy" and made the trip to Baghdad. The elevation in status came as a pleasant surprise to the young unexpecting priest. Pope Nelson bypassed the usual procedure of working with the apostolic nuncio on the appointment of a new bishop. After the mass, Bishop Ansary called the Moretti home and spoke with Anastasia.

"You won't believe it, Ana, I am a bishop. The pope flew out to Baghdad to make the announcement in person, along with Cardinal De Luca."

"Jassi, we are so proud of you. I can't wait to tell Sal when he gets home."

She was delighted to hear how great he was doing, but during the call, the newly appointed bishop learned that Sabatina had a heated falling out with her parents. They hadn't spoken with her in two months.

Bishop Ansary was shocked to hear of the rift. Anastasia refused to get into any detail about their argument, and he didn't want to push her but invited his guardians to visit Iraq.

"We would love to go, but with all the problems we are going through, it's just not the right time. But if things improve with Tina, we'll definitely make the visit."

"I understand. I'll try and see if I can go to the United States. I was stunned when Tina didn't return any of my recent calls, maybe I can talk to her when I visit."

"Hopefully. We have tried everything possible, but she just seems lost."

Bishop Ansary continued to attempt reaching Sabatina, but he was unsuccessful. Unbeknownst to him, she received the requested transfer to her firm's office in Los Angeles. He left a message with the secretary and hoped that she would eventually contact him.

The new bishop enjoyed wearing his black clerical suit and pectoral cross. He also liked the new choir dress, consisting of a black cassock with an amaranth trim and purple *zucchetto*. He was very successful, but his appointment to archbishop of Iraq helped to drive him for more achievement.

Neighboring Iran was still very intolerant toward Catholics, and he wanted to do everything within his power to change their prejudiced policies.

"Are you sure you want to venture into Iran? It won't be a welcome environment for a Catholic Bishop," President Allawi asked.

"Yes, I am ready for the trip. I have done extensive research, and I feel confident I can convince the leadership to change their policies."

"You know you have my full support, but I am not sure you know what you are getting into."

"Have faith that I know what I am doing. Let me display my vast knowledge of our neighboring country, and you will see how much I have learned. The *Ayatollah Mohammad-Reza Rafsanjani* is intent on keeping the old traditions of *Shi'a* rule in place. An eighty-member council of Islamic experts elected him as the country's third supreme leader in 2011 after the death of *Ayatollah Ali Khamenei* who came to power in 1989. The country's first supreme leader was *Ayatollah Ruhollah Khomeini*. He was a *Marja*, and his followers called him *Imam Khomeini*." Allawi was impressed. He nodded affirmatively as the bishop continued.

"The acrimonious *Ayatollah* is not interested in any Catholic expansion. He doesn't even want *Sunni* Muslims in his country. He holds the title supreme leader of Iran and is far more powerful than the country's president. It is he who is responsible for appointing most of the top political and clerical leaders in the country. Knowing all this, I am undeterred, and I intend to sit down with *Rafsanjani* in order to present my master plan to the intolerant leader. I am certain that he will accept my offer."

"It seems like my Christovert has indeed done his research. I wish you good luck. May *Allah* grant you protection from harm."

The Iraqi archbishop crossed the border into neighboring Iran. He was confident that he would be able to successfully present his case. President Allawi provided him with a bulletproof limousine and four armed escorts for the 442-mile drive to *Tehran*. When he finally arrived in the Iranian capital, the archbishop checked in at the Hotel Laleh International. The unusual exterior of the hotel was designed to look like a paperback novel being opened slowly. The bishop respectfully asked for a meeting with *Ayatollah Rafsanjani*, but the request was vehemently denied.

The *Ayatollah* flat out refused to meet with "the Catholic" who exhausted all his efforts to no avail. A member of Iran's Guardian Council, Ayatollah Hashemi Abtahi, who stood only five feet five inches tall, was curious to meet the thirty-six-year-old Iraqi bishop. The young *Ayatollah* was chubby, with a full black beard, and was considered the supreme leader's probable successor. After learning of the request, he extended an invitation to discuss the Catholic's agenda over dinner. He was intrigued by the fact that Bishop Ansary had risen to such a high position at his young age.

"Before we get to the reason for my being here, I must ask, why is it that some people say Grand Ayatollah but others say *Marja*?" Bishop Ansary asked.

"*Marja* means source to follow and is the name given to all Grand *Ayatollahs*. The position is the highest ranking of the religious leaders in the *Shi'a* tradition. The Iranian Constitution allows for the supreme leader to select six members of the Guardian Council. They are men who have achieved the rank of *Ayatollah*. The other six members are elected by the *Majlis*, which is the country's parliament. *Rafsanjani*, not the *Majlis*, appointed me. I am thought to be his successor and the future of Iran since I agree with all the supreme leader's traditional *Shi'a* policies, but who can predict these things," Abtahi said, as he threw up his arms.

The dinner was very informational to both men. Abtahi learned of the bishop's ambitions and was in awe of the young leader's passion and drive. The Iranian also had lofty goals, but the young leaders had polarizing visions for the future of the region. They both wanted peace but couldn't decide on a mutual approach. Bishop Ansary felt that Abtahi's thinking was out of date, and he left the meeting with little hope for improving relations with Iran. He still held out hope that there was a slim possibility the young *Ayatollah* could be convinced to change his views.

"I must say it was an enjoyable discussion, but I guess we'll have to agree to disagree on our plans for the future of the region. May *Allah* guide you on your journey back to Baghdad," Abtahi said.

"I haven't given up hope yet. I still believe that you will come around one day and agree with me. It was gracious of you to speak with me. Thank you and God bless you."

Abtahi knew that he needed to remain in the good graces of the supreme leader in order to gain political power, and for that reason, he didn't want to pursue a friendship with the archbishop. After talking over the phone several times, he decided to end all contact with the Catholic. During their final conversation, he began to yell at Bishop Ansary.

"You are a complete idiot. You're clearly not a free thinker. It is obvious that you are simply a puppet of the pope. I know that your aim is to rid the world of Muslims, and I won't let you accomplish your goal." Without allowing for the young leader to defend his character, Abtahi angrily hung up the phone.

The archbishop of Baghdad was upset by the harsh criticism. He assumed that the Iranian councilman was brainwashed by the supreme leader. Abtahi grew to be more conservative since his encounter with Bishop Ansary. He aligned himself with Iran's top traditionalists and became the undisputed successor to *Ayatollah Rafsanjani*. He sought the *Ayatollah's* advice on everything and plans to assure the young man's future commenced. Abtahi studied all his mentor's writings and proclamations, and his hard work began to pay off. The young *Ayatollah* became the most trusted member of the Iranian leadership.

In September 2029, *Rafsanjani* made an official state announcement naming Abtahi his successor, and the country's Grand *Ayatollahs* supported the choice. Bishop Ansary was disappointed by the fact that Abtahi didn't see a better path for the region, but there was nothing that he could do.

In November of the same year, *Ayatollah Rafsanjani* died at the age of ninety. He suffered from a severe case of emphysema, and *Hashemi* Abtahi became the new supreme leader. His first order of business was to call the Iraqi archbishop.

"I would like to apologize and ask for your forgiveness. I didn't mean what I said. I want you to know that it was all part of my grand scheme. I wanted to gain power in order for the two of us to work toward our common goal, which is why I was such a loyal follower of the old regime. The meeting that we had in *Tehran* allowed me to see that you are essential to the Middle Eastern peace process."

The *Ayatollah* still disagreed with the bishop's stance on the role of women in society, but he looked forward to beginning the daunting task of bring peace to the troubled region.

"I was disappointed after our last exchange, but I am excited to see that I have a powerful ally in my quest for peace. It is by the grace of God that you were not brainwashed."

They made plans to meet in person and discuss their future course of action. *Ayatollah* Abtahi wanted to change the world's negative perception of Iran and was angered that the country continued to be looked at as a terrorist state. He created a panel of Iranian women, whose sole purpose was to promote the continuation of the country's traditional stance. The new supreme leader was a progressive thinker on most issues, but when it came to women's rights, he would not deviate from his old way of thinking. In every other aspect of the society, he wanted to bring Iran into the modern world. It was also important to keep *Islam* as a central part of the citizen's lives, but he felt the people deserved some rights. *Shari'a* law would no longer serve as the nation's sole judicial code.

The persecution of *Sunni* minorities was also made illegal by the *Ayatollah*. Abtahi reversed his predecessor's prevention of the construction of a *Sunni* mosque in *Tehran*. It took a year for him to implement all the new progressive changes. The traditionalists were angered by his new policies, causing him to remove all members of the old regime and replacing them with more progressive minded leaders.

Ayatollah Abtahi preached religious and ethnic tolerance. The people of Iran loved him because he allowed for them to have more freedoms and he was known as the champion of the Iranian free speech movement. For the first time in their lives, the Iranian citizens were able to speak out against the leadership and not be arrested. The enemies of the new supreme leader moved away from *Tehran* and resettled in the southern part of the country near the Pakistan and Afghanistan borders. These neo-traditionalists called themselves *Khomeineists*.

They were intent on regrouping and fighting against the man whom they referred to as "Hizb al-Shaitan." The *Khomeineists* had support from the *Taliban* in Afghanistan and *Al Queda*, who were hiding out in the mountainous region between the borders.

In the spring of 2031, Iran's secretive nuclear weapons program was unveiled and dismantled. The UN inspectors controlled the operation, which served as a major sign of peace. Abtahi's removal of the "Death to America Mural" that stood in *Tehran*, constructed under the orders of his predecessor *Ayatollah Khamenei*, helped to increase diplomatic talks with the United Stated of America. The United States lifted sanctions that had been placed against the former "axis of evil" member in a show of appreciation. The American president gave a speech in which he called the *Ayatollah* "a breath of fresh air in the Middle East." The Khomeineists viewed all the supreme leader's actions as evidence that he was truly the leader of "the party of Satan."

———⊙———

Bishop Ansary's proudest moment came when he held his first mass to ordain new priests into the archdiocese of Baghdad. It was a ceremony that he would never forget since he personally mentored every member of the seminarian class, and each of the five transitional deacons served at St. John's Church in Baghdad. The bishop worked with them daily in order to mold their skills as priests and shape their theological views. They were his best pupils, and he looked forward to seeing them progress in the church. The new priests were very important to the bishop's plan of controlling the archdiocese. They were extremely loyal to him. He envisioned placing them in strategic cities, hoping that eventually they would serve as bishops under his wing.

———⊙———

At the end of the summer, *Ayatollah* Abtahi invited his friend to *Tehran* as his personal guest. He wanted to show the world that the country was no longer anti-Catholic. The *Ayatollah* also extended an invitation to the pope, who respectfully declined, stating that Bishop Ansary was his representative.

"Although I will not be able to visit on this occasion, I look forward to visiting Iran in the future, if it is the Lord's will," Pope Nelson said.

The bishop received a warm welcome from the exuberant Iranian public who believed his visit was a major step toward the country's transformation into a new progressive nation. Supporters lined the streets to cheer on the bishop's motorcade. Bishop Ansary marveled at *Tehran's* tallest structure, *Borj-e-Milad*, when his car drove past. The convoy drove further away, and he was focused on the soaring edifice's diamond-shaped windows as it reduced in size. Suddenly, out of nowhere, a powerful force knocked him out of his seat.

The jubilation was instantaneously ended by a rocket-propelled grenade, which destroyed one of the cars. Four members of Abtahi's security team were killed instantly. Bishop Ansary was lucky to survive the attack. His car was ahead of the one that was blown to pieces.

The shooter must have missed his target. *Ayatollah* Abtahi assumed the *Khomeineists* were responsible for the assassination attempt, and *Tehran* Police followed tips provided by witnesses, cornering the shooter within several hours of the attack. He was not willing to be captured. Shockingly, he pulled out a pistol from his waistband and shot himself in the head.

Ayatollah Abtahi knew that he had to send a message that religious intolerance and hatred would not be accepted. He ordered the Iranian Military to bomb the region inhabited by the *Khomeineists*. The militant group suffered many losses and was forced to flee across the border into the mountainous region of Pakistan. As a precaution, the two leaders altered their meeting location.

"I think the city of *Qom*, which is the holiest city in the country, will be a proper local."

They met for three days and devised a plan, which aimed to bring peace to the region. Abtahi asked the bishop about his motivation for the peace process.

"I have had a true calling to serve the Lord, which is why I converted to the Catholic Church. I truly believe that it is my destiny to help improve the lives of the God's children."

Bishop Ansary didn't feel the need to clue the *Ayatollah* in on the promise that he made to his grandfather because he didn't want to take away from their mission of spreading peace. The two leaders vowed not to allow the assassination attempt to deter the process. They agreed to exhaust all their resources to achieve the ultimate goal.

The one major problem that still existed between them was the bishop's insistence on improving the rights of women in Iran. On the subject, *Ayatollah* Abtahi would not waver. He quoted *Surah* 2, *Ayah* 228: "Wives have the same rights as the husbands have on them in accordance with the generally known principles. Of course, men are a degree above them in status." He proudly recited.

"You have to change your way of thinking, *Hashemi*, your views are outdated."

"That is the opinion of the prophet. And your Bible is in agreement. Are you not familiar with your own scripture?" The *Ayatollah* paused for affect. "Your religion preaches the same ideas. Allow me to quote from 1 Corinthians chapter 14 verses 33b to 35: 'As in all the churches of the holy ones, women should keep silent in the churches, for they are not allowed to speak, but should be subordinate, as even the law says. But if they want to learn anything, they should ask their husbands at home.'"

He prepared the verse prior to attending the meeting, expecting the issue to be brought up.

"Yes, it is true that the church treats women as subordinates but women should have equal rights in society."

"You cannot separate church and state. The society should follow the word of *Allah*. I will not change my stance on the role of women." Again, the stubborn men agreed to disagree. The Iraqi bishop hoped that he would one day change the *Ayatollah's* position on the matter.

On the afternoon that Bishop Ansary was to leave for Iraq, Abtahi held a press conference announcing that his capable friend would help the neighboring counties improve their tumultuous relationship.

"Our friend, the bishop, has guaranteed that his diplomatic president, Sa'dun Allawi, will meet with me so the two of us can set aside past differences and move toward a great future."

A month elapsed before Bishop Ansary set up the peace talks. The *Ayatollah* flew to Iraq and met with President Allawi. The two leaders agreed to become allies.

"I would like to thank Bishop Ansary, my Christovert, who was instrumental in helping to establish peace between Iran and Iraq," Allawi said.

Trade between the two countries opened up, allowing for both sovereign nations to flourish economically.

The following March, President Allawi, *Ayatollah* Abtahi, and Bishop Ansary were flown to Washington Dulles International

Airport for a meeting at the White House. The American president commended them for implementing the use of diplomacy to settle differences. Iranian and Iraqi forces were sent to Afghanistan to join in the effort to stabilize the war-torn nation. The use of Muslim forces to combat the *Taliban* and the lessoning of the American military operations helped to minimize the support of extremism in Afghanistan. After a year of conflict, a majority of the nation's *Taliban* fighters were removed.

Conditions in the country were improving, but more work needed to be done. After returning from America, Bishop Ansary and *Ayatollah* Abtahi continued to promote religious tolerance throughout the Middle East. The people were tired of the wars, and many of the leaders were receptive to their message of unity. There was still a lot of tension between the countries, but they didn't want to create a situation in which the United States would feel the need to get involved again. The Palestinian Israeli conflict remained a hot button issue. Jerusalem was the location of the only major conflict in the region. The leaders from the other Middle Eastern nations improved relations with one another, and the American forces were almost completely removed.

The prime minister of Egypt agreed to hold a meeting in Cairo in order to discuss the best method to deal with Jerusalem. It took place in the year 2033. Leaders from every Middle Eastern country were invited with a goal of ending the almost century long conflict between Israelis and Palestinians. The president of the Palestine Liberation Organization (PLO) sat at one end of the table; sitting opposite was the Israeli prime minister. The men met every day for a week, and negotiations sometimes became heated.

The archbishop of Baghdad was instrumental in persuading both sides to settle on an agreement. The leaders of the warring nations had no other option than to agree to end the conflict since the plan had the unequivocal support of every other Middle Eastern leader and the UN. After the particulars were ironed out, Bishop Ansary went over the fine points.

"We are all in agreement. Two sovereign nations will be created, and the capitals will be Tel Aviv and Ramallah. Jerusalem, which is located on the border between the nations, will be made into a land-locked sovereign city-state. It will be essentially like Vatican City, and neither country will have control over the state of Jerusalem. We will establish a parliament consisting of elected Israeli and Palestinian officials to run the holy city-state. The Arabs will be allowed to continue to oversee the temple of the rock and the *Al-Aqsa* Mosque. Each country will hold separate voting to elect their respective leaders.

"The parliament will consist of ten members who will advise the prime minister. Each member will serve a seven-year term and be eligible for only one subsequent reelection. The prime minister of Jerusalem will also be limited, only able to hold office for two five-year terms. All three nations will join in the election of the prime minister."

Ayatollah Abtahi further explained the details.

"Israel has reluctantly agreed to move back its borders to the 1949 Armistice Lines, known as the Green Lines. The West Bank and the Gaza Strip are to be called the Sovereign Nation of Palestine. The citizens will be allowed to remain in their homes. Israelis and Palestinians will have citizenship in all three nations. And all the citizens will be granted religious freedom.

"Israeli laws will bind those who live in Israel, and those who live in Palestine will follow Palestinian laws. Any citizen who wants to move from either nation will be allowed to and given government assistance. For the first time in almost a century, Palestinians will be issued passports. They will no longer be a nationless people.

"We have also agreed to form a new League of Middle Eastern Nations, which is to be modeled after the United Nations. The nations of the L-MEN will pay for the moving expenses incurred by Israelis and Palestinians. Every country will have equal voting power in the league, and an election will be held every four years to select a new secretary general. We will also aim to establish a single monetary system for the participating nations of the L-MEN."

A member of *Ayatollah* Abtahi's Guardian Council, Grand *Ayatollah Sadeq Bizhani* was elected to serve as the first secretary general of the L-MEN, and his hope was to completely rid the region of religious intolerance and to continue the spread of peace.

"Jews, Muslims, and Christians are all considered people of the book and should be able to live in peace with one another," *Bizhani* said.

The extremist groups had a big problem with the "lost men." There were still many incidents of violence throughout the Middle East, but the nations were all aligned in their mission to end intolerance. The hiding spots were fewer, and the groups found it difficult to operate. There were no longer any degenerate states willing to harbor terrorists.

Bishop Ansary, who played a vital role in bringing an end to the conflict in Jerusalem, had one request before the historic meeting was adjourned.

"I request to have the League of Middle East Nations' headquarters built in Baghdad. My family members were killed in the Iraqi invasion, and I want to honor them by having the headquarters built in their memory."

The leaders voted on the request and unanimously agreed to allow the archbishop to pick the exact location for the construction of the league's headquarters. They all considered Baghdad to be the cradle of civilization and felt it was the perfect home for the complex.

Bishop Ansary chose the site of the destroyed bunker in *Al A'zamiyah* as an appropriate location. Construction began a month after the meeting in Cairo, and the Ansary Complex was completed in the summer of 2034. It was dedicated in the memory of Ibrahim, Nebet, Saady, and Azfal Ansary. A large statue of the deceased family members was erected at the main entrance, and the Iraqi archbishop was brought to tears the day it was opened.

The bishop never believed he would achieve so much. Azfal would have been proud of his accomplishments. He far exceeded his expectations but was still set on completing the promise that he made to his grandfather. To the astonishment of the two accomplished leaders, in October 2036, it was announced that Bishop Ansary and *Ayatollah* Abtahi were selected as the recipients of the prestigious Nobel Peace Prize. The honor was bestowed upon them for their role in helping to establish peace in the Middle East. On December 10, the Nobel Peace Prize was given to Archbishop Jassim Ansary of Iraq and, the supreme leader of Iran, Ayatollah *Hashemi* at the Oslo City Hall in Oslo, Norway.

"The Nobel Prize for Peace is the only Nobel Award not to be given out in Stockholm, Sweden. Alfred Nobel left specific instructions in his will. The prize is handed out on the anniversary of his death, every December 10. The ceremony will be broadcast throughout the world, and you will be recognized as heroes," explained one of the representatives.

The laureates received a diploma, a medal, and a document confirming the monetary amount for the prize. The bishop donated his prize money to the Roman Catholic Church, and it was distributed throughout the various archdioceses of the Middle East. Pope Nelson thanked him for the generous gift of two million dollars and held a mass in the archbishop's honor at St. Peter's Basilica.

"I'd like to thank Pope Nelson for honoring me with this mass, but I don't feel like my job is done. We must continue to work hard to achieve the goal of bringing peace to the entire world. In Proverbs 16 verses 5 through 9, it is written:

> Every proud man is an abomination to the Lord; I assure you that he will not go unpunished. By kindness and piety guilt is expiated, and by the fear of the Lord man avoids evil. When the Lord is pleased with a man's ways, he makes even his enemies be at peace with him. Better a little virtue, than a large income with injustice.

Ayatollah Abtahi, who was already extremely wealthy, donated his prize money to the L-MEN. He was glad to be a part of the peace process.

"I want to thank you for allowing me to serve as your ally. The moment I met you, I knew that you had what it takes to get people to follow your lead. I will be honored to work with you in any future endeavor," the *Ayatollah* said.

"Thank you for the kind words, but you're too modest. Without your influence, the leaders wouldn't have agreed to meet me."

The two recipients returned to their respective cities to awaiting parades.

Bishop Ansary received a call from an ecstatic Anastasia who congratulated him on his success.

"I still haven't heard from Sabatina, but I received a letter in the mail stating that she was okay."

He was happy to hear from her but continued to worry about his friend's well-being.

Cardinal De Luca also called to congratulate his successful apprentice. "I am extremely proud of you, and I know that your grandfather is looking down on you from his eternal resting place. I wish you continued success. Remember that through God, anything is possible. Hopefully, his eminence will promote you to the cardinalate for your many accomplishments."

Pope Nelson announced the itinerary for his planned visit to the Middle East. His first stop was to be Israel, after which he would visit the state of Jerusalem, followed by a historic trip to the new nation of Palestine. The pope also arranged for a visit to Saudi Arabia, where he hoped to be allowed to enter the Islamic holy cities of Mecca and Medina. He was interested to make a stop in Iraq to see the L-MEN headquarters, and his trip was to conclude in *Tehran*. The pontiff requested for Bishop Ansary and Father Gianni to travel with him during his jaunt through the region. They flew to Tel Aviv and met him. Cardinal De Luca tagged along, and the group met with the prime minister of Israel, and the pope gave a mass at Bloomfield Stadium. The men also visited the Church of the Holy Sepulchre.

"The church is believed to sit on the site of *Golgotha*, which is the hill of Calvary where Jesus was crucified. It also contains the site of Jesus's burial and resurrection. It is considered one of the holiest places in Christendom and remains a very popular Christian pilgrimage destination. Pilgrims can touch the actual rock at the site of the Savior's crucifixion. They can also touch the spot where it is believed that Jesus's body was laid to rest inside the tomb. The church was originally constructed under the orders of the Roman Emperor Constantine. The current church has stood since AD 1885 and is topped off with a dome," the knowledgeable guide informed them.

After visiting the church, the group moved on to the Dome of the Rock on the Temple Mount. Bishop Ansary was familiar with its history.

"The Dome of the Rock houses the Rock of *Moriah* and was built to rival the Church of the Holy Sepulchre. The dome is the most recognizable building in Jerusalem. It sticks out in the otherwise bland architectural landscape of the city. The Golden Dome, which sits on top of the turquoise structure, can be seen from almost anywhere in Holy City. Muslim tradition holds that the Prophet *Muhammad* is believed to have traveled to Jerusalem in a dream. He ascended to heaven and saw the prophets Abraham, Moses, and Jesus on his way to see the Lord. The prophet ascended to heaven from the Rock of *Moriah*, which is considered the location of 'the gateway to heaven' in the Islamic tradition. *Muhammad* returned to Mecca, and when he woke the following day, he was able to describe Jerusalem even though he had never visited the Holy City. The Dome of the Rock was constructed under the leadership of *Caliph Abd al Malik Ibn Marwan* in AD 691. He began construction of the adjoining *Al-Aqsa* Mosque, which was finished by his son, *al-Walid* in AD 705. He preserved many of the remaining marble from Solomon's Temple."

The men stared up at the interior of the wonderful structure as the Bishop continued. "*Caliph Abd al Malik* had great respect for all places of worship. He considered both Jews and Christians as people of the book. The mosque was originally a small prayer house built by the *Caliph Omar*, and the Arabic writing on the walls of the interior reads, 'In the name of the one God Pray for your prophet and servant Jesus son of Mary. All people of the book join what is now the true religion.' *Abd al Malik* wanted to convert Christians and Jews to *Islam*. In 1998, the exterior of the dome was covered in eighty kilograms of gold from an 8.2-million-dollar donation from King Hussein of Jordan. He sold one of his houses to cover the expense. The Dome of the Rock is the oldest Muslim building in existence."

The visit was an experience none of the men would ever forget. His Excellency also visited the Western Wall in Jerusalem, continuing in the example of Pope John Paul II.

"Also called the 'Wailing Wall,' the structure is originally part of the second temple of Solomon. The second temple was built in the year 516 BC, and King Herod the Great expanded the structure in 19 BC. The wall was part of the outer perimeter of the expanded structure. It is customary for Jews to write down prayers on pieces of paper and place them in the crevices of the wall. In the year 2000, Pope John Paul II placed a note here. He was followed by Pope Benedict XVI, who did the same during his 2009 visit," the prime minister explained.

Pope Nelson wrote down a prayer and placed it into a small crevice. The visit to the Holy City was very important to the pontiff since Jerusalem is arguably the most religious place on earth. The pope's visit to Ramallah was even more significant because he was the first non-Muslim foreign diplomat to visit the new country. His holiness and the entourage were well received, and it seemed as if every citizen of Palestine attended the ceremonial mass.

The next desired destination for the group was Medina. Bishop Ansary was interested in visiting *Al-Masjid al Nabawi*, the mosque of the prophet. "The Prophet *Mohammad* was buried in his home, and a mosque was built on the site. I also want to visit the *Quba* Mosque, which was the first mosque of *Islam*."

The Holy City of Mecca was to be the following destination since it's the most important city to Muslims and birthplace of the prophet. The Iraqi bishop was excited for the trip and pointed to the historical significance of the city for his exuberance, but the truth of the matter was his enthusiasm to complete the *Hajj*. The pilgrimage is one of five pillars of faith to be completed by all Muslims, and the bishop was close to fulfilling that goal, but there was one major problem—the Saudi Arabian government does not allow for non-Muslims to visit the two Holy Cities.

"The Prophet *Mohammad* was forced to flee from Mecca because the leaders of the tribes there threatened his life. The prophet moved to *Yathrib*, which was later renamed Medina by his followers. The name means 'city of the prophet.' Once *Muhammad* led his followers to retake Mecca, he said nonbelievers were never to be allowed to enter," the bishop clarified.

The pope asked for King *Bandar bin Sultan bin Abdul Aziz Al Saud* to make an exception and give him permission to visit the holiest cities of Islam. Pope Nelson wanted to have a mass near the *Kaaba* or maybe in King *Abdulazziz* Stadium.

There was nothing doing. The Saudi king refused to allow the nonbelievers access to the two cities. The pontiff understood, but Bishop Ansary was devastated. He was really looking forward to completing the pilgrimage.

The group flew from Palestine to Baghdad International Airport, where they spent the first day at St. John's Church. Pope Nelson celebrated a special mass with Baghdad's Catholics. The following day, they drove to *Al A'zamiyah*, first stopping at the bishop's old home to say a prayer for his deceased family members. The men made the short drive to the L-MEN headquarters, and *Ayatollah Sadeq Bizhani* greeted them at the entrance. The touching memorial statue of the Ansary family moved everyone to tears. The remainder of the day was spent touring the massive newly constructed complex.

Ayatollah Abtahi met the pope and his associates the next day at *Imam Khomeini* International Airport. Pope Nelson gave a monumental mass at *Tehran's* newest soccer field, *Khamenei* Stadium. Although the population of Catholics in Iran was small, it was the largest Christian mass held in the country's history.

"I am honored to have the opportunity to hold this mass for the free Catholics of Iran. *Ayatollah* Abtahi has done a wonderful job of allowing non-Muslims to flourish inside of this great nation," the pope said.

With the exception of the disappointment in Saudi Arabia, the pontiff considered the trip an unbelievable success.

Chapter 16

The African pope was a welcome sight throughout the Muslim world. Relations between the Vatican and the Middle East were vastly improved. Pope Nelson and his entourage traveled to Baghdad from *Tehran*, and the Iraqi archbishop's most trusted priests deplaned, but the pope stopped Cardinal Ansary.

"You shall accompany me to Rome. I have decided to confer the 'red hat' on you."

The archbishop was overwhelmed by a sense of accomplishment and fell to his knees. He did not expect to hear the wonderful news.

He pointed to the sky. "Thank you for setting me on my path, Azi."

Archbishop Ansary knew his grandfather's plan was working. The mastermind's grand scheme was unfolding better than he could have ever imagined. President Allawi assembled a police escort to lead the priests into the city, and the pope's plane took off on route to the Vatican with the accomplished archbishop on board. He waved goodbye to Saber Stadium while he looked out the truncated window.

"The Vatican, which is located on the right bank of the Tiber River, was built on the site known in antiquity as the *Ager Vaticanus*. You should know the history. One day, it may be your home," the pope said.

"That would be an unbelievable achievement, Your Excellency, but I am content to simply serve the Lord in whatever capacity he wills."

Pope Nelson led everyone to the Apostolic Palace, which was
on the eastern section of the Vatican Hill. It was built in extreme
simplicity. He arranged for a consistory to be assembled in advance
and presented the new cardinal with his published decree of elevation. The pontiff introduced Archbishop Ansary as the new cardinal
of Baghdad. During the consistory, the new cardinal knelt before the
pope and received his ring, scarlet *zucchetto*, and scarlet *birette*, which
is the four-corner silk hat of a cardinal. Before leaving, Pope Nelson
met with him inside the Vatican Museum.

"I want you to inform Father Malandra that I have asked the
apostolic nuncio to consider him to replace you as the new bishop
of Baghdad. I also want you to know that I have taken the liberty
of arranging for your *galerum rubrum* to be fashioned for you here
in Rome."

Cardinal Ansary retrieved his elaborate broad-brimmed tasseled
hat prior to returning to Iraq. The cardinal had surpassed his lofty
goal of rising to the position of bishop. Joining the cardinalate was
not even discussed by his grandfather since it was such an inconceivable achievement. The date of his conferral was one he would never
forget—January 20, 2037.

The young cardinal was forty-four years old, and he took plea-
sure in wearing the cardinal's scarlet cassock. He was also fond of the
golden cardinal's ring given to him by the pope, which had the pontiff's name inscribed on it. The laity would kiss it whenever in the
presence of the cardinal archbishop. The Iraqi cardinal was incredibly
close to fulfilling the promise that he made to Azfal, and he no longer
had to worry about trying to impress his religious superiors in hopes
of ascending through the church ranks. He was in a peak position as
a "prince of the church." Finally having the necessary access that he
required, he focused his attention on completing the *Jihad*.

Cardinal Ansary held the esteemed position for only five months
when tragedy struck out of the blue. On the twenty-third of June,
the beloved Pope Nelson suffered a severe brain aneurysm and was

rushed to the hospital. Regrettably, he died before the ambulance arrived at the emergency entrance. Both Catholics and non-Catholics grieved the immense loss. He was a revered pope, and it was his foresight that allowed the inexperienced Father Jassim to go to Iraq. Pope Nelson would be eternally remembered for his regime's spread of religious tolerance throughout the world and his visits to many of the world's holy sites.

The citizens of Africa sorrowfully mourned the death of the first African pope. They also exuberantly celebrated his many great accomplishments. He would forever be known as Pope Nelson: "the tolerant unifier." It was the second terrible incident that occurred on June 23 in the young clergyman's life. On the infamous date in 2003, Sabatina and her parents left Italy for America. Cardinal Ansary felt maybe if the Moretti family remained in Palestrina, Azfal might have recovered.

He flew to Rome in order to meet the other members of the conclave. The election of a new pontiff didn't take much time. The growing population of Catholics throughout South America dictated that the new pope should be a representative from the continent. A Brazilian archbishop, Cardinal Miguel Francisco Godoy, was chosen.

The election room inside of the Sistine Chapel was in an uproar at the announcement of the new pontiff's regnal name. Nothing could be done since he had the authority to do whatever he pleased under the dogma of papal infallibility. The elder and more experienced cardinals were incensed by the audacity of the iconoclastic cardinal.

Twenty days after the death of Pope Nelson, the world was introduced to Pope Peter II. It was the first time that any pope chose to take the name of the Apostle Peter. The controversy created a divide between the older traditional cardinals and the younger modern ones. Cardinal Ansary didn't agree with the new pope's decision, but as a newly appointed cardinal, he didn't feel he had the tenure to voice his opinion. He thought the choice was dishonorable to the memory of the church's founding leader. Before returning to Baghdad, the Iraqi cardinal was pulled to the side by the newly appointed *Camerlengo*, Cardinal De Luca.

"Be wary of the Barcelonan cardinal. He refers to you as 'the Muslim.' Cardinal Rodriguez says that you are not a true Catholic and that you worship *Allah* when you are alone."

Cardinal Ansary was disturbed to hear the news and hoped Rodriguez would eventually change his views. Catholics throughout the world were split on the new pope's decision to take the name Peter. Yet there was one person who was extremely excited.

"Can you believe it! We are in the term of Peter the Roman, the final bishop of Rome. 'In extreme persecution, the seat of the Holy Roman Church will be occupied by Peter the Roman, who will feed the sheep through many tribulations, at the term of which the city of seven hills will be destroyed, and the formidable judge will judge his people, *FINIS*!' Malachy was right!" Bishop Malandra exclaimed.

"Do you realize you're excited that the world might end soon? I guess once we have another pope you'll say that Malachy never said there wouldn't be more than one Peter before Peter the Roman."

"Probably, I really like his prophecies."

———◦◦◦———

A month into his papacy, his holiness flew to Rio de Janeiro and celebrated a mass for over one hundred thousand crammed followers at the "marvelous city's" famous *Maracana* Stadium. Although he was formerly the cardinal of Sao Paolo, the pope was originally from Rio de Janeiro and felt a deep connection to the people of the city. The mass was the third largest event held at the stadium. Only the 2014 World Cup and the 2016 Olympic Summer Games had larger turnouts.

Pope Peter II was the pride of Brazil. The following morning, he refused the armed escort from BOPE, the city's elite special police force, and ventured up several of the infamous *favelas*. The pontiff grew up in one of Rio's poorest shantytowns and felt that the "forgotten people" captured the soul of Brazil. The *favelados*, as he called them, received His Excellency with fond admiration. Many fought through the thick crowd to touch him as he walked among them. The experience was one that the Brazilians would never forget.

The pontiff then led his entourage to the *Corcovado* Mountains. He wanted them to pray at the small chapel dedicated to the patron saint of *Brasil, Nossa Senhora Aparecida.*

"This chapel was consecrated by the archbishop of Rio in 2006 and constructed at the foot of our famous Christ the Redeemer statue. *O Cristo Redentor* is the world's second largest statue of Jesus, standing ninety-nine-feet tall on top of a thirty-one-foot pedestal. It is a few feet shorter than the *Cristo de la Concordia* in Cochabamba, Bolivia, that stands 108 feet in height. Our statue was named one of the seven new wonders of the world in 2007 along with *Chichen Itza* in Mexico, the Colosseum in Italy, the Great Wall of China, the *Taj Mahal* in India, *Machu Picchu* in Peru, and the Palace Tombs of *Petra* in Jordan. The Christ the Redeemer statue stands at the peak of the *Corcovado* Mountains and overlooks the entire city of Rio. It is the city's symbol of Catholicism and was constructed by donations from Brazilian Catholics. It took nine years to complete. A local engineer, *Heitor da Silva Costa*, designed it with the assistance of French sculptor, Paul Landowski, at the cost of 250,000 dollars. None of you will believe the view," a knowledgeable Brazilian priest informed.

Pope Peter led the procession up the 220 stairs, which led to the foot of the statue. The unrelenting Brazilian sun increased the degree of difficulty for the extensive climb, and many in the entourage stopped for several water breaks, but the experienced pontiff barely broke a sweat.

His Excellency traveled through the South American capitals for two weeks and celebrated mass in every country, ending his tour in Mexico. After celebrating an exhaustive mass in the high altitude of Mexico City, the pontiff traveled to Los Angeles. He remained in the United States for a week, visiting some of the county's finest locations before concluding his trip with a stop at the White House.

The world was stunned when the pope altered his plans and made a surprise visit to the Communist nation of Cuba. He traveled to the mausoleum of Fidel Castro in Havana; it was the first visit to capital by a pope since the 1998 visit by Pope John Paul II. The country's Catholic minority was excited to see their religious leader on his four-day expedition through Cuba. The motive for the visit was the hope that he would open the door to more rights for the citizens. There were plans to have the new Cuban president fly to the Vatican to discuss the matter in the future.

The pope landed in Rome on September 9. He viewed his first trip as a big success and enjoyed meeting the many different citizens of the world. The Vatican was not a welcoming place for Pope Peter II. While he was away, a group of cardinals, led by Cardinal Alejandro Rodriguez of Barcelona, began to plan for his removal from power. Cardinal Rodriguez was still angry by the new pope's regnal name and called for an ecumenical council to be held in Italy. All the cardinals who disapproved of the new pontiff met at the Basilica in Palermo to discuss the future of the church.

"In AD 1415, the Council of Constance created a new canon called *Sacrosancta*. This was a declaration that the council derived its power directly from God. Therefore, the council was more powerful than the pope. The Council of Basel reaffirmed the *Sacrosancta* in 1431. These councils resulted in the election of antipopes. The antipope claimed to be the true bishop of Rome, and Catholics were forced to choose between the two church leaders. The laity remained divided until one pope was able to consolidate his complete authority over the church, which usually occurred after a death. The last antipope was Felix V, who gave up his claim to the papacy in 1449. I propose that this council elect a 'true' pope."

"I know we are all angry with our colleague for taking the name Peter II. It was a very arrogant decision on his part, but I disagree with your suggestion, Alejandro. The last thing the church needs is another schism. Pope Nelson extended the church's reach throughout the world, and we cannot risk a setback. We are responsible for electing Cardinal Godoy as the new pontiff, so what's done is done. We must move forward and work with his holiness in order for the church to continue to flourish. I do not support electing an antipope," Cardinal Borgia of Florence rebutted.

He was a respected member of the conclave and one of the most honest and loyal cardinals. The pope was lucky to have his support. A vote was taken, and the overwhelming majority agreed to refuse Cardinal Rodriguez's suggestion. The pontiff was unaware of the council since the cardinals met in a secret consistory under the auspice of a theological conference.

Cardinal Ansary was not a member of the council. Although he disagreed with the pope, he was not in the good graces of Cardinal Rodriguez. He was considered one of the new progressive cardinals. The Iraqi cardinal decided it was time for him to make a visit to Boston since he was away for far too long. On September 15, he flew from Baghdad to Logan International Airport. Anastasia met him, and on the drive to the house, he learned that Sabatina was still estranged from her parents. On his first night, he enjoyed a lovely dinner with Salvatore and Anastasia, which she lovingly prepared. They were extremely proud of his accomplishments.

"Jazz-man, we always knew you were destined for greatness. If only Tina could have been here to celebrate with us."

"Yeah, hopefully, she'll get back to being the old Tina," Cardinal Ansary said.

The cardinal was hoping to see his old friend Mario and went to the new shop located in the South End. When he entered, he was told that *El Barbero* was out of the country. Mario was in Venezuela visiting his relatives. Cardinal Ansary made his way over to the Aponte house to visit Marisol and the rest of the family. He found her home alone. She was preparing a tasty dinner when he arrived. Mrs. Aponte was amazed at the sight of the young cardinal. She had always been a devout Catholic and was immensely thrilled to have him as a guest in her home.

"Mario is married with three children, a boy and two girls," she said proudly.

The cardinal felt guilty that he wasn't a part of his best friend's life. "I want to meet the new family members. The next time I return, I will call so I can insure they will be around."

"El Cardenalito" felt a sense of happiness shower over him when he discovered that Mario and Sabatina ended their affair. The archbishop agreed to join the Aponte's for dinner. He would never leave the country without enjoying her cooking at least once.

"Mi estomago pierde su comida."

"Gracias. It is an honor to cook for my *Cardenalito."*

"Chee misses the way ju eat, *Cardenal Yassi*," Mr. Aponte added.

———◈———

A mass was held in the cardinal's honor in the chapel at Saint John's Seminary. The young seminarians were encouraged to see an alumnus of the institution rise to such great heights. The cardinal also took the opportunity to pay a visit to Uncle Lu's for some tasty bread. The staff was honored by the church leader's visit, and the archbishop savored every bight of his favorite Iraqi *Khubz* bread.

Father Mike was now the head priest at Trinity Catholic. He was in attendance and celebrated the mass as the assistant. The priest was so proud of his young pupil, and they celebrated a second mass the following evening at the Trinity Catholic Chapel. Father Mike had always suspected that young Jassim had a true calling and asked him to say a few words to the youth in attendance.

"I want all of you to believe in yourselves. You're a lucky bunch because you have access to Father Mike who is a great mentor. He will help guide all of you to reach your full potential, and it is up to each one of you to put in the hard work. I will visit again in the future, and I hope to hear many success stories."

The cardinal's final mass was held in Jamaica Plain at Our Lady of Lourdes Church. The parish was filled to capacity, and everyone in attendance was excited to celebrate the return of their esteemed cardinal. After the mass, Cardinal Ansary met with some of the admiring parishioners for a trip down memory lane. He received great news from his old buddy, Mr. Hart.

"You probably won't believe it, but the soccer league is still flourishing. We have grown to thirty full squads, with children from all over the archdiocese. The championship game is held at Gillette Stadium in Foxboro."

"I'm so proud of you for sticking with these kids. Everyone is praising me, but you are the true hero. You turned your life around and have given the youth someone to look up to. I will definitely mention your achievements to the pope."

The cardinal reached into his pocket to retrieve the keys of his rental car and exited the back entrance of the church.

"Hey, seminarian. Do you remember your little wodie?"

The voice was not recognizable to him. He turned to see a young man in his midthirties standing next to a luxury vehicle, which was idling in the middle of the lot. The distinguished gentleman was well dressed and looked to be very successful, but Cardinal Ansary could not recall whom he was.

"You probably don't remember me, but I definitely remember you. My name is Mike Woodruff. I was one of the at-risk kids that you spoke to about twenty years ago. I'm the one who foolishly quoted *Smooth Killah*."

The cardinal was taken aback. The speech he had given totally escaped his mind. A sense of accomplishment washed over him as he continued to listen.

"You may not have realized it, but your speech changed my life. As I was walking home, after leaving the church that day, I thought about the way I was living my life, and I began to cry. I cried all the way to my house. For the first time in my life, I felt like someone believed in me because I never really thought that I could be successful. I took everything you said to heart and vowed to make a change. I made a list of goals for myself, writing down everything that I wanted to achieve. I then wrote down ways to attain my goals. Some of the goals were a bit outlandish, but I wrote them down anyway. From that day forward, I didn't miss a day of school, and I gave a one hundred percent effort in all my classes. I was an 'F' student prior to meeting you, but that all changed. I became the captain of both the varsity basketball and football teams, and I received numerous scholarship offers from top FBS schools." Mike stood up taller and continued, filled with a sense of pride.

"I am proud to say I turned down all the offers. I was the valedictorian and president of my high school senior class, and I accepted a full academic scholarship to Harvard University, graduated with high honors with a double major in economics and history. I went on to attend Harvard Law School, and I am currently a successful attorney, but my true passion is working with my youth group. My beautiful wife and I have two lovely girls, and they are both doing well in school. I heard you would be here today and couldn't miss the opportunity to thank you for your inspirational speech. You changed my life."

The cardinal was overjoyed to hear what Mike said. He always assumed he was able to inspire some of the children, but actually hearing how his speech improved someone else's life was incredible. He embraced Mike and couldn't stop from tearing up. Mr. Woodruff invited the inspirational cardinal to have dinner with his family, and he gladly accepted.

The Woodruff's were very welcoming, and he enjoyed the elegant dinner. Mike's success served as extra motivation for Cardinal Ansary to continue pursuing the quest to fulfill his promise to Azfal.

Although he wasn't able to reunite the triumvirate, the trip was a spirit lifting experience, and he returned to Iraq totally rejuvenated. He was excited to begin his investigation into the inner workings of the Roman Catholic Church.

Chapter 17

In late October, the pope, who suffered from a mild case of asthma, had an attack inside the Apostolic Palace. He struggled with his asthma pump, but his condition actually worsened every time he inhaled the medicine. Pope Peter II was rushed to the Polyclinic Hospital in Rome and inexplicably died during the short ride. Everyone was in disbelief. The doctors couldn't understand why the pump didn't stop the generally nonlife-threatening attack. The controversial pontiff's death was considered a freak accident, and there was no foul play reported. The pump did not contain any foreign substance, and the official toxicology report released by the Vatican also revealed no traces of poison. The general consensus was that the his eminence brought the death upon himself when he chose the name Pope Peter II.

The church officially denounced any talk about a curse, but the theory didn't die down. *Camerlengo* of the Holy Roman Church, Cardinal Giuseppe De Luca, traveled to the hospital in order to fulfill his duty of confirming the pope's death. He struck Pope Peter's cold body three times gently on the forehead with a silver hammer, each instance calling out.

"*Miguelus Dormisne.*"

After asking the pope if he was sleeping and receiving no answer, he removed the Fisherman's Ring from the pontiff's limp finger and cut it with shears in the presence of other cardinals. The *Camerlengo's* defacing of the papal seal signified an end to the pope's reign. He was also responsible for notifying the Roman *Curia* and the dean of the College of Cardinals, Arch Bishop Dominico Borgia of Florence, of his holiness's death. *Camerlengo* De Luca assembled the conclave in the Vatican, which was the second one held within a four month span.

Cardinal De Luca was also responsible for the burial arrangements. During the *Sede Vacante,* which was the time between the death of the pope and the election of a new pontiff, the *Camerlengo* serves as the head of the Vatican City State. The College of Cardinals had the responsibility of governing the Roman Catholic Church. Cardinal Ansary arrived and offered his assistance to his godfather, but all the preparations were completed.

"This is unbelievable. He only served for a few months."

"The sudden death of Pope Peter II reminds me of the short-lived papacy of Pope John Paul I, who died in 1978 after only thirty-three days in power. Like 1978, the year 2037 is a 'year of the triple pope,'" the *Camerlengo* said.

The cardinals wanted to elect a new pontiff as quick as possible so they could lessen the blow from two papal deaths in a single year.

On November 11, Cardinal Giuseppe De Luca of Milan was elected the new bishop of Rome at the age of seventy-eight. He was the third *Camerlengo* to be elected pope in the church's history. The new pontiff avoided any controversy and chose the respectable regnal name, Pope John Paul III. He always admired the great leadership skills that John Paul II possessed, and it was the aforementioned pope who was the pontiff when Father De Luca was ordained to the priesthood.

Camerlengo De Luca was rewarded for his role in the advancement of Catholicism throughout the Middle East. His mentorship and guidance helped Cardinal Archbishop Ansary to bring peace to the region. The young cardinal received one vote, but most members of the conclave felt he was not prepared for the responsibility of leading the Roman Catholic Church. The announcement of Cardinal Ansary as the new dean of the College of Cardinals was not a big surprise since most in the conclave were aware of the Iraqi's close relationship with the pope. They ultimately believed he was the best choice.

The election of the new dean did raise the ire of one member of the cardinalate in particular. Cardinal Alejandro Rodriguez of Barcelona stood up and protested.

"How can you elect the Muslim over all the other more qualified members present in this room? This is a travesty!" he yelled while he slammed his fist on the wooden table.

Many of the cardinals knew the Barcelonan disliked the acclaimed cardinal, but this was the first instance in which he had the audacity to call him "the Muslim" to his face.

Cardinal Ansary stood up and simply quoted from the book of Proverbs 18:2: "The fool takes no delight in understanding, but rather in displaying what he thinks."

Cardinal Rodriguez realized he was out of line and immediately begged for His Excellency's forgiveness before sheepishly sitting down.

"It is not only I that you owe an apology," the new pope scolded.

The envious cardinal turned to his nemesis begrudgingly. "Please forgive my rashness."

The Iraqi cardinal simply nodded in acceptance, and the cardinals gathered around Pope John Paul III to congratulate him. Bishop Malandra did not make the trip to Rome with the archbishop since he would not have been allowed inside the Sistine Chapel. He knew that only cardinals were allowed to participate in the conclave. Once notified that Cardinal De Luca was the new pontiff, he immediately flew to the Vatican.

Bishop Malandra could hardly keep his composure when the new pope named him as the new archbishop cardinal of Baghdad. He risked his life in order to help his best friend in Iraq, and he was grateful when the pontiff acknowledged his devotion. Cardinal Ansary gave his friend a tour of the Vatican after the ceremony was concluded.

"Malachy's prophecy will eventually come true. I'm sure of it," the new dean mocked.

"The ignorant ridicule because they don't know any better. 'Look over the nations and see, and be utterly amazed! For a work is being done in your days that you would not have believed, were it told.' That's a little bit of what I call H-1:5, buddy!"

"Wow! Well done, my friend. You really reached down deep to pull that one out. I can't believe you quoted from the book of Habakkuk, impressive."

———

Pope John Paul III led the church back to prominence during the period, ending in 2037 to the year 2042. He gained the reputation as "the people's pope." The pope traveled as much as he could and was rarely in the Vatican. His first venture outside of Rome was to the recovering nation of Haiti, where he marveled at the resiliency of the people. There was very little evidence of the massive 2010 earthquake's damage. The capital city of *Port-au-Prince* was completely rebuilt, and his holiness stopped at the mausoleum built in honor of the former Haitian archbishop, who was killed during the "great quake." He called for a moment of silence and celebrated mass with a great number of Haitian Catholics in the capital city, at *Stade Sylvio Cator*. The national stadium was expanded in 2015 and had a capacity of 75,000 people. Cardinal Ansary who joined his eminence on the inspirational trip to Haiti was elated to witness a full recovery of the tragedy stricken nation. He only wished his good friend Sabatina could have been at his side.

The pope had a desire to meet the laity all over the world, and his selection of the name John Paul III was fitting. Pope John Paul II was known for his extensive traveling. In only five years, the new pontiff exceeded the record number of countries visited by his namesake. His trip to the Cape Verde Islands in late July marked the 130th nation that he visited. Pope John Paul II attained the previous mark of 129 countries after a period of over 27 years.

Pope John Paul III prepared for the celebration of his five-year anniversary. He was not done traveling the globe and planned trips to other unvisited countries, but his schedule was put on hold for the festivities. He returned to the Vatican on August 2 and had a little over three months to organize for November 11. Although the pope appeared to be in perfect health, he was hiding a secret; his personal doctor diagnosed him with Alzheimer's disease in July 2004. The finding was kept a secret to avoid a worldwide panic.

The pope's condition was growing direr each month. He couldn't make it through a mass without assistance. Cardinal Ansary was one of the few people entrusted with information and the pope's health, and the dean was great at whispering some of the words to the forgetful pontiff. It became evident that the world would soon recognize his situation, so on September 30, His Excellency revealed the secret to his synod.

"It is with great melancholy that I have summonsed this advisory board. I am forced to cancel plans for the upcoming anniversary celebration due to my deteriorating health. In an effort to allow for a smooth transition, I have made the difficult decision to abdicate my position as the bishop of Rome. The *Camerlengo* has been instructed to call together the conclave. I will remain in the Vatican, and I look forward to assisting the new pontiff."

On Saturday, October 18, the College of Cardinals gathered in the Vatican City State at the *Domus Sanctae Marthae*. The cardinal electorate would be housed there during the conclave. It was the first occasion in which a conclave was held with the preceding pope still alive since AD 1294. Cardinal De Luca would have been allowed to vote since he remained in the cardinalate, but he was over the age of eighty, which excluded him. The former pope was required to announce his resignation to the College of Cardinals, and they accepted his abdication since the decision was made of his own volition.

Cardinal De Luca removed his golden Fisherman's Ring, with its depiction of St. Peter in a boat casting his net. He handed it to the *Camerlengo* Felipe Silva, who was a cardinal from Brazil. He destroyed the ring and the papal seal. Pope John Paul III was no longer the bishop of Rome. The cardinals congregated inside the Vatican City State and talked among themselves, subtly trying to influence the voting.

"It is great to see you again, my good friend," Cardinal Ansary said.

"I'm glad to be here, but I wish it was under better circumstances. Pope John Paul III was a great leader, and it is distressing that he had to abdicate," Cardinal Malandra replied.

"Yes, but luckily for us, he will continue to be around and advise the new pontiff as much as he can. It's also great that he allowed me to invite Father Mike and Reverend Cessario to assist with the ceremony. Have you prepared yourself for the conclave?"

"It's my first one. I must admit that I am worried."

"There is nothing to worry about. The Lord will guide us in selecting the new *Pontifex Maximus*."

"The thing that worries me most is the fact that we will be locked inside of the Sistine Chapel until a new pope is elected. That could take days."

"You must not be familiar with the many changes to the election process that have occurred. We will first begin with the morning mass of the Holy Spirit for the election. In the afternoon, the conclave members will gather in the hall of blessings, in St. Peter's Basilica, and then we'll enter the guarded annex of the Sistine Chapel, chanting the hymn *Veni Creator Spiritus*. After singing 'Come Creator Spirit' inside the chapel, each cardinal will take an oath."

Cardinal Malandra nodded as he listened.

"The oath is designed to protect the secret of the election process. We are to vote for the man whom we believe is the best candidate without any outside influence. Each cardinal must vote from his heart. As the papal master of ceremonies, I'll give the command for non-conclave members to exit the room by saying '*Extra Omnes!*' The curtains will be closed, and the doors sealed. We'll be locked inside only until the end of the first day's vote. It's not that bad."

Cardinal Malandra was pleased to hear about the changes.

"Pope John Paul II created the apostolic constitution called the *Universi Dominici Gregis*. He changed the tradition of locking the College of Cardinals inside the room throughout the election process. We will be allowed to return to the *Domus Sanctae Marthae* after voting, but we will not be allowed access to any media outlets. We can't have cell phones, television, or newspapers either. We are permitted to walk around the Vatican, but the workers are not allowed to talk to us. The security will conduct several sweeps to ensure that our quarters, and the Sistine Chapel along with all relevant areas are void of listening devices.

"On the first day of voting, there will only be one election held in the afternoon. The *Camerlengo* is responsible for counting the votes, along with three assistants. Pope Nelson reinstated the use of a throne, table, and canopy. In 1978, Pope Paul VI abolished the practice because there were too many cardinals. Pope Nelson decided to line up the thrones in three rows to accommodate the large number. He felt the practice was too important, so he brought it back, and each cardinal will sit on his own throne symbolizing that we all share the responsibility of governing the church during the *Sede Vacante*. The ballots will say '*Eligo in summum pontificem*'—'I elect as supreme pontiff,' and we will right down the name of the man we believe will be the best pope. We'll then walk up to the altar, where there will be a chalice with a paten. We'll hold up the paper high to show that we have voted then slide it into the chalice. Each of the assistants will read the name then read it aloud before writing it down to be tallied. The third assistant will slide the ballot onto a needle, joining them together onto a piece of thread. Once the votes are counted and a cardinal receives two-thirds majority, he will be the new pope. Who knows, maybe we'll elect you," the dean said, smiling.

"How can I be the pope? I've only been a cardinal for a short period of time."

"There are no official guidelines as to who can be elected pontiff. Any Catholic male can be elected. He must have reached the age of reason, must not be a heretic, not be involved in a schism, and not notorious for simony."

"I didn't know that. Just as well, I am guilty of simony. I paid to be named a cardinal," Cardinal Malandra joked.

"Don't say that too loud. Rodriguez may over hear you. Technically, any man can be elected pope, even someone who is not a Catholic, as long as he has the intention of converting once he is elected."

"I thought only the top cardinals were allowed."

"Many people believe that to be the case, but it isn't true. The last person to be elected, who wasn't a cardinal, was Pope Urban VI in 1379. Basically, the cardinals have the inside track, although the new pope will most likely have to know how to speak Italian because he will also be the bishop of Rome. I would say that fluency in Italian is probably the one requirement that a man must have before being elected pope."

During the first vote, several candidates received support. "The two cardinals who received the majority of the votes are Cardinal Ansary and Cardinal Rodriguez. Cardinal *Ankundinov*, Cardinal *D'alfonso*, Cardinal *Barbalho*, and Cardinal *Ngo* also received votes," *Camerlengo* Silva said.

The ballots were attached to a piece of string and burned in the fireplace. A chemical was added to the flames in order to create the smoke's color. The laity gathered in St. Peter's Square to witness the result. The black smoke rose from the chimney of the Sistine Chapel, at 7:00 p.m., notifying all in attendance that a new pope was not elected. Custom dictates that two morning elections and two evening elections were to be held each day following the first election. The ballots were burned at noon and seven o'clock in the evening.

On the second day, the votes for the first morning ballot were split between Cardinal Rodriguez and Cardinal Ansary. The Iraqi cardinal held a larger percentage of the votes but didn't have the two-thirds majority required for his election.

In the second morning vote of October 19, the *Camerlengo* announced the selection of Dean Ansary as the new bishop of Rome. The other cardinals lowered the purple canopy over their chairs. Only Cardinal Ansary's remained folded. Although it was the dean of the College of Cardinals' duty to ask the chosen man if he accepted the honor, the duty fell on the vice dean, Cardinal Luis Amado of Portugal.

"*Cardinale* Jassim Ibrahim Azfal Ansary, *non si accetta l'onore di essere il nuovo Pontefice?*"

"*Acceto,*" the overwhelmed cardinal replied.

"*Quale nome vi essere chiamato?*"

"*Papa* Ali."

Pope Ali became the 269th bishop of Rome. He chose the regnal name Ali in honor of the fourth caliph of Islam, who was the final leader to rule over both *Sunni* and *Shi'a* Muslims. He remembered Azfal's speech and thought the name was fitting. The ballots from the two morning elections were gathered and burned in the fireplace. A different chemical was added to the flames, and white smoke billowed from the chimney of the Sistine Chapel. The Bell of St. Peter's Basilica rang out resoundingly, and the laity who were gathered in the St. Peter's Square erupted in jubilation.

The new pope was outfitted in his white cassock, regalia, and insignia. Pope Ali did not wear the *triregnum*.

"The white *zucchetto* will be fine. I don't need the 'triple crown.' The three-leveled ceremonial headdress will make me look kingly, and I want to be equal to the people. For my introduction to the public, I will be in my choir dress," the new pope announced.

The protodeacon of the College of Cardinals, Cardinal *Bernardo*, stepped out onto the papal balcony of St. Peter's Basilica. He had two assistant priests on each side flanking him. The appearance of the vice dean caused an eruption of cheers from the faithful crowd. One of the assistants held out a microphone for the cardinal, and the other held a large red folder for him to read from. Cardinal Bishop Amado waved to the attentive crowd and spoke in Italian, Spanish, Arabic, English, and French respectively.

"*Fratelli sorelle carisimi, felicísimos hermanos y hermanas, habiba khoya wa oukht*, dear brothers and sisters, *chers frères et súrs.*" The crowd cheered as their respective language was spoken.

"*Annuntio vobis magnum.*" He paused and the crowd cheered wildly.

"*Habemus Papam!*" The crowd cheered even louder.

"*Eminentissimum ac reveredissimum dominum.*" The laity awaited the name of the chosen cardinal.

"*Dominum Jassimum!*" American, Iraqi, and Italian flags waved joyously.

"*Sacntae Romanae Ecclesiae Cardinalem*, Ansary." The roar of the crowd reached its highest decibel level.

"*Qui sibi nomen imposuit, Aliis Primi!*"

The vice dean waved to the jubilant crowd, and the three men stepped back inside. The balcony remained empty for a short moment, and the crowd murmured in anticipation, continuing to wave the flags of their respective countries. The large red curtains were reopened, and the first to appear was Father Mike, who was holding a golden cross. He stepped to the left side of the balcony, and Pope Ali walked forward, waving to the adoring multitude. Cardinal Gianni Malandra and Reverend Arthur Cessario flanked him on one side while his predecessor Cardinal Giuseppe De Luca stood on the other side. The new pontiff waved to his followers as they cheered. The ovation lasted a few minutes, and the assistant priest returned with the microphone. His holiness thanked the throng of passionate Catholics in Italian. He gave a brief speech followed by the traditional blessing.

"*Urbi et Orbi*."

The laity cheered as the pontiff waved to them before entering the Basilica.

"What does that mean?" asked one reveler.

"It's Latin. It means 'to the city and to the world,'" his friend responded.

The papal inauguration mass was held five days later. Pope Ali invited all his family and friends to attend, and to his delight, Mario agreed to make the trip, but he backed out at the last minute due to illness. Mrs. Aponte wouldn't have missed the inaugural mass for anything, and her three grandchildren accompanied the devout *Católica*; Mario's wife attended as well.

"It is great to finally meet you, Melanie," Pope Ali said.

"Likewise, I have heard so much about you. It's a shame that Mario couldn't make it. He was really looking forward to catching up with you. Is it true that you had to scoop out his vomit from the urinal in Victor's shop with your bare hands?"

"Yeah, don't remind me." He shivered from the recollection.

Luciana drove to the Vatican from Palestrina and enjoyed the ceremony with the others. She felt privileged to be a close friend of the two latest bishops of Rome. She was extremely proud of her godson.

The Malandras also made the trip, and the fact that his son was the new dean of the College of Cardinals overwhelmed Tomaso. He gave his word to Father *Portella* to raise his son as a priest and succeeded in his mission.

"You have made me proud, my son. Because of your devotion to the church, we have paid back, in full, the gracious help that we received."

"Father *Portella* was a great man, and I was lucky to serve as his apprentice when I returned to Florence. His funeral was one of the saddest days in my life. I have arranged for us to drive to *Fiorenze*, on Monday, so we can visit his tombstone."

Anastasia and Salvatore had mixed emotions. They were proud of Jassim but felt like horrible parents because Sabatina wasn't as driven as the new pope. She always received better grades than he did, and they couldn't stop thinking about the prominence she could have risen to if she applied herself. Sabatina was still at odds with her parents, so she didn't respond to the invitation. The pontiff still had strong feelings for her, and he remained deeply hurt by her absence.

When his eminence asked about his good friend, Anastasia broke down in tears. "I don't know what happened to her, she is not the same person."

He embraced her, but she was too distraught to explain what happened. He did his best to help her gain her composure, leading her into a private room. They sat on a couch, and Pope Ali tried his best to get her to open up, but she refused to discuss the matter any further. He was a hurt because they have always had an open relationship. Anastasia was always comfortable enough to confide in him, and his mind was racing, trying to figure out what Sabatina could have possibly done.

"I guess this isn't the right time for us to discuss, Tina. She must have done something severe for you to shut me out," he said.

The pope knew his effort was futile and stopped questioning her. Anastasia gathered herself, and the two of them rejoined the others in the hall. He was saddened by the fact that the triumvirate was unable to reunite yet again; the absence of his friends dampened the momentous occasion. Marisol received a personal request from the pontiff to prepare a meal for the group, and she was honored to serve the leader of the Roman Catholic Church.

It was at the ceremonial mass that Pope Ali received his *pallium* and Fisherman's Ring. The new dean of the College of Cardinals, Cardinal Gianni Malandra, slipped the ring onto the pope's third finger of his right hand. The other cardinals were impressed with Bishop Malandra's loyalty to the new pope and his devotion to the Roman Catholic Church. His bravery for moving to Iraq was also noted as a reason for his election as the new dean of the College of Cardinals. After the papal coronation, his holiness was joined by family and friends in the dining room, of the *Domus Sanctae Marthae*, to share the lovely meal prepared by Mrs. Aponte.

"What is a *pallium*?" asked Mario's eldest daughter Cheyenne.

"The *pallium* is this narrow band with six black crosses. It represents the good shepherd who carries the Lamb of God over his shoulders. The *pallium* is made from the wool of special white sheep that are raised by monks from the Order of the Strict Observance," Pope Ali answered.

Salvatore was uncomfortable and spoke up, "Hey, Jazz-man—I mean, Pope Jazz-man. Is it a sin to drink? Will I not be permitted to J-Walk inside the Vatican?"

Before he could finish his sentence, a bottle of Blue Label was placed directly in front of him, and he attacked it with the precision and determination of a great white shark going after a wounded harbor seal.

Two days following the inaugural ceremony, Pope Ali designed his coat of arms. He included the Tigris and Euphrates Rivers, running down the center of his ornamental shield, which was blue in honor of the Massachusetts shield. On the left side, he placed a golden yellow and maroon soccer ball, in the colors of *AS Roma*. It also symbolized his successful soccer career in high school and college. On the right side, he placed the sculpture of the Capitoline Triad, a representation of his time in Palestrina. In between the rivers, he placed a powder blue dragon, honoring the gift from Azfal.

Above the shield, he placed the papal tiara, a traditional component, that was a staple in all papal coat of arms. Behind the shield were crossing gold and silver keys. The keys represented verses 18 and 19 in chapter 16 of the book of Matthew, and they were also a traditional component of all papal coat of arms. "I will give you keys to the kingdom of heaven. Whatever you bind on earth shall be bound in heaven."

Chapter 18

Pope Ali was eager to begin establishing a trust with the Catholic citizens of the world. He gave a speech a week after his coronation in which he announced his aim to rid the church of all corruption. Transparency and serving the Lord were his goals.

"I would like to begin by introducing two exceptional gentlemen—Mike Woodruff and Zachary Hart." The pope paused while the men, standing at his side, received a rousing round of applause. "Their inspirational stories have motivated me to continue serving the Lord as best as I can. They are currently mentors to many youth in Boston, and I look forward to working closely with them in the future. The will of God must be served, not the will of man." The men returned to their seats.

Pope Ali also took the time to discuss the abdication of power by his predecessor. "I know that papal resignation is a rare occurrence since it gives the appearance that the pope is quitting on the laity, but I want to assure everyone that nothing could be further from the truth. Pope John Paul III was a great leader. He is a mentor and dear friend. He wanted to continue to lead the church, but his memory loss prevented him from being able to effectively serve the children of God. It was with great sadness that he retired, and I am grateful that Cardinal De Luca will continue to be my mentor. His abdication is not unprecedented, but in my eyes, it is the first to be carried out according to canon law.

"In 1294, Pope Celestine V was the first to resign from his position as the bishop of Rome, but his resignation was more controversial. Pope Celestine felt that power was a temptation and he didn't like having it. The pontiff had no desire to control the will of others because he was a simple man with a true calling. He is best known for reversing the decree of Pope Gregory X who ordered the shutting down of the conclave.

"Celestine's top advisor, Cardinal *Benedetto Caetani*, informed him that papal resignation was allowed by church doctrine and pushed him to retire. Pope Celestine established the proper proce-dure for a papal resignation before actually abdicating. It was later revealed that Cardinal *Caetani* was an extremely ambitious man who forced the pope to resign.

"Cardinal *Caetani* was quickly elected the new bishop of Rome and took the regnal name, Pope Boniface VIII. One of his first acts as pontiff was to arrest his predecessor. Celestine V attempted an escape, but he was quickly apprehended and held in the Fortress of *Fumone* in Italy. In 1296, he was assassinated under the order of the pope. It was Boniface VIII who established the '*Unam Sanctae*,' the pontiff's sole power over all spiritual and temporal matters. He once famously said, 'It is altogether necessary to the salvation for every human creature to be subject to the Roman pontiff. I am Caesar, I am the emperor.' Boniface adopted Pope Celestine's regulations for resignation into canon law, but as I see it, the resignation of Pope Celestine V was illegal since he was forced to resign. Canon law stip-ulates that the College of Cardinals can only accept a pope's abdica-tion if the decision was not influenced by outside forces.

"The only other incident of papal resignation was in 1415 when Pope Gregory XII abdicated. The decision was solely his, but he died before the conclave elected a new pontiff."

Pope Ali revealed that he would scour through the Vatican Secret Archives in order to expose the wrongs of the past. He vowed to set the church on a righteous path before closing the press conference.

"I leave you with a bit of scripture from the book of Proverbs chapter 1 verses 4 and 5: 'That resourcefulness may be imparted to the simple, to the young man knowledge and discretion. A wise man by hearing them will advance in learning, an intelligent man will gain sound guidance.' God bless all of you."

Most Vatican insiders were concerned after his "grand procla-mation." The pope was still in disbelief that he managed to rise to the highest position in the church because he never considered it as a pos-sibility. The thought of his grandfather watching over him helped to push him to fulfill the promise. He wanted to gather some important information before revealing his ultimate plan to *Ayatollah* Abtahi.

Pope Ali knew that Cardinal Malandra had a true faith, so he decided to keep the dean of the College of Cardinals in the dark. The pontiff's extensive research helped him to clear up some questionable actions by the Roman Catholic Church.

On Friday, November 14, his eminence held a news conference in which he announced his findings. He first blessed the laity before proceeding with the list.

"I first want to talk about some of the past inconsistencies of the church. As a seminarian, I came across a website, www.futurechurch. org/fpm/history.htm, in which there was a list brief history of celi-bacy in the church. With my access to the Vatican Secret Archives, I wanted to see if the claims were true. To my surprise, I found that everything was accurate. As far as the vow of celibacy is concerned, it is common knowledge that most of the apostles were married, and I believe if St. Peter was married, then maybe priests should be allowed to marry. In the early church, there were women serving as priests, and a majority of priests were married men, but a shift in church pol-icy occurred a couple centuries later. The new belief was that a priest could not be perfect if he were married. Yet a majority of the priests remained wedded. An interesting decree was issued at the Council of Elvira in the year 306. The members decided that priests were no longer allowed to sleep with their wives the night before giving a mass. The *Nicean* Creed later prevented priests from marrying after being ordained, and the church disallowed the ordination of women at the Council of *Laodicea* in the year 352. It was later decreed that priests could no longer sleep with their wives by Pope Siricius, who left his wife to become the pontiff.

"Priests were excommunicated if they were found with a wife as part of the new canon law, decided at the second Council of Tours held in the year 567. Pope Pelagius II decided to allow priests to stay married as long as they didn't will their estates to wives and children. The concern of the church was material possession not God's will. It was Pope Gregory 'the great' who decreed that all sexual desires were sinful, and I found documents that showed that there were still a great number of priests who were married centuries after his decree. The worst incident that I discovered was the Council of *Aix-la-Chapelle* held in the year 836. Members revealed that they had knowledge of convents and monasteries that performed abortions on the mistresses of priests. The clergy also committed infanticide to cover up the illegitimate births. I couldn't believe the church leaders committed such deplorable activities as a cover-up.

"Pope Gregory VII created the vow of celibacy in the year 1074, and many priests were forced to leave their wives. Pope Urban II worsened the situation when he forced wives of priests to be sold into slavery and left the children to be abandoned. Pope Calistus II invalidated all marriages by church clerics, but even with all the changes in church policy happening throughout the centuries, there were still many married priests and some ordained women. I didn't even want to look into the atrocities committed during the inquisition, not believing I could stomach what I uncovered. I have assigned the task of reviewing the inquisition to some of the younger priests under the guidance of a trusted colleague.

"It was Pope Pius IX who established the infallibility of the pope, and I think some of my predecessors may have used the decree to abuse the people they were elected to protect. Pope Pius veered from the old position of the church and decreed that sex can be good and holy. He allowed for the laity to consummate their marriages without the guilt of sin. It is interesting to note that Pope Pius was a married man who was previously ordained to the Lutheran Church.

"Pope John XXIII allowed for married Catholics to continue claiming their virginity, and Pope Paul VI allowed for celibacy dispensations. I guess he felt that as long as one has permission from the church, sex was okay. In the 1970s, women were allowed to be ordained in Czechoslovakia to serve females who were imprisoned by Communists. It was Pope John Paul II who ended the celibacy dispensations, maybe I should consider allowing them once again. I also found many popes who were the sons of popes. There were also many popes who had children after the practice was disallowed. I suggest to those of you who want to learn about more of the papal abuses to read *The Family* by the great Mario Puzo or *The March of Folly* by the esteemed Barbara Tuchman. Puzo tells the story of the controversial Pope Alexander VI, and Tuchman uncovers the ungodly lives of the 'Renaissance popes.'

"For those who question my decision to disclose secrets of the church, I can only say if the duty of the pontiff is to deceive the followers of Christ, through lies and deception, I would not want to be the pope. I vow to continue my search for the truth, and I will leave you with scripture from the book of Psalm 14 verses 4 through 6: 'Will these evildoers never learn? They devour my people as they devour bread; they do not call upon the Lord. They have good reason, then, to fear; God is with the company of the just. They would crush the hopes of the poor, but the poor have the Lord as their refuge.' God bless all of you."

Chapter 19

Monday, November 17, Pope Ali was astonished to learn of the secret room called *Lo scrigno del Papa*. The entrance was hidden inside of the *Cappella Paolina* in the Apostolic Palace.

"The Pauline Chapel was constructed under the order of Pope Paul III and completed in 1550. It was named after the pope. It is assessable from the palace's royal room called the *Sala Regia*. Your holiness can decide whether or not to have the chapel refurbished," the *Camerlengo* informed.

"I enjoy looking at the depictions of the conversion of St. Paul and the crucifixion of St. Peter painted by *Michelangelo*. The room is well furnished. A renovation will not be necessary because the chapel is stunning. Although it would be pleasing if you can arrange for an artist to add a piece of decorative trim around the walls, with triangles designed after the King *Abdullah* Mosque in Amman," the pope replied.

The *Oberst*, who was the commandant of the Pontifical Swiss Guard, alerted Pope Ali to the existence of the papal coffer. He arranged for his eminence to enter the secret chamber. The Swiss Guard was responsible for ensuring that only the pontiff had access to the secret room, and it was also guaranteed that no one could enter the papal coffer during the *Sede Vacante*. Once a pope dies, the *Camerlengo* removes a silk rope chain from the pontiff's neck, which is attached to a medieval key that has an oval handle with an ark carved into it. The *Camerlengo* wears the chain until the election of a new pope, but he is never informed of the key's purpose.

Other than the pope, there are only five men who knew about the papal coffer. They are the five commissioned officers of the Swiss Guard: the *Oberst*, *Oberstleutnant*, Kaplan, Major, and *Hauptmann*. Each officer had to take an oath to preserve the secret of the hidden room. The *Hauptmann's* duty was to stand at the entrance of the *Cappella Paolina* while the pope was inside with the other four officers. His responsibility was to ensure that no one entered the Pauline Chapel while the pope was inside *Lo scrigno del Papa*.

The *Cappella Paolina* has a faux floor under the first two rows of pews on its left side. The fake floor is hollow in order to reduce its weight, and the two pews are bolted to it. Even with the hollowed floor, lifting the attached pews takes the strength of four men.

The officers struggled a bit but managed to lift the large section. A set of stairs was revealed inside of the hole, and at the bottom was a plain wooden door with an ancient medieval lock. Pope Ali was excited to finally learn of the key's purpose, removing it from around his neck and carefully walking down the steep stairway. The officers were not allowed to follow him, so they sat down in the third pew awaiting his return.

The pontiff unlocked the door and noticed the room was too dark. He called up to the knowledgeable *Oberst*.

"Thomas, how am I supposed to see anything? Where is the light switch?"

"Pardon me for not informing you about the torch, your holiness. Lift the third step."

The pope lifted up the step and saw twelve boxes of matches. He grabbed the one that was already opened and struck the match, using it to light a small fanwise-shaped silver fir and pinewood torch that was supported by a bracketed cross-shaped sconce. With the lit torch, he entered the pitch-black room and used it to light six identical torches attached to the walls. The torches each had a cross on the handle, and there was an open sconce where he placed the original torch before closing the heavy wooden door. The positioning of the torches allowed for the room to be uniformly lit. He was impressed by the effective medieval technology.

There was an altar in the center of the chamber with an ark on top of it and a golden plaque on its side. "The Ark of the Covenant. Discovered at King Solomon's Temple AD 1128. Given to Pope Honorius II by the Poor Fellow Soldiers of Christ and the Temple of Solomon."

Pope Ali was in disbelief. Everything that he learned about the ark was true. It was made from acacia wood, and both the interior and exterior were plated with pure gold. Four gold rings were on the bottom of the box, with two acacia poles that were also plated with gold. It was covered by the *kapporet* with two cherubs facing each other. The *kapporet* was also made of acacia wood and plated with pure gold. The golden wings of the cherubs were touching at the tips, and from what he could tell, the dimensions were exactly as described in the scriptures. The length was forty-five inches with a height of twenty-seven inches and a width of twenty-seven inches.

The ark's wood reminded the pope of Azfal's acacia bed. He wondered in a quiet whisper. "Maybe the ark is a sign from my grandfather." Believing he was one step closer to fulfilling the promise that he made, the pontiff was amused when he thought about filmmakers Steven Spielberg and George Lucas' epic movie *Raiders of the Lost Ark*. His eyes were tightly shut, like the movie's hero Indiana Jones, while he lifted the twenty-five-pound *kapporet*. In jest, the pope wondered if the angel of death would burn his flesh in the manner he killed the Nazis during the film's haunting scene. After a few seconds, he felt safe enough to open his eyes and placed the ark's covering on top of the altar.

His holiness peered inside the opened ark and observed two stone tablets with Hebrew script on the surfaces. He removed one of the tablets and ran his fingers over the smooth face. The writing was inscribed in the stone, but he couldn't feel the letters.

This is clearly not of this world, he thought.

At the bottom of the ark were pieces of broken stone, and most of the pieces had Hebrew letters on them. It was finally confirmed, both the original tablets and the second copy were placed inside Moses's ark.

Pope Ali believed the ark looked more Egyptian than Hebrew since the lavish decorations were done in the style that was consistent with some of Azfal's art pieces. He assumed the craftsman must have learned his skill from the Egyptians, as the experts believed. After placing the tablet back inside and replacing the *kapporet*, he walked around the room. The wall consisted of seven large individual segments that were placed in a particular order, and there was a list of basic information handwritten on the wall in Italian:

I.   It is the pope's duty to ensure that a tinderbox with a fire striker, flint, and tinder is readily available.

II.   This room is solely for the eyes of the pontiff.

III.   Pope Sixtus IV constructed the room during the restoration of the *Capella Magna* between 1477–1480.

IV.   The ark has been in the possession of the pope since the Knights Templar brought it to Rome in 1129.

V.   Pope Honorius II originally hid the ark under the Lateran Palace.

VI.   The ark was secretly moved form the Lateran Palace and placed in this room by Pope Sixtus IV.

VII.   Pope Julius II felt the need to improve the room's decor when he became pontiff in 1503.

VIII. Pope Julius II commissioned seven artists to paint each segment of the story of the ark in 1505.

IX.   The pope commissioned Michelangelo, Leonardo da Vinci, Botticelli, Ghirlandaio, Perugino, Francia, and Rafael to complete the works.

X.   The segments were attached to the walls, and the room was completed in 1506.

Julius II PP. 1506

The astounded pontiff studied each painting closely, and the accompanying segments had an identification placard explaining its depiction. Each illustration of the ark, in the different segments, was unique to the artists' imagination. *Michelangelo di Lodovico Buonarroti Simoni* painted the first segment. He included Moses returning from Mount Sinai with the two tablets of the Ten Commandments in his hands and added the creation of the ark of the covenant by a master craftsman. A bright light in the sky was a depiction of the Lord. The Hebrew people were surrounding the ark as they gathered in celebration.

Leonardo da Vinci created the second segment. He painted the Ten Commandments being placed inside the ark by Moses. The second element was the placement of the ark inside the temple of King Solomon in Jerusalem.

Allesandro di Mariano di Vanni Filipepi received the commission for the third segment. *Botticelli's* addition contained the destruction of Jerusalem by Neo-Babylonian emperor, King Nebuchadnezzar II in 586 BC, in which the temple of King Solomon was demolished. King Josiah is shown hiding the ark underneath the temple prior to the siege.

Davide Ghirlandaio di Fiorenze painted the fourth segment. He added the rebuilding of King Solomon's Temple in 516 BC and also its destruction at the hands of the Roman Emperor Vespasian in AD 70. *Ghirlandaio* painted the ark hidden underground, deep beneath the demolished temple.

PietroPerugino was hired to paint the fifth segment. It contained the construction of the Dome of the Rock over the ruins of King Solomon's Temple in AD 691 by *Caliph Abd al Malik*. The ark was painted underground beneath the Dome of the Rock.

Francesco Raibolini of *Bologna* added the sixth segment. *Francia* painted Pope Urban II giving an inspirational speech to a group of the first crusaders before they left for Jerusalem. Over the pope's head in quotations were the words "*trovare l'arca, e portarlo a me.*" The first crusaders were drawn capturing the Dome of the Rock from the Muslims in AD 1099, and the ark was again painted underneath the Dome of the Rock.

Pope Julius II chose *Raffaello Sanzio da Urbino* to complete the final piece. His painting depicted the establishment of the Knights

Templar headquarters in the *Al-Aqsa* Mosque adjacent to the Dome of the Rock in the year AD 1119. Once more, the ark was painted under the dome. *Rafael's* segment also displayed a group of knights with red crosses painted on their breastplates, uncovering the ark. There were also two knights on a single brown horse with red crosses on their shields and breastplates, which was the seal of the Knights Templar. Underneath the horse, their motto was written, "Not for self, but for God." No date was painted for the discovery of the ark. *Rafael* was not privy to that information. The ark has remained hidden in the room, and its secret has been guarded ever since by each bishop of Rome.

Pope Ali was the only man alive who knew where the ark of the covenant was located, and he was angered by the fact that his predecessors decided to keep such an important historical artifact to themselves. The pope believed the ark should be placed on display so all the world's citizens could view it. He felt the story of the Prophet Moses was significant to Jews, Christians, and Muslims alike.

The ark of the covenant is not to be the sole possession of the pontiff. It belongs to the Lord's people, he thought.

The pope placed the lid on top of the ark and extinguished the torches. He locked the door of the cryptic chamber and carefully walked up the stairs.

"May we seal the entrance, Your Excellency?" asked the *Oberst*.

The pope nodded his head, and the officers of the Swiss Guard lifted the floor over the clandestine entrance. Pope Ali was curious to learn all he could about the papal coffer. He searched for more information regarding its creation in the Vatican Secret Archives. He discovered there were many references to the room from different popes throughout the centuries. In the documents, it was referred to as the "papal ark."

Vatican historians had always been baffled by the term, unable to discover what it meant. Pope Ali found out the ark remained hidden inside the Lateran Palace for centuries, and the popes only revealed the location of the ark to their most trusted advisors. Pope Sixtus IV was the one who decided the holy artifact should be more accessible for the pontiff's viewing, so he ordered the construction of the private chamber. After gathering the necessary information, Pope Ali planned a press conference for what he called a "historic revelation."

Four days later, media from every news outlet around the world dispatched camera crews to cover the pope's big announcement. His holiness sat confidently in front of the microphone, absolutely certain that he was doing the right thing.

"I truly believe that my duty as the bishop of Rome is to serve God and his people. I am the leader of the Roman Catholic Church, but I feel that it is my responsibility to look after the well-being of all God's children, whether they are religious or nonreligious. I vowed to scour through the Vatican Secret Archives in search of all past abuses of power by my predecessors and their constituency. So far, I've kept my word, and I will continue to do so. Today, my announcement is relevant to everyone but especially Muslims, Jews, and Christians because I have uncovered a secret that will interest all 'people of the book.' Our three religions are founded on the same great tradition, and it is the Prophet Moses who I will discuss today. After Neo-Babylonian Emperor, King Nebuchadnezzar II, destroyed the first temple of King Solomon, the ark of the covenant was believed to be lost to the world. Many theories regarding its location have been proposed, some more outlandish than others."

Pope Ali paused for affect before continuing.

"I have discovered the true story of the ark!" he boldly exclaimed.

The pope continued after peaking the interest of the attentive audience. "The claims by Ethiopian Orthodox Christians that they are the protectors of the ark of the covenant are untrue. The ark is not guarded inside the chapel in Axum, Ethiopia. Prior to the Neo-Babylonian siege of Jerusalem, the cunning Hebrew King *Josiah* learned of the imminent attack and ordered a secret underground storage space to be constructed beneath the original temple of Solomon. The ark was hidden in the depths and sealed prior to King *Josiah's* death in 607 BC. The great leader did not want the holy artifact to be possessed by the Neo-Babylonians.

"In 586 BC, King *Nebuchadnezzar II* led his army to sack the city of the reigning Jewish king, *Zedekiah*, who had betrayed the

Babylonian. All the men who knew about the ark's location died at the hands of the Neo-Babylonian troops, and it was lost to the world for centuries. No one even knew if it still existed. The temple of King Solomon was rebuilt in 516 but again destroyed by the Roman Emperor Vespasian in AD 70. It was *Caliph Abd al Malik* who constructed the Dome of the Rock on the site of the Jewish temples in 691.

"In 1095, Pope Urban II ordered the Catholics of Europe to unite so they could take control of the Holy City from the Muslims, and he gave special instructions for the men to search throughout the city and find the ark. The first crusaders successfully gained control of Jerusalem in 1099, but the ark was nowhere to be found. In 1119, the Poor Fellow Soldiers of Christ and the temple of Solomon established their order and founded its headquarters at the *Al-Aqsa* Mosque on the Temple Mount. The knights searched for the ark, and in 1128, it was discovered underneath the Dome of the Rock. They secretly transported the religious artifact to Rome and entrusted it to the pope in 1129. Pope Honorius II awarded the Knights Templar by giving the order an official papal sanctioning. The pontiff hid the ark under the Lateran Palace, and it remained there until the year 1477, which is when Pope Sixtus IV ordered the restoration of the *Capella Magna*. He also constructed a secret room under the Pauline Chapel, and the ark was moved to the hidden chamber.

"Pope Julius II commissioned paintings to be created by seven artists—*Michelangelo, Leonardo da Vinci, Botticelli, Ghirlandaio, Perugino, Francia,* and *Rafael.* The paintings were completed independently of one another in 1505 and placed in the room in 1506 by the pope and his most trusted advisors. The collective paintings tell the story of the ark, and each artist created a large segment, which was attached to the secret chamber's walls. The placards accompanying the segments explain the ark's history.

"The Poor Fellow Soldiers of Christ and the temple of Solomon were the only lay people who knew of the arks whereabouts. The Knights Templar were impoverished soldiers of God, which is why their seal contained two knights sharing one horse. The knights were paid handsomely to keep the secret of the ark hidden, and as a stipulation for the order being endorsed by the church, they swore an oath to keep the location of the ark a secret. The whereabouts of the ark of the covenant has remained undisclosed for centuries, believed to be lost forever. Pope Clement V disbanded the order under pressure from King Philip IV of France in 1312, and the leaders of the order were rounded up and killed in order to preserve the secret. Both the pope and the king shared a mutual desire to strip knights of their power. The French monarch was almost penniless and indebted to the Knights Templar, and he desired to seize their riches. The Muslim forces had regained control of Jerusalem, so the knights were no longer needed to protect Christian pilgrims who traveled the dangerous route to the Holy Land.

"Pope Julius II was obsessed with art among his many vices, which is why he commissioned the secret paintings. He also decided the secret should remain with the pope, so after his trusted advisors helped him complete the papal coffer, he arranged for each of them to be murdered. In the year 1506, the guilt-ridden and paranoid pontiff established the Swiss Guard, whose singular purpose was to ensure his protection from any future acts of retaliation by the families of his advisors. The guard has since remained the personal protectors of the pontiff.

"Pope Julius also established a method to keep the knowledge of the secret chamber solely with the pontificate. He entrusted the *Camerlengo* with the duty of protecting the 'ark key,' while the officers of the Swiss Guard were responsible for guarding the location of the hidden chamber. Pope Julius's flawless system has kept the ark a secret since his reign.

"I feel that the ark is for everyone to view, which is why I am revealing its secret today. I will arrange for an encasement to be built so the ark and the accompanying paintings can be properly displayed. The housing will be a permanent 'wilderness tabernacle,' and the city state of Jerusalem will be its new home. This concludes my announcement, and I will not be taking any questions. Be assured that I will continue to search for more revelations. Thank you all for giving me the oppurtunity to hold this press conference. I leave you with verse 28 from chapter 18 in the book of Sirach: 'Any learned man should make wisdom known, and he who attains to her should declare her praise.' God bless all of you."

The news was stunning. It was the major headline throughout the world, and Pope Ali decided to allow one camera from CNN to film inside of the papal coffer. He knew the world would not be able to wait for the encasement to be erected before seeing the ark. CNN broadcast the interior of the room to a record audience. It was the single most significant news event since British journalist David Frost interviewed disgraced American President Richard M. Nixon in 1977.

Many experts in the world of art agreed that the paintings were probably the most essential works ever uncovered. It was anticipated that the *Mona Lisa* would be surpassed as the most famous painting in the world. The Vatican received a barrage of calls from interested museums, all offering to buy the exclusive ark collection. The first offer was for five hundred million dollars, but it was instantly turned down, and the amount continued to rise into the billions. The prime minister of Jerusalem agreed that the Holy City was the proper home for both the artwork and the ark, and construction on the structure was commenced. Pope Ali was moving in the right direction, and he hoped to continue uncovering more hidden church secrets.

Plans for the ark of the covenant's new home were finalized a month after the pope's astonishing announcement. A greenish bulletproofed glass structure was to be constructed outside of the Dome of the Rock. The prime minister discussed many different options with the Vatican, Jewish leaders, and Muslim leaders as to the best location for the structure because logistically the interior of the dome was not able to provide the necessary space. They all agreed to use the empty space outside the Dome of the Rock to construct the large glass encasement.

Construction of the beautiful bulletproof structure lasted three months. The ark, along with the seven paintings, was heavily protected as it was transported to Jerusalem. The new structure was impenetrable with armed security guarding it around the clock. The ark was placed in the center of the tinted glass structure, and the paintings were lined up behind it. The two stone tablets were placed on each side, and the encasement was officially opened on Saturday, March 21, 2043. Spectators from every corner of the globe traveled to the Holy City to view the ark and its accompanying paintings.

Rubbing the bottom of the tablets became the new tradition for all followers of the Prophet Moses. Pope Ali was focused on trying to unearth more church secrets, so he planned to visit the site in the distant future. The ark of the covenant became the most visited artifact in the world as anticipated. The money generated from ticket sales was divided between the government of Jerusalem and the League of Middle Eastern Nations.

Chapter 20

Pope Ali continued to look through the archives while the government of Jerusalem was constructing the encasement for the ark, making several significant discoveries and arranging for another press conference. The pope sat in front of the world media, on Friday, March 27, and revealed information that would shake the foundation of the Roman Catholic Church to its core. The pope's enlightening announcements became known as "the Friday revelations."

"I was pleased by the reports of the vast number of people, representing all the world's religions, who are making the pilgrimage to see the ark of the covenant. I feel the world is becoming a more spiritual place, which is my aim. Today, I will discuss three controversial topics.

"The first topic I want to deal with is pedophilia. I reviewed many church documents, and I was greatly disturbed by what I discovered. In the past, the Vatican has been too lenient with priests who have been accused of pedophilia. I have issued a papal bull stating that any priest, who is to be a pedophile, will be immediately excommunicated from the church and the proper authorities will be instantly notified. The Roman Catholic Church will offer its full cooperation to all investigations. I cannot allow the earlier practice, of dealing with the matter internally, to continue. We must send a strong message to the world that the Roman Catholic Church is vehemently against pedophilia. I assure you that the crime will no longer be associated with the Vatican.

"I also want to discuss homosexuality. I personally do not have any problems with anyone who is a homosexual because I believe that we are all children of God. I am not sure if sexual orientation is a choice, and I understand that the official church stance on the subject is that homosexuality is a sin, but I want to keep an open mind about the matter. The church should not be exclusionary toward any group of people, and I have assembled a panel of cardinals to look into the matter further. They will report their findings to me, and I will decide on the proper course to pursue, but at the present moment, I am not ready to make any changes to the church's current policy concerning homosexuals.

"I have one more topic that I want to discuss, and it is the most explosive of the three. In the Vatican Secret Archives, I have discovered some books that have been lost to the world. I haven't had time to go over all the content, so I decided to focus on a few themes. The most important of my discoveries is the "original Bible," which predates the first Council of Nicaea held in AD 325. It was at the council that the leaders of the church agreed on which gospels should be contained in the canon. It is common knowledge that many books were omitted, but they also edited some of the content throughout the books of the New Testament."

The murmuring audience was stunned, and hoped the Pope would be able to substantiate his controversial remark.

"One of the major corrections is the description of the death of the apostle Judas Iscariot, who was in charge of holding the group's finances. In the original Bible accounts, Judas kills himself in a slightly different manner than the New Testament description. When I read the actual events, I understood why the council members felt the need to edit it because the graphic violence was bone chilling. I will allow you to read it for yourselves, but I give a stern warning. It is not for the faint of heart."

The pope lifted up a pamphlet, containing the story of the disgraced apostle. "Following my announcement, these will be available for anyone who wishes to read about Judas.

"The original Bible has revealed a massive cover-up. As far as Mary Magdalene is concerned, I want to ensure all of you that she was not married to Jesus, nor did he have any sexual relationship with her. There has been much debate over Mary Magdalene's association with the Savior since the discovery of the Dead Sea Scrolls, and I have uncovered the truth about her role in Christianity. Some of the roughly nine hundred or so books that were discovered between 1947 through 1956 in the caves of the *Qumran Wadi* are actually contained in the original Bible, but most are not. The most controversial argument is over the Gospel of Philip, which is contained in the original Bible. While talking about Jesus, Philip writes, 'He used to kiss her often on her...' The document found in the caves of *Qumran* is missing the essential word.

"I have looked at the passage in the original Bible and found it intact. There were experts who added the word *pirw*, which means mouth to the Gospel of Philip in order to make it appear as if Jesus and Mary Magdalene had a sexual relationship, but the assumption was wrong. The missing word is actually *ni[alauj*, which is coptic for feet. Mary Magdalene was Jesus's favorite disciple and his most trusted follower. She kissed him on his feet in order to display her utter respect and undying loyalty to the Lamb of God. She was widowed before meeting Christ, and her husband left her a substantial amount of wealth. Seven different demons possessed her, each representing one of the seven deadly sins—gluttony, fornication, covetousness, anger, dejection, sloth, and pride. Mary Magdalene was guilty of all seven, and her sister Martha convinced her to seek out the Messiah in hopes of changing her life. She was healed and forgiven for her sins by Jesus, and Mary became his most trusted follower, growing to be his favorite disciple. She used her wealth to fund the spreading of the teachings of Christ.

"Mary Magdalene was always at Jesus's side, and she is the 'beloved disciple' referred to in chapter 21 of the Gospel of John. The members of the Council of Nicaea changed the gender of the disciple to disguise the fact that Mary Magdalene was 'the disciple whom Jesus loved.' They also edited the last supper described by the apostle Paul in 1 Corinthians. In the unedited version contained in the original Bible, St. Paul describes a different event. Jesus told his disciples that one of them would betray him, and St. Paul noticed that

Mary Magdalene, who was present, immediately looked at Judas. It was as if she knew he would be the traitor. St. Paul also wrote what Jesus revealed to Mary Magdalene: 'You will be the foundation of my Church.' Mary was at the foot of the cross when Jesus was crucified, and she was also the first person that he appeared to once he was resurrected. She remained at his tomb and was the only apostle who immediately believed that he was alive. Jesus didn't have to display his wounds to her as proof of his identity. The Savior once again reiterated to her that she was the chosen leader of the apostles, leading them after the Messiah ascended to heaven.

"Mary Magdalene eventually traveled to Rome, and in the year AD 37, she revealed to the Roman Emperor Tiberius news of Christ's resurrection. Most of the apostles agreed to use the *Ichthys*, colloquially referred to as the 'Jesus fish,' as the official symbol of the church. But Mary, on the other hand, decided to wear an ivory cross around her neck to honor Christ's sacrifice.

"During the meeting, the emperor replied that Jesus was as much alive as the ivory cross was pink. Mary held the cross in her right hand, and it slowly turned pink. Tiberius was afraid of her miraculous powers and allowed for her to live in Rome under the protection of the emperor. Mary established the Christian Church and was the first bishop of Rome. She held the position of pontiff, from the year 37 to 60, when the apostles St. Paul and St. Peter arrived in the city to assist her.

"The two disciples were constantly arguing over the new church's policies. The main disagreement was whether or not to continue the old Jewish traditions. St. Peter wanted to force converts to the new Christian Church to adhere to the old Jewish laws. Most notably, he wanted the converts to become circumcised. St. Paul believed that the new church should simply adhere to the teachings of Jesus and not worry about keeping the old traditions. He definitely didn't see the need to force grown men to become circumcised. Mary Magdalene was in agreement with St. Paul's position and chose him to be the new bishop of Rome.

"St. Peter had always been her harshest critic since he was against the involvement of women in the church. The other apostles believed if the Messiah felt Mary was their equal, then they didn't have the right to disagree. When the church leaders edited the Bible, at the Council of Nicaea, St. Peter was named the first bishop of Rome as a reward for his stance against the involvement of women in the church.

"St. Paul led the church as the second bishop of Rome, and Mary Magdalene traveled to the south of France to the city of *Marseille*. Her brother Lazarus and sister Martha were living there at the time, and the devout siblings helped Mary convert the entire region to the new Christian Church. She appointed Lazarus as the region's bishop and spent her remaining years living in the caves of *Sainte-Baume* outside of *Marseille*. Legend has it that a shepherd was traveling in the area and saw Mary Magdalene being carried to heaven by an angel, but I haven't found any evidence to authenticate the story.

"Roman Emperor Nero killed the apostles St. Peter and St. Paul in the year 67, leaving Pope Linus as the choice to serve as the third bishop of Rome. Mary Magdalene was the true first pope of the Catholic Church. I am no longer the 269th bishop of Rome. I am the 270th pope. Mary Magdalene was purposely removed from the scriptures in order to keep the church in the hands of male leaders. I have discovered 269 instances in which she was omitted from the New Testament. For centuries, Mary Magdalene was erroneously considered a prostitute, when in fact, she was the best of the apostles. The apostle St. Paul wrote that she sat at Jesus's side during the Last Supper. I have already disclosed to all of you in my previous announcement that there is a long history of women priests in the church, but I do not know how I am going to reinstate women clergy. I can only assure you that it will happen. The logistics have to be worked out first, but I have made it a top priority of mine." There was a murmur through the crowd.

"I am not finished. I also want to look into allowing priests to marry since the vow of celibacy was introduced for the sole purpose of greed. The church didn't want its priests to will their property to their children, so the leaders banned the clergy from marrying. Allowing priests to marry will benefit the Catholic Church immensely, but allowing the priests to marry requires some planning, so it will also take time before a change in policy is made.

Pope Ali grabbed a document and lifted it up so it could be visible to the cameras.

"I have issued a papal bull, declaring that the original Bible will supercede the previous copy as the new Holy Book of the Roman Catholic Church. I will also forgo the canonization process. I have declared Mary Magdalene a saint, and I've already instructed the Vatican press to begin producing copies of the 'real bible,' which will be sold to the public at cost. I'm not interested in making a profit based on the deceptions of past church leaders. The copies will be made available in a month's time.

"I will continue to search through the archives, and I hope to uncover the lost Gospel of Bartholomew. The original Bible makes many references to the private conversation between Jesus and St. Bartholomew, prior to the Savior's ascension into heaven. The gospel may reveal the last words of Christ. Thank you all for your attention, and please refer all questions to the *Camerlengo*. I leave you with the first verse from chapter 13 in the book of Wisdom: 'For all men were by nature foolish who were in ignorance of God, and who from the good things seen did not succeed in knowing him who is, and from studying the works did not discern the artisan.' God bless all of you."

Pope Ali stepped away from the microphones and exited the press conference. Many of the cardinals were in agreement with the actions of the new pontiff. They believed that revealing the past wrongs of the church would lead to a better relationship with the laity.

"It is better for his holiness to empty out the skeletons in the church's closet before an outsider gets a hold of the information," Cardinal Borgia remarked.

The one staunch opposing opinion came from Cardinal Rodriguez, who was incensed by the pope's transparency.

"The Muslim is attempting to take down the Catholic Church," Rodriguez said to the few cardinals who were in agreement with his views.

When Pope Ali learned of the cardinal's comments, he asked Dean Malandra to be mindful of the Barcelonan's actions.

"I will keep a close eye on him. He seems to have an evil spirit," the dean said.

"Rodriguez's comments are merely the result of a personal grudge that he has against me. Realistically, I believe him to be harmless."

Most of the pope's ardent supporters denounced the disgruntled cardinal's views.

———◦◉◦———

At the entrance to St. Peter's Basilica, near the front steps, were statues of the apostles St. Peter and St. Paul. Pope Ali invited a local sculptor, named *Pietro Galligani*, to the Apostolic Palace.

"I want you to erect a statue in honor of St. Mary Magdalene, the true first bishop of Rome. The statue will stand along the other two leaders of the Roman Catholic Church."

"Are you referring to the two statues in front of the Basilica?" *Galligani* asked.

"Yes, and I want St. Mary's statue to be slightly larger," Pope Ali said.

"I would be honored. Is St. Peter's the largest Basilica in the world?"

"St. Peter's Basilica was the largest church in Christendom, until the construction of the new Basilica of Our Lady of Peace of *Yamoussoukro*. The Colossal Basilica is located in the Ivory Coast and is inspired by St. Peter's. Pope John Paul II consecrated the massive church in 1990, and construction of the thirty-thousand-square-meter complex cost three hundred million dollars."

Pope Ali continued his investigation of the secret archives, and the new Bibles were distributed throughout the world. Some Catholics didn't agree with the change, but they bought the book anyway, simply out of curiosity. Fears of a new schism swept through the Vatican, but his holiness remained undeterred in his effort to remove corruption from the church. An anonymous supporter of his sent an army-green *zucchetto* because of the pontiff's comparison to the United State's Army Green Berets, whose motto was "Liberate the oppressed."

Chapter 21

The pope knew he had to dig deep into the archives in order to find information that would keep the church unified. On the twenty-fifth of May, without any explanation, Pope Ali made a stunning decision. He revoked the power of every sitting cardinal. New cardinals were appointed to replace the previous church leaders. The new cardinalate consisted of young priests who hadn't served as bishops. The pope wanted a group of cardinals that was untainted by the influence of past regimes. An overwhelming majority of the new Synod of Bishops was from Middle Eastern countries. The only cardinals who didn't lose their authority were Archbishop Malandra and the retired ex-pope Cardinal De Luca.

The paranoid pontiff explained that the two men were the only ones whom he could truly trust.

Cardinal Malandra retained his position as the dean of the College of Cardinals, but he was confused by the pope's decision. "Are you sure this is the right move? You're already clouded by controversy with the Friday revelations. Expelling the cardinals will only add to your list of enemies."

"I assure you that I have only acted out of necessity. I am acting in the interest of the church, and I will explain my decision to remove the sitting cardinals when the appropriate time arrives."

Pope Ali didn't give a reason for his drastic action to anyone. He simply stated that his life was in imminent danger, which was why he acted so swiftly. Even in the face of danger, the determination that he had to complete his *Jihad* was undying.

Most of the displaced cardinals were very upset. The decision to strip the cardinalate of their authority did not come easy to the pope because he knew that many of the men were truly honorable shepherds of the Lord. Those whom he considered his dearest friends were given a handwritten letter with the papal seal, explaining that he didn't have a choice in the matter; he was forced to act immediately. Most notably was the eldest of the group, Cardinal Borgia of Florence, whose devotion was undeniable. He was a man who had always placed the interest of the church before anything else, and Pope Ali wrestled with the decision to allow him to keep his position but ultimately decided another exception would further anger the other cardinals.

Former Cardinal Alejandro Rodriguez of Barcelona was the most outspoken of the discontented group. He held a press conference on the twenty-seventh of May, announcing that he was seriously considering organizing the election of a "real pope."

"I demand to know the reason behind the Muslim's decision to remove the cardinals from our positions of power."

In response to the cardinal's demands, Pope Ali announced, "All will be explained in a press conference at the end of the week."

Prior to retiring to his quarters for the night, the pope received a letter from Sabatina, which was the first contact from her since he left for Iraq. His holiness held the letter in his hand for several minutes, but he didn't have the nerve to open it. He couldn't decide whether to read it or have Cardinal Malandra read it to him, ultimately deciding to sleep on the decision and placing the unopened envelope on an antique mahogany desk in his papal chamber before turning in.

The following morning, he gave the situation some serious thought, and the more he contemplated opening it, the more furious he grew. Pope Ali taped a piece of paper around the sealed envelope and wrote on it.

"Thanks for attending the inauguration!"

He added his seal to the document and placed it into a large manila envelope before ordering the letter to be mailed to the return address. The pope had no desire to talk with Sabatina. He already exasperated every avenue in an attempt to find her and had more pressing matters to attend to.

———◦———

On May 29, the pontiff held another press conference. It was his fourth Friday revelation. Once again, he sat in front of a large number of microphones and divulged his latest unearthing. His Excellency was clearly despondent. The news he was about to reveal would further compromise his safety, and it was the first press conference in which ten soldiers from the Swiss Guard stood at his side.

"I would like to thank all my former cardinals for allowing this difficult transition to happen without incident. I want to say that I know in my heart, most of the men are in fact great servants of God with a true calling. It broke my heart to strip them of their authority."

The pope was visibly shaken by what he had uncovered. His eyes began to tear up as he spoke.

"When I embarked on my journey to repair the integrity of the Roman Catholic Church, I never envisioned discovering the type of treachery that I recently uncovered. When I converted to Catholicism, as an eleven-year-old boy, I held the pope and his cardinals in the highest esteem. These men were true followers of Christ, in the example of the Savior's disciples, and I looked up to them as role models. I never imagined that I could one day join their ranks, but through my faith in God, I am here to serve his flock as the Lord's shepherd. It is with great sorrow that I make my announcement today."

Pope Ali was having second thoughts about continuing with the announcement, but he knew there was no turning back.

"I have discovered a dangerous secret society, whose members include some of the Vatican's most trusted cardinals."

There was a distinctive murmur through the crowd, and the pontiff paused to gather himself. Many in attendance had always suspected the existence of an evil secret society inside the Vatican. The overwhelming assumption was that the pope was about to reveal his discovery of the *illuminati*.

"It is a far more treacherous institution than the Italian mafia. *La Cosa Nostra* is a group of choirboys compared to these men. The order was first called *Il Sinodo di Basilea*. The name Synod of Basel was later changed to *Cardinali di Basilea*. The members changed the name because a synod is designed to assist and advise the pope, but these men were intent on serving their own avarice.

"The members of the cardinals of Basel have secretly controlled the Vatican City State and the Holy See, a massive betrayal of the Roman Catholic Church. On December 18, 1431, Pope Eugene IV dissolved the Council of Basel, which was assembled during the tenure of his predecessor, Pope Martin V. Basel Switzerland, was chosen as the site of the council in order to allow the cardinals to meet outside of the Holy Roman Empire. Pope Eugene IV was disappointed with the council's progress, which led to the dissolution, but the cardinals refused to leave. They believed the pope was trying to prevent them from creating new reforms.

"The council, which was led by Cardinal *d'Allemand* of Arles, reestablished the *Sacrosancta*, which was a canon introduced by the Council of Constance in 1415. The new canon decreed that the power of the cardinals was superior to that of the pope.

"In hopes of weakening the strength of its members, Pope Eugene IV moved the council from Basel to Ferarra, Italy, but twelve of the cardinals remained in Basel, and they elected Amadeus VIII as the new pope. He chose the regnal name Pope Felix V.

"Felix reigned from 1439 to 1449 in opposition of Pope Eugene IV, and he was considered an antipope. Pope Felix V eventually relinquished his claim to the papacy after the election of Nicholas V. The new pontiff agreed to name the former antipope a cardinal on April 17, ending the dual papacy.

"It was Cardinal Amadeus VIII who established *Cardinali di Basilea* in 1450. The society's purpose is to uphold the wealth and power of the church. Members swear an oath to prevent the diminishing of power by any future pope. They believe that their authority is greater than the pope's and that their power is derived directly from God. The cardinals of Basel have been responsible for most of the scandals involving the Roman Catholic Church since its inception in 1450. Today, I will mention a few of their acts that I have uncovered."

Everyone listened intently as the pope divulged the horrible details.

"In 1972, Pope Paul VI announced to the laity, 'Through some fissure the smoke of Satan entered into the temple of God.' The pope had uncovered the secret society of cardinals, but he only was able to identify three of its members—Cardinals *Villot*, *Benelli*, and *Casaroli*. Pope Paul VI began to further investigate the cardinals of Basel in order to expose all the members.

"In 1975, before he could gather enough information, the cardinals of Basel began the process of poisoning him and replaced his holiness with an imposter. Pope Paul's health slowly deteriorated, and the devil's cardinals arranged for an actor to receive plastic surgery so he could serve as an imposter pontiff. No one noticed the cardinal's biggest blunder. The imposter had green eyes, but the real pope had blue eyes. The imposter pope adhered to the will of *Cardinali di Basilea*, and the real pope was hidden in Florence while he drew closer to death. From 1975 until the death of Pope Paul in 1978, the cardinals of Basel controlled the Roman Catholic Church, and they were able to keep their existence a secret. A few people unsuccessfully attempted to point out that the pope was an imposter, but the truth remained hidden. The imposterpontiff was murdered once the true Pope Paul finally succumbed to the poison.

"In 1978, the newly elected Pope John Paul I, known as the 'the smiling pope,' announced that his aim was to rid the church of corruption. He was also a believer in diminishing the church's wealth and wanted to reduce the power of the cardinalate. Pope John Paul I was in poor health, so the cardinals knew that the poison would kill him quickly. The sincere pontiff was given exceedingly small doses until the thirty-third day of his reign, in which the dosage was significantly increased. His term as the bishop of Rome only lasted thirty-three days, which the cardinals of Basel felt would be symbolic, marking one day for every year that Christ walked the earth.

"*Cardinali di Basilea* was also behind the celibacy dispensations that were issued by Pope Paul VI in 1966. The secret order of cardinals gave the pope false information about a planned schism, and he was told that unless the dispensations were ordered, members of the College of Cardinals were planning to elect an antipope. He agreed in hopes of saving the church.

"Pope John Paul II discontinued the celibacy dispensations in 1978 once he uncovered the truth behind the decision of his predecessor. He also believed that there was a secret evil organization of cardinals within the Vatican and discovered that they were responsible for the assassination of his antecedent, but he felt the revelation of such a scandal would probably bring down the church. The pope knew his life would be in grave danger, so he decided to keep silent. I haven't found any evidence to suggest that the evil order was behind the assassination attempt of Pope John Paul II, but I'm sure they had a hand in it."

Pope Ali slowly wiped away tears from his cheeks and paused for a moment. He was having a difficult time making it through the announcement. It wasn't easy for him to imagine that such evil was able to penetrate the Vatican, and after taking a few moments to gain his composure, he continued.

"I have also found evidence that leads me to believe *Cardinali di Basilea* was responsible for the assassination of the controversial Pope Peter II. The Vatican did not allow for an autopsy to be performed on the body by an independent medical examiner. I have discovered documentation, which points to the fact that the pope's asthma pump was switched, prior to it being handed over to the responding medics. It appears he was breathing in poisonous gas instead of the medicine that could have saved his life. The original report from the hospital revealed that the inhaler found at the scene, by the EMS workers, was full. It is safe to assume that a member of the cardinals of Basel wrote the falsified medical report. From what I can ascertain, Pope Peter II was murdered."

The crowd was shocked by Pope Ali's claim. The existence of a murderous order of cardinals was a difficult concept for many of them to grasp.

"*Cardinali di Basilea* has also generated an immense wealth through gambling. There is verification that its members are working in conjunction with professional gamblers to bring illegal money into the Vatican. I have evidence of secret phone conversations between the Vatican and known criminals. The worst gambling offense began with the election of Pope Benedict XVI. The cardinals placed bets with London oddsmakers on who the new bishop of Rome would be. They put one hundred thousand euros, stolen from the Vatican Bank, on the election of Cardinal Joseph Ratzinger, a long shot at 12 to 1 odds. The Basel cardinals used their influence to insure Cardinal Ratzinger would be elected. The hundred thousand was quietly returned to the Vatican bank before its disappearance was noticed, and the profit was evenly distributed between the society's members. I haven't found any connection between Cardinal Ratzinger and *Cardinali di Basilea*, but his appointment to the cardinalate occurred in 1977 during the reign of the imposter pope. I will give him the benefit of the doubt and assume that he was not connected to Satan's cardinals.

"The practice of betting on the conclave has continued since, and the cardinals of Basel earned a comparatively small profit of three hundred thousand euros during my election. The largest profit was the four and a quarter million euros they collected during the election of Pope Peter II."

The enormous figures stunned the gasping crowd as the pope reeled them off. Again wiping his tear-drenched face, the fearless pontiff continued.

"It's the discovery of this secret society that forced me to remove the entirety of the sitting cardinalate, and the reason I acted so swiftly was the shocking discovery of small traces of poison in my bloodstream. Some conniving person has been giving me small dosages of a toxin with my meals. I had to act quickly in order to protect myself from the evil that has penetrated the Vatican."

Dean Malandra walked closer to his friend and embraced him. "I'm sorry I questioned your motives. I didn't know they were attempting to assassinate you."

"I should've told you when I found out." He gathered himself and concluded the announcement.

"It's obvious this discovery has been very difficult for me to handle, but it was important for me to stand before all of you and deal with this problem. I won't be taking any questions, but I assure you all that I will continue my search for the truth. I will not let intimidation deter me from my duty. Let me leave you with a few prophetic words from the book of Psalm chapter 12 verses 2 and 3: 'Help, Lord, for no one loyal remains; the faithful have vanished form the human race. Those who tell lies to one another speak with deceiving lips and a double heart.' Thank you and may God bless all of you."

The pope retired to the Vatican Palace, both physically and mentally exhausted. The information traveled through the media like a powerful tsunami. Pope Ali's courage in dealing with the cardinals of Basel and the dragon that was on his coat of arms earned him the titles "the dragon pope" and "God's dragon." His eminence was proud of the new monikers. They reminded him of Azfal's gift.

The cardinals of Basel were removed from their lofty positions in the church, but the group's presence was still felt. Pope Ali woke up to find his Fisherman's Ring missing from the papal chamber, but he assumed that he must have misplaced it and ordered the creation of a replacement. Foul play never crossed him mind until he spoke with the dean.

"Do you think *Cardinali di Basilea* is responsible for the missing ring?" Cardinal Malandra asked.

The pope quickly denounced the accusation. "They no longer have the ability to affect the inner workings of the Vatican."

The new gold ring was given to the pope within a few days, and a week later, he received an anonymous package. Inside was an envelope with the year 1450 written on it, and it contained the missing Fisherman's Ring, a clear message from the cardinals of Basel that the pope would not be able to get rid of them so easily. The pontiff quietly suspected his old friend Cardinal De Luca since he was the only remaining member of the old order, unless the secret society was able to corrupt one of the new cardinals.

His Excellency revealed his suspicions to Cardinal Malandra, but he was not convinced. There was no way that Cardinal De Luca would ever betray his godson.

"I think we have to focus on the possibility of Satan's cardinals influencing one of the new cardinals. There is also the likelihood that a member of the Swiss Guard might be assisting them."

Pope Ali agreed that his friend's assumption seemed more plausible. "I still want you to investigate everyone, but don't let anyone in on what you are doing."

"I will look into the matter and let you know what I uncover."

The pope was heartbroken when the damning evidence, gathered by the dean, was revealed to him. The Vatican phone records proved that Cardinal De Luca was busy contacting many of the displaced cardinals. Once he saw the evidence, the pope remembered what his grandfather told him when he was an eleven-year-old boy.

"Our friend, the helpful priest, will guide you with your assimilation into their culture, but remember that you can never trust him." Azfal was right; Cardinal De Luca was a deceiver. Pope Ali also remembered what his godfather said to him prior to leaving for Iraq.

"Take care, my child. Your future will be bright. If you do well, the cardinals will be grateful."

His mentor was obviously preparing him for his initiation into the secret society but must have decided to turn on him once he realized his godson would not be corrupted. His holiness knew at that moment that Cardinal De Luca was clearly a member of the cardinals of Basel; he was most likely the leader.

Dean Malandra was furious since he also established a great relationship with the mentoring cardinal. "We have to remove the last minion of Satan from the Vatican," he exclaimed.

The pope was upset with himself for not following his grandfather's advice. He let down his guard and allowed Cardinal De Luca to betray him.

"I can't believe he had the audacity to serve as my godfather. I will never let down my guard again." He confidently told the dean, and they both wondered if the cardinal used the Alzheimer's diagnosis as nothing more than a scam.

"I don't want to alert him that we've uncovered his true identity, so we have to devise a plan to delicately convince De Luca to move back to Milan," Pope Ali said.

The pope immediately had his blood checked for traces of poison, fearing that his godfather might have continued lacing his food with toxins.

Pope Ali met with "the devil's cardinal" the following morning and was infuriated by the sight of his old friend. He wanted to quickly remove the evildoer from the Vatican.

"Old friend, you have been a great mentor to me, and I have always sought your counsel whenever faced with a difficult challenge. You were always there to guide me, but as you know, my life is in danger, and I cannot risk your life as well. I think it is best if you return to the Archdiocese of Milan, where you can escape the treachery that exists inside St. Peter's."

Cardinal De Luca was not himself. He understood what the pope said, but his fading memory didn't allow him to recall the recent events. "I don't understand why my life is in danger, but I will trust your guidance and follow your holiness's suggestion."

The next day, the pope received the results from his blood test, and they revealed small traces of poison in his bloodstream. His trusted friend and mentor Cardinal De Luca had continued to poison him. The news brought Pope Ali to his knees because he couldn't bear the thought of his godfather's treason. His weeping made him realize how much the relationship with his mentor meant. Cardinal De Luca was basically his family and one of the last people on earth that the pope would have expected to be influenced by the devil. The eye-opening incident crushed Pope Ali's heart, and he was unable to deal with the pain, remaining in a cavernous depression for a few days. He cried almost as much as when he lost his family members.

When he finally recovered, the angered pope's heart became numb with blackness, and he was even more determined to carry out the promise that he made to his grandfather. Cardinal De Luca was sent to Milan on June 19. He would never step foot inside the Vatican again. It took everything within his power to keep the pope from strangling his disloyal mentor.

"The Vatican is finally rid of Satan's evil influence," he declared.

With Cardinal De Luca back home, the influence of the cardinals of Basel ended. There were no more "strange" incidents. A third test result revealed the pope's blood was clean and void of any traces of poison. His holiness was finally excited to have the true support of the remaining cardinalate, and he gathered his Synod of Bishops.

"I want to thank all of you for your loyalty. From this day forward, we will join together in our quest to defeat Satan. We will spread the word of the Lord. Let me quote from 1 Corinthians chapter 12 verses 25 and 26: 'So that there may be no division in the body, but that parts may have the same concern for one another. If [one] part suffers, all the parts suffer with it; if one part is honored, all the parts share its joy.'"

Pope Ali suspected Cardinal De Luca to be the leader of *Cardinali di Basilea*, and he also believed that Cardinal Rodriguez of Barcelona was a key member. It was the former Barcelonan cardinal who organized another Ecumenical Council to be held on August 22. In the meantime, the pope continued to research the Vatican Secret Archives.

The Council of *Brianza* was held in the province of Milan at *Besana in Brianza*, in the *Basilica Romana Minore*. The ex-cardinals discussed the possible election of a new pope, and once again, Cardinal Rodriguez was among the minority.

Cardinal Borgia of Florence remained an ardent supporter of Pope Ali. "The pontiff is only doing what is in the best interest of the church. Many of us would have done the same thing if we were placed in a similar situation. There is no need to worry. As soon as the cardinals of Basel are exposed, we will once again have our authority. It is the duty of the cardinalate to support the bishop of Rome in his quest to uncover the truth."

Cardinal Rodriguez wanted to continue his argument but decided to let the matter go. He knew that he was the main suspect as a member of the secret society and wanted to avoid adding fuel to the fire. The council was disbanded, and the ex-cardinals returned to their respective dioceses, without an antipope being elected.

Chapter 22

"The past few months have been an extremely emotional time. It isn't easy to deal with the discovery of a treacherous plot aimed at assassinating me. I was blindsided by the betrayal of those whom I trusted most, but through the grace of God, I have made a full recovery. I am pleased to announce that I've been receiving a weekly blood test and there are no more traces of poison in my system. The cardinals of Basel are still out there, and I'm sure they are planning their next attack on the church, but I assure you that their members have been successfully removed from the Vatican," Pope Ali said, as he stood triumphantly in front of the laity during his solemn September 4, 2043 Friday revelation. The large gathering hung on every word, looking up at the balcony of St. Peter's Basilica.

"I am prepared to announce another surprising unearthing. In my latest research, I've discovered a plot by past Vatican leaders to mislead the laity. I'm sure most of you are familiar with the story of Our Lady of Fatima. For those of you who are not, I will give a brief summary. On May 13, 1917, the Virgin Mary, Mother of Jesus Christ, appeared to three young children in the village of Fatima, Portugal. Lucia Santos was the eldest at age ten, and her two cousins—Jacinta and Francisco Marto—were helping her tend to sheep at *Cova da Iria*. The children revealed to the townspeople that they saw a vision of the Virgin Mary, reporting that Our Lady of Fatima revealed three secrets to them, but they would not disclose what the secrets were, and many of the skeptical adults didn't believe the story.

"On the thirteenth of October, the same year, the Virgin Mary performed the 'miracle of the sun,' which proved to the almost hundred thousand in attendance that the children were telling the truth. Many of the spectators reported seeing the sun fall from the sky and perform a dance. The children were vindicated by the miracle. However, Jacinta and Francisco were victims of the influenza endemic that plagued Portugal, and they didn't live much longer. Francisco died on April 4, 1919, and Jacinta succumbed to the illness the following February. They are both buried at the Our Lady of Fatima Basilica in Portugal. Lucia survived the influenza epidemic, and in 1941, at the urging of Jose da Silva who was the bishop of Leira, she revealed the first two secrets in a letter.

"The first secret was a vision of hell that the children were shown by the Blessed Mother. The second secret was the prediction of an end to World War I, along with the coming of a worse Second World War, during the pontificate of Pius XI. Lucia refused to reveal the third secret. She said that she didn't have permission from God, but in 1944, the bishop of Leira convinced her to write down the third secret in the event that she passed away before it could be revealed. She wrote down the secret and sealed it in an envelope, which wasn't supposed to be opened until 1960, the year the secret would be better understood. The letter remained in the possession of the bishop, until 1957, when he finally sent it to the secret archives of the holy office. Sister Lucia made the bishop of Leira promise to open the letter either on the day of her death or in 1960.

"In 1960, the Vatican released a statement: 'Most probable the secret would remain, forever, under absolute seal.' Pope John XXIII read sister Lucia's letter, and he resealed the envelope, returning it to the archives. In 1965, Pope Paul VI read the letter and did the same as his predecessor. Pope John Paul II did not read the epistle until after a lone gunman failed to assassinate him in 1981. The pope was wounded, and *in lieu* of the attack, he finally decided to look at the document. It wasn't until the year 2000 that Pope John Paul II exposed the third secret of Fatima. The announcement was made on May 13, the eighty-third anniversary of the Blessed Mother's first appearance at Fatima. The pope's explanation connected the memo to his assassination in 1981. There has been much controversy over the interpretation. Many people believed that the pope created a false document in order to keep the true secret hidden. Former Cardinal Ratzinger, who succeeded Pope John Paul II and took the name Benedict XVI, wrote an adjoining correspondence to the note, which confirmed that it was indeed the actual letter from Sister Lucia. Many people believed that the truth would remain forever hidden when Sister Lucia died at the ripe-old age of ninety-seven in the year 2005.

"Today, I am delighted to report that I have uncovered the truth behind Sister Lucia's letter. It was not the four-page document revealed to the world by John Paul II in the year 2000." An assistant priest handed a letter to the pope. The crowd was hushed as if his holiness had asked for a moment of silence. "I will now read the English translation of the one-page letter written by Lucia:

> I write in obedience to you, my God, who commands me to do so through his excellency the bishop of Leira and through your most Holy Mother and mine. After the two parts in which I have previously explained, we saw a vision of two identical bishops dressed in white. The first was laying on his deathbed. His eyes were filled with pain as he inched closer to his final moment. He was screaming from the bites of venomous snakes. It was his own bishops who released the snakes.
>
> An imposter bishop was standing in front of his flock. He was preaching to them the words that the bishops were feeding him. The twin bishops were then tied together and eaten by a large serpent that we assumed to be Satan. We were frightened when the serpent turned and began to chase the people, but the light of the heavenly Father protected them and drove the serpent away.

We then saw men on opposite sides of the Holy Land. They were holding large guns that shot out a flashing light. Flames were striking down men that stood in the path of the guns. Two men stood at the top of the city. Their presence led the armies of the Holy Land to end their conflict. One man later appeared in the white dress of a bishop. We believed that he was a future pope. He led his people on a long journey, over mountains through many rivers, and past a vast wilderness. He brought them to a mountain top where the light of the Lord was at its brightest. We were blinded at first, but the Holy Mother adjusted our eyes. The second man, wearing a strange wrapped headdress, led his people to the same mountain. The first bishop was revealing the true words of the Lord to his people. The second leader joined him. They instructed their people to listen to the words of the Mighty Father. Other evil bishops appeared holding flaming swords in their hands. They were dressed in red bearing the mark of the serpent on their breasts. They were preventing the people from reaching the Lord's mountain. The people stopped in their tracks. They were frightened. Some people followed the bishop in white while the others listened to Satan's bishops. The bishop in white urged them to keep the faith. He called for them to fight against the minions of the devil. The people who believed in the bishop made it to the Lord's mountain. The ones who were afraid were overtaken by darkness. The bishop attempted to save them, but he was struck in the back by the sword of his most trusted friend. Only those who followed the bishop were saved. With the bishop betrayed, Rome became the throne of the antichrist. He will bring on the world's third major conflict and its eventual destruction. After the three visions, the Blessed Mother told us that in Portugal, the dogma of the faith will always be preserved and salvation will come to those who follow the peacemaker."

The pope held up the single sheet of paper along with the original Portuguese document for the people to see.

"I guess Pope John Paul II didn't want to spread fear throughout the world by revealing the true third secret of Fatima, and Sister Lucia was coerced into confirming the authenticity of the fake document. She believed that the pope was God's messenger on earth and didn't question his judgment. She assumed that he was acting in the best interest of the church and prayed to the Virgin Mary for guidance. In her mind, the pontiff had the ultimate authority on earth, but I don't think we have to fear the secret. If we follow the teachings of the Lord and adhere to his laws, we will all be saved. Evil can only thrive in the absence of good, and I will do my best to lead the church on God's path. There will be those who oppose me, but together, we can prevent the rule of the antichrist. Ultimately, it is up to the people to follow my lead. As is my custom, I will not be answering any questions. A copy of the document will be distributed to everyone in attendance. Thank you for your undivided attention. Remember the book of Sirach chapter 14 verses 1 and 2: 'Happy the man whose mouth brings him no grief, who is not stung by remorse for sin. Happy the man whose conscience does not reproach him, who has not lost hope.' May God bless all of you."

Pope Ali returned to his apartment in the papal palace, but he was unsure what his next course of action should be. The third secret of Fatima was a lot to take in, and the faith of God's children rested in his hands. For the first time in his adult life, the pontiff was scared. He was confused as to where he was to lead God's people.

Should I continue with the Jihad? he mused. *There is a strong possibility that the instructions I received came out of spite.*

His eminence cleared the papal schedule in order to spend a week alone in Palestrina, contemplating the life-altering decision. Supporters of Pope Ali began to call him the "peacemaker." It was obvious to them that he was the bishop dressed in white, and they were confident that the reference to the conflict in the Holy Land was describing the role he played in ending the conflict between the Israelis and the Palestinians. The reference to the antichrist was apparently about the cardinals of Basel, and Catholics throughout the world knew the pope's life was in danger.

Eight days following his speech, Pope Ali returned to the Vatican after the week in his favorite city. The time away was exactly what he needed; he was rejuvenated and ready to complete his lofty task. The pontiff truly believed that he was destined to lead the Catholic people on a new path toward God. Prior to his departure, he met in private with his most trusted cardinal.

"My good friend, please arrange a meeting with my friend the *Ayatollah*. It is essential for him to visit the Vatican as soon as possible."

"I will contact him immediately."

The announcement of the Iranian leader's visit in the Holy See Press Office's Bulletin created angst among the laity.

In an effort to gain a larger support base, the disgruntled ex-cardinal of Barcelona, Alejandro Rodriguez, warned Catholics that the pope was preparing to allow the *Ayatollah* to serve as a new cardinal. Pope Ali quickly dispelled the superfluous rumor and assured followers that he had no such plan. Yet many of the people remained wary of the pontiff's actions.

The urgent meeting was set for the twenty-first of September, but before having the important discussion with the *Ayatollah*, the pope wanted to show his old friend the Egyptian Museum. The pudgy Ayatollah did not like to walk, but he did enjoy the tour of the Vatican.

"This museum was opened in AD 1838 by Pope Gregory XVI. This is my favorite location in the Vatican because it reminds me of Azfal." The Ayatollah could see the admiration in his friend's eyes as he spoke. "I often spend several hours looking through the papyrus manuscripts. There is just something about them that is near and dear to my heart," Pope Ali said.

The *Ayatollah* enjoyed the many exhibits, but he was anxious to find out why he was summoned to Rome. The influential leaders met for several hours inside the Vatican Gardens. It was a mild winter day, and the pope was quite comfortable outdoors. He wanted absolute privacy for the controversial chat, but the *Ayatollah* wasn't accustomed to the coldness and shivered under the snuggly goose-down coat that he promptly requested. His chubby body was no match for the frost. He suffered a great deal but knew the meeting was important and toughed it out. They strolled through the lush greenery and discussed his holiness's plans for the future of the Catholic Church.

The ambitious pontiff could not complete his grand scheme without the help of the *Ayatollah*, so he revealed his interpretation of the third secret of Fatima.

"My good friend, I cleared my schedule for a week and spent the time in deep thought. My mission was to figure out how to translate the secret, and I have come to the conclusion that the Lord called me to lead the followers of Christ to his true word. It is I who will convert every Catholic to *Islam*."

The *Ayatollah* was startled by the pope's objective. He couldn't believe what his good friend was saying.

"I don't understand. How can you convert the entire Roman Catholic community? You will create another schism because a majority of the laity will not follow you. I think you are making a monumental mistake. This is exactly what your enemy Rodriguez was waiting for."

"Don't worry about Rodriguez, he doesn't have any support, he is not a leader. The people will follow me, and I have a plan that will ensure it. Sister Lucia's true vision makes it perfectly obvious that I am the bishop in white who will lead the followers to God's Word. Muslims believe the *Qur'an* is God's true word, and it is my mission to lead the people from the interpolations of the Bible to the truth of the prophet's teachings. My plan will work, but I need you to assist me in completing it. Together, we can accomplish anything."

"I agree that we can accomplish a great deal, but this doesn't seem possible. I know that I said I would always follow your lead, but you have to think about the consequences."

"Have faith, my friend. No one believed that we could end the conflict in the Holy Land, but we persevered and brought peace to Jerusalem. We will shock the world once more and bring the followers of the Prophet Jesus to *Islam*. I have devised a plan that will help me gain the complete trust of the laity. I was inspired to attempt the mass conversion after I discovered an old *Qur'an* inside the Vatican Secret Archives."

The vigilant *Ayatollah* was not sure they would be able to succeed in carrying out such a daunting task because he felt it was way too dangerous. "I think you are misguided. The vision of the bishop in white is not you. I believe it is of some future pope who will lead the people to some mountain. Where is your mountain? I think you are trying to mold your life to fit the prophecy, which is dangerous. There are many different ways to interpret the third secret. The twin bishops could be describing a future schism in which two popes will rule, and the conflict in the Holy Land can mean anything. People have been fighting in Jerusalem for millenniums. Throughout history, there have been thirty-four major battles at *Meggido* alone, and there is no way that I can be the second leader because I only lead Iran, not all Muslims. I have to say that I don't agree with your plan."

"I know you don't truly believe everything that you just said. You are speaking out of fear, because deep down inside, we both know that we can convert the church. I have garnered the trust of the laity, and I am certain they will follow me. I need you to use all your contacts in order to create a false document. It will be the document that ensures the loyalty of the people. We will succeed! Trust me."

The Hoover Dam would have succumbed to the pressure the *Ayatollah* felt. His gaze shifted from the massive oak desk to the filled book case against the wall. With a sense of trepidation, he unenthusiastically agreed to help, not wanting to let down his good friend. "What document do you want me to counterfeit?"

"I will give you the pertinent information. Let us go to my library."

It would not be an easy undertaking. Catholics were very trusting of the pope, but a conversion to *Islam* was unfathomable. It would require more than trust. His eminence had Lucia's letter to lean on, but he knew that he needed to generate more faith from the laity, and he knew exactly what had to be done.

"I will announce to the people that I am taking a trip in order to decide on the church's future. But the truth is, we will use the time to plan out our strategy for the conversion. After our meeting, you will meet with the members of the L-MEN and deliver the details of our plan. Hopefully, they will agree to help us."

Pope Ali led the *Ayatollah* to the papal library where he handed him the information needed for the fake document. His holiness poured himself a glass of Blue Label 1805 and offered one to his friend.

"This bottle was a gift from King Harry of England. He gave me twelve 'Special Edition' Johnnie Walker bottles when His Highness visited the Vatican. The 1805 Blue Label is valued at approximately thirty thousand dollars a bottle. I sent one to Sal, and he still hasn't stopped thanking me. I swear it's his new child!"

The look on Abtahi's face revealed that he wasn't at all impressed. In fact, it was as though the pope was instantly reminded of Azfal's face on the day of Salvatore's crass comment.

"I'm sure you remember the story about Sal's offensive comment. I apologize for making the same *faux pas*." He was guilt-ridden by the realization of his rude action. "I now can understand how Sal must have felt after seeing the look on your face. Here I am with my glass of Blue Label, making the same mistake. Please excuse me."

The *Ayatollah* nodded his head in agreement. "I recall you telling me that story. It was Sal's comment that made his action offensive, but you simply acted as you would naturally. I am not offended. There is no need to apologize."

The men left the meeting with a great sense of responsibility and purpose. They each knew what had to be done, and prior to leaving the Vatican, the *Ayatollah* received a special limited edition pen from the pope.

"This pen is modeled after the *baldacchino* over the main altar of St. Peter's Basilica created by *Gian Lorenzo Bernini*. The pen is a traditional gift given to foreign dignitaries during their visit to the Vatican," Cardinal Malandra informed him.

For the next five months, the two leaders gave total devotion to the plan.

Chapter 23

O
n February 19, 2044, Pope Ali held a press conference. It was another of his Friday revelations, and he had three agendas. The first was to reveal the discovery of the old *Qur'an*. He also wanted to discuss his interpretation of the third secret of Fatima. Most importantly, the final topic was his discovery of a lost gospel.

"Dear brothers and sisters, I have given Sister Lucia's letter a great deal of thought. And after serious consideration, I have devised a plan for the future of the Roman Catholic Church. In my hand, I hold an ancient text—a copy of the *Qur'an*. After months of etymological analysis, scriptologists and experts in Arabic calligraphy have determined that it's the oldest existing *Qur'an* in the world. I will give a brief history of this monumental text. The book dates back to the year AD 653. Twenty-one years after the passing of the Prophet *Muhammad*, the *Caliph Uthman* completed four official versions of the *Qur'an*. The copies were thought to be lost forever, but this is one of the originally sanctioned *Uthmanic* manuscripts. It predates the *Samarkand* manuscript, which is located in the *Tashkent* library in Uzbekistan, and the *Topkapi* manuscript, located in the *Topkapi* Museum in Istanbul, Turkey. Those two manuscripts were written in the *Kufic* script, but this *Qur'an* is written in the *al-Ma'il* script. It was taken to Spain and eventually placed in the palace of the ruling *caliph*.

"In AD 936, *Umayyad Caliph Abd al-Rahman III* began the construction of the spectacular Palace of *Madinat al-Zahra* outside of

Cordoba, Spain. It took forty years to erect and was completed by his son, *Abd al-Hakim II*. The palace was an architectural masterpiece, and the Muslims were very tolerant of the native Christians and Jews since they were considered people of the book. *Islam* was well received in Spain and quickly spread throughout the region, making Cordoba the most sophisticated city in Western Europe.

"Eventually tensions increased, and the Muslims began to mistreat the indigenous *Berber*. Even those who converted to *Islam* were treated as second-class citizens. The *Caliphal* residence stood for a short time but was destroyed in eleventh century by *Berber* troops who were against Islamic rule.

"This *Qur'an* remained in Spain and ended up in the possession of Queen Isabella during the Treaty of Grenada in 1492, which granted rights to Muslims, ending centuries of war in Spain. Queen Isabella and King Ferdinand began the process of unifying Spain under Catholic Rule while explorer Christopher Columbus was discovering the New World. Pope Alexander VI named them 'the Catholic monarchs,' and the text was sent to Rome as a gift to the supportive bishop of Rome. In 1534, Pope Clement VII commissioned his ambassador, French bibliophile *Jean Grolier de Servieres*, to add the leather covering to this manuscript."

Pope Ali held up the Islamic Holy Book to display the decorative leather covering, with its gold lettering. Pamphlets, with photos from the text and further information, were made available to the crowd.

"It was the discovery of this *Qur'an* that inspired my interpretation of the third secret of Fatima. Clearly, Sister Lucia wanted the bishop of Leira to wait until 1960 before he opened the letter. I believe the year was significant because of the 1957 founding of the Palestinian Liberation Committee, known as the *Fatah*. Prior to 1957, there was no central leadership with any hope of gaining independence for Palestinians, and by 1960, the world was more aware of the conflict between the Palestinians and Jews.

"I believe 'the two identical bishops' is in reference to Pope Paul VI and the imposter pope. It's also apparent to me that the two leaders are the *Ayatollah* and myself. The vision obviously describes our accomplishment of bringing peace to Jerusalem. The *Ayatollah* must lead Muslims to the Lord, and I must lead Catholics." The pope paused for effect. "I interpret the Holy Mother's vision as the unification of the two religions."

The crowd gasped at the thought of *Islam* and Catholicism coming together, but their attention shifted to the pope's mention of the discovery of a lost gospel.

"There have been many references to the Gospel of St. Bartholomew. If you remember my announcement last year on the twenty-seventh of March, I mentioned my hopes of finding the lost gospel, and I am pleased to say that I have discovered the original text in the Vatican Secret Archives. There are many important new revelations from St. Bartholomew, but the most important is Jesus's prophetic words given to his disciple."

The pope thumbed through the original copy of St. Bartholomew's Gospel and read to the dumbfounded crowd. "In the gospel, the apostle writes, 'Turning to me in private, the teacher said, my teaching is not my own, but from the One who sent me. I say to you my disciple, an evil and unfaithful generation will degrade the word of the Lord; blessed are the ears that hear what you hear. Among those born of women there were none greater than those who are willing to lose their lives for my sake. My disciples will faithfully preach the Gospel to all nations, but the evil ones will add their own words; misleading the Lord's flock. An angel will appear to a future prophet of the Lord, and the word of the Father will be restored.' I have cross-referenced many of the stories in the gospel, and Bartholomew tells the same stories as the other apostles. The gospel has been dated and is confirmed to be authentic.

"St. Bartholomew also gave the most detailed account of the death of the Apostle Judas, which matched the portrayal of the event that was written in the other gospels. He wrote that the shamed apostle tied a lengthy rope around a pillar of salt, atop a cliff overlooking the 'salt sea.' The salt pillar was located near the site of the shattered town of *Bab edh-Dhra*, on the ruins of the ill-reputed biblical city of *Sodom*. Judas then jumped to his death. Bartholomew notes witness reports, which describe history's most infamous suicide. The rope unfurled as Judas plummeted toward the sea, and when it tightened, the disgraced apostle's head was severed from his body. The body was never recovered from the Dead Sea, but the head was buried at the foot of the pillar along with the rope. The gospel corroborates the assumption that *Bab edh-Dhra* is the sight of *Sodom*, which I would assume means that *Numeira* is the site of *Gomorrah*."

The account of the apostle's death was chilling but necessary to prove the authenticity of the gospel.

"A decision must be made on the future of the church, and I will travel to meet with the *Ayatollah* so we can further discuss the best course of action. I do not want anyone to jump to any premature conclusions. A decision has not been made yet, and we will discuss the matter thoroughly before deciding how to proceed. I plan to visit Jerusalem on my trip, and I will bring this *Qur'an* with me as a gift to be placed in the *Al-Aqsa* Mosque. The trip will give me an oppurtunity to visit the ark of the covenant, and upon my return from the Middle East, I will announce my decision on the plans for the future of the church. I'll return to Rome in time for the celebration of Easter."

The pope displayed one of the many reproductions of the gospel to the people.

"A copy of the Gospel of St. Bartholomew will be distributed to those who wish to examine it, and the *Camerlengo* will answer any of your questions. Thank you for your attention. Take the lesson from the book of Proverbs chapter 1 verse 7: 'The fear of the Lord is the beginning of knowledge; wisdom and instruction fools despise.' God bless all of you."

The announcement of St. Bartholomew's gospel was a shock to Catholics around the world. Many of them were afraid that the pope might decide to convert the church to *Isla*m, making it the most controversial of his Friday revelations.

The *Ayatollah* was correct in his assumption that the adversarial ex-Cardinal Rodriguez would use the pope's controversial conversion plan as his platform for change. He assembled an Ecumenical Council on Sunday, the twenty-first.

"My fellow displaced cardinals, I have organized this council in my hometown of Barcelona, here in the *Catedral Basílica Metropolitana de Santa Creu i Santa Eulalia*, because we must act fast to prevent the destruction of our church."

The former cardinals were joined by many of the sitting cardinals, who were also concerned with the pope's intent. In attendance were both of Pope Ali's most trusted friends, Cardinal Gianni Malandra and Cardinal Giuseppe De Luca. As usual, Alejandro Rodriguez called for the immediate election of a new pontiff, but Cardinal Dominico Borgia of Florence again unequivocally opposed him. "Be patient, my overzealous Alejandro. We must wait for an official declaration to be issued by his holiness before acting in haste."

A vote was taken, and the overwhelming majority sided with the influential Cardinal Borgia.

Rodriguez was livid. "I cannot sit around and wait for this council's permission to act. The Muslim is the antichrist, and he is leading the church toward its destruction. Are all of you under his spell? Can you not see the signs? He is not the only one who reads the Bible. Remember the book of Revelations chapter 12 verse 9: 'The huge dragon, the ancient serpent, who is called the Devil and Satan, who deceived the whole world…' Also chapter 13 verse 4: 'They worshipped the dragon because it gave its authority to the beast.' And chapter 19 verse 5: 'The beast was given a mouth uttering proud boasts and blasphemies, and it was given authority to act for forty-two months.' We don't have much time!" he screamed, slamming the thick wooden table with his fist. "I think the Muslim is attempting to prepare the world for a fight against heaven. He is attempting to amass a large army that will speak the same Arabic language. God previously prevented this from happening in the story of the Tower of Babel in chapter 11 verses 1 through 18 of the book of Genesis: 'The whole world spoke the same language, using the same words. Then the Lord said: "If now, while they are one people, all speaking the same language, they have started to do this, nothing will later stop them from doing whatever they presume to do. Let us then go down and there confuse their language…" Thus the Lord scattered them from there all over the earth, and they stopped building the city.' The actions of the Muslim are described perfectly in these verses. The true mission behind his trip to the Holy Land is to prepare the people to unite at *Har Megiddo*, the site of the Apostle John's description of Armageddon. He is flying to the Middle East to prepare for the battle against heaven. I know his true destination is Mount *Megiddo*, which is located thirty kilometers southeast of *Haifa* at the strategic entrance to the Eastern Camel Hills. We cannot hesitate! I don't know how much time we have left."

An exasperated Cardinal Borgia stood up. He still believed in the pope and didn't think a conversion would happen. "What is it that frightens you, Alejandro? Even if what you say is true, do you not feel that you will be saved during the rapture?"

The undeterred Barcelonan responded, "You believe in the pre-tribulation rapture. I believe in the post. Either way, you have nothing to worry about."

Cardinal De Luca, who didn't understand what they were referring to because of his Alzheimer's, stood up. "What are you talking about, pre- and post-tribulation rapture?"

Cardinal Borgia explained, "Rodriguez is speaking in reference to the tribulation, which will be a period of seven years of suffering on earth, and the rapture is when God saves all the devout people before bringing destruction to the world. Catholic scholars are divided as to when the rapture will take place. Some believe that it will occur before the tribulation while others think it will happen after it."

An undeterred Rodriguez continued, "It doesn't matter. We only have to look at your pope's coat of arms to uncover the true identity of the dragon described by the Apostle John in the book of Revelations. I have made up my mind. Those of you who want to wait for your pope's announcement are free to leave, but I will not sit idly by while the Muslim destroys the church. This council will not end until we elect a true pontiff."

The room was filled with the clamoring of chairs being moved back and forth. Many of the clergy in attendance got up and left, unwilling to participate in the election of an antipope. The former Cardinal Rodriguez was left with only twelve supporters.

"It appears that the unlucky thirteen will stand alone." Cardinal Borgia ridiculed before leaving.

The remaining members of the council enacted the power of *Sacrosancta*, and Alejandro Rodriguez was elected the "true" pope in opposition to the rule of Pope Ali. He chose the regnal name, Nelson II. His namesake was the pontiff who elevated the Barcelonan to the cardinalate. He was referred to as antipope Nelson and received little support from the laity. Most people didn't believe his eminence would ever make the decision to convert the church because the idea seemed implausible.

Antipope Nelson issued a statement. "The Father has chosen me to lead his people against the rule of the antichrist, and I await the recognition of my authority from Catholics around the world once the Muslim betrays our Lord and Savior."

The consensus held by most Catholics was that antipope Nelson, and his supporters were the members of the cardinals of Basel. The remaining cardinals feared the Roman Catholic Church was headed for a schism. The few followers of Nelson II, who criticized Pope Ali, routinely referred to the pontiff as the antichrist, a distinction given to his holiness by the new antipope.

"Pope Ali is following in the infamous line of Napoleon and Hitler. Prophets such as the famed *Michel de Nostredame*, commonly known as *Nostradamus*, predicted the coming of the third antichrist, who would cause the 'end of days.' We must band together and fight against the Lord's enemy!" the antipope announced.

The pope's itinerary for his Middle Eastern tour was completed. He would first travel to Tel Aviv, a Saturday night flight on the twenty-seventh of February, allowing for his holiness to observe Ash Wednesday in St. Peter's. Pope Ali would spend time in both Israel and Palestine before traveling to the state of Jerusalem to see the ark's new impenetrable encasement. Following his brief visit to the Holy City, his eminence would fly to Iraq and meet with the *Ayatollah* at the L-MEN headquarters in *Al A'zamiyah*. The leaders were to discuss plans for the future of the church before the pontiff returned to Rome for the beginning of Holy Week, celebrating Palm Sunday on the third of April.

"Before I leave for the Holy Land, I want you to arrange a meeting with the Egyptian Cardinal *Luqman Marzouk*, the president of the Pontifical Commission for the Vatican City State," Pope Ali said.

"I will see to it that a meeting is set up for Monday, the twenty-second, but why do you want to meet with the leader of the legislative body of the Vatican City State?" Cardinal Malandra asked.

"My good friend, you must have faith that I will make the proper decision. Soon, all your questions will be answered. Please be patient."

Chapter 24

On the Monday, the twenty-second of February, following his controversial Friday revelation, Pope Ali entered the palace of the governorate to meet with the charming cardinal president who also had executive authority over the Vatican and a second title: president of the governorate of the Vatican City State.

"Cardinal *Marzouk*, thank you for taking an hour out of your busy schedule to meet with me. I have an important issue to discuss with you," the pope said.

"Your eminence, of course, I will always clear up time to meet with you. It is an honor."

"I want to ask you to accompany me on my trip to the Middle East because you are originally from Egypt. I can use your advice as I contemplate the future of the church. You must know how difficult a decision this will be. I don't want you to get involved if you have any reservations."

"Of course, I will join you on the trip. I am flattered that you are asking me to be a part of your entourage. You can count on my full support for any decision that you make. A conversion to the teachings of the Prophet Mohammad will help to mend the relationship between me and my parents. They have disowned me since my conversion to the Catholic Church," Cardinal *Marzouk* said.

"There is no guarantee that I will go through with the conversion. We will decide during the trip."

The powerful men ironed out plans for the his holiness's upcoming Middle Eastern visit. Pope Ali was pleased to have the undying support of the cardinal. Satisfied with the final plans, the pope left the meeting and made the short walk back to the papal palace.

On the morning of Ash Wednesday, Pope Ali met with his most trusted cardinal. "I am looking forward to celebrating mass to mark the beginning of Lent."

"You will enter the packed St. Peter's Basilica, leading a convoy of your cardinals, and the procession will head to the altar for the start of mass," Cardinal Malandra replied.

To everyone's surprise, while the procession slowly made its way to the altar, a deranged woman, dressed in a red-hooded sweatshirt, jumped over the wooden barrier and attacked the pontiff. Pope Ali landed awkwardly on the round porphyry slab set into the floor. He fell at the foot of the bronze statue of St. Peter, enthroned in the northern corner of the nave, and damaged his right knee. Thankfully, the Swiss Guard apprehended the insane woman before she could cause any further injury to his eminence.

"The woman's name is Anna Sue Maio. She was the daughter of the crazed lady who attacked Pope Benedict XVI, at St Peter's Basilica, during the Christmas Eve mass in 2009," said a police officer from the *Corpo della Gendarmerie* of Vatican City. "By the grace of God, Pope Benedict escaped without being harmed, but it appears that the psychotic woman raised her impressionable daughter in preparation for today's attack. Apparently, they are against the Catholic Church's stance on abortion, which both Pope Benedict and Pope Ali vehemently support."

Pope Ali was taught that abortion is murder, and his views were strengthened during his rise through the ranks of the church.

"What injuries did his holiness suffer?" asked a concerned Cardinal Malandra.

"He was not as fortunate as his predecessor. The pope suffered a grade three MCL tear in his right knee. The recovery will take three to four weeks, but luckily, surgery is unnecessary," the officer informed.

The pontiff had to wear a knee immobilizer and also required the use of crutches for the first ten days. The mass was celebrated by the dean of the College of Cardinals in the pontiff's absence. The monumental trip to the Middle East was not affected by the attack because Pope Ali's personal doctor would accompany him on the excursion.

On Saturday morning, Cardinal Malandra entered the papal chamber and awoke the sleeping pontiff. "There is a special guest waiting for you in your library."

The pope was surprised since he didn't have any planned appointments. He thought the request was strange because he specifically cleared his schedule for the day to prepare for the evening's flight to Jerusalem.

"Is it some foreign dignitary?"

"I think you would rather see for yourself, my good friend."

Pope Ali threw back the Egyptian cotton covers and stepped into his slippers. It took twenty minutes for him to get ready. He briskly walked into his large cold library, trembling because his papal vestments didn't shield him from the cool air. The pontiff preferred to be back under his warm covers but was astonished to see a woman seated at his desk. Her face was turned from his view, but he recognized her long flowing auburn hair. *It couldn't be*, he thought.

He immediately knew who it was. "Sabatina?"

The woman stood up and turned to face the familiar sounding voice. She was older but had the same attractive face and perfectly maintained athletic physique. At the age of fifty-two, she was stunning. Sabatina didn't look a day over thirty, and his holiness was in awe of her beauty, but he was full of mixed emotions. She wasn't sure how he would react to her unexpected visit and wondered whether he was excited to see her or angry.

"I received the returned unopened letter and figured you didn't want to see me, hence me showing up without warning. What do I call you? Your Highness? Your eminence?" the pope's befuddled friend asked.

He was still in a state of shock. "Jassi is fine."

"Sorry for showing up unexpectedly, but I figured you wouldn't have answered my call, and please don't blame Gianni—I forced him to help me out," she said nervously.

"What are you doing here?"

"I wanted to write another letter, but you probably wouldn't have read it, so I figured I would have to show up unannounced."

He couldn't look her in the eye and stared at the blue Namixin Gold Dragon fountain pen on his desk. He had no response.

She continued uneasily. "I want to apologize for not attending your inauguration. I know my absence must have angered you, but I guess as the pope, you have no choice but to forgive me. I honestly don't blame you if you are mad at me. I've been through a lot in my life, and I was embarrassed to see you. I know it isn't a good excuse, but it's the truth." She looked him over. "You're still looking handsome as always. I must look like a mess," she said, running her fingers through her hair. "I rushed over here and didn't get a chance to do my hair."

He continued to avoid looking at her.

"Anyway, I don't know if you care or not, but I ended things with Mario the day after you left for Iraq. I realized I was wrong for hooking up with him, but you have to remember that I was vulnerable and heartbroken. I guess the fact that you didn't want me, made me feel undesirable—Mario was there to console me, and things just went too far. We only hid the relationship from you because we didn't know how you would react once you found out."

She paused for a reaction, but he didn't even flinch.

"My life kind of fell apart after you left. I began to hang with the wrong crowd and got mixed up in drugs and alcohol."

Pope Ali was hurt to hear that she chose to use illegal drugs. He wanted to show compassion but continued to sit at his desk, arms crossed and a stoic look on his face.

"I guess I was looking for something to fill the void that your absence created, and I made the mistake of turning to drugs. I couldn't face my parents anymore, so I asked my boss to transfer me to Los Angeles. I barely was myself. I ended up losing my job and was forced to move back home, but all I did was fight with my parents. I felt like a failure. Things got worst one day when my mom walked in on me using heroin. I was so high, I didn't even care, and when I finally sobered up, I was so embarrassed that I left home. I was too afraid to go back, so I just crashed with friends. I was working at the mall before my mom found me using, and my career was completely over. I finally went to rehab about seven years ago, and I'm proud to say that I've been clean ever since.

"I now work for a youth organization, helping young girls avoid the same mistakes that I've made in my life, and I'm finally happy again. I feel like I'm living for the first time in a long time. The people I work with are great, and they've been so supportive. I also just closed on my first house, which was a wonderful feeling. When I received the invitation to your inauguration, I ignored it because I didn't want to face you. I wasn't proud of all the mistakes that I've made, and I was too embarrassed to see you."

There was still no reaction from the pope.

"I guess I'm here to try and convince you not to go through with your crazy plan. Attempting to convert the Catholic Church to *Islam* is too dangerous. I heard the announcement last week, and I decided to come here and ask you not to go through with it because you are putting your life at risk. You already created so many enemies once you began revealing secrets of the church, and those evil cardinals will continue to target you. This will just make things worse. Please don't go through with the conversion!"

The pope uncrossed his hands and ran them through his black hair, but he didn't have anything to say.

She continued to plead her case. "I know I haven't been a good friend in recent years, but I'm still in love with you. I think that you should consider retiring from the Vatican and moving in with me because I know you still have feelings for me. I'm begging you not to go to the Middle East. You have too many people who love you, and you've been an inspiration to everyone. We wouldn't be able to deal with you being harmed.

"You don't know how hurtful it was when you turned me down. I was upset that you considered the night we shared a sin. I'll never forget Isaiah chapter 1 verse 18. I have it tattooed on my arm because I never wanted to forget the pain that I felt while we sat at the top the million-dollar stairs. To me, what we had was true love. I may not know all the Bible quotes like you, but I know that God wants people to fall in love. You even pointed out that priests should be allowed to get married." She looked into his eyes and saw a vast emptiness. "Don't you have anything to say, Jassi? Are you just going to stand there like an emotionless robot and let me ramble on?"

Pope Ali listened intently to every word, trying to figure out a proper response. He already had a lot to think about with the impending conversion, and her showing up was the last thing he needed. Sabatina's timing couldn't have been worse. He didn't want to deal with the situation, and without saying a word, he stood up and left the room. She was astonished by his reaction. Four Swiss Guardsmen entered the room shortly after the pope's exodus and led her to the exit.

"Stay away from the Vatican City State. You will be arrested if you attempt to return," one of the guards said.

Sabatina wasn't upset by the fact that the pope was angry because she knew that he was offended after she blew off his inauguration. She hoped he would eventually forgive her and felt the way he treated her was colder than the iciness of the Italian winter afternoon, totally unnecessary. She felt the least he could have done was speak to her even if he yelled.

The pope was silent during the evening flight to Tel Aviv. The plane landed safely in the capital of Israel, and he met with the prime minister in the morning. On the trip, he only brought along Middle Eastern cardinals, including Cardinal President *Marzouk*. Pope Ali did not allow for Cardinal Malandra to accompany him, believing that his faithful friend had a true calling. He didn't want the dean to be involved in any corruption. He also wasn't sure if the trip would be safe and wanted Cardinal Malandra to remain at the Vatican in case of a tragedy.

The warm Israeli weather was a pleasant respite from the frosty Italian winter. The flimsy unbuttoned designer jacket was a stark contrast from the massive winter coat that he wore as he boarded the plane. The visit to Israel lasted two days before the convoy flew to Ramallah, Palestine.

The pontiff received a king's welcome from the independent Palestinian public who hailed him as a hero for his role in the peace negotiations. During his visit, Pope Ali made a stop in Bethlehem, the birthplace of Jesus and King David. The town was also where the biblical hero David was crowned the king of the Israelites. He was the father of the brilliant and reasonable King Solomon and the architect of the first holy Jewish remple built by the latter. Pope Ali remained in the new nation for two days before moving on to Jerusalem.

The pontiff's plane landed at the newly renovated and expanded *Atarot* Airport, in the Holy City on Thursday, March 3. He desired to spend a significant amount of time in Jerusalem, not wanting to rush the experience. Saturday, the fifth, was exactly ten days after his knee injury, and the pope was able to wear a hinged knee brace. He switched from the crutches to a walking stick, which was gifted to Pope Benedict XVI.

"That's a staff. Where did you get it from?" asked Cardinal *Marzouk*.

"It was in the Vatican. Former U.S. President George W. Bush gave this walking stick to the pope during his visit to the Vatican in 2007. The stick is inscribed with the Ten Commandments and was carved by a former homeless man. It is five feet in length and made out of cedar wood. It's commonly known as the 'Moses stick.' The walking stick's natural off-white color with the commandments colored in green is one of three options. The lettering also comes in red and black. It is interesting to note that controversy arose when the *Camerlengo* pointed out the Ten Commandments were inscribed in the Protestant tradition. The designer carves two different versions of the stick, one for Catholics and one for Protestants. Not surprisingly, President Bush erroneously purchased the wrong version."

"Who would have guessed. Bush made a mistake? I can't believe it!" Cardinal President *Marzouk* joked. "I never knew that the Protestants had their own version of the Ten Commandments."

"Yes, Catholics combine the first two Protestant commandments into their first commandment, while the Protestants combine the Catholic ninth and tenth commandments into their tenth, but the words remain the same."

The encasement that housed the ark of the covenant had a mural with Pope Ali's photo inside. He was praised for returning the ark to its home. During the visit, the pontiff revisited many of the country's holiest sites, but the trip was marred by the thoughts that were in his head. He couldn't stop thinking about Sabatina's visit and began to question whether or not he was doing the right thing. His holiness thought about how much he influenced Mike Woodruff and Zachary Hart, along with all his other great achievements. He wondered if it was justifiable for him to attempt converting the institution that helped him accomplish so much. The realization of the church's great value began to seep in, and the pope was not in the right mind state to meet with the *Ayatollah*.

He wasn't ready to go through with the conversion and decided to make an improbable request. Pope Ali asked the respectable Abtahi to speak with the new king of Saudi Arabia, Sultan *Ahmed bin Sulayem*, brother of the previous king.

"I want you to ask him to grant me permission to visit Mecca," the pope requested.

Abtahi didn't think the king would agree, but he honored his friend's request. Astonishingly, the progressive Saudi Arabian king agreed to allow the pope to enter the Islamic Holy City. King Sultan *Ahmed bin Sulayem* granted the request on the grounds that the pontiff was born a Muslim. The king also wanted to encourage the pope's possible conversion of the Roman Catholic Church to *Islam*.

The exception pleased Pope Ali, and *Ayatollah* Abtahi flew to Jerusalem in order to join his friend on the historic visit to Mecca, but the king set conditions for the papal visit. He would be the only member of his entourage allowed, and he would not be permitted to enter the city of the prophet, Medina.

On Monday, March 7, Pope Ali and *Ayatollah* Abtahi landed via the Saudi king's private airbus A380-900 at the small Mecca East Airport in *Makkah*. King Sultan *Ahmed bin Sulayem's* limousine met the private jet and escorted the men to Mecca. The king's motorcade navigated through the crowded streets of the Holy City while throngs of well-wishers lined up to greet the praiseworthy pontiff.

Pope Ali recognized the call of a *muezzin* as they headed toward the *Ka'bah*. "When did the *muezzin* become part of the tradition?" he asked the *Ayatollah*.

"The tradition of the *Muezzin* originated during the life of the Prophet *Muhammad*. *Bilal ibn Ribah* was the first to hold the position. He was an early follower of the prophet and had the duty of walking the streets and calling the followers of *Muhammad* to his home for instruction. The modern-day *muezzin* calls people to prayer from the mosque's amplified minarets, and each mosque chooses a professional *muezzin* who is to face the *Kiblah*, which is the direction facing the *Ka'bah*, when calling out to the people."

The pope was looking forward to finally completing the *Hajj*. Tradition holds that Muslims must walk in a counterclockwise direction around the *Ka'bah* multiple times. Although Pope Ali wasn't sure he was going to convert the church, he wanted to honor his grandfather by following in the tradition of the prophet. Deep down inside, he felt like a true Muslim and was unable to control his emotions. As he circled the *Ka'bah*, he thought about Azfal and began to cry.

His devout grandfather told him about the indescribable feeling of completing the *Hajj*, and his holiness was glad that he was able to take advantage of the king's decision, remaining in Mecca for five days. King Sultan *Ahmed bin Sulayem* became a true friend of the pontiff and was invited to visit the Vatican. Pope Ali and *Ayatollah* Abtahi were allowed to use the king's private jet for the flight to Baghdad. They would finally have their significant meeting. The pope's entourage would fly from Jerusalem and meet him in Iraq. He was in the right mind state and back on course. The pope refocused his attention to the promise that he made to his grandfather. It was the experience in Mecca that helped to remind him of his true goal, and he was once again excited about planning the conversion.

Chapter 25

On the lengthy flight to Iraq, things began to slowly unravel for the pope. He thought about Sabatina's speech and all the people that he influenced. He continued to reflect on the positive influence he had on Mike Woodruff. The pope accomplished a great deal through the church and didn't want to tarnish his legacy.

Pope Ali and the *Ayatollah* met privately inside the headquarters of the L-MEN. They sat in the luxurious founder's room, discussing conversion plans, while they looked up at their massive pictures adorning the main wall. The pope was impressed with *Ayatollah* Abtahi's falsification of the Gospel of Bartholomew.

"How did you get that document authenticated?" he asked.

The proud *Ayatollah* answered frankly, "I first hired a forgery specialist from Dubai. He used different methods to create the parchment and aged it using secret techniques. To the naked eye, his reproduction is undetectable, and the craftsmanship is flawless. As far as the authentication goes, I called in a favor from one of the members of my guardian council who has a cousin from Yemen that works at the German lab. We sent a payment, and he was able to create a false data report. The people were excited to hear another great discovery, and they believed it was an independent laboratory. No one will be able to trace the man back to me, so the plan worked perfectly."

"Indeed, it did. Let us now discuss the conversion."

The *Ayatollah* had many questions for the pope because he wasn't completely comfortable with the plan. His efforts to improve the world's perception of Iran would all be unraveled if they failed, and he didn't want to take such a great risk.

The pope noticed the *Ayatollah's* lack of enthusiasm. "I can see that you still have a lot of concerns. Let me be completely honest with you. There is more to the story than I have let on. I have an ulterior motive."

The *Ayatollah* listened intently as his friend revealed all the details of the promise that he made to his grandfather.

"I see. I was on the fence before, but now I must say that I can no longer support your plan. We cannot risk everything that we have worked so hard to achieve simply to fulfill a promise that you made when you were an eleven-year-old child. You need to focus on improving your church and forget about the promise. Now you can truly become President Allawi's Christovert."

Pope Ali sighed and shook his head in agreement. "I always knew the conversion was wrong. I think I was so focused on the task at hand that I never stopped to consider whether or not it was the right thing to do. I never took into consideration my grandfather's true motives. He was very angry when we had our talk, and it wasn't until I recently spoke with Tina that I began to question my plan."

With the decision to end the conversion agreed upon, the talk shifted to new policies. Pope Ali was against the affluence of the church.

"There is no need for a wealthy church. We can't have billions of dollars at our disposal while many of the followers are suffering. I must deal with the problem of greed that has existed inside of the Catholic Church. For centuries, indulgences were given to people in return for money. The practice led to the Protestant Reformation under Martin Luther. Are you familiar with Luther?"

"I know he is the main figure in the Protestant Church, but I do not know his story."

"The *Ninety-Five Theses*, written by Luther, in 1517 disputed the Catholic Church's claim that freedom from God's punishment for sins could be bought. Pope Leo X excommunicated him in 1521.

The holy Roman emperor, Charles V, agreed with the pope and condemned Luther as an outlaw. In 1520, the two leaders met with Luther in Worms. The meeting is known as the Edict of Worms. Luther taught that salvation came through faith in God and not through the purchase of indulgences. He translated the Bible into German so the lay people could read it for themselves. The church's policy was for priests who were taught to read Latin to read the Bible and interpret it to the people. After his death, Luther's followers went on to found the Protestant Church."

"It seems that he was a very courageous man. Why is he not more popular?"

"His legacy was tarnished because he was an anti-Semite. He preached that the homes of Jews should be burned down and the Nazis used his writings as propaganda during the Holocaust. The practice of selling indulgences has since been removed from the church, but the leaders have developed a new method to extract money from its followers. We now focus our attention on guilting people into donating money regardless of their economic condition. We have become more of a business than a religious institution. Obviously, we need the laity to help fund the church, but we have taken too much money from them over the years. I have to change the policy and find a way to share the wealth. I want to use all the excess money to help improve the lives of the impoverished. A new shift in policy may possibly bring back our Protestant brothers and sisters. The first thing I have to do is apologize to the people for considering the conversion."

The two leaders continued to talk for the remainder of the day, and they agreed to leave things as they were; there was no need for a conversion. The plan was for the two religions to form a bond and work together in an effort to bring peace to the world. March 12 was the day that Jassim Ansary truly became Pope Ali, the supreme pontiff of the Roman Catholic Church. He felt that his grandfather was wrong for asking an eleven-year-old boy to make a lifetime commitment but understood why Azfal wanted him to complete the *Jihad*.

The *Ayatollah* agreed with Pope Ali's decision to share the church's wealth, but they decided not to reveal that the Gospel of Bartholomew was a fake; it would create distrust among the followers. The pope focused on creating a different interpretation of the text and prepared to reveal his plans to the people on Easter Sunday. The remainder of the his holiness's time in the Middle East was devoted to traveling and meeting the people. The pontiff was proud of his role in the expansion of Catholicism and even more prideful of the peace that he helped spread.

Pope Ali called Cardinal Malandra and asked him to clear up some time during Easter Sunday.

"We look forward to hearing what you have decided, but I must let you know that some of the other cardinals are very angry about the conversion. You don't have to worry because there is still a majority willing to support whatever you decide. Most of the cardinals trust your judgment."

Pope Ali was grateful to hear of the cardinal's support. "I don't want you to worry about my safety, I will be fine. Everything will work itself out through the grace of God. Thank you for continuing to be my trusted friend."

"I know that you would have stood by my side if our roles were reversed. Have a safe flight."

Prior to his departure for Rome, the pope wrote a letter to Sabatina and fastened it with the papal seal. Mailing the envelope was his last act before boarding the plane. The Vatican Press released an official statement that his holiness was returning to Rome with a decision concerning the future of the church. Many of the anxious cardinals, who accompanied Pope Ali on the trip, feared for their lives. They all assumed that the forces of Satan would arrange for the plane to be blown to pieces, causing the flight to be consumed by an atmosphere of fright.

The return to Rome was nerve-racking but uneventful. The Middle Eastern excursion ended on April 4. The papal security team was on extra high alert, and Cardinal Malandra was overjoyed to see his friend return safely. They met in the papal library and ironed out the plans for Easter.

"Your holiness will address the laity in St. Peter's Square following the celebration of Easter mass."

"It was an eventful trip, and I look forward to making my announcement. The visit to Mecca will remain with me forever."

On Easter Sunday, Dean Malandra entered the papal chamber and presented him with a gift from all the supportive cardinals. He was not aware what Pope Ali was preparing to announce, but the cardinal assumed that the plan was to go through with a conversion to *Islam*. While the pope was away, a majority of the cardinals agreed that a conversion was inevitable due to the contents of his latest Friday revelation. The vacillating cardinals wanted to show a sign of support even though they were not completely sure whether or not the pope was making the proper decision for the church.

Cardinal Malandra handed the pontiff a three-foot diamond-encrusted platinum cane. It had the Islamic crescent moon and star centered inside of the Roman Catholic cross.

"This gift is from the cardinalate. We want to show our undying support. This cane will forever mark this glorious announcement."

The pope was touched. "I am grateful to have the support of my bishops. This gift will help to give me the strength to make my historic announcement."

"As the dean of the College of Cardinals, I want to relay our vow to help with any transition that may be coming."

"I never questioned the support from the cardinals. When we removed the cardinals of Basel, we created an atmosphere of unity throughout the Vatican. And there is nothing that Satan can do to break our strong bond."

Easter Mass marked the end of the celebration of the Passover. Following the mass, the anxious pope returned to the Apostolic Palace to prepare for his speech. The new platinum cane was more to his liking and easier to use than the lengthy walking stick. He also loved its symbolism.

Prior to the announcement, Pope Ali asked Cardinal Malandra to stand by his side on the balcony, but the dean didn't want to take away from the pope's limelight.

"This is your moment. I will remain here and pray for the people to have faith in your judgment. I know the Lord has guided your decision," Cardinal Malandra said.

The pope graciously thanked his faithful friend for his loyalty, and the two embraced. "You have always been a trustworthy friend. Let me quote from the book of Sirach chapter 6 verse 6: 'Let your acquaintance be many, but one in a thousand your confidant.'"

Chapter 26

The enthusiastic laity filled *Piazza San Pietro*, awaiting the pope's appearance. The monumental colonnade by *Bernini*, containing 140 statues of saints, outlined the square and remained visible from the balcony, providing protection from evil forces. Pope Ali emerged before his people, on the balcony of *San Pietro in Vaticano*, and waved to the adoring crowd as they cheered for him. It was a lovely day, and a gentle wind blew across his brow. The beautiful Italian spring morning was the perfect setting for his announcement. It was as if the Lord removed all the clouds from the sky so the souls in heaven could have a clear view. Although he was aborting the promise that he made to his grandfather, he knew Azfal was looking down on him proudly.

His eminence looked out to the Egyptian in the center of St. Peter's Square. "I feel like the luckiest man in the world. I have the oppurtunity to lead the people and carry out the will of the Lord. I look out at the multitude of followers gathered here today for this momentous announcement, and I feel that we are on the right course. I am reminded of my grandfather as I look at the Egyptian obelisk. It was originally placed in Rome at the site of the wall of the Circus of Caligula in AD 37. The circus was later named *Circo Vaticano o di Nerone* after the Emperor Nero. Pope Sixtus V later moved it to the square in 1586. I know Azi is looking down on me today and he is proud of the man that I have become. I have the full support from the cardinalate, and I want to display this lovely gift that they have bestowed on me," Pope Ali announced.

The pope held up the cane and diamonds gleamed in the glistening sun, almost blinding the anticipatory crowd. His announcement would be the most significant event in history.

Suddenly, an explosion sent everyone scurrying in a horrific frenzy. The people were filled with dreadfulness as they looked up to see the obliterated balcony. The tremendous blast caused one witness to look to the sky in search of the Enola Gay. The pope was instantly killed along with several of the laity who were standing closest to the building. Ironically, Cardinal Ansary was introduced to the world as Pope Ali from the very same balcony.

The official Vatican investigation speculated the assassination was possibly the work of an unknown anti-Catholic terrorist group. Most people suspected the members of the cardinals of Basel.

A week later, the world was stunned when the Vatican unexpectedly announced that antipope Nelson was found dead in his apartment. Barcelona Police discovered a suicide note attached to his decaying body. In the note, the antipope confessed to the murder of Pope Ali and admitted that he was unable to live with the guilt. The *Camerlengo* quickly acted to assemble the conclave, and the College of Cardinals unanimously selected Dean Gianni Malandra as the new bishop of Rome.

"Those of you who know me best know that I have always been a big fan of the prophecies of St. Malachy. As a matter of fact, my good friend and predecessor, Pope Ali, enjoyed mocking me for believing them to be true. I can't say that they are true, but they were very intriguing, so I have decided to take on the regnal name, Innocent XIV. I want to honor Pope Innocent II who received the prophecies from St. Malachy in 1139.

"In recent years, there has been an emphasis on calling the pope his holiness or his eminence. I think those are perfectly fine ways to address me, but I also want to bring back the title 'Holy Father.'"

Pope Innocent's first act was to expel the ali-appointed cardinals from the Vatican. He reappointed the former cardinals, except for the twelve supporters of antipope Nelson.

"There is no reason to punish the former cardinals. They will be acquitted from the charge that they were members of the evil secret society."

Pope Innocent XIV identified the twelve supporters of the anti-pope as the members of *Cardinali di Basilea*. They were excommunicated form the Roman Catholic Church and handed over to the authorities as conspirators in the murder of Pope Ali. Cardinal De Luca was also excommunicated for his betrayal of the late pontiff, but his Alzheimer's prevented him from fully comprehending what was happening.

Pope Ali's body was blown half to pieces, but the Holy Father ordered whatever could be gathered up to be flown to Iraq in order to be buried in *Al A'zamiyah*. The mournful President Allawi began construction of a mausoleum in honor of the great pope, which was to be built on the grounds of the L-MEN. Pope Innocent declared a rebirth of the church and praised Pope Ali for all that he had accomplished, vowing to continue his predecessor's work of removing corruption from the Vatican.

The pope met with his Synod of Bishops, and Cardinal Dominico Borgia stood up. He began a slow clap before turning to the newly elected pontiff. "You have done well, my son. Your actions have prevented the antichrist from leading the Lord's people astray. It is only fitting that you are the man who sits before us as the new Holy Father."

Following the meeting, Pope Innocent met privately with Cardinal Borgia. ********* to Florence after his ordination into the priesthood, and it was during his return that he was recruited to join *Cardinali di Basilea*. He learned about the history of the secret organization and agreed to be a member.

"The Council of Basel was eventually moved to Florence. It was originally held in Basel, Switzerland, because the cardinals wanted to meet outside the Holy Roman Empire. With the society's new home in Florence, the cardinals secretly meet monthly in order to conduct our business. We arrange for young Italian boys to be groomed for service in our secret society. Each boy is chosen at the age of three, and the selected families are sent to different cities throughout the world, where they are prepared for the priesthood. The council chose you, and your family was sent to New Jersey. Your devout father Tomaso was given sufficient money and sworn to secrecy. He didn't know who was behind his selection but knew that betrayal was punishable by death," Father *Portella* informed.

"I see. Why did you wait until I became a priest before revealing this information?" Father Gianni asked.

"We had to allow you to find the Lord for yourself. Many people believe us to be an evil society, but the truth is that we are the ones who carry out the Lord's work. We ensure that his will is carried out at all cost."

Father Gianni always knew that the church helped his family, but he didn't have knowledge of the agreement that his father made. Tomaso was not given all the details; he just knew that he was getting a better life for his family. The only stipulation was for him to ensure that his son joined the priesthood. The family was extremely poor while living in *Firenze*, so it was an easy decision for him to make. The aim of the cardinals of Basel was to preserve the wealth and power of the Roman Catholic Church, and Father Gianni truly believed the cardinals were carrying out God's will. He didn't think twice about betraying his good friend. To him, the future of the church was more important than their friendship.

Pope Ali's attempt to convert the church to *Islam* did not sit well with Cardinal Malandra or the leader of the *Cardinali di Basilea*, Archbishop Emeritus Borgia of Florence. Upon his initiation, Father Gianni immediately identified Father Jassim as a potential problem. He let the cardinals know that his best friend had an inner drive that would lead him to greatness. *Cardinali di Basilea* arranged for Father Gianni to stay close to the ambitious Iraqi priest in order to monitor his actions.

Cardinal Malandra and the other secret society members believed that God worked through them to ensure the glorious future of the church, and it was Cardinal Malandra who planted the bomb inside of the his holiness's new platinum cane. *Cardinali di Basilea* also arranged for antipope Nelson to be framed for the assassination; a forger was paid to write the suicide note. It turned out that the antipope actually had a true calling and was simply attempting to preserve the traditions of the church.

Cardinal Malandra was also instrumental in another sinister plot of deception. He led Pope Ali to believe that his godfather betrayed him. The truth of the matter was that Cardinal De Luca was simply making phone calls because he missed his close friends. The dean took advantage of the oppurtunity to frame the retired pope for the poisoning. Cardinal Malandra actually was the one who mixed a drop of cyanide into the pope's meals on a daily basis.

Cardinal Borgia patiently waited for the perfect oppurtunity before getting rid of Pope Ali. He purposely challenged Cardinal Rodriguez to make it appear as if the Barcelonan was a member of *Cardinali di Basilea,* and the Spaniard fell for the trap. The accusations against the antipope turned out to be a red herring. The glib Cardinal Borgia was considered for the papacy on several occasions because of his devotion, but he never wanted to be the face of the church. He always arranged for the Basel cardinals to vote for the same bishop and meticulously selected the new pontiff. He already held the power in the Vatican and didn't need a title to substantiate it. Most people associate Italian crime and power, with the Mafia. The true power resides in the *Basilica di Santa Maria del Firoe in Firenze* with *Cardinali di Basilea,* under the guile of Cardinal Archbishop Borgia.

Chapter 27

A few days after the assassination of Pope Ali, an express mail parcel arrived at Sabatina's residence. Her quaint home was located in the tranquil New England town of Wayland, Massachusetts. She excitedly opened the package to find a large manila envelope inside and noticed the papal seal. She opened it anxiously, pulling out a handwritten letter from the late pontiff.

My Dear Sabatina,

I am writing this letter because I fear for my life. The actions that I have taken have infuriated some very powerful people, namely the cardinals of Basel. They are determined to kill me, and I know they will stop at nothing to achieve their goal. I do not know the identity of the members, but I suspect that my "friend" Cardinal De Luca is the leader, and I believe that his first commander is antipope Nelson. They are very upset with the possibility that I may convert the Roman Catholic Church to *Islam* and are eager to remove me from power through any means necessary.

I want to sincerely apologize for my reaction in the Apostolic Palace. You poured out your heart, and I reacted coldly. I want you to know that I listened to your words with an open heart, and I want you to know that I am very proud of you. I don't judge you for the mistakes of your past. I am very impressed with the way you turned your life around. It's wonderful that you are helping young women to better their lives. As far as we are concerned, you have always known that I love you, but you have to understand that I never chose the priesthood over you. I was simply fulfilling a promise that I made to my grandfather. I have now discovered that it was unfair for him to have asked me to make such a grand pledge at that young of an age. I now realize that I am responsible for choosing my own destiny.

I cannot leave the church and marry you because my calling to serve the Lord is true, but if I am able to make it back to the Vatican safely, I will make the necessary changes to allow for clergy to marry. We can get hitched and live in the Vatican with you as the foremost "First Lady of the Roman Catholic Church." Nothing would make me happier than for us to finally be together. Nothing will keep us apart from then on.

We always talked about sharing a lovely dinner at *Monte Caruso*, my favorite place in Italy, and I would love to finally have that oppurtunity. I also hope to reconcile with Mario. It pains me that the two of us haven't been able to become friends again. I want the triumvirate to unite once more because friendship is very important to me, especially now that I am having difficulty finding people who I can trust. I met Mario's beautiful daughters, Cheyenne and Brie, and his energetic little boy, Kevin. Most importantly, I look forward to recapturing my title as "the grand champion of race at the

Spanish Steps." Marco was upset that I defeated him during our race, and he grabbed my shirt, allowing for you to have an unfair advantage.

My grandfather was a very defeated man, and I think the death of my grandmother changed him. His heart grew even colder after my parents and my uncle were killed. He convinced me to set forth on a *Jihad* against the "crusaders." while on his deathbed. He spoke to me privately and explained what he wanted me to do.

"De Luca has been a good friend. I can't dispute that fact. The question is, what is his motive? Was he sent by the Catholic Church to keep an eye on us because we are Muslim? I don't have proof, but I am sure of it. I believe that De Luca tricked Luciana into introducing us, and I don't believe she is a conspirator in his evil plot. Since De Luca deceived us, we must deceive him. As a Muslim, you must learn about *Taqiyya*, which was taught to me by Nadje. I never knew what it meant since it is a *Shi'a* term. *Taqiyya* is essential for the survival of our religion."

"The word means fear or to guard against. The first thing you must know is *Shi'a* and *Sunni* Muslims are the same people. Both groups follow the teachings of the Prophet *Mohammad* and have the same aim of righteousness.

"They follow in the traditions of the prophet and his 'true' successor *Ali*, who converted to *Islam* at the age of eleven, and eventually married the prophet's daughter *Fatima*. *Shi'a* theology, namely *Taqiyya*, allows for believers to conceal their faith when under threat, persecution, or compulsion. Friendship to nonbelievers must be shown outwardly but never inwardly. This concealing of one's faith is designed to save oneself or people from physical and/or mental injury. The aim is to gain an element of surprise over an opponent.

"This is what you must do. It is a sign from *Allah* that you are eleven years old. As *Ali* converted to Islam at age eleven, you must convert to Catholicism at the same age. You will appear to be a true follower of Christ, but in your heart, you must always remain a Muslim. We are under attack from the 'crusaders' and must apply *Taqiyya* to prevent our demise. The only way to stop the 'crusaders' is to expose them and their deceitful ways. The world must know that the Catholic Church has lead *Allah's* people astray.

"The pope's power must be removed. The people of the book must be allowed to join and follow the proper teachings of *Allah*. You must not allow ignorant people to confuse you. God and *Allah* are one in the same. The lofty goal I am setting before you is to join their church. You must learn all that you can about their customs and become an ordained priest.

"You must rise as high as you can through their ranks, and when you are in a position to acquire their secrets, you must expose them to the world. The one thing you have to understand is that it will take many years for you to become a high-ranking priest. De Luca is the key. He is the vehicle that you will use in order to complete the task set before you.

"You must appear to be a true Catholic. Remove all your own beliefs, and accept what they teach. Never disclose your true aim to anyone, and follow their laws to become a 'true' follower of Christ. They cannot suspect that you have an ulterior motive. It is essential that you appear genuine, and with De Luca's help, you may one day be promoted to bishop. That's unlikely, but if you adhere to their laws, it may be possible. Even if you cannot ascend to that position, you must befriend a bishop and use him to gain the necessary knowledge.

"Our friend, De Luca, will guide you to the pertinent information, but you are never to trust him. When you are in a position to prove what you uncover, reveal their wicked ways to the world. The black heart of Satan, not the hand of *Allah*, guides the Catholic Church. Once the truth is revealed, the 'crusaders' will be defeated. You are destined for greatness, but it will not be on the football pitch as you had hoped. It is through you that *Allah* will spread his word.

"This will be your *Jihad*. You must remember that the Catholic Church is designed to keep people poor. The followers are coerced into giving to the church even if they have nothing. They are encouraged to remain poor and promised to be rewarded in heaven once they are dead. The church is not designed to improve the lives of its people.

"You must always strive to be a good Muslim and follow the teachings of the prophet. The 'greater' *Jihad* is a lifelong struggle. I have given you instructions on the 'lesser' *Jihad*, which will be your struggle against the 'crusaders.' They are the ones who are responsible for the deaths of many Iraqis, including Nebet, Ibrahim, and Saady."

My grandfather's last wish was for me to promise him that I would complete the *Jihad*. I was only eleven, and the promise became the most important thing to me. I had just lost my parents, and the hurt helped to drive me. I assured Azi that nothing would keep me from my goal.

The most difficult choice in my life was the decision to turn you down. I have struggled with being away from you the entire time, and when I saw you and Mario together, I was torn apart. I didn't know how to handle it. I now realize that I played a role in your spiraling out of control, and I want for us to put the past behind us and enjoy the rest of our lives together!

I want you to know that the Friday revelations were all true. I found all the documents in the Vatican Secret Archives. The only false document was the Gospel of Bartholomew. *Ayatollah* Abtahi arranged for it to be counterfeited because we felt that it was necessary in order to ensure the faithfulness of the people. I had to make them trust in my judgment, but in the meeting with the *Ayatollah* in Baghdad, we decided to cancel the conversion. It was during our conversation that I first revealed the *Taqiyya* to him. We have agreed to continue leading our people separately, and we hope to promote peace and tolerance throughout the world. We believe that religion does not have to be a divider of people, and our faiths will coexist, serving the Lord as a united community.

In my attempt to destroy the Catholic Church, I realized that the institution was responsible for all the good that I have achieved. My true aim will be to rid the church of corruption and to lead the people to God. I previously believed that the church was unnecessary, thinking that people could serve the Lord in any fashion that they saw fit, but I now understand that although the church is not the only road to salvation. It does serve an essential role in bringing people to the Lord. It is better to serve God as a community than as an individual, and together, we can work to assist the helpless citizens of the world.

The important thing to remember is the Lord will judge us by how we live our lives. I believe that even atheist will be allowed to enter heaven. They don't have to believe in the Lord in order to serve him. If an atheist lives a decent life, God will reward him or her.

I am not certain that I will be alive by the time this letter reaches you, and in the event of my untimely death, I have arranged for a trusted friend to pass on secret documents to you. They will disclose more of the church's past atrocities! *Cardinali di Basilea* will attempt to tarnish my legacy by creating vicious lies, and you must let the world know what my true aim was. Their secret society will stop at nothing to try and prevent you from exposing the documents, so you have to be careful. An associate of mine is currently compiling a list of their members, which will be given to you along with the other documents. Please be selective in who you trust. Satan has infected the Vatican. It was Father De Luca who attempted to poison me, and Gianni is the only cardinal that I can truly trust. Be careful!

"Bear one another's burdens, and so you will fulfill the law of Christ" (Galatians 6:2).

Love,
Aliis I PP.

Sabatina cried while reading the letter. She removed references to her and Jassim's relationship and the section about the false document before making a copy, which she placed into a manila envelope. It was a beautiful New England spring afternoon, and the sun warmed the brick walkway that led up to her front door. A graceful squirrel collected a pine cone from the lawn and scurried up the towering coniferous tree that bordered her neighbor's front yard. She walked down to the corner of the quiet street to the blue mailbox and opened the slot. Before dropping it in, the stunning auburn-haired *Italiana* double-checked the mailing address. It was correct:

> His holiness, Pope Innocent XIV P.P.
> 00120 *Via del Pellegrino*
> *Citta del Vaticano*

The slot slammed shut, and Sabatina proudly sauntered back to her home.

Terminus

Afterword

I really don't like Pope Benedict XVI. Nothing personal, I just think he owes me a big apology. I understand that religion is a divisive topic and many people get offended easily, so I won't write exactly how I feel about the ex-pontiff.

Please allow me to explain why I have a major beef with the man who was chosen by his Lord and Savior to lead his flock. This novel took a great deal of blood, sweat, and tears to produce. In order to create my story, I did some extensive research and discovered that there were a couple examples of popes who actually resigned from their leadership position, a fact that is not well-known. The chapter in my novel with a pope who quit would have been ground breaking, but it now looks as if I stole the idea after Benedict quit. Please let the record show that I wrote the book a couple years before he quit!

I am patiently waiting for a handwritten letter from the ex-pope, and I expect for him to be apologetic and sincere.

About the Author

Peter Teixeira is a native Bostonian who earned a diploma from the prestigious Boston Latin School. He continued his studies at Seton Hall University, eventually transferring to the University of Massachusetts Boston, where he earned a degree in history and completed a minor in anthropology. His parents emigrated from Cape Verde, an island nation off the West Coast of Africa. He now lives in Los Angeles as a refugee who escaped the unbearable frozen climate of the northeast. He is no longer interested in being cold.